7/09

Tomato Rhapsody

Tomato Rhapsody

A FABLE OF LOVE, LUST
AND FORBIDDEN FRUIT

Adam Schell

DELACORTE PRESS

Published in the United States by Delacorte Press, an imprint of The Random House Publishing Group, a division of Random House, Inc., New York.

DELACORTE PRESS is a registered trademark of Random House, Inc., and the colophon is a trademark of Random House, Inc.

Library of Congress Cataloging-in-Publication Data
Schell, Adam.
Tomato rhapsody : a fable of love, lust, and forbidden fruit /
by Adam Schell.
p. cm.
ISBN 978-0-385-34333-6—ISBN 978-0-440-33861-1 (eBook)
1. Magic realism (Literature) I. Title.
PS3619.C347T66 2009
813'.6—dc22
2008051835

Printed in the United States of America on acid-free paper

www.bantamdell.com

9 8 7 6 5 4 3 2 1
First Edition

Text design by Catherine Leonardo

For Noodle and Asher.
Truly, my heart is full.

Tomato Rhapsody

Parte Uno

TOMATOES

In Which We Become Acquainted With:

Davido, a young *Ebreo* tomato farmer

Mari, a young *Cattolica* olive farmer

Nonno, grandfather to Davido

Cosimo di Pucci de' Meducci III, Grand Duke of Tuscany

The Good Padre, the village's new priest

Giuseppe, the villainous owner of the village
olive orchard and oil factory

Benito, henchman to Giuseppe

Bobo the Fool, the village fool

Luigi Campoverde, chef for Cosimo di Pucci de' Meducci

Bertolli, altar boy at the Good Padre's church

SETTING

Late August, sometime in the 16th century. A small village in the Tuscan countryside. The tomato has just arrived in Tuscany by way of a group of newly countrified *Ebrei* from Florence. Tomato sauce has yet to be discovered.

In Which We Learn
How an *Ebreo* Travels
Best in Tuscany

Nonno looked east across the roll of his farm at that particular moment in a late-summer dawn when the soon-to-be-risen sun threw an expectant hue of orange and purple across the horizon. It was a beautiful sight, indeed, but the day-breaking spectrum held a bit too much uncertainty for Nonno's comfort. The old man scrunched his eyes for better focus and continued his gaze outward, searching the horizon for some small harbinger affirming that their travels today would go safely and that he was doing what was best for his grandson. Then, in the distance, it lumbered into view.

It was the obstinate old stud, the one inherited along with the farm and the one Nonno loved the most. The donkey paused along the eastern border of the land, atop a slight knoll and between a pair of ancient fig trees. This alone was a sublime image, but when the gnarled beast suddenly dropped its prodigious *cazzone* to dangle before the horizon, careened its head upward and let go with an impassioned bray, Nonno knew the God of Abraham would be with him and his grandson as they traveled to Florence.

The mournful cry erupted from the donkey's mouth and filled Nonno's ears as profoundly as the sounding of a shofar on Rosh Hashanah. Against the still morning it was a sound of such magnitude that it rose from the horizon like a gust of wind billowing a ship's sails and drawing all hands to deck. Songbirds quieted and competing roosters halted in mid-crow as the lonely bellow ballooned to a mass, teetered on its own enormity and began to roll across the land. The sound, robust, anxious, a touch melancholy, tumbled across the farm, hurdling row upon row of tomato plants before leaping the old farm's wall. It rambled down valley and over hill. It combed through grape vineyards and rustled about olive orchards. It rumbled up the road and breached the village walls. It echoed through narrow streets and wide piazzas. It moaned in wine barrels and whistled through empty oil jugs, moving every like creature to concur until the entire countryside rang with the chorus of a thousand lonely donkeys.

Allied with the crisp dawn air and amethyst horizon, the bray had a supernatural quality that affected and connected all of our tale's characters. To begin with, it put a smile on the face of the Good Padre as he tended the church's vegetable garden. It eased the anguish of Cosimo di Pucci de' Meducci the Third, Grand Duke of Tuscany, after an awful week in Rome. It disturbed the stomach of Chef Luigi Campoverde as he stuffed ground pork and veal into sausage casings with fennel, sage, salt and yellow raisins. It startled and annoyed Giuseppe, as did anything that seemed to emanate from a power greater than himself, while it thrilled both Benito and Bobo the Fool for the very reason it unnerved their boss. With amorous serendipity it caused our heroine, Mari, to pause while stirring a batch of her favorite olives at the very same moment our hero, Davido, paused as he loaded a basket with tomatoes.

But for Nonno, the sound of an obstinate and misunderstood beast of burden wailing against an uncaring world was a physical and aural incarnation of what it meant to be an *Ebreo* in a gentile world, and a tear of both sadness and joy streaked the old man's face. By ways unexpected and through loss unimaginable, Nonno had managed to relocate his family and closest of kin from the ghetto of Florence, with its vicious plagues and politics, to a safer home and farm in the country. A place, he wished, where his extended family could peaceably prosper.

Though all the children who lived on the farm called him Nonno, his one true grandchild, Davido, was soon to be married, which meant Nonno would have something real to leave him—land and a wife. Nonno hoped that under Davido's leadership the farm would blossom into a place where *Ebrei* from Florence, Siena, Pitigliano, even as far away as Venice and Rome could seek refuge, flee the ghettos and create a new life. Nonno understood that this late-coming dream would not reach fruition in his lifetime. He could feel his power waning. His body was still fairly limber and his mind still somewhat sharp, but he knew it was Davido's time to come to the fore and prayed daily for the strength of his grandson.

He was an odd boy, his Davido, odd in ways Nonno admired and also feared. Goodness knows, Nonno was pleased by the seriousness with which his grandson took to farming. The boy was coming into his own. A year of hard country life had toughened up his grandchild and put a bit of muscle on his skinny frame, but Nonno found the boy's devotion to the tomato a bit obsessive. He had no problem with his grandson's newfound love of the earth, but he didn't want the boy turning into one of those half-crazed farmers he knew from the markets of Florence. The kind of folk who mumble and grumble when conversing with another human, yet speak clearly and sweetly when talking to the vegetables upon their stand. Truth be told, the way Davido would talk to the tomato plants—his nose pressed closely against the leaves as if to inhale their entirety into the depth of his brain—Nonno was concerned some of this countrified madness had already beset the boy. Nothing a good wife and some children wouldn't cure, thought Nonno. God willing, their trip today would help see to that.

☙   ☙   ☙

Il Raglio Sacro, the Holy Bray, echoed into oblivion and returned Davido's thoughts to the day at hand. Woefully, he lowered his gaze from the horizon so as to look into the basket held in his hands. His eyes could not help but mist with tears—the tomatoes were that beautiful. His first true crop: lush, round, slightly ribbed, a shade of red unmatched in all of nature, with a melding of yellow as the fruit bent and crinkled toward its green stem. What a shame, he thought to himself with an earnestness more appropriate to how the old look upon the young as they're sent off to die in a pointless war. He would rather be doing anything than traveling to Florence today to visit with the girl and the family who in sixteen short days would respectively become his wife and in-laws. Davido brought his thought full circle. He had already met the girl once and the notion that fruits so glorious were bound to waste their goodness and vitality upon an ignominious cause pained his heart exquisitely.

Davido took a few steps forward and set the basket of tomatoes onto the rear of the wagon, sliding it forward so to brace it against another basket. The wagon was nearly full with a dozen similar baskets: presents for old friends and a wife-to-be in Florence. She wasn't at all like Davido's late sister—shrewd, strong-willed, adventurous, beautiful—and she was nothing near what Davido had hoped for in a spouse. On the contrary, she was shy and skinny and she reminded Davido of himself when he was about her age—a puny schoolboy of Florence holed up in the lightless *Seminario di Ebrei* for hours on end—and for this he could not stand being in her presence. She was a child, just fifteen or so, a good five years

Davido's junior and the youngest daughter of a successful merchant more than pleased to pawn off the last of his progeny to the grandchild of a legendary *Ebreo* like Nonno.

Though Nonno had explained to Davido a hundred times that this was the way things were done—that family knew best, tradition dictated the way—Davido was not convinced. He was repulsed by the girl, and the fact that their *Chituba*[1] stipulated that they would spend the first year of marriage living together in the home of her parents, *in Florence,* was a thought so horrible it brought bile to his throat every time he thought it, and he thought it often.

Davido turned and walked to the rear of the barn. He knelt down and took a handful of hay and set it in the bottom of another wood basket. He slid himself a bit closer to the large burlap cloth stacked with ripe tomatoes—close enough so that he could catch one more whiff of their beloved fragrance—and then, one by one, he began to gently set them into the hay-lined basket. A layer of hay, a layer of tomatoes, a layer of hay, a layer of tomatoes, two deep and well cushioned for the bumpy three-hour ride ahead. It would be a hot journey too, and though the sun had just begun to rise, Davido found himself sweating uncomfortably beneath the heavy robe he wore. With a curt sniff, he caught an anxious undertone in his sweat that always reminded him of rotting onions. Of course, a heavy wool robe worn in summer made him perspire, but it was the girl who caused his sweat to stink.

The monk's robe was a necessary burden that Nonno had thought up many years ago while hiding about the cities of Tuscany. Nonno realized then that nothing protected a traveling *Ebreo* like the brown robe of a mendicant monk, a heavy wood cross dangling about the chest and a few well-said phrases in Latin. Hence, whenever Davido or Nonno or any of the extended family members living on the farm traveled to Florence, Pitigliano, Livorno or any other city, they did so draped in the hefty robes of Franciscan monks and pulled along by humble donkeys.

[1] *Chituba* (key-two-ba): an *Ebreo* marriage contract.

"By and by!" Davido shouted to his grandfather to let him know the wagon was just about set. Davido spread a large burlap cloth over the back of the wagon. The tomatoes would be fine exposed to the sun, but it would be imprudent for a pair of false monks to openly travel with a cart full of Love Apples. It was unlikely that anyone they happened to cross paths with would know what a tomato was, but nonetheless, as Nonno often repeated, it was always best to keep suspicions at bay. Davido then walked into the barn to load a basket with some provisions: a loaf of bread; a hunk of cheese; a few bottles, some with water, others with wine; a handful of figs and a half dozen peaches. He and Nonno would have tonight's Sabbath meal with the family of his betrothed, spend the night with friends in the ghetto and then leave early Sunday morning for the return home, but they would need food and drink for the journey there.

Nonno heard a touch of anger in his grandson's voice and it bent his lips into a wry smile. As of yet, the boy expressed no excitement for his pending nuptial. The day would be trying, Nonno was certain of that, and he took one more solid gaze upon his donkey for inspiration, when something about the absurd sight triggered his memory. *"Mio Dio,"* Nonno whispered as the bizarre and often heartbreaking life adventure that brought him from Toledo to Tuscany flashed suddenly before his mind's eye: the three-month-long voyage aboard Cristoforo Colombo's ship in search of a new route to the Orient, and the stroke of pure dumb luck (Colombo's greatest virtue, Nonno always felt), whereby they happened upon an entirely new world instead. Nonno's ten desperate years after being abandoned by Colombo on the island of Guanahani. His life, *his wife,* among the island's natives. The return trip with Colombo back to Europe and his escape to Tuscany. The decade spent in semi-hiding while Spanish operatives searched tirelessly to discover the former finance minister who had so brazenly robbed Colombo of nearly half his treasure. The plague that ravaged Florence some fifteen years past—a horrendous scourge that took the life of his second wife, only son and daughter-in-law, and left him to raise a grandson of seven and a granddaughter of thirteen. But most raw upon Nonno's memory was the life sacrifice his granddaughter had made, dead now nearly two years. Nonno closed his eyes and let his past wash over him with the first breeze of the day.

It was time, time to head to Florence, and Nonno inhaled deeply to inoculate himself against the ghetto's summer stench with the farm's good air, when, suddenly, the strangest notion crossed his mind. It was a thought so visceral that his hand almost mimicked the gesture he had witnessed ten thousand times, and he contemplated how, if he'd been born a *Cristiano,* this would be a perfect time to cross himself. Alas, *Ebrei* have no gesture like that, and as Nonno stepped to the wagon, he looked toward the heavens and sighed a slight "Oy"—perhaps an *Ebreo*'s equivalent to signing the cross.

"Hurry up!" Nonno barked to his grandson in a tone more playful than serious. "Your wife awaits." Nonno was sitting on the wagon seat with the reins to the pair of donkeys ready in his hands.

Davido did not smile back. He set the basket of food between them and took his seat.

Nonno laughed nonetheless as he snapped the reins, and the pair of donkeys began to trot down the carriageway. "Come, now," said Nonno, "bad enough we're dressed as monks, must you be as silent as one too?"

Davido looked away. He didn't want to give Nonno the satisfaction that his foul mood could be so easily cracked. "You're jingling," he said after the urge to smile finally passed.

"What?" said Nonno.

"Your money vest." Davido pointed to Nonno's midsection. "I doubt a marauder's sense of charity would extend to monks who forgo poverty," he mumbled.

"Oh, dear God," said Nonno as he simultaneously rearranged his robe to quell the noise and shot his grandson a disapproving glance. "Don't start that nonsense."

"What?" said Davido defensively, though he knew he was guilty.

"You very well know what."

"I have no idea," Davido lied as convincingly as he could.

Nonno frowned. "The rhyming."

"Oh." Davido smiled guiltily. "That. Sorry."

But he wasn't really sorry at all. True, the local village's nasty old padre had prohibited Nonno and his kin from setting foot in *his* town, but they were nevertheless living among rhymers now and Davido felt he should do his best to master the odd local dialect. The funny thing about *rimatori,* Davido recalled from the country farmers who would set up their fruit and vegetable stands at the weekend markets in Florence, was how they clearly felt their way of speaking made them smarter than the city folk. To the citizens of Florence, however, Nonno included, the rhyming, antiquated Italo-Etruscan they spoke made them appear like bumpkins. As far as Davido understood it, all public and formal speech was meant to rhyme, and all intimate conversation—well, Davido had never had one so he couldn't say and didn't much care. The truth was, Davido liked rhyming; it was just one more thing about country living that set it apart from life in the ghetto.

"How much is it these days to buy a bride?"

"Plenty," chuckled Nonno. "Her father charged a hefty *prezzo della sposa.*"

Davido frowned as he turned his head to gaze over the land. The idea of having to *buy* something he did not want in the first place was beyond absurd to him.

"Tsst," Nonno clucked, "the problem with youth is that you think of love and marriage like a lucky fool who goes for a stroll and happens upon a delicious fruit hanging ripe on a vine and prime for the plucking. All the sweetness with none of the sacrifice."

Davido opened his mouth to speak, but no words came out. What difference would it make? The die was cast, the bride's price to be paid this weekend and the *Chituba* already drawn up. Nonno would never understand his aversion to marrying that skinny-ankled little girl.

"Good God," said Nonno, breaking the silence, "do you think I am so old that I cannot hear what the young think?"

Davido couldn't take it anymore. "But what of love?" he blurted.

"Love?" Nonno raised an eyebrow sardonically. "Look at me, I have had two wives in my life and I couldn't stand either one."

This time Davido could not help but laugh.

"Davido," said Nonno, adopting a more thoughtful tone, "one does not love a seed, one plants a seed and tends to it. A plant grows, the plant bears fruit and we come to depend on the fruit for sustenance. God willing, after much effort and sacrifice you will at least come to acquire a taste for the fruit. And if you are truly blessed, like I was twice, the fruit will taste sweet and you will come to love it."

Davido sat in silence as they trotted along the road that led to Florence. He had met this girl already and the only taste he could ever imagine was bland—bland with a bitter aftertaste.

In Which We Are Introduced to the Theories of Pozzo Menzogna & Learn of Apoplexia

"**M**ake heavy their hearts and burden their minds," wrote the renowned 14th-century Italian dramatist Pozzo Menzogna[2], whose eloquent treatise on drama, *Il*

---

[2] Pozzo Menzogna [b. 1247–d. 1311]: Scholar, composer, actor, playwright and mentor of Dante Bocchino Alighieri. Born to an illiterate cobbler in the village of Cacasenno. At the age of twelve, Menzogna was sold by his father into servitude in the Court of Salvestro de' Meducci. Young Menzogna had nimble fingers and a keen ear for music, learned to play the lute and mandolin, and by 1268 attained the position of Court composer—a post he held with distinction until his untimely death. Self-educated, Menzogna taught himself Latin, French, Greek and Spanish and became a prolific writer of plays and essays. He is universally recognized as the creator of dramaturgy. His great treatise on theatrical and narrative philosophy, *Il Trattato Definitivo sul Dramma*, was completed in 1301 and became the formative text upon which the Renaissance theater and modern novel were largely based. Tragically, during a visit to Bagni di Lucca with a troupe of thespians, Menzogna overindulged in the region's renowned grappa while soaking in one the village's famous hot springs. The combination of relaxing geothermal water and alcohol proved fatal, as Menzogna fell asleep and drowned.

Trattato Definitivo sul Dramma, we will from time to time refer to. Menzogna was speaking, of course, about the importance of layering the lives of a story's heroes—lovers, in our case—with encumbrances and heartaches. Make it so, Menzogna would surely have encouraged, that when Davido and Mari finally do meet, they see in each other the remedy to all that heavies their hearts and burdens their minds.

And it was indeed with a heavy heart and an agitated mind that Mari carried the two wooden buckets filled with water toward the room her mother shared with her stepfather. She arrived before her mother's door, took a deep breath and lowered onto her knees. She pulled the cross out from underneath her blouse, clasped her hands and lowered her head for prayer. Her private moment with *La Virgine Benedetta.* True, part of her thought it was quite silly to kneel before her mother's door and pray, but she hated the task so much and *she hated herself for hating it* that she felt little choice but to beseech the Bless'd Virgin for strength. The sad truth was, her mother's body was dying—for years from the outside in, more recently from the inside out—and it needed cleaning.

Certain her stepfather was already out for the day—she had heard him leave at the crack of dawn—she knocked softly on the door. A groan issued from inside the room, a groan being the only sound her mother could muster.

"*Buongiorno, Mama,*" Mari said with what she hoped was a believable cheerfulness as she entered and approached her mother's bedside. Mari's mother looked at her daughter and with the half of her face that could still manage, she smiled. Mari set down the buckets of water, the washcloth and the bar of olive oil soap. She stepped to the window and drew back the curtains, spilling the room with morning sunlight. The room had two beds set a good eight feet apart. Her mother and stepfather did not sleep together. In fact, most often, he slept on a feather-mat in his study. Mari pulled over a chair for her mother to brace herself, then bent down and, with a heave, lifted her mother upright and seated at the edge of her bed.

Mari tried her best not to make a face, but her mother was not so broken that she could not perceive the tiny flutter of revulsion that rippled her daughter's countenance. The smell was that bad.

Now Mari smiled and brightened her eyes, doing everything she could to protect the dignity of her mother. "Did *La Regina* have a good sleep?" Mari asked playfully. She always called her mother The Queen before she bathed her. It was what Mari's father had called his wife, *La Regina,* and Mari *La Principessa.*

Mari's mother pressed her good right arm into the mattress as her daughter supported and pulled from under her mother's lame left arm. Working together, *La Regina* was brought to her feet. In a practiced motion, Mari smoothly slid the chair closer so her mother could brace herself upon its sturdy back. Subtly, Mari stepped to her mother's side to block her view in case she turned her neck to see what Mari caught in the corner of her eye and what she'd come to realize over the last several months to be something of a doleful morning certainty. Once again, her mother's cream-colored sleeping gown was stained.

The breakdown of her mother's body began acutely, some ten years ago, when Mari was just nine years old, three weeks after the death of her father. Her mother, overwhelmed with grief since her husband's undoing, had barely brought a crumb of food or a drop of water to her lips. Her misery, however, was not enough to keep the nasty old padre from informing her that if she did not find a new husband within one hundred and twenty days, the farm, the mill—all of it—would be confiscated by the church, *for your own protection, of course.* In a fit of anguish, Mari's mother wandered off into the olive orchard to be among the trees her husband had tended for nearly all his life. It was an unusually warm day for early October and, by the late afternoon, Mari's mother collapsed to the ground, burnt, exhausted and severely dehydrated from a full day in the sun. When she regained consciousness, some two weeks later, nothing about her was the same.

Apoplexia: struck down with violence, was how Hippocrates first defined it. And the violence had struck Mari's mother with a heartless ferocity. The whole left side of her face wilted, like a candle left out in the sun. Her left arm hung, near-useless, and her left leg had but a fraction of its former vitality, encumbering her with a dramatic limp. She could walk, yes, but her gait was slow and plodding, and if there was any distance to cover, she required a cane in her right hand and a strong body on her left. Her speech and tongue too seemed to have lost their way. But saddest to Mari was the state of her mother's will, seemingly more damaged and depressed than any part of her body. In the months and years that followed, the limp abated slightly, her eye strengthened to open a fraction wider and her left arm grew just strong enough to hold a broom or help out a bit on market day. Her spirit, however, never recovered. Neither did her tongue or speech, and Mari knew why. What retarded her mother's recuperation was not solely the misfortune of her past, but the reality of her present. One day shy of the four-month anniversary of Mari's father's death, her mother remarried, to a man so rotten and heinous that Mari imagined her mother wished she were blind and deaf too. God knows, Mari often wished she were.

Quickly, Mari now knelt down and gathered up the bottom of her mother's gown. "Ay!" Mari joked as she rose up and lifted the soiled garment off her mother's body and over her head and then tossed it toward the door. Mari knelt back down, wet the bar of soap, dunked the washcloth into the bucket, then worked the one against the other to create a lather—the soap's smell of bay laurel thankfully scenting the air. Her gaze traveled from her mother's bare, puffy feet and swollen ankles all the way up to her backside—once farm-strong skin, muscle and bone, now a travesty of weathered and atrophied naked flesh. Mari set the soapy cloth upon her mother's left leg and moved it in an upward motion, cleansing the leak of excrement that stained her thigh and wondering how a just and good God could heap one more indignity upon a woman already so buried in grief?

In Which We Learn
the Recipe for
Melanzane con Pesto di Erbe

The late-morning sun poured through the stained-glass
window of the village's medieval church and seeped
through the tight weave of the confessional's lattice. Inside the
small wooden abode the light dripped a bluish hue upon the
rather concerned countenance of a pudgy twelve-year-old
altar boy named Bertolli. The boy was panting, overwrought
with anxiousness, and squeaked a pathetic-sounding "Ay" as
he laid his hand upon his heart. It had all happened so suddenly. Up until a few moments ago, it had been a pleasant
morning, a morning in which Bertolli had been feeling especially proud of himself. He had been diligently attending to
his morning chores and, more important, he had not committed a single act of mischief for three full days. In fact, since

meeting the Good Padre some six months ago, Bertolli had begun to feel that his lifelong fascination with disobedience was waning. That was, at least, until the exotic trio came riding in and laid temptation in the palm of his hand.

Inside the confessional, Bertolli knelt and removed a rather formal-looking letter from inside the fold of his simple cream-colored cassock. The boy's pale and chubby hands trembled as he ran his fingers across the letter's fine parchment and over the intricate indentations of its crimson wax seal. "Oh," groaned Bertolli as he mulled over the events that had transpired only a moment earlier, "*merda.*"

It all had started innocently enough. Bertolli had been busy sweeping the front steps for the imminent Sunday evening mass when he heard the clatter of hooves and looked up to see a *Corriere di Vaticane,* escorted by two *Guardia Nobile di Meducci,* gallop through the village's open gate and halt their stallions before the church's entranceway. *Mio Dio,* thought Bertolli, Meducci guards, a Vatican courier, here?

"*Ragazzo,*" said the severe-looking courier with deep-set eyes and a turtle-like nose, which bent disturbingly to the right. "Come here."

"Eh? Me?" Bertolli pointed to himself, astonished that such an important person desired to communicate with him.

"Yes, you, boy."

Certain he was in trouble for something he had done, Bertolli descended the church steps and approached the courier. As he neared, Bertolli found himself overwhelmed by the fierceness and regalia of the trio. Sitting upon his huge horse, the courier appeared majestic. He wore a fine red tunic tied around the waist with a sash of gold silk. His horse was so spectacularly muscled and well groomed that its deep auburn paint shimmered in the sunlight and caused Bertolli to squint. Though the village was the kind of place far more familiar to the mule, Bertolli had, of course, seen horses before, but not like this one.

"This is a far-off little village, isn't it?" said the courier.

"I wouldn't know, sir."

"Why is that, boy?"

"I have never been much beyond the village walls, sir."

"Ah," nodded the courier, seemingly impressed by the boy's self-awareness, "I see. Well, you appear well fed in this little village, well fed, indeed. Perhaps there is no point in venturing out, perhaps none at all. But," the courier lowered his voice as he leaned over toward Bertolli, the leather of his saddle squeaking against his trousers, "beyond these walls, boy, there are wonders and adventures beyond your wildest dreaming. There are bodies of water wider than a hundred days' journey by ship, and sea creatures so awesome they eat boys like you by the dozen and shit forth your bones cleaned of every morsel of muscle and organ. There are mountains higher than a hundred days' walking can crest, mountains lorded over by giant snow beasts whose fangs and nails are the size of daggers and whose thirst for blood—particularly young and virgin—is insatiable. And while you may be too young to appreciate this now, there are women—beguiling creatures of such beauty and mystery that in a fleeting look you will be smitten forever. They will steal your heart, take over your mind and tantalize your flesh to heights of pleasure your young brain can hardly fathom. Oh, yes, there are wonders and mysteries all across this broad, flat world. And one day, boy, when your balls grow hairy and your spirit craves to eat more from life than the home-grown grass, if you are so inclined, you will breach these village walls and make a great adventure of your life."

Bertolli was mesmerized and confused. The *corriere* spoke without a stitch of rhyme. Bertolli could only comprehend half of what the man said, but even that was enough to enthrall him.

Having had enough of their comrade's charade, one of the Meducci guards cleared his throat.

The noise broke the magic and the courier sat upright in his saddle when something in the near-distance caught his eye. "Bless'd Virgin," said the courier with a surprising softness as his vision beheld the statue of the Virgin that sat above the church's entrance.

"Faccia di stronzo," said the Meducci guard who had just cleared his throat, "would you get on with it."

"Yes, yes," said the courier dismissively. "You are an altar boy of this humble church?"

"Yes, sir," said Bertolli.

"Good," said the courier. "And has this church a priest?"

"Yes, sir. Shall I fetch him?"

"No need. You seem like a capable youth." The courier removed a letter from his leather satchel. "Have you any idea what this is?"

"No, sir," said Bertolli.

" 'Tis an official papal decree, written and signed by His Holiness Pope Leon XI and His Eminence Cosimo di Pucci de' Meducci the Third. It is of the utmost importance. The will of God Himself, conducted through the Holy Pope and honorable Meducci and set to parchment. Handed directly from His Holiness to yours truly, with the express command that I hand-deliver this decree to the padre of this little church and every like church throughout Tuscany. But since my men and I are ravaged by thirst and hunger and desirous of visiting the tavern, I will entrust final passage of this ordinance to you, altar boy. Do you understand me?"

Bertolli was speechless. He could feel the energy building inside him, the devilish curiosity.

"Ragazzo," said the courier, snapping the altar boy back to attention. "Do you understand me?"

"Yes, sir."

"Good." The courier motioned with the letter toward Bertolli, but as Bertolli reached up for the letter, the courier pulled it back. "Now, altar boy," said the courier, "under no circumstances are you to open the letter. Do not let curious fingers chip the wax from its seal. Do not unfurl one crease of its fold. Do not even hold it to the light to make out its contents. Remember, from God's will to Pope's quill, from Pope's charge to my duty, from my duty to your honor." The courier then set the letter in Bertolli's outstretched hand. "Now off you go, *ragazzo*, off you go."

    🍅   🍅   🍅

Inside the confessional, Bertolli ran his nervous, chubby fingers over the fine papal letter and not-so-innocently flaked away at the elaborate wax seal. It was a perplexing time in his young life. His *Confermazione* was fast approaching and he was having great difficulty rationalizing his boyish instincts against his pending manhood. For reasons unbeknownst to him, many of the actions that had brought him so much joy, and he had given hardly a thought to, now brought him far less joy and provoked far more thought. Such contemplation was not pleasant and the idea of giving up the antics that had defined his youth was not easy for him.

Indeed, tormenting the old padre had been the highlight and focus of his last four years. Evidence of his former antics and triumphs was all about him. Even inside the confessional, a deep inhale through the nostrils could still catch the slight aroma of the rotten eggs Bertolli had hidden two years back. It had taken the old padre four vexing months, in which he'd thought a demon had inhabited the sacred domain, before he finally discovered the source of the fetid sulfuric odor.

Oh, but times had changed, and much to Bertolli's current consternation, the new Good Padre, as he was commonly called, existed so far beyond Bertolli's limited understanding of the world that the poor boy's mind was in crisis. Even his altar boy responsibilities, which had always been a perfunctory duty forced upon him by his grandmother, were now a service he secretly relished. He was spending so much time at the church that his grandmother had come to suspect he'd discovered a key to the wine cellar and was up to no good.

After all, pondered Bertolli, who was this new Good Padre? He'd simply arrived in town the very day after the old padre died. But how? Bertolli wondered. He knew everything that went on at the church, and no one to his knowledge had notified the diocese in Florence that the village was in need of a new priest—and so quickly. As far as Bertolli could recall, in the four years he'd been an altar boy, no one informed the diocese about anything, ever. But there he was, at the door of the church, so Bertolli did what everyone else in the village did: he let him in, fearfully assuming that the Holy See had a far greater vision than anyone had previously imagined.

The timing of the new priest's arrival was just one of the many mysteries that perplexed Bertolli. The man was, without a doubt, the most confounding person Bertolli had ever laid eyes upon; a man whose voice seemed to echo from Bertolli's bowels to his brain like a sacred hymn chanted by a hundred monks; who spoke in metaphors that only made sense after a day's pondering; who cooked meals for him with flavors well beyond anything his own grandmother ever prepared; who was as big as a water buffalo, yet gentle as a ewe; and whose eyes glowed with a magnanimous joy that transfixed the boy.

But more than anything, Bertolli's mind was gripped by the utter incomprehensibility of the Good Padre's appearance. It was possible to describe the size of the Good Padre's shoulders, the thickness of his chest, the bellow of his voice; however, his complexion seemed to defy thought itself. Every time Bertolli was in the presence of the Good Padre, his brain would flutter with a vague, foggy notion that the Good Padre was as dark and shiny as a profoundly purple eggplant[3]. But the thought would not stay still and the more Bertolli tried to comprehend it, the thought would slip and twist and become even more incomprehensible. It was like trying to draw water with a sieve. Every time Bertolli attempted to confirm such a thought out loud, either to himself or another, the thought would simply drain from his mind and the words evaporate from his tongue.

The courier's charge now clanged like an Easter morning church bell in the belfry of Bertolli's mind. He was trying to change, he was trying to be good, but old habits, even for young altar boys, were not so easily undone. The parchment of the letter was so fine, the wax seal so intricate. He felt

---

[3] Historical Note: throughout medieval and Renaissance Italy, the word black, *nero,* was not considered a color, rather the absence of color, and was used only to describe inanimate objects. Vernacular of that day commonly used fruits and vegetables as a means for describing the skin color of an individual or ethnic group. For example, travelers from the British Isles were described as having skin the color of cow's cream; Ottomans, the sun-bleached hue of dried apricots; and Africans, the profoundly purple sheen of a ripe eggplant.

himself growing intoxicated on the faint scent of rotten eggs. His thumbnail flaked away a small fleck of wax. It was too much, all the unsettled questions spinning about his brain. Might the letter hold some insight about the Good Padre? Might it?

❀   ❀   ❀

Meanwhile, in the church's garden, kneeling on the slim strip of upturned earth between the rows of zucchini on his left and eggplants on his right, the Good Padre contemplated which of several splendidly ripe eggplants he should pluck for the evening's supper. The other day a new idea for eggplant preparation had come to him and he was eager to try it out. The recipe, as he imagined it, would begin with eggplant, cut width-wise into finger-thick slices. Next, the Good Padre planned to dip the slices into egg batter and then dredge them in chestnut flour with coarsely crushed walnuts, pignoli, sea salt and red pepper flakes. Filling a skillet half-knuckle deep with olive oil, he would then fry the slices until their outsides were golden and their innards soft. Next, the Good Padre planned to lay slices of a particularly pungent, semi-firm cow's-milk cheese upon the fried eggplant pieces. Finally, he would set the skillet in an oven to soften the cheese and bake the eggplant.

To dress the eggplant slices, the Good Padre conceived of a new version of pesto. He would still use olive oil, salt, pepper, pignoli and a little squeeze of lemon, but diverging from the recipe made popular in Genoa, he would complement basil with an equal amount of fresh mint and even a few sage leaves. Overall, he imagined the fried eggplant meat, nutty coating and ripe cheese would blossom nicely under the sage and mint pesto's zest.

The Good Padre was fortunate in that his arrival in the village had coincided with the spring planting season and he was now reaping the verdant benefits of late August in Tuscany. He viewed the success of his small plot as an affirmation of his faith and a harbinger of good things to come. At the center of the church's garden stood a lovely, five-foot-high replica of the same Virgin Mary statue located above the church entrance. In designing his garden, the Good Padre had intentionally created a nimbus-like shape, with all twelve planting rows angling outward from the feet of the Virgin.

Reaching his decision as to which eggplant to try his recipe upon, the Good Padre set his grip around a fine specimen. It was a slight, gentle action that lent a keen perspective to the Good Padre's size and complexion, as the bulbous deep-purple eggplant nearly blended with the color of the Good Padre's skin and disappeared beneath the girth of his palm and width of his fingers. The Good Padre was a huge man, but it was not so much the Good Padre's height that was overwhelming, as he was only a few fingers' width taller than the average man; it was his thickness.

The Good Padre's chest was like an old walnut tree trunk and his arms were like the thick lower branches that had first matured and born fruit three centuries ago. If, in passing, one happened to gently lay a hand upon the Good Padre's knee or shoulder, he would find it to be the size and oblong roundness of the largest late-summer honeydew melon he had ever touched. The Good Padre's fingers shared both their size and slightly bulbous shape with a soon-to-be giant squash halfway through its growing season. His nose had the width and slope of a small pear from Piedmont. His nostrils, each the circumference of a colossal green olive from Sicily, and his head, the girth and glabrous sheen of a Mantuan pumpkin in late November. His teeth were like the large acorns that dropped from white oak trees in November, and when he smiled, which he often did, his mouth curved and broadened to the size of an August carob bean hanging from a tree in Lucca. His wide eyes emanated both the wholesome allure and the glint of playfulness that can only be understood if one has sliced a ripe Umbrian fig through the belly of its width and gazed upon its starry innards. Indeed, the Good Padre was a man of startling and perplexing complexion, but as part of his curse (more of a magical enchantment, really), certain physical and temporal details evaded his perception and he had not the slightest idea that his size and color were the least bit unusual.

❋   ❋   ❋

"Gli Ebrei," uttered Bertolli as he lowered the letter from his eyes. A thousand invectives the old padre had spewed burst inside Bertolli's head. His heart began to pound so loudly it clogged his ears from the inside out. "Oh, God!" Bertolli cursed himself as he darted from the confessional. "Why did I let the Good Padre teach me how to read?" But Bertolli's mind was so astir from the shocking news that his eyes saw not what they had seen a thousand times before, and he promptly crashed into the wood bench of the church's rearmost row.

A vivid terror overtook Bertolli as he looked up to see the church pews toppling upon one another, one by one. In the stillness of trauma, Bertolli knew exactly what to do and he clearly envisioned he had the strength and agility to stop the toppling rows. However, fate was far more ironic, and as Bertolli sprang to action, he failed to release his grip upon the papal letter, which had gotten pinched between the fallen rows, thus causing him to tear the fine parchment entirely in two.

❋   ❋   ❋

"Bertolli," the Good Padre sighed as he heard the spectacular racket echoing from inside the church. He began to count the seconds until the spirited boy would appear before him, panting, all too ready with a fanciful excuse. At roughly the count of four, the Good Padre heard the distant shout of "Padre!" crackling from the boy's prepubescent larynx. By the count of nine, the voice was right behind him.

"Padre," Bertolli said, gasping for breath, "urgent news."

Ignoring the boy's frenzy, the Good Padre remained on one knee alongside the row of eggplants. With great care, as if detaching a newborn from its mother's umbilical cord, he separated the eggplant he'd been holding from its vine, lifted it to his nose and gave it a sniff.

"Take heed of this eggplant's vital glow." The Good Padre spoke out loud, though not at his altar boy. "But what was key to its bountiful growth? By water and sun both fruit and man can survive, but what are the means by which we thrive? For in richness of man and richness of earth, there is one special nutrient that gives bounty birth. And this nutrient so natural to her soul," the Good Padre gestured to the statue of the Virgin, "does too make man and land whole."

"But Padre—" Bertolli attempted to speak.

"You see, young Bertolli," said the Good Padre, "this eggplant grows more splendid than another 'cause it grows by love of the Sacred Mother. And when by love, man or fruit does render, we blossom to beings of utter splendor." Taking no particular notice of the torn letter, the Good Padre stood up, handed Bertolli the eggplant and took a deep inhale.

"*Boun Pa . . .*" said Bertolli, until the word suddenly deflated upon his tongue. He was halted by the length and depth of the Good Padre's inhale and how his already massive frame seemed to expand like a sail catching wind. The sound too was overwhelming, a great drawing in of air that played before the ear like a giant bellows stoking a blacksmith's kiln. "Urgent tidings," the boy said meekly, his fervor undone by awe.

"Ah, do you smell this morn's fine air?" said the Good Padre. "Oh, the joy to be young and without care! Now, young Bertolli, listen to your padre and the wasted youth that I'll attest, less time in church and more at play would do you best." The Good Padre paused as it occurred to him he couldn't exactly remember his own youth.

"But Padre, urgent tidings from Holy Rome."

"Rome," said the Good Padre with a wave of his hand. "For youth, Rome can wait."

"But Padre, please. This is serious."

"Well," chuckled the Good Padre, "then 'tis a fine day even better that Vatican courier hath entrusted you with papal letter."

Bertolli groaned in dismay.

"Oh, Bertolli," said the Good Padre, his attention suddenly fixated on a bee as it disappeared between the petals of a burgundy rose in full bloom, "nothing is so serious 'til man think it so." He bent over and brought his nose dangerously close to the bee's endeavoring then gently sniffed the air. "Do you see, Bertolli, is it not sublime, this interplay of life? Do not all actions, be they elaborate or random, seem governed by divine accord? For the rose will choke upon its nectar unless extracted by the bee, and the bee that takes the nectar gives honey to man." The Good Padre turned his head and looked directly into Bertolli's eyes. "Who could imagine sweetness to arise in such a manner?"

⊛   ⊛   ⊛

"Bertolli," said the Good Padre, breaking the extended moment of silence.

"Yes, Padre," the boy said faintly.

"Speak. Speak."

"Oh," said Bertolli, with hardly the fervor of a moment ago. *"Gli Ebrei, Gli Ebrei sono liberi."* The *Ebrei* are to be free.

In Which We Learn of
Truffles & Other Mushrooms

With a knowing snort and a taut yank on the leashes around his wrist, Benito knew his little pigs had caught a whiff. This was the moment of the hunt and Benito shouted through the forest, *"Tartufi! Tartufi!"* to share his joy with the one he both loved and hated.

It was early Sunday morning and though Benito had already been up for hours, he felt stiff and unprepared to match the morning vigor of his *little ladies*. He belched as he struggled to keep control over the three knee-high sows leashed to his right wrist, and tasted an acrid teaspoon of last night's drink as it sloshed back up from his belly. He feared he might vomit. Benito knew why his boss desired to go truffle hunting at such a premature time—Benito wasn't as stupid as people thought him to be—but he never imagined that his trio of adolescent female pigs would actually catch a scent in late August. Last evening, at the tavern, as he ordered one, two and then three more pints, he did so figuring that today's endeavor would prove nothing more than a futile walk in the woods with his lazy sows and greedy boss. But Benito's truffle-hunting sows most certainly had caught scent of something and the familiar feeling of both joy and dread shot through Benito's ale-bloated body.

Though it might seem more logical for Benito to balance the stress by holding two of his sows' leashes in his left hand and one in his right, or vice versa, he knew better. He had never forgotten his first truffle hunt, when he mistakenly held two of his sows' leashes in his left hand and one in his right and was left helpless as the fervent creatures divided around an oak tree, pulled his arms in two directions and ran his splayed-out body directly into the knobby old tree. The impact did poor Benito's appearance no favor and furthered the expansion of a nose that had already faced numerous hardships.

It was amazing to Benito how creatures with such short legs and small strides could move at a clip so challenging to match. For the most part, sows were lazy animals, but once they caught a truffle's scent, the little creatures went through an utter transformation: a demeanor marked by reluctance and sloth suddenly became one of vehemence. Thighs and hindquarters that moments ago jiggled like spongy adipose now snapped and shimmered with sinewy muscle. The rapture, though, was not without a certain grace, and no one could attest to that more than Benito.

⁂   ⁂   ⁂

For those unfamiliar with the near-narcotic flavor of a truffle, it may come as a surprise to learn that the most expensive and sought-after food in all of Italy is foraged by such unlikely creatures. There is, however, nothing ordinary about truffles. On the chance that the reader has never eaten a truffle of the Tuscan variety and quality, let it be known it conveys both a flavor and a sensation unlike any other food. In the most tangible sense, a good truffle tastes something like a cross between porcini mushrooms, roasted garlic and fresh-shelled walnuts. However, it's the intangible that makes the truffle so resplendent. Along with the earthy flavor of porcini, garlic and walnut, truffles exude a profound and slightly unnerving gaseous musk. A scent that is unique among all the foods of the world.

The authentic truffle experience begins in the olfactory gland as the clump of fungus (about the size of a garlic bulb) is shaved over a steaming plate of fettuccine in sweet butter or a puree of wild mushroom soup with roasted barley. Caught in the steamy vapors, the truffle's aroma enchants the nostrils with an otherworldly quality, at once sublime and disturbing. In some cases, a deep whiff or mouthful of fresh truffle has been known to cause women of weak constitutions to faint and men to awkwardly contend with a sudden *bastone* tenting up their trousers and colliding against the underside of the dinner table. In fact, the age-old Tuscan adage for good luck—*Tocando Legno* (knock wood)—was widely believed to have originated with ancient truffle hunters who equated good fortune with truffle-inspired erections knocking against wooden tables.

In order to maintain the truffle's elevated allure and price, truffle hunters have historically exaggerated both the mysteries of the fungus and their own prowess to excavate it. But, in truth, a truffle hunter can only be as good as the pig he has trained. Pigs have extraordinary olfactory capabilities, and well-trained truffle-hunting sows, like Benito's, are skilled enough to locate the faint gaseous aroma of a ripe truffle from five hundred paces out, all the more impressive considering truffles grow an average of six inches under the forest bed.

    🍅   🍅   🍅

Benito's call of *"Tartufi!"* shot through the forest and pierced the bull's-eye of Giuseppe's ire. The animalistic echo of his underling's voice startled Giuseppe and his toes instinctively clenched inside his boots. This slight, near imperceptible twitch of muscle and tendon aroused Giuseppe's gout and sent a painful spasm up his nervous system. His trigger finger quivered at the worst possible moment and he watched his ivory-tipped bolt[4]—purchased in Pistoia at some cost—miss its target and lodge irrevocably into the thick bark of a chestnut tree.

"*Vaffanculo!*" Giuseppe murmured unpleasantly as he lowered his crossbow and watched his would-be prey bound into oblivion. "Benito." Giuseppe said it like a curse word. It was bad enough to lose a good kill and the opportunity to torment his stepdaughter by forcing her to skin and roast a *rabbitte bunnio;* but to waste such a fine and costly arrow was especially irksome.

"*Merda,*" huffed Giuseppe as he finally relented in his struggle to remove the impacted arrow when something caught his eye. "*Merda,*" Giuseppe said again, this time with an inquisitive tone. There, just to the side of the tree, basking in a slender stream of sunlight and growing up from the loose, decomposed forest bed, sat an enormous patch of some two hundred mushrooms. "*Sacra merda!*" By their shape—slim two-inch stems and smallish, wavy caps—he knew precisely what he had found.

Giuseppe removed a small cloth from his pocket and spread it on the ground. He hadn't seen this type of mushroom in years, but remembered it well and knew this patch he'd come upon, once extracted of its toxins, would make enough poison to turn half the village into a drooling mass of idiots. Giuseppe reached inside his right boot and removed a gleaming, ox-bone-handled seven-inch dagger. He used its sharp tip to loosen the soil under the mushrooms, pluck them up and set them on the cloth.

While these particular fungi had not the gastronomic value of the truffle, they were still quite valuable. *Fungi di Santo,* they were called: Saint's Mushrooms. The name, rightly or wrongly, was attributed to a sect of 12th-century Gnostic monks, *Il Ordo Fratrum Risata,* Order of the Laughing

---

[4] A crossbow arrow.

Brothers, who were believed to use the mushrooms as part of their religious practices. The fungi were a poison of sorts, and while not wholly lethal, once ingested they brought on visions and dementia, fits of laughter and a special kinship with nature. The intoxication typically lasted six or so hours; but a highly concentrated dose, by Giuseppe's recollection, could severely alter the mind for an extended period of time and, in certain instances, cause permanent derangement.

As a teenager in Rome, Giuseppe had helped his uncle use *Fungi di Santo*-tainted wine to turn a cadre of pompous French diplomats into a choir of giggling girls. On another occasion, he and his uncle used the same fungi-laced wine to transform a reserved and ruthless bishop into a babbling fool before the Pope. However, when the irate bishop discovered the whereabouts of the boy who'd delivered the tainted wine, it was a fifteen-year-old Giuseppe who took the fall for his uncle and the Meducci Cardinal who hired them. For the offense, Giuseppe spent two years in a dank prison cell, where he was intermittently beaten and abused, and ironically, after his release, it was a bottle of wine infused with *Fungi di Santo* that Giuseppe used to bludgeon his uncle to death.

"Tartufi, tartufi!" Benito's voice rang through the forest.

"Yes, you idiot," Giuseppe mumbled as he collected the mushrooms, tucked them into his satchel and made his way in the direction of Benito's voice. My God, Giuseppe thought with some surprise, could those little pigs have really caught a scent of a truffle in late August?

Benito was relieved to see Giuseppe approach, as his sows had been halted by a new chest-high wood fence that cut through the forest. Benito couldn't remember his pigs ever behaving this excitedly. Such commotion would have normally thrilled him, but he found the circumstances before him quite conflicting and he looked to Giuseppe for direction.

"Ebrei," said Giuseppe as he stepped aside the pigs and gazed over the wood fence protecting a patch of recently cleared land and a lone tombstone marked with strange letters and a six-pointed star. *"Gli Ebrei,"* Giuseppe repeated, lips crinkling with disgust.

Benito's sows snorted anxiously as they dug with their snouts about the base of the fence, where the wood planks ran into the earth. Benito found this unsettling and though the muscles of his lower back ached and his belly gurgled with nausea, he mustered the strength to pull the hot-blooded creatures back.

Giuseppe could excuse the snorting and salivating of the sows as a bestial sound common to their nature, but he found the labored panting of Benito intolerable. To Giuseppe's never-ending vexation, Benito was always making some disgusting and distracting noise, be it his heavy mouth-breathing, his habit of humming and singing songs to which he hardly knew the words or, even worse, the combination of moaning, lip-smacking and belching that accompanied his eating.

"Will you stop your Goddamn slobbering!" Giuseppe spat out the words like rancid wine. He needed to think. How, Giuseppe pondered, as he'd pondered over much of the last year, could a sorry handful of *Ebrei* have come into possession of such a fine parcel, which had belonged to the Meducci for as long as anyone could remember?

Over the course of summer, Giuseppe's curiosity had grown to the point where he could no longer ignore it and, under the guise of hunting for game and foraging for truffles, Giuseppe began bringing Benito and his pigs to the forests southeast of town to get a clearer sense of just how much property the *Ebrei* possessed. Though Giuseppe had no information on how the small clan of Florentine *Ebrei* had managed to acquire the land, experience had taught him that only guilt, greed or love could cause a man to blatantly ignore and contradict every law and tradition that governed property ownership in Tuscany. But what does one as rich and powerful as the Meducci feel guilt or greed over, especially from a lowly lot of *Ebrei*? It must be a woman, thought Giuseppe. One of the famed *Courtesane Ebreane*[5], perhaps? The reason hardly mattered, for what was now clear as day was that Giuseppe

---

[5] *Ebreo* courtesans, sometimes referred to as *La Sorella di Ester,* the Sisters of Esther, a secret association of exquisitely trained courtesans who operated in many of Europe's leading cities and were rumored to have infiltrated the highest reaches of society.

was no longer the preeminent landholder in the area and this was entirely unacceptable to him.

Grave-robbing, chided La Piccola Voce, the little voice inside Benito's head, which so often spoke in opposition to Giuseppe's wishes, *is a task for only the truly wretched.* Benito had foraged for truffles in many places and under a variety of circumstances. He had dug his hands into all kinds of soil, but never had he done so in such proximity to a tombstone, particularly an *Ebreo* tombstone.

Benito had never actually met an *Ebreo.* According to the village's recently deceased padre, *Ebrei* in general, and this clan in particular, were especially worthy of suspicion and contempt. They had planted their fields with a strange red fruit that the old padre derisively referred to as Love Apples straight from the Garden of Eden. Benito had no idea what a *Pomo di Amore* was, nor did he fully recall what transpired in *Il Giardino di Eden,* but he knew it wasn't good and the little voice inside his head told him to let the dead rest in peace.

Benito turned to his boss for a cue. He had known Giuseppe since the very first day he arrived at the olive orchard, and the decades of familiarity had bred their share of contempt. Like many other itinerants looking for a few weeks' work harvesting olives and pressing oil, Giuseppe and a then thirteen-year-old Benito were randomly assigned as harvesting partners and given the none-too-pleasant task of denuding the fecund olive trees of their fruits. Six years Benito's senior, Giuseppe was from day one something of an older brother figure to Benito, albeit an often sadistic and corruptive one.

Despite his arrogance and wicked temper, Giuseppe possessed a trait that Benito had never seen in any of the villagers: ambition. Within a few weeks of their first meeting, Giuseppe quietly and seductively shared with Benito how he planned to one day own orchards, and that maybe, *maybe,* he would bring Benito along as foreman. Such talk captivated Benito. He had never been considered in anyone's plans, not even his parents', who, until the day they died (an earthquake caused their hovel to collapse on them as they slept), had scarcely set a place for him at the dinner table. Hence, his inclusion in Giuseppe's schemes and dreams was enough to secure Benito's desperate adolescent devotion.

Giuseppe demanded this devotion, and throughout much of Benito's youth, he doled out severe punishment upon Benito for even the slightest show of disloyalty. *La Punizione,* Giuseppe called it, as his uncle had called it before him, and he used this disciplinary tactic to such effect that by the time he finally did come into possession of his own vineyard and olive orchard, he had molded Benito into an entirely devout and dependent underling—or so he thought. In actuality, their relationship was bound by odious abuse and a villainous secret, and as unions of guilt are often marked by contempt, rancor and bizarre dependency, so too was the relationship between Giuseppe and Benito.

🍅   🍅   🍅

Benito swallowed hard as the little voice inside his head shouted, *You coward! You servant to a murderer! Don't do it!* But as the heel of Giuseppe's finely crafted brown boot came crashing down upon the rickety wood fence, Benito did indeed do it. He squelched the little voice, trampled the fence and gave in to the sows' euphoria as they charged at the truffle-scented spot of earth. Oh, how a part of him, a part that he'd come to hate, still loved to make Giuseppe happy!

Six inches under the soil Benito's fingertips grazed the bulbous heads of two extraordinarily large truffles. He wriggled his digits deeper to snap the truffles from the root they grew upon. It was a strange-feeling root: smooth, straight, ivory-like, unlike any he had ever touched. In the midst of his delight Benito was able to suppress his suspicion, but for days afterward the root's imprint upon his fingertips proved indelible. No matter how often he grated the tips of his fingers across his rough wool trousers, Benito could not scrub away the unnerving thought that he had unearthed the two most splendid truffles he had ever seen from the thigh bone of a recently dead *Ebreo.*

In Which We Learn
the Shared History
of the Tomato & the Ebreo

S unday was a special day on the farm, a year-old family ritual in which Nonno, Davido, his six aunts and uncles, their five children and any guests would gather around the table for a relaxing afternoon feast. Considering that in two Sundays Davido would be married and living in Florence for the next twelve months, the moment he and Nonno returned from Florence Davido went straight to the kitchen, doing his best to cook away all the anxiety that simmered inside him.

Waiting for him there, Davido found a surprise—the best thing he'd come upon in the last three days. Rabbi Lumaca and a small entourage from the town of Pitigliano were visiting to discuss wedding plans and they brought with them a fine pair of bronzini, just pulled from the waters that very morning and packed in salt. Fresh fish was a splendid treat for all, especially Davido, as it afforded him more leeway with the restrictive *Ebreo* dietary laws than did preparing a meal with meat. How it was that a few brief biblical passages stating that one should not cook a calf in its mother's cud got extrapolated into a set of food laws so elaborate that one could not even place cheese and meat upon the same table, not even with poultry, was beyond Davido's sense of logic and gastronomy. How could one cook a chicken in its *mother's milk*?

Fish, on the other hand, gave Davido the opportunity to work with cheese, which he enjoyed greatly. Ever since he and his kin began raising their own animals, Davido had rather lost his taste for meat. The idea of eating one of the cows, goats or sheep that he had helped rear and could not help but adore now had little appeal. Thankfully, the farm's five sheep, four goats and two cows were needed for their milk, not their meat. Even the farm's thirty or so chickens—more valuable for their eggs, soil-nourishing manure and insect-eating prowess— got to live a long life before finding their way into the cook pot or onto a spit. While meat had become of less and less interest to Davido, vegetables and cheese—vegetables he grew and the goat, sheep and cow's milk cheeses he and Uncle Uccello had begun to make—had never before been so precious and delicious to him.

Cooking too. Since moving onto the farm, the preparing of food had taken on a whole new attraction for Davido, and he threw himself into it with all his heart. It was the culmination of the cycle of life that so enamored him: earth, seed, plant, blossom, vegetable, fruit, cutting board, cook pot and finally table. It was also something that came naturally to him and that he did exceedingly well, the one thing he understood and did better than Nonno ever had.

Back in Florence, Davido's grandfather seemed to have a mastery of everything in which Davido struggled and *Ebrei* were judged by. Though they lived humbly in Florence (best not to raise the suspicion of the ruling gentile class), every

Ebreo knew that Nonno was the richest man in the ghetto and the de facto leader of the *Ebreo* community. His life story was legendary. At age twenty-three, little older than Davido, back in Toledo, Nonno's skill with numbers had vaulted him to the position of finance minister for Ferdinand and Isabella. He had voyaged with Cristoforo Colombo and spent ten years living among the island natives before returning to Europe. The man was smart beyond comprehension; in addition to *Italiano,* he spoke *Spagnolo, Francese, Portoghese, Tedesco, Latino,* even the ancient *Ebreo* language which was only used for prayer. And sometimes, when his grandfather's siesta slumber was especially deep, Nonno could be overheard mumbling in that bizarre tongue that he claimed to have learned from the *Indiani* of *Il Nuovo Mundo.* But when it came to the farm and kitchen, Nonno was all thumbs and none of them green. True, the old man loved his tomatoes and was singularly responsible for introducing them to Europe, but his expertise was only in eating them. Here, among the trees and plants, fruits and vegetables, cook pots and roasting fires was where Davido shined, and his illustrious Nonno had little choice but to defer to his knowledge and instinct.

※   ※   ※

Despite an early rise, a three-hour donkey ride from Florence, a two-hour effort in the kitchen, a full belly and the cool weight of tomatoes shading his eyes and perfuming the air around him, Davido couldn't sleep. This was especially disconcerting to him, as just being around his tomato plants tended to calm his mind and deepen his breath. There was something about the smell of tomato plants that Davido adored so profoundly that from first planting in early May through last picking in late October, he would sneak away to siesta in between their rows every day, with the zeal of a young lover off to visit his paramour. With certainty, he could be found just a few dozen meters from the barn, between the first and second rows of plants, lying on his back with a ripe tomato upon each eye to block out the sun and young green leaves under his nostrils to sweeten his suspiration. To him, the plant's fragrance was sublime and sacred. A scent that transcended his olfactory organs to purify his heart and cleanse his mind.

Now, as any wise parent will attest, few things create quite as much curiosity in children as the quietly confident and completely abnormal behavior of an adult, and it wasn't long before Davido's siesta habits were mimicked by most of the farm's children. The youngsters were Davido's cousins, the children of his aunts and uncles who had moved onto the farm at Nonno's insistence. As such, few of their parents took umbrage to the tangle of limbs and leaves that slumbered away the afternoons. And on the occasion when his curious siesta practices were called into question, Davido simply replied that they were a recipe for sweet dreams. And indeed they were. After growing up amongst the reeking, congested labyrinth of Florence's ghetto, these rolling acres of farmland and forest that Davido now called home carried a breeze so restorative that in thirteen months a lifetime of foul smells had been nearly eviscerated from the corridors of his nostrils. That was, at least, until this last visit burned the ghetto's stench back into his nose.

Beyond all of the other bad memories, Florence in the summer carried an especially rancorous odor that undid any and all peace of his afternoon siesta. Yes, he was satisfied with the preparations he'd made for lunch that day—indeed, the fish was especially delicious—but something about the pasta wasn't quite right. The flavors were too thin and ill-combined. Noodles squirmed upon the palate from the virgin lubrication of olive oil. Tomatoes slid across the tongue and burst under tooth, diluting the other flavors. The piquant dried goat cheese and the fresh basil were a nice touch, but, as a whole, the dish was strangely unsubstantial, inconsequential and ultimately disconnected. The pasta neither left the mouth with a robust impression nor stuck to the ribs with satisfaction. This culinary inadequacy very much undermined the quality of Davido's rest. Lying there, under the weight of the plant's fruits and leaves, Davido could not help but feel that the tomato and the pasta could be better combined.

The truth was, despite his complete adoration of the tomato, Davido didn't entirely understand it. Neither did Nonno.
None of the books on farming he'd bought in Florence even
knew the tomato existed. True, while growing up in the ghetto
he and his sister would propagate a few seeds each spring
and grow a dozen tomato plants from pots in the courtyard
of their building, always collecting the seeds from the largest, best-looking and best-tasting fruit. But that was hardly
the large-scale production he was into now. Everything about
the tomato was a process of experimentation, and while the
crop was producing this year in spectacular fashion, it was
the phase after the tomato was ripe and picked that troubled
Davido the most.

There were thousands upon thousands of tomatoes to be
dealt with. Just keeping up with the demands of harvesting
such a bountiful crop, let alone the myriad other farm-life
demands, was a near full-time affair, and Davido was placing great pressure on himself to conjure up other uses for
tomatoes. The trouble was, besides precious little spare time
for experimentation, when it came to cooking the tomato,
Davido was flummoxed. The fruit emitted a great deal of water when heated and while this was acceptable for the braised
bronzini—the sauce more on the brothy side—for pasta it just
wasn't right.

Neither was this whole business about marriage! The
weekend had been awful. Florence was hot and stunk like
shit and piss, just like it did every summer. The visit with
his bride-to-be had been a fiasco, burdened by the enormity
of the commitment placed on the two young people. And if
there had been even a flicker of hope in Davido's mind it was
emphatically extinguished after he presented her with a gift
basket full of ripe tomatoes. Her reaction was one of utter
indifference, and she three times refused her father's invitation to indulge in one of the sweet fruits in front of their
guests—a deflection that slammed the barn door of Davido's
heart. Fine, Davido begrudgingly recognized, she wasn't a
monster, but she was a girl, a child still, and she had none
of the earth in her that Davido craved. Her skin was fair and

her demeanor meek. Her wrists and ankles were so thin that Davido imagined they would snap beneath the toil of working a shovel into the soil. And as the moments of their visit dripped by, her continual glances at Davido's hands—which, despite much scrubbing, still held remnants of the farm under his fingernails—made clear her fear of country life. She would never make it on the farm, and though she and Davido shared few words with each other, they both seemed to know it. Likewise, Davido would never make it in Florence. Florence was death to him, the death of his mother, father and sister. If he had to leave the farm to marry and live in Florence for a year, he would die as well.

Abruptly, Davido sat up from his troubling siesta, causing the tomatoes that had been covering his eyes to roll down his torso and bounce off the heads and limbs of several slumbering children. He needed to forget about Florence and skinny ankles. He needed to practice his rhyme. He needed to come up with a proper tomato sauce!

"Wake up, wake up," urged Davido as he began to shake, jostle and tickle bellies. "Wake up and listen to me, children." Davido reached across the row and plucked a ripe tomato from its vine. " 'Tis time you learn the history of our fruits, 'cause in it lies our roots."

The half-dozen children awoke with a giggle. They had heard this story several times over the last year, but no one seemed to tell it like their *zio* Davido. "Now heed well, children, this story here, of why we hold this fruit most dear." Davido held the tomato in his hand before the children and lowered his voice as if revealing a secret. "A thousand years past by Imperial Rome's hand, we were scattered from the Holy Land. Thrown to the desert to find our own way, and a new land where the *Ebreo* could stay. And after centuries of hardship and pain, our ancestors arrived in Spain. Toledo is where our family history did first grow, with the Golden Age of the Spanish *Ebreo*. A time in which our people reached their finest hour, and our Nonno sat among the halls of power. Don Judah el Hebreo was then our Nonno's name, and he was chief accountant for King Ferdinand, Queen Isabella and all of Spain. But after years of service at the king and queen's side, there arose a hateful tide. This awful spell was called the *Inquisition,* and it put all Spain's *Ebrei* in a horrible position."

Davido squeezed hard and burst the tomato in his hand, sending juice and seeds squirting. The children shrieked and giggled. Davido leaned in. "But the king and queen did not want Nonno to go, for no one counted the bean better than their *Ebreo.* However, in that year ending in nine and two, something else was a-brew. A man named Colombo was about to set sail upon a voyage thought destined to fail. You see, Colombo believed the world was round, and to the west new lands to be found." The children's heads turned quickly as Davido pointed his finger in the direction they all mistook for west. "So, to save our Nonno from the Inquisition, Ferdinand and Isabella appointed him chief accountant of Colombo's expedition.

"The ship set sail and after thirty-three days reached the new shore, where Colombo and his men went forth to explore. They went in search of gold and treasure, leaving Nonno behind, as their greed would bear no measure. But alas, Colombo was sorely mistook, for our Nonno did more than keep the book. Resilient, adventurous and contemplative, Nonno used the years to study the land and befriend the native. He learned of their speech and custom and dance, and then one fateful night, as if by chance, the natives shared their sacred fruit, the very one that here takes root. When Nonno departed this mysterious place, the natives, in an act of friendship and grace, gave him a sack of tomato seeds most fine, so one day he may start his own vine.

"Now, Colombo, an Italian, spoke fondly of his home, and the fertile lands 'tween Milan and Rome. So with survival and the tomato on his mind, Nonno decided this region he would find. And off the coast of Genoa Nonno bid a secret adieu, to Colombo and his loathsome crew. And as Colombo described, indeed, Nonno found this perfect plot to lay his seed. So for our family and fruit, dear cousins, always revere, for it's been sacrifice and love that brought us here."

Davido finished his history lesson and allowed the children to bask in the rich, imaginative silence. Let them believe, he thought. Let them believe in a little magic. In time they will come to know all things: of Davido's sister, of *La Sorella di Ester* and of her life sacrifice; of their Nonno and of how he stole away from Colombo's ship with not only a sack of tomato seeds but enough gold and riches to bribe half of Italy.

6

In Which We Meet
Cosimo di Pucci de' Meducci III,
Grand Duke of Tuscany, &
Learn of His Decree

It was that moment of the day, the day in which we meet
Cosimo the Third, when the sun's first rays cracked
the horizon, sifting through the fine lace curtains of Cosimo's
four-horse-drawn carriage and falling upon his face. Behind
closed eyelids, Cosimo's pupils constricted, rousing him from
the enervating state that sadly passed as his nightly sleep.
Slowly, Cosimo opened his eyes and his vision came to rest
upon a grapevine-combed horizon glistening under Sunday
morning's late August dew. My God, thought Cosimo, with
the day's first workings of his mind, if only I were a farmer.

Cosimo di Pucci de' Meducci, who governed under the title
Cosimo the Third, was descended from, as he often put it, the
lesser lineage of a long and dubious line of inbreeds, half-wits,

THE GRAND LINEAGE OF THE PUCCI DE' MEDUCCI FAMILY

(* Indicates held Grand Duke title)

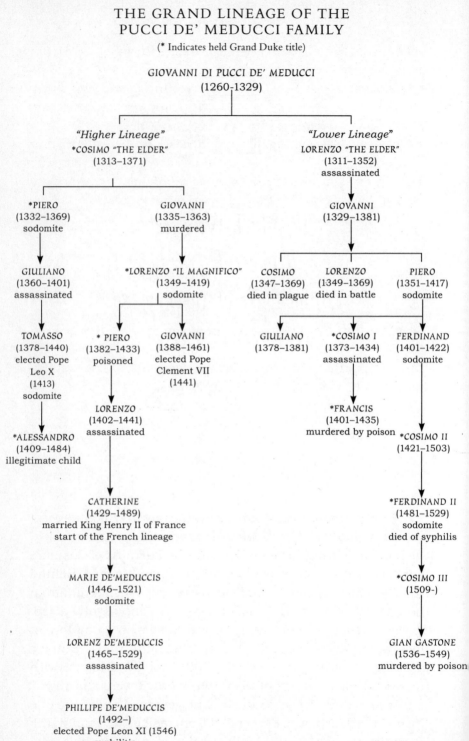

GIOVANNI DI PUCCI DE' MEDUCCI
(1260–1329)

"Higher Lineage"
*COSIMO "THE ELDER"
(1313–1371)

"Lower Lineage"
LORENZO "THE ELDER"
(1311–1352)
assassinated

*PIERO
(1332–1369)
sodomite

GIOVANNI
(1335–1363)
murdered

GIOVANNI
(1329–1381)

GIULIANO
(1360–1401)
assassinated

*LORENZO "IL MAGNIFICO"
(1349–1419)
sodomite

COSIMO
(1347–1369)
died in plague

LORENZO
(1349–1369)
died in battle

PIERO
(1351–1417)
sodomite

TOMASSO
(1378–1440)
elected Pope
Leo X
(1413)
sodomite

* PIERO
(1382–1433)
poisoned

GIOVANNI
(1388–1461)
elected Pope
Clement VII
(1441)

GIULIANO
(1378–1381)

*COSIMO I
(1373–1434)
assassinated

FERDINAND
(1401–1422)
sodomite

LORENZO
(1402–1441)
assassinated

*FRANCIS
(1401–1435)
murdered by poison

*ALESSANDRO
(1409–1484)
illegitimate child

*COSIMO II
(1421–1503)

CATHERINE
(1429–1489)
married King Henry II of France
start of the French lineage

*FERDINAND II
(1481–1529)
sodomite
died of syphilis

MARIE DE'MEDUCCIS
(1446–1521)
sodomite

*COSIMO III
(1509–)

LORENZ DE'MEDUCCIS
(1465–1529)
assassinated

GIAN GASTONE
(1536–1549)
murdered by poison

PHILLIPE DE'MEDUCCIS
(1492–)
elected Pope Leon XI (1546)
syphilitic

perverts, pedants, scoundrels, tyrants, sodomites and syphilitics, who seemed to have both an extraordinary love of the arts and an uncanny proclivity for getting themselves assassinated. Amongst Cosimo's direct ancestors and relatives were three popes, two queens of France, nine dukes of Tuscany, plus more cardinals, princes, princesses and foreign royalty by way of arranged marriage than he cared to recollect. Quite frankly, though, he despised almost all of them and harbored a great deal of contempt for his own family name.

For as long as he could remember, Cosimo was envious of the rural peasants who tended the land and populated the small towns and villages throughout his province. Yes, they were an ignorant lot, but from what little he knew they seemed to possess an honest joy and bawdiness for which Cosimo would have traded all his useless power and privilege. Even the lyrical and jubilant peasant dialect, *Etruscanato Antiquato*[6], rhymed and rolled from belly to tongue. It was a far cry from the reserved and gestureless *Nuovo Italiano* spoken by the nobility, which Cosimo was the lax, ineffectual and reluctant leader of. He had been educated to speak the New Italian, but he hated the dialect of the gentry whose forked tongues managed to freeze and crack even the warmest of Italian vowels. It was a sound, particularly as spoken by his wife, that would drive icicles into his ears. Great spells of silence were Cosimo's most common recourse, days on end when he would do little more than grunt and point, all the while dreaming in silence of how he'd gladly forfeit his title and a lifetime of speech if but for a day he could work

---

[6] *Etruscanato Antiquato* (Old Etruscan): the early-Italian dialect that evolved in Tuscany in the centuries after the ancient Etruscans were conquered by Rome (396 BC) and their indigenous language combined with Latin over the centuries to form Italian. Like many of the earliest languages (Aramaic, Greek, Hungarian, Basque), developed and spoken before the advent of writing, Old Etruscan was a largely rhyming idiom.

Linguists and anthropologists theorize that rhyming language developed as a means to facilitate memorization before the emergence and widespread understanding of written language. The conceit was elevated to an art form by traveling poets who used rhyme for the creation and performance of their epic poems (Homer). With the creation of the printing press (Venice, 1426), and by the time of the Renaissance, *Nuovo Italiano* had replaced its rhyming precursor as the official dialect of the educated, elite and city dwellers. By the sixteenth century, *Etruscanato Antiquato* was considered a quaint dialect spoken by rural peasants and eccentrics, commonly called *rimatori* (rhymers), and a sure sign of illiteracy.

amongst the rows of grapes and speak with the rapture and rhythm of a peasant.

For Cosimo, royalty and reputation seemed to serve up far more sourness than sweetness. In his first twenty years of life, Cosimo had endured the murder of two uncles, three assassination attempts upon his father (which ended up killing two food tasters, one of whom young Cosimo was especially fond of), two short yet brutal wars against the powerful Milanese clans to the north and, cruelest of all to a thirteen-year-old boy, the disappearance of his favorite cousin and only childhood friend.

Over the next twenty years, Cosimo endured the syphilitic demise of his father; the ravages of two plagues in Florence; a fierce and drawn-out conflict with the Spanish, who forever used Tuscany as their battleground with the French; an unwanted, politically arranged marriage to an aloof Austrian princess who expressed not an inkling of love for him (nor he for her); the usurpation of nearly all his power by his cousin the Queen of France; and, most recently and significantly, the poisoning of his beloved *courtesane.* She'd been poisoned by arsenic-laced honey she drizzled upon her chestnut polenta as she and Cosimo enjoyed a late-morning breakfast. Murdered a mere two weeks after Cosimo had given a less than enthusiastic recommendation that his eldest cousin, then a cardinal, would make a fine and pious Pope.

Of late, Cosimo had even come to feel that his own loins mocked him, as with the onset of his son's pubescence came the seemingly irrefutable evidence that his sole progeny had acquired the familial trait of being born a man more meant to be a woman. So much so that ever since the ravishingly beautiful and surprisingly maternal Queen Margarita of Naples visited Florence, young Prince Gian had taken to wearing his mother's dresses and calling himself Princess Margarita.

His son's peculiarity was but one of many anomalies, indignities and heartbreaks Cosimo had endured since he'd inherited the Dukeship of Tuscany. It was a title he neither coveted nor felt particularly worthy of. Despite the pomp, power and privilege, the title was a hellish burden and his near two decades as duke had been marked by fits of horrendous depression. Though he'd largely managed to keep Tuscany out of war, great violence had nonetheless been perpetrated against him. And over the course of two years (three months, thirteen days and seven hours) since the death of his courtesan, time dripped by like winter sap oozing from a dying chestnut tree, every moment a torment caught between the nostalgia of memory and the reality of her non-existence.

However, on this morning, as his speeding carriage blasted the grape-sweet air into his nostrils, Cosimo could feel the death-grip of melancholia recede and, for the first time in two years, he grinned. He was returning from Rome, where he had just successfully completed an official errand commissioned by his eminent second cousins, the King and Queen of France. By all appearances, his charge had been to travel to the Vatican and negotiate a series of religiously tolerant and economically inclusive papal decrees regarding the French-controlled Kingdom of Tuscany. However, the King and Queen of France were not so foolish as to leave the construction of important documents up to a mumbling, milk-hearted, whoremongering, bucolic dreamer like Cosimo. Cosimo was entirely aware that his real task was to play the part of official baby-sitter. He was the imperial pawn put in place by the King and Queen of France to undermine the Vatican and guarantee that the reluctant signature of his other cousin, Pope Leon XI, would grace the handful of documents.

Though Cosimo could have cared less, the stakes were rather high. The powers that controlled Europe were in flux. The Polish Empire was gaining strength and had begun to expand southward, encroaching into lands long controlled by the Turkish Empire. The Polacks wanted access and control over a southern port city, namely Venice, and they'd recently won a decisive victory over the Turks at Budapest, a major step in their march to the sea. This was not good for France, as it meant that Venice, an independent and important trading partner with France, could soon be under the sway of France's most significant European rival, the dreaded Polacks. Along with strengthening the army and readying for war, France needed to make its own ports and markets more attractive to foreign investment, and the only way to do so was to guarantee, as in Venice, that every *Moro, Greco, Turco, Ebreo, Gipsi, Africano, Indiano* and *Orientale* banker, shipper, trader, merchant, mercenary, charlatan and scoundrel would be free to conduct commerce without religious-based restriction and taxation. So, in the name of self-preservation, spurred on by greed and rivalry, sponsored by a heartless king and queen and signed into law by a hate-mongering Pope, Tuscany had just passed its most liberal laws to date, granting commerce a divinity not even the Church could molest.

🍅   🍅   🍅

The morning's dew cooked to vapor and carried the slight aroma of rosemary through the carriage windows, filling Cosimo's nostrils with the musk of nostalgia. For rosemary was *her* scent. In the years since her death, the shape of her face and contour of her body had begun to slip from his mind's grasp, but her aroma never left the tableau of Cosimo's dreams. The sweet perfume eased away the eight days of tension and conjured up memories of his courtesan so acute that Cosimo could feel his flesh tingle beneath the caress of his reminiscence. Oh, lamented Cosimo, who had never had the courage to tell her how dearly he loved her, she would have been so pleased by the news he had to tell!

Cosimo undid the first few buttons of his trousers to allow the restorative breeze to better circulate about his body. He closed his eyes and, from the safety of his carriage, recalled with vivid detail the sweet irony of his unintended revenge. He had not meant nor planned to enact a vendetta upon his cousin, which was why he deemed the events that transpired to have been divinely inspired. Oh, it was a slight reprisal in relation to the bloody retributions that marked his family name, but his love had known well that Cosimo had little taste for blood or family tradition. It was a poetic revenge, the kind of which his mistress would have approved: a soul-stirring sign that the eyes of his angel were still upon him.

Cosimo could still hear the echo of his cousin's footsteps

as he approached the aft chamber of the palace where Cosimo and the French entourage waited. Outrageously, they had been waiting for eight days and had grown fat on a constant diet of excuses about the Pontiff's "regrettably" busy schedule. Each day their meeting would be planned, delayed and then inevitably postponed. Through the days of monotony, Cosimo seemed to lose a degree of control over his mind, always waiting for the meeting to occur, always on edge.

The pervasive lack of light in the interior Vatican chambers trapped Cosimo in the dank shadows of memory. There, Cosimo spent much time revisiting and lamenting over that which had been stolen from him. He had little doubt that it was then *Cardinale* Meducci who "disappeared" his cousin and only childhood friend, just as it was the newly ascended Meducci Pope, Leon XI, who had destroyed his beloved paramour.

Despite Cosimo's desire to ponder more pleasant thoughts, he was unable to meditate on anything but the pending meeting with his cousin and all that this horrible man had stolen from his life. It was a cloudy meditation, one that wavered between vengeance and cowardice, anger and despair, and it culminated as Cosimo turned and caught sight of the flowing bloodred robe and the face that seemed to eat the light around it. Adrenal-laced fear flushed through Cosimo's veins with such a sudden hotness that he nearly loosed his bowels. It was his cousin.

Pope Leon XI was a fairly tall man marked by a gaunt and severe countenance that sunk his eyes into pools of shadow beneath the quarry of his brow. His nose was long and slender with a flat bridge in the most Roman of ways; it seemed always to cast a mountain of shade upon one pronounced cheekbone or the other. Even his temples, devoid of hair, seemed to fall off into shadow. Cosimo imagined not even Lucifer himself could carry so much darkness upon his face.

Cosimo had not seen his cousin for some time, but he recalled him as a man who seemed to thrive on hate. Hate was the breath and food of his existence and Cosimo could hardly imagine how the prospect of being the first Pope to grant freedom of movement, ownership and commerce to every godless *Moro, Greco, Turco, Ebreo, Gipsi, Africano, Indiano* and *Orientale* in Tuscany must have twisted his cousin's wretched gut. But, alas, as Cosimo knew, even Pope Leon XI had his superiors, and should the Polacks come to dominate Europe, a Franco-Italian Pope would need a legion of food tasters to protect him.

Pope Leon entered the room without looking up to greet his cousin nor any member of the French/Tuscan envoy. Despite his lack of acknowledgment of the guests, all in attendance rose until His Holiness took his official seat at the enormous marble table right alongside Cosimo. It was the closest physical proximity Cosimo had shared with his cousin since he was a child.

Immediately, the Pontiff began to feign perusal of the documents awaiting his signature. He knew full well what he was about to sign, but he continued the charade if not for the appearance of piety then at least to unsettle his cousin. Pope Leon leaned into the document, as if scrutinizing a particular passage, when the oddest thing occurred: sunlight fell upon his profile.

The arrangement of the room was such that the only shaft of direct sunlight came from a slender, western-facing rectangular window located a few feet behind and to the right of where the Pope sat. The window couldn't have been much larger than a foot in width and three feet in height, but it was just large enough to catch a sliver of the afternoon sun and undo the darkness that Pope Leon seemed to so covet.

Drained of shadow, a new light was cast upon Cosimo's fear. He had not seen his cousin for years, but in contrast to what Cosimo recalled from his youth, his cousin appeared to have not only aged, but veritably rotted. In the light, Cosimo noticed the age-spotted epidermis of his cousin's hand and how his skin looked thin as paper. How unsightly tributaries of blue veins spidered across his bald head and ashen complexion. How the white of his eyes appeared jaundiced and bloodshot, and how his once piercing blue irises had faded to gray. In the light, Cosimo could see all the joy this hateful man had taken from him.

As Pope Leon reached for his quill, Cosimo observed a tremor in his cousin's hand. He was unsure whether age or rage had caused the palsy, but he imagined it was both. Methodically, the Pope dipped the quill into the inkwell and then brought his hand to the portion of the paper that would soon turn a mere document into a papal decree. Black ink from the quill tip leached onto the parchment like dye suddenly cast into a pool of clear water as Pope Leon XI began his Holy Roman imprimatur. It was a long, slow signature, and as the Pontiff's quill formed the curves and angles of his name, Cosimo noticed a slight trickle of blood careen down his cousin's nostril. Ever so briefly, the droplet paused, trapped in the sharp triangle of cartilage that defined the inner tip of the Pope's beak; and then, with the final stroke of his quill, the droplet gave way, punctuating Pope Leon's signature with sanguinity.

Mortified, the Pope set down his quill and ran his longish middle finger across his nostril. It streaked his pale digit with red blood. Incredulous, the Pope turned and glared at Cosimo. It was a look of such venom that Cosimo felt his heart spasm with fear, yet he could not turn away. In the light, Cosimo saw the twitch of his cousin's brow, the swelling of the veins across his left temple and the rupturing of blood vessels that latticed his eyes. It was the first time Cosimo had seen blood run from someone's eyes since the arsenic poison ate through the tear ducts of his courtesan. Instantly, Cosimo felt the torment in his heart relent and an overwhelming feeling of sadness sweep through his being. If only I were a farmer, he thought, if only I were a farmer.

⊛   ⊛   ⊛

Now, in case the reader is wondering what an aristocrat like Cosimo di Pucci de' Meducci the Third, Grand Duke of Tuscany, has to do with our provincial romance, rest assured: Cosimo the Third serves a purpose. The reader should note that our tale is not a love story, not at all, but a romance, and according to the renowned 14th-century Italian dramatist Pozzo Menzogna, "There's a significant difference between a love story and a romance."

In a love story, the obstacle(s) to achieving love lie primarily within the protagonist(s), usually in the form of an overly inflated sense of pride. This excessive conceit puts the lovers at odds with each other, while the characters who surround them mock and rejoice in the foolery and antics of such prideful persons as they desperately try to avoid what everyone knows to be ultimately unavoidable. Hence, the love story is predisposed to comedy.

In a romance, however, the love between the protagonists is never in question—from the moment they first set eyes upon each other they know their hearts have been pierced by Cupid's arrow, or rung by *Il Tuono dell' Amore,* the thunder of love, as Menzogna put it. A romance's conflict, unlike a love story, stems not from self-created issues of pride, but from the more severe burdens that family and society place upon the lovers. 'Tis why the romance is predisposed to tragedy, for the whittling away of one's vanity is often a comical affair, but the confronting of deeply held societal and familial prejudices, resentments, laws and traditions is an altogether different and all too often tragic set of challenges. Hence, in a romance, time and place are critical to understanding the familial and societal forces that the lovers must confront and circumvent in order to finally unite.

So, while Cosimo di Pucci de' Meducci the Third, Grand Duke of Tuscany, may or may not have much to do with our story, the decree he and his cousin Pope Leon XI just signed into law helps establish our romance's setting, and is the instrumental stroke of serendipity that will soon unite an *Ebreo* tomato farmer and a *Catollica* olive grower at the Monday morning market of our fair hamlet. Not to mention, had we not briefly peered into Cosimo's world we never would have met his chef and come to know the story of pizza.

⊛   ⊛   ⊛

"I want to smell it! Let me smell it!" blurted the queerly dressed boy as he reached up and tried to grab the earthen-like clump currently in the hands of the family chef.

"Patience, patience," the chef replied while raising the truffle out of reach of the boy's grabby hands and smiling inauthentically. "Now, off you go, and put those melons back."

"But Papa loves truffles and you always let me smell them."

"Shh," said the chef, hastily pressing his forefinger to the boy's lips. "Best not to disturb official business."

"Father does not care what I disturb," replied the boy.

"And who might Father be?" asked the older and more pompous-looking of the two truffle-selling rhymers standing just outside the kitchen door.

"Cosimo di Pucci de Meducci the Third," the boy said proudly. "Grand Duke of Tuscany."

"Is that so?" said the rhymer. "And that would make you . . . ?"

"Princess Margarita, heir to Duke—"

"Oh, stop it," the chef interrupted. "Your name is nothing of the sort." The chef could see the smirk on the smug rhymer's face and this bothered him immensely. "Oh, very well, Prince Gian," said the chef as he handed the large truffle over to the boy, effectively conceding the negotiations before they had even begun. "Sniff away, if you must."

Though Prince Gian's young mind could hardly fathom such a thought, it wasn't easy heading up the kitchen for the Meducci family and Chef Luigi was in a bothered state for several reasons. First, ever since meeting Queen Margarita of Naples, his boss's *curious* child had not only taken on the queen's name, but the mortifying habit of wearing his mother's dresses and stealing the melons Chef Luigi planned to use for lunch to fill out the gown's vacant breast pouches. Despite himself, Luigi couldn't help but feel a bit flattered by the prince's attention, but what if, Luigi thought often and with great concern, the child should trip over the gown and hurt himself in the kitchen? He would most assuredly be out of a job then. Nonetheless, it wasn't the antics of the prince that currently vexed Luigi (he had grown well accustomed to Gian's behavior); it was the vulgar duo of *rimatori* who had sought out the royal kitchen in hopes of selling some truffles.

They were a rank pair, one pompous and the other slovenly. The kind of rough-hewn village folk who might have bullied and abused Luigi when he was a young boy at the orphanage and sent to market for the day's shopping. They would never have made it past the villa's guards had not the pair of early-season truffles in their possession been so extraordinary. The truffles were unlike anything Luigi had ever seen or smelled, and he had to have them. The problem was, the pompous rhymer knew it, and if there was anything Luigi hated, it was parting with money, even if it wasn't his.

"Oh, Chef Luigi," young Gian chirped as he dreamily sniffed the pungent clump of fungus, "I know Papa will love them." The boy leaned against the kitchen door, jostling a wreath of garlic bulbs and causing a few sheaths of garlic skin to flake off.

"And in which dish, young *Princess Margarita*," asked the pompous truffle seller, "does your father most like truffles?"

Repugnant, thought Luigi as he scraped his clog against the wooden floor to whisk the garlic peelings out the door. "Mustn't make a mess of my kitchen, now, young prince."

"But," from out of nowhere the more slovenly of the pair of truffle sellers stammered, "but you're dressed like a princess?" The man seemed genuinely overcome, as if the mass of his bafflement suddenly slipped through a crack in his discretion.

Luigi stiffened.

Leaning against the frame of the door, Prince Gian continued to sniff the truffle, then replied nonchalantly, "So, what of it?"

"Well," the slovenly man continued, eyes wide and transfixed upon the boy, "it just seems not proper."

The pompous truffle seller turned to his underling: his

eyebrows raised in disbelief, his lips bent with rage. "Shut your mouth!" he snapped.

Now the young prince stopped his sniffing and looked contemptuously at the pompous truffle seller. "You do not," the prince said with a surprising authority, "tell anyone to *shut his mouth* before the Prince of Tuscany."

There was a pause, heavy and tense, as Prince Gian held his gaze upon the pompous truffle seller. Luigi's blood froze in his veins. The man did not appear to take kindly to his remonstration. Finally, a forced smile broke the man's lip-lock and he lowered his eyes. "My apologies, young lord," he said, though Luigi didn't believe a word of it.

Satisfied, Prince Gian now turned to address the slovenly truffle seller. "May I," he asked the man rather sweetly, "see your hands?"

"My what?" the man asked, seemingly more confused than ever.

"May I," repeated Gian, "see your hands?"

The man nodded nervously as he moved his hands from behind his back to before the prince's eyes. His hands were thick and calloused; dirt dusted and colored his skin and impacted in black bands under his fingernails.

"I tell you," said the boy as he simultaneously assessed the man's hands and fondled the truffle he held, "what seems not proper. It was your hands that dug up the truffles, no?"

Sheepishly, the slovenly truffle seller nodded.

"And from the smell of it," Gian continued, "it was your hands that wrangled and led the sows?"

Seeming to wilt under the boy's doe-eyed gaze, the man nodded, again.

"Yet," the boy let his eyes wander from the slovenly one's hands to the pompous one's boots, "from the looks of it, the profits are all his."

Mio Dio! Luigi could not help but smile, suddenly feeling as if the negotiations had not gone totally awry. Now, thought Luigi, if only the boy would put on a pair of trousers, he'd one day rule all of Italy.

Awkwardly, the pair of rhymers stood there, the wind sapped from their sails by a twelve-year-old prince in a dress, when suddenly—thankfully for the duo of truffle sellers—the air filled with the clanging of a large bell.

Young Gian gasped and his eyes blossomed with excitement. "Papa!" he squealed, sounding very much like a young girl.

"The duke!" a voice echoing from inside the house began to shout out. "The duke approaches." A pair of guards scrambled and began to push open the enormous entrance gates. The young prince and the pair of truffle dealers momentarily forgot their business and turned their attention to the open gates. In an instant, the great home awoke from its lazy Sunday slumber to a bustle of activity. Butlers, servants, stablemen and a contingent of *Guardia Nobile di Meducci* began to emerge from the villa's numerous exits, hurriedly neatening their appearance as they fell into position alongside the arching carriageway that swept before the colossal home's main entrance.

Unstirred by the commotion, Luigi took the truffle from the distracted prince just as the boy ran off in the direction of his father's carriage. Luigi brought the truffle to his nose and gave it another sniff. How had this conceited rogue and his rank companion, who dressed and smelled like a barnyard mule, managed to come up with truffles so grand, particularly two months before the start of the truffle season? From the looks of them, Luigi wondered if the fungus hadn't sprung from the more slovenly one's navel.

"I'll be back," Luigi said to neither one in particular as he left the pair of *rimatori* waiting outside the kitchen door. With the servants otherwise occupied, it was an opportune moment to have a look about one of the lesser-used rooms of the villa and choose some meaningless trinket of the duke's or lady duke's that Luigi could use to barter for the truffles.

❀   ❀   ❀

Meanwhile, the duke's horse-drawn carriage coursed through the open gates of his country villa and passed the kitchen entrance. Upon seeing his father's carriage, Prince Gian Gastone, sole heir to the title, ran eagerly from the kitchen of the chef he adored to greet the father he worshipped. As he ran along the carriageway, Gian tripped over his dress twice and crushed one of the ripe melons against the tender young flesh of his chest. He gathered his feet and made it to his father's carriage as it came to pause, just before the master butler could position himself at the coach's door.

Panting and full of expectancy, young Gian opened the carriage door to the greatest sight his young eyes had ever beheld. It was a shocking image, but it filled the remaining sixteen days of young Gian's life with strokes of bliss. And on the morning of the seventeenth day, when the organs of his body finally succumbed to the virulent poison laced within the fig jam he'd eaten, it was the image from earth that young Gian took to heaven. For Gian Gastone di Pucci de' Meducci, sporting a dress and dripping fresh melon, opened the door of the carriage to find his father fully naked, *bastone* in hand, and dreaming of the *Courtesane Ebreane* he had so loved.

7

In Which We Learn the Recipe for Insalata di Pomodoro e Menta

"Cousins," said Davido, abandoning the storytelling tone he'd just been using. He sat up and turned his head in the direction of what caught his eye. "Go tell Nonno a visitor approaches."

Even at their young ages the children had inherited a suspicion of strangers and they sprang up like a five-headed hydra from between the rows of tomato plants. Each head popped up in order of age, from eight to three, and mimicked the sudden shift in countenance of their next elder kin.

"Go on," Davido snapped his fingers, "now."

Heeding their cousin's charge, the five children sprang from the field and ran off toward the large stone and wood barn.

Davido stood, to better size up the odd sight advancing in the distance. At first glance he registered an equine lope and what looked like the brown cassock of an itinerant monk. He squinted and shaded his brow for better focus, but still couldn't tell whether the man was upon a donkey or a mule, though from the ears, large and pointy, he knew it wasn't a horse. That mattered to Davido greatly, as *Ebrei* were subject to a degrading law of the land that only permitted them to own and ride upon donkeys. Even the humble mule was off-limits. However, what really confused Davido, and what he thought must be an illusion of the late-afternoon sun, was the apparent skin color of the figure in the distance.

With the man still eighty paces down the driveway and presently waving, Davido turned and began to walk toward the barn. The handling of church envoys was something usually done by Nonno, and Davido thought it best to let his grandfather know that it looked as if a lone priest was approaching. A priest, who in the distance appeared the color of a late-summer eggplant—but Davido wasn't exactly sure he'd mention that.

⊛   ⊛   ⊛

At just the moment he climbed into his tub and began to lower his old bones into the hot water for his Sunday afternoon bath, Nonno's eardrums rang as all the grandchildren hollered his name from somewhere outside the barn. The old man's peaceful sigh transformed into an obstinate grunt and Nonno paused for a moment to reconcile himself to the inevitable disturbance of his Sunday ritual. After the three-hour wagon ride from Florence, his old bones needed a good soaking.

Because the creature was nearby and seemed to have the emotional capacity to appreciate the sanctity of a Sunday bath, Nonno looked to the old donkey standing beside his tub. Signore Meducci was his name, called that because he seemed to have been left behind from when the Meducci winemakers owned the property. Plus, the donkey treated just about everyone but Nonno the way a fallen monarch might treat his keepers—with equal parts disgust and disinterest. From the onset, the old beast had taken to standing in the barn during Nonno's Sunday bath, apparently enjoying the fire's warm embers and herb-scented steam. Nonno did not object to the donkey's presence and felt a certain empathy for him, figuring that when one reaches a certain age he should be able to do whatever he likes. Knowingly, Signore Meducci returned Nonno's gaze, as if the donkey also had no desire to see his Sunday respite disturbed. As the children's voices grew closer, Nonno inhaled deeply and grinned at the donkey, and then submerged himself entirely underwater.

It should be noted that Nonno's tub was not a traditional bathtub. It was an enormous cast-iron cauldron left by the Meducci winemakers that could easily hold a hundred buckets of water as well as a grown man. The cauldron had most likely been used in the production of jams and vinegar, where vast amounts of wine and/or grapes were boiled down; but with some repair and a good cleaning, Davido had managed to convert it into a fine bathtub. A gift to Nonno, who, after growing up frequenting the *Ebreo* bath houses of Toledo, enjoyed a weekly hot soak above all else.

What made the tub extraordinary was not so much its size or proximity to a waterspout, but its maneuverability. The cauldron was attached to a weighted cantilever, allowing it to be easily swung from an iron fire ring to an iron cooling ring, making the process of heating entirely less arduous. This was a well-known idea in blacksmith shops used for cooking and cooling ore, but for bathing, as far as Davido knew, it was a first.

On Sunday afternoons, much like this one, after the family meal Davido would fill the cauldron with water, stoke the fire to heat it and then swing the cauldron atop the cooling rack so Nonno could take a long hot bath. The only problem in adapting the device had been that the cauldron, shaped like an enormous soup crock, could get a little too hot on the feet. Davido remedied the problem by placing two large hempen sacks, filled with the dried and shredded bark, leaves and needles of pine, cypress and bay laurel trees, as well as significant bunches of dried rosemary, lavender and peppermint, on the cauldron's bottom. The pillow-sized sacks cushioned the cauldron's sloping base and took the heat off Nonno's feet. They also acted like two enormous tea pouches, scenting the water and releasing their rejuvenating properties.

Nonno's Sunday ritual was as well established as any ritual on the newly reclaimed farm, and the children were certain they would find Nonno in the midst of his Sunday soak. They entered the barn shouting his name and headed directly to the tub. But something seemed wrong and the children quieted. The embers under the cauldron glowed, Signore Meducci stood nearby, steam wafted off the water as usual and the air had its familiar moist, herbaceous scent. But Nonno's bearded, wrinkled face was not resting above the bathwater.

Underwater, Nonno still had several seconds' worth of air inside his lungs, but he knew time flew quickly to expectant children, and at just the instant Davido entered the barn to find his cousins held in nervous silence and felt his own heart drop, Nonno burst up from the water howling like a loon. "Who dare disturb Poseidon while he bathe," Nonno splashed the giggling children with warm bathwater, "shall bear the fury of water and wave!"

⊛   ⊛   ⊛

Outside, the Good Padre brought his mule to a halt at roughly the spot where the young man who had been scrutinizing him just a moment ago had been standing. He dismounted, reached into the fold of his frock, removed a carrot and fed it to his sturdy mule. As the mule ate from his hand, the Good Padre let his vision wander. "Bless'd Virgin," the Good Padre uttered, "how glorious."

The land was fecund. At a glance, the Good Padre estimated at least thirty rows of green-leafed, semi-vine-like plants, ripe with clusters of large red berries. Speckled about the farm, from distant horizon to barnside proximity were decades-old olive, fig, peach and plum trees. Behind him lay three sizable vegetable patches. In a glance he could tell they were bursting with life. He saw the green shoots of garlic and onion tops; the yellow, green and purple bellies of fat late-summer squash, zucchini and eggplant; slender fingers of green beans hanging from a trestle; the bushy tops of fennel and carrots; the marbled purple and white of radicchio; and the crinkled emerald-black of loose-leafed cabbage, his favorite sautéing green in all the world.

The barn, some fifty paces from where the Good Padre paused, appeared recently rehabilitated and was of a goodly size, forty feet square by twenty feet high. Masonry work had been done; the mortar between the stones appeared young, still cream-colored. The barn's upper two-thirds looked newly painted in reddish ocher. Mature cypress trees, forty feet high, shaded the barn's western side, with lavender, rosemary and rosebushes planted between the trees. Flanking the barn's southern wall, a pair of bushy bay laurel trees, whose leaves the Good Padre found delicious for the flavoring of soups and stews, had been planted. All around him life abounded.

The Good Padre turned his vision to the Love Apple plants before him. He left his mule's side and knelt before a plant to have a closer look. Running his fingers over the stalk and leaves of the knee-high plant, he discovered they had a slight tacky prickle to them—not quite as harsh and cellulose as a zucchini vine, nor as woody and smooth as an eggplant. He moved his hand across the taut skin of a single tomato and then glanced toward the barn to make sure no one approached. He was alone. There was a meaty weightiness to the fruit that seemed to beckon one to eat it. It felt like the cheek skin of a month-old infant, who, though lovely to touch with the fingers, one felt impelled to kiss with the lips. The Good Padre brought the fruit to his nose to breathe it in as deeply as possible. The fragrance was sublime and if he could have inhaled the entire fruit into the circumference of his nostril he assuredly would have. By smell alone, the fruit seemed to belie the dangers of which Bertolli warned: the blisters, boils, blindness, bleeding, retching, reeling horrid death that the old padre foretold for anyone blasphemous enough to even touch a Love Apple.

The Good Padre now heard a commotion coming from the barn; it sounded like children laughing. He thought of all the fear and superstition of which Bertolli had spoken and the old padre had preached, stories that so many in the village construed as fact: the ludicrous idea that Man's fall from grace was the fault of a fruit of this earth—a fruit now planted and growing just beyond their village walls. If only Bertolli could hear this sound, the sound of children laughing. If only the fearful and superstitious could smell this fruit, the smell of earth and herbs and goodness. *"Assurdita,"* the Good Padre whispered as he snapped the fruit from its vine and hid the Love Apple inside his frock: "Utter absurdity."

🍅   🍅   🍅

"A mule?" said Nonno as he emerged from the tub. The grandfather and grandson had just sent the children off to their home, a large converted wine mill at the farm's other end, where they lived with their parents. "You are sure it was a mule?"

"Well, it certainly wasn't a horse," Davido said as he handed Nonno his robe and sandals. Not wanting to seem delusional, Davido decided to omit the fact that the visitor appeared to be the hue of a well-ripened eggplant. "And he most definitely wore a brown garment, I know that."

"Oy," groaned Nonno as he laced his arms through his robe and made for the barn's side door. He and Davido had been through this once before. About a year ago, shortly after moving onto the farm, a nasty old priest and a small contingent of Vatican guards had come to roust them from the land on charges of illegal occupation. However, when Nonno presented the envoy with a *Magno Sigillo di Meducci*[7], the local priest had no choice but to abandon his plan. "I thought they rested on Sunday," said Nonno as he exited the barn, a hint of anger in his voice.

The old man walked briskly and let his robe remain open

---

[7] Grand Seal of the Meducci: a ring and document that verifies the holder has a direct relation to the Meducci and is afforded privileges and protection by the Duke of Tuscany.

for his first few steps toward the row of tomatoes where he saw the visitor squatting. The afternoon air felt cool and refreshing as it commingled with his overly heated body; but refreshment was hardly Nonno's motivation for leaving his robe undone. It was a secret expression of hostility, no doubt, one Nonno wouldn't have admitted even to himself. Nevertheless, somewhere in Nonno's psyche arose an urge, both spontaneous and rebellious, to give a member of the Catholic clergy a defiant glimpse of his old, haggard and very circumcised *Ebreo cazzone.*

As many an old wife will attest, few things hang as pendulous as the poached scrotum of a skinny old man recently emerged from a hot tub. Thus, indelicate and hostile as Nonno's intention may have been, the act was lost on the Good Padre. He turned and saw the entirety of the old man's gesture, dangling and jangling from skinny thigh to thigh, and thought not of the genital distinction between *Ebreo* and *Cattolico* and all that it had come to signify, but rather of overripe figs, still clinging to their branch in late October and swaying in the breeze.

The old man closed his robe at twenty paces, just as the Good Padre rose up from kneeling beside the tomato plant. "Greetings, neighbors," the Good Padre called to the approaching pair.

Nonno, whose mind was sharper than his vision, looked up from the tying of his robe and promptly felt the faculties of his brain grow cloudy. The man before him was physically enormous, a near water buffalo sheathed in a humble mendicant's frock. Nonno felt an impulse, a vague notion scurrying about his mind that somehow evaded full comprehension. He had difficulty locating a reply and after a dumbfounded moment he heard himself say, "And greetings to you, my friend."

Davido remained a step behind his grandfather. The late afternoon sun lay at a perfect angle, cutting long shadows and painting the land in golden light—the kind of light that makes old sights appear new and new sights appear magical in their amber clarity. The kind of light that's easy on the eyes and beckoned Davido to stare longer and harder than he normally would. Davido had seen people of all shapes and colors over the course of his life in Florence and during his many visits to Venice. He had seen Moorish slave traders the color of sand, and Indian spice dealers the color of red earth. He had seen old Greek sailors lashed and baked by a lifetime of wind and sun to the texture and hue of dried apricots. He had seen English society women the porcelain shade of pure cream just wrung from a cow, glistening bluish-white. He had seen slaves from the Dark Continent the color of roasted carob beans brewed to liquid, some with a touch of milk, some without. He had seen turban-wearing silk merchants from the East with skin the color of walnut shells. He had seen Orientals with complexions the color of cheap, second-pressed olive oil, more yellow than green. But never in his life had Davido seen a man as singularly unique as the one before him now. For Davido and only one other in the village could see and comprehend the Good Padre's true color: purple, deep, dark, entirely eggplant purple.

The Good Padre smiled broadly at the approaching pair, acknowledging the older man first and then the younger one with a gracious nod. Briefly, he closed his eyes and inhaled deeply through his nostrils. " 'Tis a sweet and piquant air," he said, gesturing to the tomato plants at his left, "and the flavor?"

"Oh, good visitor," said Nonno through his mind's fog, "most fair."

"And is it a fruit or vegetable?"

" 'Tis a fruit, I believe, but eaten more like a vegetable," answered Nonno.

"Aha," sighed the Good Padre, "and is it a fast-taking seed?"

"Oh, yes, good shepherd," Nonno answered, his wits returning. He would show this *Cattolico* rhymer a thing or two. "Like a weed."

The Good Padre continued his line of questioning. "And is it like the pepper that when green is tart, but ripe'd to red means ready?"

"Indeed again, good pilgrim," said Nonno, "most heady."

"Hmm, and is this fruit truly called a *Pomo di Amore?*"

"Not by us," said Nonno with emphasis. "We share not your fixation with that story."

The Good Padre chuckled.

Davido glanced a bit sideways at Nonno. He had no idea his grandfather was such a good rhymer.

Nonno continued, "And while it indeed be lovely and a color not unlike a ripe apple, we call it an *apple of gold.*"

"Pomo di oro?" said the Good Padre.

"Nearly," replied Nonno. *"Pomodoro."*

"Pomodoro," repeated the Good Padre as he let the *R*'s and *O*'s roll about his tongue. *"Pomodoro. Pomodoro.* 'Tis a good name. Yes, yes, a good name, indeed."

Enthusiastically the Good Padre turned to look over the sprawl of ripening rows. "And where shall these ripe *pomodori* find a home?"

"Well," said Nonno, "what the church forsakes, we sell to the *Ebrei* of Florence, Venice and Rome."

It was an innocent question, spoken with the sincerest curiosity, but from the old man's reply the Good Padre knew it had been misperceived. Bertolli had told him full well how the old padre had been quite nasty toward the *Ebrei* and personally forbade them from bringing their "Love Apples" anywhere near the village.

Nonno said nothing and let the air thicken for a moment. He was dubious of gentile inquisitiveness. Such pleasantries were usually veiled threats that cloaked a desire to be the recipient of a bribe. "And now, my pleasant and curious friend," said Nonno, "let us bring this papal inquiry to an end. Report this to your diocese and village priest, it should suffice, this *serpent's* fruit still be solely an *Ebrei* vice."

"Papal inquiry?" said the Good Padre. "Oh, sir, please, 'tis not the reason of my visit."

"What a pleasant surprise t'would be if it isn't," said Nonno. "Now, if you will be so kind as to wait here, we shall fetch our papers of proprietorship." Nonno stepped in the direction of the barn.

"Please, sir!" the Good Padre called after Nonno. "I did not come to question your legitimacy."

Nonno had been satisfied by the way he'd handled the priest thus far. It was a good lesson for Davido too, but something about the priest seemed so imminently likable. "No?" asked Nonno, turning back around to face the priest.

"No," repeated the Good Padre. "I do not care to see your papers or question your legitimacy. I come only with well wishes and good tidings."

Nonno's brow furrowed doubtfully. "Very well, say your piece."

"Well, sir, I am the town's new priest."

"And what happened to the shepherd of old?"

The Good Padre paused for a moment as his enormous mouth lit up with the beginnings of a smirk. "Perhaps, fair gentleman, this will put you at greater ease, but that *honorable* old herder was undone by a horrid disease."

Nonno's face, mapped with lines of loss and laughter, grew toward the latter. "Is it so?"

"I'm afraid," said the Good Padre, lowering his eyes, "indeed."

Nonno stepped toward his grandson and grabbed Davido's elbow with a squeeze of excitement. "What a shame," said Nonno, "how unfortunate. We are so sorry."

"Yes, unfortunate," said the Good Padre, "unfortunate, indeed."

"Now, tell me, noble priest, did he suffer in his passing? Surely, there must be details?"

"Well, gentle neighbor," said the Good Padre with an intentional clearing of his throat, "for one so pious and respected it seems both ironic and absurd, and though my eyes did not see, I will, for new love, repeat what I have heard. 'Twas that horrid New World disease—the Spanish scourge, wrought upon those who could not control the urge. And as these things travel, from a conquistador's phallus, to a Naples brothel, to a Tuscan palace; like the wind scatters yeast, all the way down to our village priest came the ghastly menace that eats from *cazzone* to brain, devouring one to incontinent shame. Now I say this knowing he will be sorely missed, but our former shepherd died, ball-less, brainless, in his own shit and piss."

"*Sifilide*." Nonno drew in a short, quick breath. His stomach muscles tightened. He knew the disease well. Half of Cristoforo Colombo's crew had contracted it. He heard the words repeat inside his head: *ball-less, brainless, in his own shit and piss*. Feeling his old bones and body go suddenly young, he began to laugh; he could not help it. A rich laugh, a deep laugh, a laugh that jiggled the belly, shook his organs and opened the Pandora's box of pain that lay at the very bottom of his soul. And what emerged was a vengeful laugh, a healing laugh. The kind of laugh that takes on a life of its own, sweeping up both Davido and the Good Padre, buckling their knees, bending them at the belly and causing family and stranger alike to hug and cling to one another as they crumpled to the earth. Laughter that affirmed one's belief in God, that somehow there is an absurd and perfect order to the universe. A laugh so rapturous one forgets what one was originally laughing about. A seizure of joy: contagious, delicious, divinely incorrigible.

"Now," attempted the Good Padre for the fourth time as he lifted himself from the ground and brushed the hay and dirt from his robe, "as the sun does ebb and your hot tub awaits, let me share my tidings."

Davido helped Nonno to his feet.

"By all means." It hurt Nonno's sides to speak.

"As politics oft be the Church's tide," said the Good Padre, "good news in the current does here reside. Ironically, politics, competition and greed have spurred a noble edict to be decreed. Hence, the ruling Meducci with their power to persuade have moved the Church to declare Tuscany now a land of free trade."

Nonno's brow crinkled in disbelief. It was one thing to share a laugh and heartfelt moment with a gentile—a priest, no less—but to believe that decades of economic restriction had just been lifted, well, that was too much.

"Oh," said the Good Padre recalling the document he carried. He reached into the fold of his frock and, careful not to dislodge the tomato he'd hidden there, took out the papal letter. "Here."

Nonno furrowed his brow as he reached for the letter and realized that it was in two pieces—torn imperfectly in half.

"Long story," said the Good Padre apologetically to the old man, who, by facial expression, seemed to understand that some things in life were beyond explanation.

Nonno held the two pieces of the letter as if it were one document. Davido leaned toward his grandfather so he too could read the decree and immediately felt a jolt of nerves. He recognized the signature. It was that of the Meducci. Both he and Nonno had seen that signature before. It graced the bottom of a very sad letter written to them some two years ago and signed in just the same way, though that signature had been streaked and smudged by tears.

"Your *pomodori*," the Good Padre said after a moment's pause, "by law, are now welcome at any market in Tuscany, including ours."

Davido waited for his grandfather to take the lead, but Nonno seemed a bit confounded and had yet to look up from the letter. Davido knew why and took it upon himself to continue with the priest. "You are saying we are free to sell our fruit?"

"That and any other economic pursuit," answered the Good Padre.

Davido turned to his grandfather to be certain that he'd fully heard the news. While he did seem to register what the priest had said, the old man did not look nearly as pleased as his grandson.

"Hmm," said Nonno with a skeptical frown as he folded the letter and handed it back to the priest.

"Well," said the Good Padre, tucking the tattered letter into the fold of his frock, "peace be with you." He stepped toward his mule and vaulted his enormous thigh over his mount with a grace surprising for one so large. The Good Padre paused before prompting his mule. He felt uneasy about leaving them with little more than words upon a torn parchment. "Neighbors," he said, "have you ever set foot in the village?"

"No," answered Davido.

"Not in all your time here?"

"Your predecessor did not encourage it," said Davido.

"Ah." The Good Padre nodded contritely. "I have heard. Well, despite the failings of the few, there is much goodness in these villagers."

"I do not doubt that," answered Nonno, "but goodness of heart, so often, is little match for malice of head."

"True, dear man, true," said the Good Padre as he turned and looked directly into Davido's eyes, "but the question is, from which organ do you wish to be led?"

Davido felt a sudden burst of energy hit him right in the heart. He felt his knees go momentarily weak and his eyes flush with tears as he heard the priest's voice repeat itself inside his head: *But the question is, from which organ do you wish to be led?*

"Who's to say," the Good Padre continued, "how this news here, come evening mass, will bode upon the rabble's ear? But there is much goodness in this little village. As I too am new to this hamlet and can attest. And if tomorrow's market you're brave enough to attend, perhaps we can move this superstition to an end. Now, as for me, at mass and market, I'll preach my part, that buying your produce be the way to start." The Good Padre gave a gentle prod to his mule. "Now peace be with you, and Godspeed with tomorrow's dawn. I will wait at market."

Davido was stunned, his pulse raced and his eyes were still misty with something like delight. The whole meeting with the Good Padre had been overwhelming and he wanted to shout, *Yes,* he would be there at market with a thousand *pomodori,* be anywhere but Florence. "Wait, wait!" Davido yelled.

The Good Padre slowed his mule and turned back over his shoulder.

"Do you like vegetables?" asked Davido as he hurried over to the closest tomato vines.

The Good Padre smiled—a smile of a thousand words.

Quickly, sliding a pruning knife from his back pocket, Davido snipped off a cluster of a half dozen or so ripe tomatoes. "Here," he said, catching up to the Good Padre's slow-moving mule. "Take these *pomodori*. Eat the first few plain, they're delicious, maybe with a touch of salt and olive oil." Davido placed the tomatoes into the priest's enormous hands. "Then take the others and slice them into bite-sized wedges. Toss with olive oil, a squeeze of lemon, salt, sheep's cheese and fresh-cut mint. Remember, it's mint that lends the dish a summer's hin—"

Davido heard a thud and felt a tremor through the tendons and muscles of his feet and ankles, like that of a small earthquake. A prickle of fear now shot through his body as he scrambled to and knelt over the fallen priest. Thank goodness, thought Davido, that it wasn't a far fall off his short mule, that the earth was soft, his back quite large and there was no rock to hit his head upon.

After a few seconds of ecstatic darkness—his entire being tossed and glistening with tomato, mint, cheese, olive oil and the *entusiasmo* and love in the boy's gesture—the Good Padre opened his eyes and his vision came to focus upon the sweet face of the young *Ebreo*. "The *Pomo di Amore?*" he asked dreamily.

"Yes," answered Davido.

"Are they injured?"

Davido glanced down and saw that the cluster of tomatoes had taken the fall gently, cradled between the priest's huge hands and belly. "No."

"*Grazie Dio*," said the Good Padre with a deep sigh that deflated his belly and freed the illicit tomato hidden in his cassock. "Thank God."

How wonderful, thought Davido, as he noticed a lone tomato gently roll from the folds of the Good Padre's garment. A priest has stolen the forbidden fruit.

In Which We Learn
the Origins of
Our Heroine's Name

Nearly twenty-two years past, a troupe of Neapolitan minstrels, who had been hired to play for the newly ascended Grand Duke of Tuscany, got lost en route somewhere between the undulating hills, mountainous peaks and vineyards of central Tuscany. By early evening, the disoriented and disheartened players headed up a twisty road, rolled by an olive orchard, continued under a medieval archway, trotted past a small stone church with a striking statue of the Virgin and wound up in the middle of our village's piazza on what happened to be the hamlet's most raucous and significant feast day.

The minstrels were from Naples and therefore quite familiar with the drunken antics ritually celebrated in the honor of

one saint or another; but the troupe found the festive antics
of our particular village, which combined drinking and donkey racing, so absurdly captivating, they stayed to observe
the outcome. It was a heated competition eventually won by a
strapping and inebriated young man. Upon victory, the young
man professed his love for his sweetheart and asked for her
hand in marriage. When she said yes, the crowd erupted with
such intoxicated glee that the minstrels got swept up in the
merriment, assumed their instruments and began to play.

Tuscans have historically been gifted builders, artisans
and winemakers, but when it came to the making of music,
no one in all of Italy could compare with Neapolitans. Accordingly, as the feast neared its end, the villagers begged the
players to leave them with one of their glorious songs. It was a
simple ballad, one renowned throughout Naples, entitled "Oi
Mari." It told of a lovesick young man as he stood before the
window of the woman he loved. It was sunrise and the young
man lay in hiding, praying for his love to arise, come to her
window and open it to let the sun in so he may gaze upon her
splendor.

The day's champion was so moved by the song that he
decided right there, if his first child was a girl, Mari would
be her name. Ten months later, he and his wife did have a
girl and they named her Mari: the very Mari who is the heroine of this story. However, it didn't become tradition to serenade Mari with her namesake song until after the untimely
death of her father and the laming of her mother, some ten
years ago. It began one market day in spring when the Cheese
Maker, a plump-bellied and sweet-natured man whose stand
occupied the first slot in the market row, took notice of the
little girl's vacant eyes and lost expression as she entered
the piazza. Recognizing her sense of loss, the Cheese Maker
spontaneously began to serenade the young girl. Well, it has
never taken much prodding to bring a Tuscan to song, and no
sooner had the first verse of "Oi Mari" left the Cheese Maker's
lips then, one by one, all the vendors at market took up the
ballad.

Like a good bit of village folklore, what had begun as a

lark had grown into a tradition, and as Mari's donkey-drawn wagon rolled into the piazza this morning, just as they had for the last ten years, the vendors lifted their voices to sing. It began in the same fashion, with the Cheese Maker, who was still the first vendor in the line of stalls and who had matured and fattened into a full-throated tenor. The heroic implications of singing to a heartbroken little girl were no longer pertinent, but the vendors and villagers had come to relish the tradition. It was a constant, something they did every Monday morning, and since the arrival of the Good Padre, consistency was something the villagers desperately clung to. For change was at hand, more change than most of the villagers could handle. Word from last evening's mass had spread quickly amongst the assembled villagers that their most unusual padre had invited the *Ebrei* to market. So the villagers sang with more than normal vigor, sang to bind them with their past and distract the mind from the disturbing notion that *Il Serpente* and his *Pomo di Amore* might soon enter their lives.

"Oiiiii, Mari!"

Mari looked up and smiled at the Cheese Maker as she always did. She hadn't been to church last night and therefore chalked up the day's voluminous singing to the fine weather. Mari was no longer so set against the Church as she had been for many of her teenage years, though she dared not share that sentiment with anyone. The awful manner in which the old padre had died restored some of her faith in God, and the Good Padre, well, he was just so baffling and sweet a man that Mari could not help but adore him. So much so that she'd even begun to take weekly confession, fabricating sins and exaggerating peccadilloes just for the pleasure of being in his company. He was also an ardent consumer of Mari's olives and olive oil and was usually among her first customers at the Monday morning market. Thus, she'd had every intention of being at church last night; indeed, she made a point of escorting her mother to Sunday evening services. It was just that last night, as she was prone to do, Mari let her olives get the best of her. There was prepping for the market to be done and the all-important mixing and marinating and spice-blending for the nine varieties of olives her stand sold—a task she entrusted to no one but herself. When she finally stepped out from the mill, it was well past dark, the service was over and she was certain her stepfather would be griping for his supper.

Hence, with no knowledge of the Good Padre's shocking announcement, Mari simply did this morning what she always did: conduct her donkey-drawn wagon along the row of stalls and gently take up the song herself. She knew full well that she was merely part of a ritual, not the point of it, but on the inside, the song still struck Mari as profoundly as when she was a little girl. As a child, Mari's father would often personally sing "Oi Mari" to her. After the spring solstice, when the evenings grew longer and lighter and the olive trees began to bud their new fruit, Mari and her mother would arrive at the orchard to fetch her father for supper. Then Mari would take her father's hand and follow him about the orchard and mill while he finished his tasks. Her father's hands were as large and powerful as his work was toilsome, but his constant proximity to olive oil lent them a suppleness that little Mari found delicious. He would hug her tightly as he sang the song of her namesake and, as the lyrics emerged from his sturdy chest, the vibrations would pass directly into her body, stirring her heart and tingling her belly.

It had been nearly ten years since her father's death and though with each passing day the remembrance of his hands' buttery touch and tickle of his beard grew fainter, the vibrations never left her. And as she entered into market on Monday mornings like this one, her namesake song bouncing off cobblestones and buildings, Mari would flush with memories of her father, and for a moment it was as if he'd never left her.

In Which We Learn the Meaning of *Cucinare con Collera*

Painstakingly, Luigi Campoverde, chef for the Meducci, worked the fine, soft bristles of his mushroom brush over every pore and crevice of the enormous truffle he'd acquired earlier in the day. While brushing a truffle clean was not an especially difficult task, Luigi had already been working for hours, and the pressure of knowing that one grain of grit or dirt in the lady duke's meal and he could very well be out of a job certainly exacerbated his mood. The lady duke very much loved to hate that which gave her husband any joy, and, after this morning's embarrassment, Luigi was preparing himself for the worst.

She'd already changed his menu once, "requesting" that he switch the truffle preparation from risotto to *ancini di pepe—ancini* being an excruciatingly difficult-to-make hand-made pasta, whereby tiny pinches of fresh dough are rolled between the thumb and forefinger to the exact size and round-ness of a small pearl. And to think, each of the three bowls he would have to fill for supper this evening required at least one hundred and fifty of the tiny, hand-rolled *ancini di pepe*. Worse still, the lady duke would have hardly a spoonful: though she squawked like a gull over preparations, she ate like a hummingbird. True, cooking for the duke and young Gian was not without pleasure and reward, but the lady duke evoked in Luigi a very old and cultivated rancor. And before he knew it, the cramping in his fingers and ache of his legs brought the indignation that he constantly struggled to keep at a mere simmer to a furious boil.

The irony was, it didn't have to be this way. Luigi could very well have become an honorable man had certain events not irreparably altered his path. He was a quiet and sensi-tive country boy who'd been orphaned at age six when an ungodly plague swept through his village and the outlying farms. Somehow, young Luigi's constitution had withstood the scourge, but his parents and two older sisters were not so fortunate. Following a lonely and frightening seven-week period in which Luigi subsisted on the remnants of food to be found on his family's small farm, he was discovered by a pair of traveling monks on their way to Florence. After un-successfully inquiring if the boy had any close-by relatives, the monks took young Luigi to a Franciscan monastery in Florence. There, for the next twelve years, he was trained in the kitchen arts by an angry and aging Sicilian brother, who along with being extraordinarily tightfisted and somewhat unscrupulous, instilled in his young apprentice a tenet that was unspoken, but most prevalent amongst chefs throughout the world, namely *Cucinare con Collera:* to cook with anger.

The idea of *Cucinare con Collera* is as simple to under-stand as two piles of fava beans. First, imagine you need to shell, blanch and peel just twenty or so pods of the broad beans for a group of ten people you care about and love to feed. Then, while you set about the slightly tedious task of shelling, blanching and peeling the beans, you busy the mind with the pleasant thought of how you're going to mash the fava beans with cream, butter, salt, white pepper and roasted garlic. You imagine how the finished puree will appear like light green angels of deliciousness upon the plate, how the *Romano*-style hint of roasted garlic will thrill the taste buds of the ones you love and complement the meat you have decided to serve along with it. As you finish peeling the last broad bean you imagine humbly receiving your loved ones' accolades as they say things like, "Only you, Luigi, could make the lowly fava bean taste as if it sprang from the Cornucopia of Bacchus."

Now imagine the number of beans you need to peel is no longer twenty to feed the ten people you love, but two thousand to feed five hundred monastic persons you have never met. The muscles running from your neck through your shoulders to your arms and into your hands will begin to burn with the fire of five hours of repetitive motion. Your fingers, stained a sickly green, will feel as if they're likely to fall off. You'll attempt to do the shelling with a small knife to relieve the ache, only to have the head chef chastise you, denouncing your work as slow and sloppy and performed with the dexterity of a hoofed animal. Your feet, knees and legs will throb and cramp from standing in the same position for hours. You will recall the swollen ankles, gnarled knees and varicose veins of an old cook you once worked with and wonder if one day your legs will also look as ravaged. Out of boredom you will begin to snack on any food item that crosses your path until you are disgustingly bloated, and food and flavor have been rendered tasteless and meaningless. You will begin to resent the monks you are preparing to feed, as you know between their vows of silence and severe ideas of humility they will offer you no praise. You will begrudge your low wages and lack of respect, and deem the people for whom you labor as slothful, sanctimonious, overindulged and unworthy of their lofty positions. Your mind will meander through every subject imaginable, but always return to the torturous thought that the pile of fava beans seems to be multiplying. You will begin to hate each and every bean. You will begin to cook with anger.

This concept of *Cucinare con Collera* could very well have evolved naturally over the course of young Luigi's difficult apprenticeship, but in his case, it was most definitely a lesson he tacitly gleaned from his kitchen mentor at the monastery. Luigi's mentor of ten years had been a rather salty and disagreeable Sicilian chef, forever embittered by the traveling monks who'd tempted him off his small island three decades earlier with tales of Florence's *beautiful seaside location,* assurances of good pay and promises that he'd rarely have to cook for more than a handful of monks. Not surprisingly, by the time young Luigi was introduced to his mentor, the man boiled with indignation over having to feed one hundred thirteen monks three times a day, with neither a squid nor shrimp to be found in less than a day's journey. Nonetheless, Luigi's mentor was a skilled chef and knew better than to seek revenge upon the food he prepared and risk unemployment. So what the old Sicilian did to offset the rage and iniquity that ate through his daily routine was to steal.

It was a sophisticated and therapeutic form of thievery that the old chef practiced, closer to bartering, and it had no effect upon the quality of the meals that the kitchen turned out. The only catch was the old chef bartered items that were never his to begin with. As chef for the monastery, he was allocated a budget in gold and silver coins to keep the kitchen supplied, and as long as the meals were good and tasty no one paid any mind as to how the money was spent. In fact, the monks had such regard for the Sicilian brother and his rich and spicy southern cooking that they never even suspected it might be their chef who was behind the random disappearances of artifacts, ancient books and other property that seemed to plague the monastery. But indeed it was, for rather than use the majority of gold and silver coins he was budgeted, the Sicilian brother often chose to pay his suppliers in small, highly valuable gold-laid crucifixes, ancient religious texts, artifacts, even the occasional painting.

It was this lesson, though never directly taught, that Luigi learned from his mentor as well as any recipe and had taken to practicing in his own professional life. And while it has only a peripheral effect upon our story, it certainly explains how a relatively petty landowner such as Giuseppe could have come into possession of a lovely three-segmented telescope that originally belonged to Cosimo di Pucci de' Meducci the Third, Grand Duke of Tuscany, in exchange for two absolutely splendid early-season truffles.

⊛   ⊛   ⊛

The cool morning air stung Giuseppe's lungs as he drew a breath and stepped onto the balcony of his stepdaughter's room. The bedroom's balcony was situated at such an angle that he could see both the town's entrance archway and a significant portion of the piazza. The only problem with the balcony was that his stepdaughter's room was attached to it and he had to wait until the obstinate bitch left the house before he could use it. He would have married her off years ago and taken the room from her entirely but for two reasons: one, the idea of putting *his* money toward *her* dowry sickened him; and two, she knew the workings of the farm and mill better than any paid employee and that saved him a great deal of money.

Though Giuseppe never let Mari know it, she was a near-genius when it came to grapes and olives. She did the work of three men, invented new blends of grapes and techniques for fermenting the wine and new cures and marinades for olives, prepped for the local market, kept the books, managed the orchards, vineyards and mill and didn't cost Giuseppe a cent, as he didn't pay her a penny. Not to mention, she wasn't a bad cook, either. But unlike her mute and maimed mother, she was a truculent little *vacca*. She had a temper, a quick wit, a sharp tongue, and Giuseppe knew that taking her meager room from her would have been an incredible pain in the ass. But now—now that he owned a telescope—maybe he *would* take over her room, for its balcony was an excellent vantage point from which to spy.

Reluctantly, Giuseppe could not help but feel that Benito was on to something when he pulled the enormous truffles from the earth and declared them fit for the Duke of Tuscany.

Giuseppe was concerned that traveling halfway to Florence to the Meducci summer villa on the slim hopes of selling the truffles to the royal kitchen would prove to be a great waste of time. Obviously, judging by the exquisite telescope he now held in his hands, he was wrong. Who could have imagined that so much of the royal underbelly would be revealed so quickly? The young Prince of Tuscany, an obnoxious little twit and queer as a three-legged donkey; his father, the duke, a masturbating buffoon; the royal chef, as unscrupulous as a gypsy whore—and a weak negotiator, to boot.

So excited was Giuseppe with his new toy that on the return journey from the Meducci estate he immediately put the telescope to its first furtive use. Halfway between the Meducci villa and Giuseppe's village, there was a fork in the road. To the left, a smoother, more direct route to the village; to the right, a longer, meandering, bumpier road, which, before leading back to the village, passed the *Ebrei* farm. Giuseppe instructed Benito to take a right at the fork. After a half hour's travel, the *Ebrei* land was in sight, however, not very clearly. The wagon's incessant bouncing and the jostling about of Benito's three truffle-hunting sows in the wagon-bed made it nearly impossible for Giuseppe to get a good, steady look at anything. This frustrated Giuseppe greatly, but as Benito directed the wagon down the ridge line, situated along the northeast high ground above the former Meducci vineyard, the road smoothed for an instant, the sows settled and Giuseppe, to his surprise, caught a glimpse of the Good Padre several hundred paces down the road, riding upon his odd mule, just as he turned onto the *Ebrei* property.

Giuseppe shushed Benito and had him stop the wagon behind a tall poplar tree so to better spy on the Good Padre as he made his way up the *Ebrei* carriageway. Through his enhanced vision, Giuseppe could not help but notice, enviously so, how much the land and barn had been rehabilitated in the year since the *Ebrei* moved in. What used to be nothing more than a blight-ridden bramble of weeds had been transformed into an exquisite piece of farmland.

After a few moments a pair of *Ebrei* emerged from the barn

to greet the Good Padre, one young, the other old. It was the perfect moment, thought Giuseppe, with the *Ebrei* occupied by their visitor, to get a closer look at the strange red fruit they grew.

"Benito," Giuseppe said whilst keeping his eye to the telescope.

"Eh?"

"Are you hungry?"

"Benito is always hungry, but not so hungry as to eat one of those wretched Love Apples."

"Have we known each other so long and well that you claim to know my mind?" said Giuseppe.

"I would sooner claim to know the mind of this here horse than to know of your mind's course. I only know to follow patterns. When my sows lift their noses and scratch their feet upon the ground, I brace, as a truffle scent's been found. Too much rain in summer makes the wine watery and weak, and when Giuseppe inquires of Benito, a task he does seek."

"And what task would that be?"

"Here? Now?" said Benito. "Could be only one."

"And is Benito daunted by such a task?"

"Need you even ask? That fruit will set flesh to blister and belly to boil."

"Is that what you've heard?" asked Giuseppe.

"Indeed," grumbled Benito.

"Well," said Giuseppe, making a special point to quash any bumptious ideas Benito may have gotten from the uppity young prince, "I have heard that fouling sheep will break your shins and rot your pecker to a pus-hewn canker, yet you still walk and frolic with whores." Giuseppe took his eye from the telescope and removed a pair of leather gloves from his rear pocket. "Here," said Giuseppe as he tossed them before Benito, "now go."

⊛   ⊛   ⊛

At last, the rising sun breached the buildings surrounding the piazza and the vision before Giuseppe's telescope grew crisp at precisely the instant the singing began. Oh, no, thought Giuseppe, not that stupid ballad. On Monday mornings he made it a point to arise early and flee to the countryside or at least to hide his head beneath several pillows to avoid the turgid tune. For him the song was a facile, pompous, bloated Neapolitan trifle, sung by a chorus of swollen-tongued, tone-deaf mongrels. Worst of all, it was an ugly reminder of a day he'd sooner forget.

But not even the annoying echo of "Oi Mari" could undo all that pleased Giuseppe this morning. Benito was on time, appearing more or less sober, and he had remembered the all-important satchel. Satisfied, Giuseppe continued to move his vision about the readying piazza. He made a mental note about whom of the thirty or so merchants could be easily riled should the day go accordingly. According to what, Giuseppe was not yet entirely certain. However, should the *Ebrei* actually be so foolish as to arrive at market with their forbidden fruits, Giuseppe had decided to improvise a little introduction. To this end, he had made certain after last evening's mass to stop by the tavern and enlist the servile brawn of Benito and the feral, provocative wit of Bobo the Fool. It was a motley duo to rely upon—one churlish, vulgar, slovenly, drunkenly and resoundingly stupid, yet entirely controllable and loyal; the other, churlish, vulgar, slovenly, drunkenly and supremely intelligent, yet entirely uncontrollable and beyond any semblance of loyalty to anything but the promise of a few coins and goblets of wine, and even then one could never be certain with Bobo. But such were the pawns with which Giuseppe had to play.

Giuseppe scanned the piazza to see if he could locate the fool, when, by the law of ill attraction, his telescopic gaze happened upon the Cheese Maker. Now, there was a person Giuseppe certainly couldn't count on. A pathetic being in that uniquely Italian capacity, who both looked and acted like a winged little Cupid perched on a cloud, all roly-poly, dizzy-eyed and soft-hearted. Giuseppe jerked his vision elsewhere to avoid witnessing the Cheese Maker bellowing "Oi Mari" when the real thing suddenly rolled her wagon before his eye. There she was. The little *vacca* herself, looking as nonchalant as ever and in her casual beauty reminding Giuseppe of his own shortcomings and past failures. Oh, how much Mari looked like her mother when she was around that age, the age at which Giuseppe sought after her and was in turn rejected. Oh, how much Mari looked like her father too when he was around that age, the age at which Giuseppe lost the Race of the Drunken Saint to him, and the hand of the woman he had so desired.

Mari's image was noxious to Giuseppe, a lowly, self-loathing, addictive narcotic. Truth was, he had more than enough money to pony up a dowry and marry her off, and at nineteen she was well of marrying age. But the thought of marrying her to some local peasant or having her marry and move away was as anathema to him as selling off his own kidney. He needed Mari. She was the kindling that fed the fire and indignation that drove him, and he secretly desired to do to her what her father and mother had done to him: ruin his life. He followed her past several vendors to their slot in the market row, where Benito awaited her. Giuseppe couldn't help but gloat as he witnessed all the melody in Mari's countenance fall flat as she laid eyes upon the pig. Now, Giuseppe pondered, with twenty-some years of retribution gurgling in his psyche, what part shall she play in this plot?

10

In Which We Learn
of Carciofi alla Judea &
Il Fodero di Moses

By Nonno's standards, the village market was nothing compared to the giant markets of Florence, Venice and Rome, which stretched for hundreds of stalls and were crowded with people, produce and goods from all parts of the world. In Venice alone you had more fishmongers than this market had vendors, but despite its relative paucity, Nonno could not help but think that the market, piazza and surrounding village were not without a modicum of charm. In the Etruscan tradition, streets were narrow and had a slight bend to them before flowing into the piazza. The piazza itself was small, Nonno estimated sixty paces in diameter. The encircling buildings were uneven in height but stood at roughly two stories. They were covered in various tones of amber-colored mortar, which in many places had begun to crumble, revealing the brick and stone beneath. Vines crept up walls, and in the sunnier spots, flowers bloomed from pots and hung from balconies.

As in many towns Nonno had seen throughout Tuscany, a sculpture stood at the center of the piazza. Only this statue was no bombastic recounting of Neptune's adventures or some biblical epic. A slightly larger than life-sized figure of a monk gazed benevolently, if slightly dazed, at passersby. He sat upon a donkey and drank eagerly from a goblet in his left hand. A wine jug was slung across the monk's chest, wine grapes hung from his mendicant sack and by facial expression—rather cherubic—one could reasonably assume the monk was drunk and happy. Though obviously *Cristiano,* the statue appeared blatantly pagan, a left-handed Bacchus draped in a monk's frock. To punctuate the incongruity, the monk's robe was fashioned in such a way that he seemed to have no right arm.

"Thank God," Nonno mumbled to himself after pondering the statue for a moment. Experience had taught him well, and he preferred when *Cristiano* religious art conveyed some lightness of spirit. Goodness knows how the sculptures throughout Spain, with their fixation on the devil and sin, persecution and crucifixion, used to unsettle him. Hardly a surprise that the Inquisition found such ripe soil there. Thankfully, thought Nonno, this sculpture differed from those in Spain and suggested that the village might have the necessary sense of humor that would allow a pair of forbidden-fruit-selling *Ebrei* to escape the day unscathed.

Regardless, Nonno was hardly comfortable with what he'd gotten himself involved in. The village padre had *not* been there to greet them, and their entry into market was one of the more mortifying instances in Nonno's life. He should have just conducted his wagon right through the piazza and headed home, but by some foolish impulse he did not rightly understand, he followed the pointing of his grandson's finger and parked their wagon at the last spot in the market row.

Faccia di merda, thought Nonno as he considered the sheer stupidity and danger of their current situation. Have I grown senile? At one point in his life he'd been considered the shrewdest man in all Toledo, but at this moment he seriously wondered whether he was beginning to lose his mental faculties. How could he have been so foolish as to consent to his grandson's desire? Of course the village priest wasn't present to greet them—if that odd character had even *been* the village priest. Only a priest bent on excommunication would be reckless enough to escort a pair of *Ebrei* and a cart full of Love Apples to market. Nonno considered whether the whole thing wasn't a ruse, a humiliating setup by the nasty old padre. And if it was, how could he have been so stupid as to fall for it? Why didn't I do, Nonno cursed himself, what I have always done? Send in some scouts, a few of Rabbi Lumaca's men from the nearby lesser city of Pitigliano, to assess the situation and report back their impressions of the village.

It was a grievous mistake, he feared, one of many. All stemming from the original mistake of entertaining the bizarre padre's invitation in the first place. It had always been Nonno's idea to introduce the *pomodoro* to the *Ebreo* markets of Florence, Venice, Siena and eventually Rome. These larger urban markets were often visited by gentiles, where locals came to snack upon *carciofi alla Judea,* a ghetto delicacy of battered and fried baby artichokes, eaten with a sprinkle of salt and a squeeze of lemon. Nonno had witnessed how *carciofi alla Judea* had become a guilty pleasure amongst the citizens of Rome and Florence, and not just the common folk. By late spring, when the wild artichokes were plentiful, priests, bishops and even the occasional cardinal could all be found lining up before the vending stalls of the ghetto, squeezing lemons and licking oily lips as they devoured platefuls of the delectable *Ebreo* specialty. This was how Nonno wanted things to progress: to expose the new fruit to their kin in the ghettos and let the more sophisticated urban gentiles who frequented the *Ebreo* markets be introduced to it at their discretion. Eventually, Nonno assured his grandson, just like fried artichokes, ivory dentures, *Il Fodero di Moses*[8] and a hundred other *Ebreo* inventions, the *pomodoro* would one day be highly regarded.

Davido, though, felt differently and made a compelling argument. "This is not Florence, Rome or Venice," Davido rebutted his grandfather. "In these parts, *Ebrei* and gentiles do not live in proximity to one another, and the more we are strangers to them, the more we live in harm's way. We'll sell only tomatoes at market, so not to compete with any of the village's existing fruit or vegetable vendors. It only makes sense, Nonno. How are the locals to gain any familiarity with us or with tomatoes unless we take up this kind padre's offer? Besides," Davido added for emphasis, "what does it say of us if we do not?"

Well, that was yesterday and as Nonno now reflected on the idiocy of his grandson's reasoning he couldn't stand to keep his mouth shut. "So much for your *kind padre*," said Nonno to Davido as the old man set an empty basket on the rear of the wagon. The market had begun to bustle, but their stand was empty of customers—as empty as if they were selling the plague.

Davido paused before he set a tomato in its place on the pyramid of tomatoes he was arranging upon the stand. "The day is not yet done."

"No?" Nonno whispered sharply. "The day is wasted and done as sure as it was foolishly begun. I only pray this day knocks a daft idea from your mind and you see, finally, an *Ebreo*'s place is best among his kind."

My God, thought Davido, *what a good rhyme!*

⊛   ⊛   ⊛

---

[8] Precedent for the modern condom, the Sheath of Moses was a prophylactic made of bound sheep intestine, preserved and lubricated in olive oil. After being pulled over the erect penis, the Sheath of Moses was held in place by fastening the intestines' open end in a figure-eight-like pattern around the testicles and base of the penis, and then tucking the remaining end into the anus. Its creation is credited to Moses Goldone, a 15th-century Roman *Ebreo* who owned a kosher butchery and sausage shop.

For their part, the villagers reacted to the entrance of the *Ebrei* like a pair of lepers in their midst, stealing glances at the odd beings, but never, never for goodness sake, daring to approach their stand. Those villagers who attended last evening's mass had heard, or at least thought they heard, the Good Padre announce the new decree and mention he'd invited their *Ebreo* neighbors to Monday's market. It was just that most of the villagers were hesitant to believe anything uttered by such an enigma, especially something so outrageous.

Nonetheless, the people of the village were not so closed-minded that they would not accept the arrival of a new person. Heaven knows, countless souls, and not all of them ordinary, had come and gone through town. Even Giuseppe and the odd and irksome Bobo the Fool had wandered into town years ago and grown to become village fixtures. But the Good Padre was different. Being in his company seemed to fracture the relationship between time and constancy, eyes and brain, thought and tongue, and forced upon one and all the stupefying idea that the world was larger and more mysterious than their ability to comprehend it.

For most in the village, including Vincenzo, Mucca, the Cheese Maker, Augusto Po and Signore Coglione (all characters we will soon come to know), this was not a welcome notion and for the first six weeks of the Good Padre's tenure they kept their distance. In fact, over those initial Sundays, only the blind, nearly blind and those consigned to escort the blind attended mass. The Cheese Maker, like virtually every other villager, did his best to dismiss the disconcerting fact that young children and infants were drawn to the Good Padre as if he were made of butter and honey, and that his mere presence would calm a crying toddler and cause a gaggle of youngsters to follow in his wake, laughing and giggling with delight. However, when Vincenzo's mother, old Signora Donnaccia, whose pupils had long ago been obscured by milky cataracts and whose anus had long been painfully obstructed by bloody hemorrhoids, awoke the morning after Good Friday mass to behold in crystal clarity the greatest bowel movement she'd had in thirty-five years, well, even the most obstinate villager took note.

Slowly, with great hesitancy and pulled by opposing forces of hope and fear, the villagers returned to church. They sat in the dim candlelight with their eyes closed, too fearful to look upon the priest who both warmed the heart and roasted the brain, yet too superstitious to miss out on the chance of a miracle. Even as church attendance grew and small miracles seemed to be occurring throughout the village, there was very little public talk of the new Good Padre. Yes, Mucca found it possible to speak of the Good Padre's sonorous voice and his melodic way with Latin, and Signore Coglione praised how well he'd trained his nephew, Bertolli, and the other altar boys to sing. But these were superficial topics that merely masked the gnawing, voracious desire everyone felt to speak about the one thing that, when attempted to be spoken of, disappeared into the ether and, for reasons they could not comprehend, left them disoriented, tongue-tied and staring at one another in awkward silence.

Hence, word of the decree and the Good Padre's shocking invitation did not spread with the fervor that one might usually associate with big news in a small town. It was uncharacteristically not blabbered about by Mucca or conspiratorially whispered by Augusto Po. No, much like the Good Padre's presence itself, the idea that foreign *Ebrei* and their illicit fruit would be appearing in town seemed incomprehensible. And though the temptation to be the bearer of foreboding news was as pressing as ever to Mucca and Po and many others, the uncertainty and embarrassment of speaking about the Good Padre was enough to quell the urge.

Work seemed to be the beleaguered villagers' only recourse. And so they took to their morning tasks with a special fastidiousness. Vincenzo fussed excessively over how thin he could slice the prosciutto, sharpening his knife again and again and cursing with dissatisfaction. Signore Coglione overscrutinized each onion and head of radicchio he placed in his basket. Augusto Po made certain to remind each and every one of his tenants exactly how overdue on rent they were. Mucca haggled over prices with people she had known too long and too well to expect any kind of discount. And the Cheese Maker set and then reset and then set once again his freshest and ripest Gorgonzola, each time thinking he'd found the perfect angle to display his favorite cheese. Yes, all the villagers pretended as best they could to be consumed by their tasks and dared not utter a word to one another about the new arrivals. The only thing Mucca, the Cheese Maker, Vincenzo, Augusto Po, Signore Coglione and just about every other villager could do was peek, stealing glances at the *Ebrei* with all the trepidation of a hedgehog peering up from its hole to see if it's safe to come out.

But not Mari. She stared like an owl at midnight: brown eyes wide open, transfixed by the move and bob of the boy's chestnut curls and the red fruits piling up there down the market row.

In Which We Learn
How to Properly Care
for Chamomile

The eggplant dish the Good Padre had thought up in the morning, with its crunchy herb and pine nut crust, rich and smoky innards and mint-basil-sage pesto looked and smelled delicious. The bread too, garlicky, crisp and sprinkled with coarse salt, appealed to eye and appetite. Yet despite great hunger and pride in their efforts, Bertolli and the other altar boys could not bring themselves to set their plates with food. Their bellies were full with fear, as there, inches before their noses, glistening in olive oil, specked with mint and chunked with cheese, sat a bowl of Love Apples.

Bertolli and the boys loved their new ritual of cooking and eating with the Good Padre after Sunday evening mass, but the idea that their Good Padre was soon to be killed ter-

rified them. The old padre had told them more than once
and most fervently that within an instant of a *Pomo di Amore*
touching the tongue, death was imminent. So Bertolli and
the boys waited, guts gripped, for the painful writhing and
devilish seizures to begin. But as the Good Padre chewed, he
moaned not in pain or panic, but in delight. It was a sound
that Bertolli and the boys knew well, a sound they often made
when eating the Good Padre's food, and as the Good Padre
reached for the tomato salad and ladled another helping on
his plate, another horrible thought flooded Bertolli's mind—
what if I'm missing out and there might not be any left to eat?
This was an overwhelming notion to Bertolli and before his
mind fully registered the action of his body, his chubby fingers were dripping olive oil, his mouth suddenly stuffed with
tomatoes, mint and cheese.

"Mmm," Bertolli hummed through a full mouth, eyes
blazing with joy. He had hardly swallowed when his hand dug
into the bowl for another scoop. Bertolli's brazen act freed
the hands of his three mates, who rose from their chairs to
likewise scoop from the bowl. With bare hands, they stuffed
tomatoes into their mouths. Juices ran between their fingers
and down their chins; olive oil shined upon their lips as they
smiled and cooed with pleasure. Their cooing quickly turned
to laughter as they dug their hands into the bowl for a second,
third and fourth time. Laughing as they stuffed tomatoes in
their mouths, laughing as they swallowed, laughing as they
sunk their teeth into the hot eggplant and crisp bread. Tears
began to well up in their eyes as their bliss transmuted into a
weeping of sorts. And while their young minds did not realize
it, for the very first time, Bertolli and his mates laughed and
wept as adults. They had opened Pandora's box to find it held
a false demon.

The Good Padre, in his seemingly oblivious wisdom, just
allowed the boys to be, offering no words or comfort beyond
the quiet, unspoken calm he seemed to naturally exude. And
when the festival of laughing and weeping and eating was finished and every tomato, eggplant and crust of bread devoured,
the group fell silent, prayerfully so. And there they remained

for several moments, heads bowed in reverence, tears of joy drying on their cheeks, bellies tingling with delight.

"*Buono*," said the Good Padre, finally fracturing the silence.

"*Buono*," the boys repeated.

⌖   ⌖   ⌖

Good it was, indeed, and as the Good Padre slept that night, so too did a goodly amount of liquid fill his bladder. The day's excitement, the rigors of traveling by mule in the hot sun, and the evening mass had left him parched. He had been thirsty beyond measure, and during the preparation and consuming of his evening supper he drank two bottles of wine, the first one white and the second one red. For many, this would have led to an awful night's sleep, ruined with sweats, spins and vomiting. But unbeknownst to the Good Padre, ever since his divine curse some centuries back, he'd become largely indifferent to the negative effects of alcohol and tended to sleep even more soundly after a bottle or two of wine. Regardless of intoxication, or lack thereof, it was a great deal of fluid to ingest so shortly before bed, and as the Good Padre set his head to hay for the evening he had more than a bucket of liquid swishing about his belly.

As the Good Padre slept, the fluids meandered the length of his intestines and slowly filled the cistern of his bladder. The liquid, however, kept coming. It occupied every nook and cranny until the final droplets trickled down and pressured the cantilever of his nether regions. As the night wore on, the Good Padre's internal pulley drew taut, steadily growing and swelling into a volatile, voluminous and unbendable *bastone.*

Finally, the morning sun slivered through the muslin curtains of his open window and roused the Good Padre. He awoke in a leisurely fashion that belied the urgency of his engorged member and swollen bladder. He yawned, stretched and opened his eyes with a smile, silently thanking God for the gift of another day. True, the Good Padre desperately needed to flow his water, but there was no need for panic, no need to rush to the outhouse. He'd experienced this problem before and recently worked out what he felt to be a fine solution.

What the Good Padre used to do was place his left hand against the outhouse's rear wall and lean at the most acute angle possible to reduce the degree to which he'd have to force his obstinate *bastone* downward. Alas, such a posture was strenuous to the point of undermining all the pleasure to be had as the bladder emptied. There was little choice, though, and over the course of his first weeks at the new parish, he withstood this morning ordeal until the day his support hand, in mid-release, broke through the outhouse's old wood boards. Instantly, his arm sunk to the hilt of his shoulder and his barrel chest crashed against the wall. His personal mass was far too great and sudden a weight for such a flimsy structure to endure and, before the Good Padre realized what was happening, he was lying on the ground, the outhouse toppled over and broken to pieces, warm urine spouting up his nightshirt.

Now, peacefully, in accord with his new routine, the Good Padre rose from his bed, shuffled to his window, slightly parted the curtains, lifted his nightshirt, perched his *bastone* on the windowsill and relaxed his body's floodgates. Though his window was not entirely private, the release was guilt-free as he usually woke at an early hour, well before sunrise, and knew that the chamomile patch he'd planted below the window benefited from the properties inherent in horse and human urine. This morning, however, just as he reached that delicious halfway point in his urination, a glimmer of sunlight suddenly illuminated more than just his yellowish water. He looked up to assess the angle of the mid-morning sun. "Bless'd Virgin!" the Good Padre gasped as the panic of oversleeping pinched his stream to a dribble. *"Gli Ebrei!"*

🍅 🍅 🍅

Bertolli and the other altar boys had hardly slept a wink all night. Supper's euphoria, come midnight, had regressed to fear and shame. Surely, if they closed their eyes to sleep, the Love Apple's poison would take hold and they would wake to find themselves roasting in the fires of hell. Spontaneously, with the dawn's first light, Bertolli and the boys found one another gathered and hiding outside the church's garden, all gripped by the same paranoia. Filled with awful thoughts the old padre had planted deep inside their heads, they had come to see if their Good Padre survived the night. But when he appeared in the window, Bertolli and the boys did not sigh with relief that he was alive and well. Neither did they think of hell or transgression, Original Sin, serpents or forbidden fruit. They had no thought but one: that maybe, one day, if they were as pious and kindly and good as their Good Padre, their bare and diminutive *cazzoni* would also grow to such staggering proportions.

In Which We Learn
the Meaning of
Il Tuono dell' Amore

D avido felt strangely good, better than he dared admit
as he busied himself in the construction of a tomato
pyramid upon his stand. He was terrified, of course—he
really had believed the priest would be there to greet him
and Nonno as they rolled into market—but Davido found the
terror oddly exhilarating. He'd been raised with the stories
of Nonno's travels and, in comparison, his life had been an
utter bore thus far. He had heartache and heartbreak, but
none of the excitement. Now, however, as Nonno must have
felt aboard the deck of Cristoforo Colombo's ship as it sailed
into uncharted territory, Davido felt his bodily senses adren-
alized and heightened. The tomato in his palm had never felt
so soothing, so varied in tones of crimson and red, nor so

piquant to his nose. To his ear, the readying market squawked and flapped like a flock of geese breakfasting on a riverbank at dawn. He could hear the fracturing of crust as a peasant tore a chunk from the bread she'd purchased, the clinking of wine bottles, the crowing of roosters and the chatter of bartering. Clove bud being sold down the market row tickled his left sinus. He could smell the deliciously unkosher aroma of roasted pork through one nostril, while catching the floral perfume of late-summer lavender in the other. Exuberantly, his nose deciphered patchouli, frankincense, myrrh, cedar wood, cinnamon, oak moss, bergamot and all the sacred oils wafting through the market's air. And though he could not encase such thoughts in language, he felt engaged in the world, as if the adventure before him was finally his!

🍅   🍅   🍅

Down the market row, Mari was struggling to stay focused on her duties. It was still early, but a decent-sized crowd was waiting before the olive stand to have their old wine bottles filled with oil and their clay pots replenished with any one of the dozen varieties of cured olives her stand offered. It was a busy morning, too busy for Mari's sake. She was feeling flustered and distracted and, much unlike herself, her mind wasn't entirely focused on olives and oil. Yes, it was always draining to have Benito around, as he did nothing to help and plenty to hinder. However, the cur had been around for as long as she could remember and while his behavior had grown increasingly repulsive in the years since her father's death, she could handle him without a problem. Although, if she was being perfectly frank, she had even less patience with Benito on days like today, when her mother joined her at the stand. Mari's mother knew she wasn't good for much. She was content to sit on half of a wine barrel at the rear of the stand and watch her daughter work, but even the idea that Benito might try any of his antics in front of her mother had Mari especially on edge.

But more than Benito and her mother's presence, what was most on Mari's mind and undermining the usual attention with which she managed her stand was the enticing sight of those red fruits down the market row and the loose curls of brown hair moving behind the growing pyramid of produce.

"How's your mother?" whispered a full-breasted and semi-toothless peasant woman who'd been called Mucca for so long that hardly anyone in the village remembered her real name. Mucca extended Mari her empty olive oil bottle.

"I don't know," Mari answered with an obvious lack of enthusiasm. She couldn't stand it when people pretended her mother was deaf as well as mute. "Let me ask her." Mari turned over her shoulder. "Mom, Mucca wants to know how you're feeling?"

Mari's mother frowned and tilted her head to the side.

Mari turned back to face Mucca. "There, you see," said Mari, "the same." Mari took hold of Mucca's empty bottle and the pair held eyes for a moment. Mucca had known both Mari and her mother since they were babies. Like almost everyone in the village, Mari found Mucca to be a pain in the ass, but she also knew the woman had a heart of gold. "Maybe a bit worse," Mari added softly.

"Sorry, dear," Mucca looked at Mari contritely. "Well, the good news is a husband can't be too far off."

"Oh, good God, Mucca." No subject annoyed Mari more. "Must you?"

"Surely," Mucca laughed, then continued, indifferent to Mari's protest and loud enough for Mari's mother to hear, "that stepfather of yours is gonna find you a husband?"

Mari raised her eyebrows and shrugged as she set the bottle under the olive oil spigot.

"I imagine," chimed in Signore Coglione, who was waiting in line behind Mucca, "that's the problem."

"True," laughed Mucca as she lowered her voice conspiratorially, "never trust a *magnaccio*[9] to find you a mate."

Not that something so true struck her as funny, but Mari chuckled anyhow.

---

[9] From the Etruscan *magnare*, meaning "to eat," i.e., "someone who eats with other people's money."

"Nevertheless," Signore Coglione said with smile, "a husband and children can be a happy fate."

"Perhaps," Mari retorted, hoping to end the conversation, "but I'd rather choose the food upon my plate."

"Ay." Signore Coglione nodded and raised his eyebrows in a conciliatory fashion. A triple rhyme always trumped.

"What's the matter," Mucca said with a wave of her hand, "no boy in town strike your fancy?"

Mari had had enough. She corked the oil bottle and set it down with a clunk. She felt her blood heating up. "Saving myself for Benito," she said flatly, hoping that would shut Mucca up.

"Goodness, dear," Mucca said as both she and Signore Coglione laughed, "you can do better than that!" Mucca handed Mari her olive jar. She pointed to the olives she wanted.

Mari took hold of a large wooden spoon and began to fill the jar with olives. She knew full well why she didn't have a husband yet. True, she didn't find any young man in town remotely worth marrying, but that was hardly the issue. Her stepfather couldn't care less about love or her desires. He was indeed a *magnaccio,* and had made his life—a *good* life— eating with other people's money. She ran his olive and grape mill, took care of his crippled wife and made his supper, and why in the devil's name would he give that up and pay a dowry to do it?

Mari caught some motion in the corner of her eye and her instinct system went on alert. She tightened her grip upon the large spoon she held. Despite the dozen or so villagers waiting with empty bottles in hand behind Mucca and the presence of Mari's mother, Benito left his position alongside the olive oil barrel and picked up the weighty satchel he'd brought with him to market. "Back in a bit," he snorted at Mari.

"Not on my account," Mari retorted as she powerfully whipped the wooden spoon behind her buttocks.

"Ow!" yelped Benito as the spoon whacked the knuckles of his right hand. *"Faccia di merda!"*

"Ha! Serves you right," said Mucca as she, Signore Coglione, Mari's mother and the handful of villagers surrounding the stand burst into laughter. "Best keep your fingers where they're less likely to get hit," Mucca said whilst handing some coins over to Mari. "Either stuffed in your nostrils or scratching about your dangling bit."

Benito jutted his chin in Mucca's direction. *"Vaffanculo!"* he spat as he shook the sting from his hand and shuffled off into the market.

"Oh, tell it to the sheep," Mucca yelled after him to more laughter—forever reminding Benito and villagers alike of his most infamous moment of adolescence, some twenty years past.

It had been a solid connection, the sharp rap of wood upon knuckle, and though Mari's pride flared from the perfection of her timing, she shared little of the crowd's joy. It was a tired routine to her. She had experienced enough of Benito's pats upon her backside to know exactly when his hand was most likely to make its wanton move, always in public and always as he parted her company.

Truth be told, Mari was fed up with Benito for many reasons, foremost of which was that she found him contradictory to her fundamental belief in the purity of the olive. He was always scratching the whiskers about his chin, picking his ear and then thoughtlessly sticking his vile fingers in the olive jars and stuffing olives in his mouth—olives that she had worked tirelessly to cure, marinate and stuff. Worse still, she would catch him—in the midst of servicing customers—reaching inside his trousers to adjust his genitals. True, there was no other olive oil vendor in town, but Mari still imagined Benito's presence caused more than a few people to abstain from having their bottles refilled with oil or olives for the week, and this was a horrible affront to her. She loved her olives too much to stomach such degradation.

Over the years Mari had tried to distance herself from the fortunes and follies of the olive orchard, but she had been unable to do so. Olive oil ran through her veins. Indeed, she felt that by honoring the olive she honored the memory of her father and the orchard and fruit that her family had nurtured for generations. In the years since her father's death she'd been overworked, unpaid and treated indignantly, but Mari still cared about olives—cared with a vengeance.

🍅   🍅   🍅

"Are you paying attention?" Giuseppe said as he snapped his fingers before Benito's nose. But Benito wasn't paying attention. He couldn't stop thinking about the other day, how a boy, a queer little boy wearing a dress, so easily silenced his boss, and how, once again, it was Benito charged with the dirty work.

"Listen up!" Giuseppe leaned in, his pitch controlled but fervent with enthusiasm. "Three dozen Love Apples to do the deed, to sow the soil and plant our seed. 'Tween now and tomorrow, Benito, play it cool and aloof, then when market starts to bustle, make your way up to the roof. Splatter these forbidden fruits upon random heads, hams, breads and lambs; off cheese panino and dried sheets of *papiro*[10], upon roasted pigs and pies, figs and dyes; hit the butcher and baker and candlestick maker. Wail and paste arms and limbs, baskets and shiny knife blades; plant one solidly on that fat prick who sells spades. Better yet, don't waste the time on direct aim, pelt the young, the old, the vigorous, the lame. Quick as you can spread bedlam and fear, disorient the eye and confuse the ear. Let Love Apple drip from noses and off statues in poses, making soggy crisp crusts of bread and speckling clothing in watery red. Tainting white pails of heavy cream, splashing the gypsy who interprets the dream. Let it cling to short eyelashes and the hair on horses' asses, to peaches and plums and off the tip of farmers' thick thumbs. Bombard the marketgoers head to boot with the juice and pulp of an illicit, forbidden fruit. Rejoice, Benito, take your vengeance upon the crowd, do the deed well and make me proud."

That was what Giuseppe had instructed yesterday evening, just before leaving Benito at the tavern with a full mug of ale, a purse full of coins and a belly full of fear. But as Benito, now perched upon the roof of the bakery overlooking the bustling market two stories below, opened up his leather

---

[10] Papyrus paper used for writing and wrapping.

satchel and peered into it, he felt his throwing arm go suddenly numb. There they were, thirty-six deathly and deadly
Love Apples. Worse still, Benito had forgotten Giuseppe's leather
gloves, the only thing, he was certain, that saved him from ca-
tastrophe yesterday when he picked them from their vines.

As Giuseppe had instructed, Benito was to launch the
Love Apples into the crowd as quickly as possible. Giuseppe
felt it was critical for the bombardment to be rapid so as to
create as much confusion as possible. Giuseppe suggested
throwing them two by two, and although it would be a great
temptation, he urged Benito not to take particular aim at any
one person, as it would only slow the process; under no cir-
cumstance was he to throw one in the direction of the *Ebrei*.
It had to appear that *they* were throwing them.

Slowly, with a nervous tremor to his hand, Benito reached
into the satchel and pulled out a Love Apple. Instantly, its
dreaded poison began to burn the tips of his fingers as if he'd
just scooped up a handful of lye. He felt his pulse quicken,
his brow break with sweat and his heart beat unnaturally
fast. Good God, he thought to himself, I'll be dead before I
manage to throw all of these. Then he rose up onto his knees,
still mostly hidden behind the bakery's wide chimney, and
gazed intently at the market below, searching for the perfect
target. His hand still ached from where Mari had whacked it
and he gave a moment's thought to hurling the first one at
her, but the little voice inside his head wouldn't allow him
to hurt what he loved so much. Who then, Benito pondered,
entirely ignoring Giuseppe's order. Quick, before this devilish
fruit incinerates my hand. Mucca? Vincenzo? *"Vaffanculo,"*
Benito whispered, "there's the face of Bobo the Fool." Feeling
his upper limb suddenly come back to life, Benito cocked his
arm and with all the vengeance a dozen years of snide com-
ments and putdowns can instill, he hurled the overripe tomato at the slender, hairless face of Bobo the Fool.

⁂   ⁂   ⁂

Mari slid Signore Coglione's coins into her apron pocket as
they said, *"Ciao,"* to each other in near-harmony, though he

always added *bella.* As the tavern owner, he was her best customer, and without any help at her stand, it took Mari nearly
ten minutes just to put his order together: eight bottles of olive oil, six earthen jars filled with olives. The wine he ordered
from her was delivered separately, usually on Wednesdays:
one barrel of red, one half barrel of white. As Mari looked up
to greet her next customer she noticed with aggravation the
backup at her stand; at least ten people were waiting. She
looked over her shoulder to see if her mother could help, but
her poor mama was so exhausted from the short walk between her apartment and the piazza that she'd fallen asleep.
It wasn't a pretty sight. Her mother, once so beautiful, looked
like a fat little toad as she sat there asleep on the half barrel,
chin collapsed into her bosom, a thin stream of saliva drooling from the permanently numb left corner of her mouth.

Mari cursed Benito's name silently as she took the next
empty bottle before her and turned to face the large olive-oil-
filled barrel to her side. She placed the bottle under the olive
oil spout, turned the lever and watched for a moment as a
thin line of green-gold oil flowed into the bottle. She estimated how long it would take to fill then lifted her head to
look across the market in the direction of her curiosity, when
something prodigious caught her eye and in an instant all
the anger and heartache that pestered her mind vanished.

Whether it was the lone hand of the Divine or the gods
acting in collusion or a mischievous Cupid out to cause a stir
was impossible to say; but at the very second Mari lifted her
head, the crowded market appeared to part and Mari and
Davido found each other's gaze. Naturally, the jolt of Eros
simultaneously stunned the eyes and enthralled the loins of
our two lovers-to-be; but at a moment such as this it would
be too easy to speak solely of beauty and youthful lust, as the
couple's shared vision was more than that. Indeed, what they
found in each other's eyes shot through them from the inside out and sent a hot, sublime sensation bursting up their
spines, causing the world around them to melt away, as if the
eye had just beheld the image of what the soul had previously

known and craved to know again. A vision that revealed a shared destiny and a burning desire to manifest it. It was a vision that came with a great clamor that only Davido and Mari could hear: *Il Tuono dell' Amore,* as Menzogna put it. The thunder of love.

13

In Which We Learn How the Mind Stills Itself in Moments of Trauma

Across the piazza, oblivious to Benito's orders and Mari and Davido's rapture, Luigi Campoverde stood with his mouth slightly agape, staring at the beautiful array of purple and green figs on the stand before him. Luigi was deep in thought, envisioning how delicious the ripe figs would be once he sliced them lengthwise, spread them with whipped ricotta and set a balsamic-caramelized walnut atop each for a bit more sweetness and crunch, when the recipe suddenly burst inside his brain.

Twenty-four hours ago Luigi never would have imagined that he, esteemed chef for Cosimo di Pucci de' Meducci the Third, Grand Duke of Tuscany, would have ventured a rough two hours by mule to attend the market of an inconsequen-

tial little village he'd never even heard of. One of the luxuries
about being the chef for the Duke of Tuscany was that food
vendors came to *him*. However, despite the breach of protocol,
the duo of *rimatori* who'd arrived at his kitchen the other day
with the exquisite pair of early-season truffles had aroused
his curiosity about what other gastronomic treasures the hilltop hamlet might offer. His interest had been further stoked
by how willing the one pompous scoundrel had been to accept payment in a manner other than money. Should such
sentiments be shared by other vendors at the out-of-the-way
market, well, Luigi reckoned, it could make for the perfect place
to covertly resupply his kitchen.

Surreptitious thoughts of delectable produce bartered for
some of the useless bric-a-brac overflowing from the duke's
villa was what Luigi had been thinking about all morning.
Until now, at least, when a rude, spindly, drunken fool cut
before him and obstructed Luigi's view of the mouthwater-
ing collection of figs. As if that weren't offensive enough, the
fool reeked of soured wine, and his continual bobbing and
bending, as he sampled amply from the stand, had Luigi at
his wits' end. Finally—*suddenly*—just as Luigi was thinking
of knocking the twit out of his way, the fool once again bent
over, and a tomato, hurled by one and meant for another,
came spectacularly crashing into Luigi's face.

It has long been known how the mind stills itself in moments of trauma so that details may be recalled afterward
with an absolute clarity, and it was with this heightened
sense that the instant of impact played out in Luigi's mind.
The sound hit Luigi first. That unmistakable whistle of the
wind breaking across a hurled projectile. Then the sharp slap
of fruit skin upon human skin. It was a funny sound and
Luigi wondered where it was coming from. Next, a squirting
noise, like a wide boot stepping into a fresh pile of mud, as
the tomato's moist innards broke across the upper bridge of
his nose, right between his eyes. Of course there would be
pain, but that sensation would have to wait. For as the splattering of pulp, seeds and juice blinded his eyes, blew into his
open mouth and registered upon his taste buds, there was

flavor. My God, there was a flavor the likes of which Luigi had never tasted.

⊛   ⊛   ⊛

Across the piazza, Cosimo di Pucci de' Meducci, Grand Duke of Tuscany, was still in something of a daze and had yet to notice the stand laden with nostalgic fruit or his filching chef prowling about. It had been a difficult evening for Cosimo. The indelicacy of being caught *in flagrante delicto* by his child had been most awkward. The embarrassment was greatly compounded by the fact that his wife and entire staff had all been present, standing at attention to receive their returning duke when young Gian pulled open the carriage door, exposing, quite literally, his father.

The family meal that evening proved unbearable. The cavernous dining hall, sparsely filled with three Meduccis and three attending servants, crackled with tension. Cosimo and his wife sat at opposite ends of the table, twenty-six feet apart. Splitting the distance sat young Gian, merrily cooing over a bowl of wild mushroom *ancini di pepe,* copiously infused with the wafer-thin shavings of fresh truffle.

The boy sounded happier than Cosimo could remember, as if a great secret had been revealed to him, and he ate with a demonstrative relish, his feet dancing and tapping upon the floor. God bless you, thought Cosimo, I only pray the aristocracy shall fall before you inherit such a burdensome heartache. Cosimo wanted to look up. To smile at his boy and tell him how much he loved him. To laugh with his wife at the farce that fate had made of their lives. But he could not bring himself to do so. He knew his wife would never share in such a joke. The sad reality for Cosimo was that he had no one with whom to share anything of feeling or meaning, no true friend—no trusted confidant. The one person he did have, the one who would have laughed with him, his beloved courtesan, had been stolen away.

Oh, dear God, thought Cosimo, as he rose up from the table in a fit of melancholy and without a word slid out the kitchen entrance, if only I were a farmer. *Yes,* he repeated to himself, if only I were a farmer. And then he strode over to the stables, awoke the snoozing stable-master and demanded not only the most decrepit mule of the lot, but that his servant disrobe and lend him his well-worn and far less regal boots, trousers, tunic, vest and long stableman's jacket. If only I were a farmer, mused Cosimo as he left the villa behind, rode through the night, past his old vineyard, and loped into a small hilltop village at dawn, I could have led the life I was meant to lead and she, she would still be alive.

That's what Cosimo had been thinking until he noticed a blur of red hurl through the market and explode across the face of his chef. *"Mio Dio,"* Cosimo sighed, it was a *pomodoro!* The same precious fruit his courtesan used to feed him.

14

In Which We Learn
How Davido & Nonno Came to Be
Invited to *La Festa del Santo Ubriaco*

T he scream was horrendous, a bloodcurdling yelp, the
desperate cry of a man in his death throes.

The acid-scorch of Benito's fingers was unbearable and
he could only bring himself to throw one more tomato, despite
his nearly equal superstitious fear of displeasing Giuseppe.
Nevertheless, his second throw had found its mark. He'd
blasted that blubbery pork-selling piglet good, and despite
the arsenic pain ravaging his throwing hand, the scream
now playing before his ears made it all worthwhile.

Certainly, the hurled projectile exploding solidly into
his ear stung and stunned the pork butcher Vincenzo and
sent him crashing against his rack of sausage links like a
lumbering drunkard. But he didn't realize it was a mortal

wound until his senses sorted out that it was a Love Apple that struck him and he saw the red juice and aghast expression splattered across the tunic and face of his closest customer, Augusto Po. Instantly, Vincenzo felt the forbidden fruit's deathly seeds and juice drip into the cavity of his ear and his brain set fire as he clasped his head, keeled over and yelled bloody murder.

Petrified, the crowd around Vincenzo's stand leapt back. Men hollered and women screamed. Vincenzo rolled from his knees and fell to the cobblestones like a pigeon shot mortally in one wing. Drained of life, his screams receded to ghastly moans. He began to writhe and reel upon the ground, the acid burning down his ear canal and eating away his brain. The crowd surrounding him doubled, tripled, quadrupled, until nearly half the market was there to see Vincenzo take his final breath and his body go lifeless. Killed by a hurled Love Apple impacted solidly in his right ear.

Instantly, there was silence, dead silence that spread from the surrounding crowd to the entire market. Heads turned, people left their shopping aside until nearly all the marketgoers, all but Mari, Davido and Nonno, were gathered around Vincenzo. Close enough to see what happened, but far enough back to keep clear of the murderous poison that had killed him.

"*Gli Ebrei,*" a lone voice in the solidifying crowd shouted out. "*Gli Ebrei del Pomo di Amore.*"

The crowd took to grumbling. Heads began to now turn in the direction of the *Ebrei* stand. Eyes narrowed, expressions went cross. A pair of men slid on their thick leather gloves, stepped forward, grabbed Vincenzo from under his arms and dragged his lifeless body fifty or so feet and then dropped him before the *Ebrei.*

"Oy, *merda,*" babbled Nonno as he became terribly aware he and Davido were no longer going to be ignored. Nonno turned to look at his grandson. He saw the bewildered expression on the boy's face, the nearly completed tomato pyramid before him and the ripe fruit gripped in his left hand. Could he have been so foolish, thought Nonno?

"*Assassino!*" Mucca took a half step into the semi-circle

surrounding Vincenzo's body and the *Ebrei* stand. "Murderer!"

A hot burst of adrenaline shot through Mari and roasted what remained of her amorous goose bumps. She heard the angry words and saw through a fracture in the crowd the prone body of Vincenzo. Mari squinted to better observe the shocking sight and could have sworn she saw his eyes twitch. *Mio Dio,* thought Mari as she continued to focus her vision upon Vincenzo, does that *cacasodo* have no shame? Suddenly, a scenario flashed before her. Where was Benito? How odd that he should shuffle off so shortly before all this. And what was in that weighty satchel of his? Oh, no, thought Mari, as she grabbed a bucket of water from under her stand and made her way over to the scene, what had Giuseppe put the ogre up to?

A horrible silence thickened the air as Davido looked upon the body before him and the soft tomato: smashed, splattered, destroyed upon and into the man's ear. What happened, he wondered, that my eyes could so quickly go from gazing upon that beautiful girl to looking upon this? Davido swallowed hard. He thought of his young cousins who would often have fights with the overripe tomatoes they found upon the ground, and wondered if he'd ever see them again.

"You," said Mucca as she pointed to the tomato in Davido's hand, "you killed him."

Davido followed the squat woman's finger and looked oddly at his own hand, which he wasn't even certain was part of his body, and wondered why it held a tomato. His defense left his mouth like a wounded whisper: "No."

"You did!" Mucca yelled. "I never liked him much, but he was one of ours and you killed him."

"No," Davido repeated faintly, shaking his head in dismay.

"Of course," blurted a man in the crowd, "of course the *Ebreo* would seek to kill a pork merchant!"

"No."

"Then how did this happen?" Mucca asked while pointing to the dead man on the ground.

Davido was speechless and he returned the peasant woman's contemptuous gaze with a look of dumbfounded apology. Their eyes held each other in an awkward pause until an egg flung from the rear of the crowd suddenly hit Davido upon the neck. The shell stung and burst upon his collarbone, its innards quickly sliming down his shirt like a fast-moving slug.

The blow to his grandson, though harmless, erupted the stomach acid in Nonno with a sickening force. He had been in these situations before and was fearful that the barrier between angry words and action had just been broken.

A clamor erupted from the crowd as a second piece of produce, a baton-like green zucchini, crashed before Davido, toppling his tomato pyramid and sending a hundred tomatoes bouncing to the cobblestones. To a chorus of jeers, the floodgates of retribution opened. Instantly, the air was filled with other fruits and vegetables as the villagers reached for whatever produce was near at hand. Soft peaches, overripe plums, soggy figs and heads of loose-leaf radicchio began to crash and bang all around and upon the foreigners in their midst. Thank goodness, for Davido and Nonno's sake, it was late August, a time in which most of summer's fruits and vegetables were well ripened and the hard tubers of autumn were still a few weeks from harvest, and the villagers were too inherently frugal to throw any more eggs or the expensive and delectable *melone del cantalupo*.

Panicked and concerned for his grandfather's safety, Davido glanced over to discover that the old man had lifted a large wicker basket from the wagon and was using it to protect his face and head. It was a ridiculous sight, his skinny old grandfather warding off an assault of soft fruits and vegetables behind a flimsy shield of wicker, and he felt a rather bizarre impulse to laugh. That was, at least, until a large cabbage broke across the side of Davido's head, knocked him off balance and caused him to slip and fall upon a soft tomato.

"Basta!" a voice moving through the crowd shouted out and brought the bombardment to a halt. *"Basta!* Enough!"

To Davido, disoriented and lying upon the cobblestones under his stand, the voice, so firm, so feminine, sounded as if it issued from the lips of an angel. Davido blinked a few times to sort out his vision as the crowd parted to reveal the calves, ankles, feet and sandals of the dissenting voice. She walked to the center of the crowd and paused next to the body of the dead man. Davido had never seen such wonderful extremities. Her feet were perfect—salt-of-the-earth perfect—strong and shapely with a slight arch shaped like a cantaloupe's curve. She had beautiful toes, like baby eggplants—sleek, tapered and slightly bulbous around the tips. Her ankles were strong, not too thick, nor too skinny, and they grew gracefully into muscular calves that seemed shaped by hours of standing on tiptoe to pick peaches or knock olives from trees. Just below the hem of her skirt, Davido could make out a small scar, right below her left knee, shaped like a scythe. It was a beautiful imperfection existing in harmony with the perfection of her skin, and Davido longed to crawl out and give the little scar a kiss.

"*Basta!*" she yelled one more time, and then promptly dumped a bucket of water over the face of the dead man.

"Huh!" The crowd gasped at such disrespect for the deceased.

Immediately, the dead man sat up and began to cough.

"*Madonna mio!*" a hundred voices rang out as nearly half the assembled group dropped to their knees and made the sign of the cross. "*Un miracolo!*" shouts rang out, "a miracle!"

"Nothing of the sort," shot back Mari. "If any of you had been as concerned about Vincenzo as you were about vengeance, you might have noticed that he was breathing the whole time."

"I was dead," protested Vincenzo, gasping for breath. "Sure as *Cristo* died on the cross, I was dead!"

A frown curled Mari's mouth as she sunk her gaze into Vincenzo.

Vincenzo withered, lowering his head sheepishly. "Well, I thought I was as good as dead."

Mari did not relent.

"Regardless," Vincenzo flicked his thumb in the *Ebreo* boy's direction, "what kind of monster attacks a man in his own village?"

"How do you know it was him?" asked Mari.

"How do I know?" Vincenzo responded indignantly. "Who else could have done this?" He pointed to his tomato-splattered right ear.

Despite the safety of his current position and the lovely view of the woman's feet, knees and ankles, Davido drew a deep breath and, though motivated more by curiosity than courage, rose up from under his stand to face his many attackers and lone defender.

"Vincenzo," Mari said with a confidence that made him feel a bit like a little boy, "did you actually see this man throw his fruit at you?"

"What?" said Vincenzo indignantly as he lifted himself up from the ground.

"Did you actually see this man throw his fruit at you?"

Vincenzo's lips pursed. "No, but need I more proof than what lies lodged in my ear and resting in his hand?"

"Vincenzo," said Mari, "do you think anyone so foolish that they would attack the locals with the very fruit they wish to sell?"

"Foolish?" Vincenzo repeated. "Surely those who nailed our *Cristo* to the cross could be so foolish as to give their fruit a toss."

Good God—Nonno rolled his eyes—must it always come back to that?

The villagers erupted in agreement. Even the more open-minded and sensitive among them, like the Cheese Maker and Signore Coglione, could not rightly doubt the depths of evil and foolishness to which an *Ebreo* could stoop.

"Vincenzo," Mari said calmly, adopting a new tactic, "in which direction does your stand face?"

The question flustered Vincenzo as he regarded his stand. He was prepared to argue about Judas and *Cristo* and the profound injustice dealt to the pig, not about direction. "West, I think. But what has that to do with anything?" Vincenzo said brusquely.

"Mmm, west, indeed," repeated Mari. "And in what direction does this stand here face?"

Vincenzo took in the angle of the tomato stand. The market row had a slight bend. "North, split with west," he said, not sure what Mari was getting at.

"Mmm, north split with west," Mari said, parroting Vincenzo. She had never done anything quite like this before. What prompted her to speak from her heart had become an equation for her head and she now strained mentally to organize her point. "Now," said Mari, "in which ear were you hit with their fruit?"

"My right ear," Vincenzo said, again pointing to his ear.

"I know your right ear," Mari affirmed, though she was still not certain her own logic was on target. "But when you stood outward, doling the sausage from your space, in which direction did your right ear face?" Mari set her feet as if she were tending Vincenzo's stall, then pointed to the *Ebrei* at her left and gave a slight tug on her right earlobe, which lay clearly on the opposite side of her head from the *Ebrei's* stand.

Vincenzo, keener in geometry than in confidence, finally got Mari's point and he lowered his eyes like an admonished schoolboy.

Davido watched in amazement as ears were tugged and conversations flared up between those who understood the girl's point and those who didn't. But to Davido an altogether different point was being made—*this was quite a woman!*

"What if," a rather slow and slippery voice in the crowd spoke out, "Vincenzo had turned around?"

"What?" said Mari as the crowd quieted.

Incensed by an unsightly globule of tomato stuck upon the breast pocket of his Venetian silk tunic, Augusto Po repeated his challenge. "What if Vincenzo had turned around for a moment, let's say, to fetch a sausage off his rack?"

Oh, God, thought Mari, I hadn't considered that.

The crowd parted to better reveal Augusto Po, his smooth

bald head and corona of white hair glimmering in the sunlight. "Sweet girl," he said after a moment's pause, "you have
used logic and reason to defend this here *Ebreo* from treason.
But what say your eyes? Surely, your eyes must bear some
witness to your defense?"

The crowd hushed. Augusto Po was a nasty old fox and it
was rare for him to make a scene in public, especially since
the death of his uncle. Po was not native to the village. He
was the nephew of the town's recently deceased old padre,
and had, many years ago, moved to the village to help his
uncle manage the church and its landholdings. Most considered his a well-paid but dubious position, which Po managed
to exploit for great personal gain. He was known to engage
in usury, and he owned a good many of the rental dwellings
about town.

"I am sure," Mari responded directly to Augusto, "because
my eyes were upon him."

A murmur ran through the crowd.

Oh, no. From the corner of his eye, Nonno caught his grandson battling a smirk. Great tragedies have stemmed from
lesser lines.

Giuseppe, who had descended from his balcony to witness the action, really wasn't as patient as he believed himself to be and he didn't like the nature of this standoff. "Oh,
Mari, my daughter," said Giuseppe as his face parted with a
put-on smile, "who, as a child, at a mouse's pain took pity, as
a woman protects even the donkey of our fair Italy."

Her name is Mari? Davido felt his heart jump.

"Oh, God bless the good Italian heart," the Good Padre
said on top of the crowd's laughter as he stepped enthusiastically to the center of the crowd. He looked at Mari and smiled.
"I see news of the decree has been well spread and well received. Yes, welcome, neighbors, welcome." The Good Padre
rubbed his hands together as if sizing up a holiday table set
with a delectable feast. "Now, Mari, who has tried this new
fruit and can attest its flavor?"

Mari bit the corner of her lip. The crowd fell stone silent.

"Come now," the Good Padre said, attempting to prod the

villagers, "no need for shyness." He pointed to the crimson-speckled villagers before him. "You, Signore Po, seem to wear its juice upon your blouse, and you, Vincenzo, though, 'tis off your mouth, upon your ear. Indeed, by appearances, it does look like a sloppy feast hast happened here. Now, who shall step forward and tell me of its flavor?"

The public recognition of a blemish upon his tunic, coupled with his disturbing inability to comprehend the Good Padre, caused Po to slither back into the crowd.

"Good Padre," Giuseppe said, fracturing the pause, "we have not partaken of this fruit."

"No? Then why the mirth? Why the merry? Did I not enter in mid-joviality?" The Good Padre paused his eyes on Vincenzo. "You mean, not a single one has tried this fruit?"

Vincenzo looked at his feet.

"Oh, good God," said the Good Padre with a chuckle as he stepped over to the tomato stand. "I tell you, just last night, after visiting with our lovely neighbors, I ate several of their fruits. And they were delicious."

The crowd gasped at the revelation.

"O, bless'd Virgin," said the Good Padre as he lifted a tomato from the stand and held it up for inspection, " 'tis a fruit, nothing more and nothing less. Here," the Good Padre handed the tomato to Davido, "good lad, cut me a slice of this one here."

Davido reached across his stand to take the *pomodoro* from the priest. He cleared a small space before him upon his disheveled stand and began to slice the tomato in half.

"And if I," said the Good Padre as Davido handed him the sliced half tomato, "a man of the cloth, be cut down, then we know here evil be found. But if I emerge in salubrious splendor then forever fear not the fruit of this vendor."

"No! No!" shouted the Cheese Maker, "don't do it, Good Padre." "It will be the death of you," another villager called out. "No, no, *Boun Padre!*" other shouts rang out in protest.

The Good Padre smiled as he unveiled his acorn-sized teeth and, to a chorus of gasps usually reserved for the swallowing of a sword when the Gypsy circus came to town each spring, bit into the fruit and began to chew.

"Oh, my!" the Good Padre uttered upon swallowing. Immediately, the breakfast possibilities the *pomodoro* offered flooded his mind. He thought of how lovely softly poached eggs laid atop sheep's-milk-cheese-smeared toast, with sliced *pomodoro,* sea salt, chives and a drizzle of olive oil would be for a late breakfast. "Put fear and anxiety to waste, dear neighbors, for here is a heavenly taste," said the Good Padre as he opened his mouth wide and tucked the rest of the tomato inside.

With the sting from the blow finally wearing off his face, yet the flavor still lingering on his tongue, Luigi Campoverde found the Good Padre's expression too compelling an affirmation to ignore. Luigi knew a good eater when he saw one, and he decided to take advantage of the crowd's distracted state and gather a few of the fallen fruits lying about the piazza's cobblestones. He reached between legs, under skirts, around canvas bags and wicker baskets and quickly gathered up nearly a dozen of the Love Apples into his sack. While slinking about at ankle-level, Luigi noticed a wonderful bottle of olive oil resting inside some preoccupied peasant's basket. The small market seemed to possess a wealth of gastronomic charms and he was curious if it extended to the local olive oil. The oil had a robust color—a perfect hue of green-gold—and Luigi couldn't help himself. Slyly, he dropped a pair of the lady duke's pearl earrings into the peasant's basket and then slid the stolen oil into his satchel.

"Dear cousins," said the Good Padre as he motioned for Davido to hand him the other half of the tomato, "t'would be a shame to let fear and superstition impede this delight. Indeed, this fruit is delicious." The Good Padre took the half tomato from Davido and stepped closer to Vincenzo. "Come now, Vincenzo," said the Good Padre as he put his arm around the pork merchant. "Since you appear the most aggrieved, you above all will be the most relieved. Have a bite."

Ever since the miraculous Good Friday disappearance

of his mother's cataracts and hemorrhoids, Vincenzo had attended church regularly, but he was, nevertheless, hardly comfortable in the Good Padre's presence. "Bbb . . . Bbb . . . But . . ."

"Oh, Vincenzo," assured the Good Padre, "two full mouthfuls now and half a dozen just last night, and I am here and healthy as ever."

"Go on, Vincenzo," said the squat, bosomy hag Mucca, *"mangialo!"*

A single affirmation was all it took for the crowd to let loose. "Eat it!" was the first. *"Si,* Vincenzo, *mangialo!"* rang the second, as the third, fourth and fifth voices reiterated the same call of *"mangialo."* Then, inevitably, from deep in the crowd, having finally descended from the rooftop, came the tormenting prompt that followed Vincenzo throughout his life and that drove him to this situation in the first place. "Go on," the somewhat disguised voice of Benito rang out, "you pig-loving bastard, *mangialo."*

Seeing that no ground remained sacred before the Good Padre, the crowd broke into a chorus of pig-like snorts.

Vincenzo's jaw dropped and his expression turned cross. "Who said that?" he asked, though he knew full well who said it. *"Va il piacere una pecora!"* Vincenzo yelled.

With his slight shoulders, protruding potbelly, oddly short neck, errant right eye and the absolute toothlessness of his threats, Vincenzo's curses, especially his standard retort to Benito—*Go pleasure a sheep*—carried the very opposite effect he desired and the crowd howled with laughter.

Truly, thought Nonno, the Lord is great.

"Ah, go on, Vincenzo," Mucca repeated herself, this time more loudly and audaciously. "Eat it."

Vincenzo's wandering eye shot to Mucca. "Not a chance, you beslubbering old cow. *You* eat it!"

"Blah." Mucca waved the back of her hand as if swatting the insult away. "Since when does a pig give such a thought to what it scoffs?"

"Nor a cow to what it cuds," Vincenzo said sharply.

"Oh, for goodness sake," chimed the Good Padre, "won't either of you try one?"

"But what if it's like hemlock and cuts slow to the chase?" Mucca answered the question with a question.

"Aye! True. True. For not all poison is quick to kill," added Vincenzo with an affirming nod.

"I doubt that's the case," said the Good Padre.

"With all due respect," said Vincenzo, as he squirmed from under the Good Padre's arm, "I will not let that Love Apple cross my lips."

The Good Padre eyed Mucca.

"Nor I," gasped Mucca as she brought her hand to her prodigious bosom in mock offense. "I have lived long and well enough without this fruit. If you're so excited about it, why don't you eat another one?"

"*Si,*" several voices in the crowd rang out. "*Mangialo un altro, Boun Padre.* Eat another one."

"Ay, ay," said the Good Padre, still surprisingly unflustered. "For the sake of my nervous brother I will gladly eat another." He turned to Davido. "A pinch of salt, perhaps?"

Davido's lips pursed into a held-back smile as he fetched a small container of salt from the rear of his wagon. He really couldn't help but adore this priest. He unfastened the leather tie that held the cloth atop the earthen jar of salt, took a pinch, reached across his stand and sprinkled it upon the Good Padre's half tomato.

The Good Padre liked the look of this: the way the whitish-blue bits of sea salt glistened and dissolved upon the tomato's moist innards. "Witness," he shouted to the crowd and then gracefully slid the salt-speckled tomato into his mouth and began to chew.

Mucca, who stood barely chest-high to the priest, poked her knobby little forefinger into the Good Padre's stomach. "You feel not an ounce different?"

"Not even a pinch," said the Good Padre.

"But you're the size of a barnyard ox," said Mucca.

"*Eh,* true, true. He's big as a cow," agreed a voice from the crowd.

"And broad as a bull," added Vincenzo.

"I have heard," continued Mucca, narrowing her eyes

suspiciously, "that Sicilians can eat fire, fart smoke and shit ash."

"*Eh,* true," said Vincenzo, wagging his finger. " 'Tis well known, Sicilians have a gut of iron and a bowel of bronze."

"Sicily?" said the Good Padre with a raised eyebrow. He didn't think he was from Sicily.

Mucca, ignored by her husband as a libidinous nag, but appreciated by the villagers as a foul-mouthed wench, was very much enjoying herself and continued as the crowd's mouthpiece. "How are we to know a pleasure in the morning won't be a poison by the dusk? For we know nothing about this fruit."

"Is it even a fruit?" asked Vincenzo. "Looks like a vegetable to me."

Curious himself as to the *pomodoro*'s origin, the Good Padre turned to the old *Ebreo*. "Neighbor," he said, with a questioning tone.

Nonno took a moment to clear his throat. "Well," he said, "as it's yet to be marked by the botanists of Florence or Rome, its delineation is still officially unknown."

"But what of the fruit's nature?" said the Good Padre. "How does it grow?"

"For that answer, ask my green-thumbed grandson," said Nonno. "Davido."

Davido, Mari's heart leapt as she repeated the name to herself, *Davido.*

"Well," said the Good Padre, "what say you, young Davido, how grows it?"

Davido felt his flesh get hot and his mouth go dry as all eyes turned in his direction. Since when does Nonno defer to me in public, he thought? This was certainly more than he'd bargained for and he was sure he would sound like a fool before her—he'd never had to rhyme in public. " 'T . . . 't . . ." Davido's voice crackled with uncertainty. " 'Tis a small seed." He kept his eyes upon the tomatoes before him as his mind searched desperately to find the rhyme. "Best planted from mid-spring to early summer in rich, well-draining soil. It likes a good, strong sun and a once-weekly rain. From a small, scentless yellow flower comes a fruit, green at first, which ripens to red. About eighty days, from planting to harvest. Its skin is soft and its flesh easily bruised, and after picking, it's not to be abused." *Oh, thank God,* thought Davido, having finally coupled a sentence the way locals do. "And though it may sound a bit contrary, *pomodori* grow like a pepper, yet are juicy like a berry."

He loves the earth, thought Mari. She could hear that in his voice, see that in his eyes. He looked at his tomatoes the way she wished he'd look at her.

The crowd was silent, not knowing what to make of it all.

"Well," said Mucca, "that's an odd combination."

"*Eh,* true," added Vincenzo. "Berries are oft poisonous, and peppers oft sorcerous."

Many in the crowd hummed and nodded in agreement.

"Neighbors," said the Good Padre. He had no tolerance for the ignorant maligning of the earth. "What do you know of poisons and sorcery? For surely," the Good Padre gestured to the onion and garlic farmer standing nearby, "had Renzo here come upon this fruit and seeds, who'd suggest such evil deeds?"

"Exactly the point!" said Vincenzo. "For Renzo is as common to us as the garlic he grows."

"And as stinky," blurted Mucca.

"Oh, good God!" The Good Padre threw up his hands. "Hast not anyone the bravery to try this fruit?"

Mari looked apologetically toward Davido. She felt a jolt as her eyes met his and the two fought against their smiles in unison. She would have gladly taken up the Good Padre's challenge and eaten a hundred of the boy's fruit. A hundred hundred she would have eaten. But Mari was smarter than that and knew her village well enough to understand what would be perceived as principle and what as promiscuity. So, against her heart, she held her tongue.

It was time, thought Giuseppe, as his eyes scanned the crowd for Benito. He located his underling and gave him a subtle nod.

"Bobo the Fool will eat it," Benito called out. "Bobo will eat anything!"

A grand idea! The crowd reacted with rousing support and the air filled with an array of calls for Bobo to step forward. Here was a perfect time to put one on the fool who so often put one on them all.

"He'll do it for a mug of ale," said Mucca, as if revealing a little-known piece of information.

"Or a goblet of wine," seconded Vincenzo through the ruckus.

"Well," said the Good Padre, "where is this brave Bobo?"

The idea of the words *brave* and *Bobo* existing in the same sentence sent a roar of laughter through the crowd.

"Here's the *brave* fool!" shouted Benito. He pointed underneath the statue of the Drunken Saint where Bobo the Fool was curled into a fetal position, sleeping. Bobo had awoken briefly to sample a few figs from the Fig Farmer's stand, but once food started flying about, Bobo quickly took shelter, desirous of more sleep.

Benito now poked the toe of his boot against Bobo's buttock. "Wake up, fool," he chided.

"Go away," groaned Bobo, swatting at Benito's foot. "Bobo sleeps."

Cosimo di Pucci de' Meducci the Third, Grand Duke of Tuscany, had been gratefully distracted by these provincial antics until a voice in the crowd landed upon his heart like an anvil. "My God." Cosimo's mouth fell open and his knees went weak under the weight of so many memories. He hadn't seen Bobo for almost thirty years.

"But 'tis time for your breakfast, fool." Benito felt a disconcerting tingle in his loins as he reached under the statue, grabbed the belt of Bobo's trousers, dragged the rather slight fool to his feet and flung him into the crowd. Benito often felt that tingle whenever he manhandled Bobo and it bothered him immensely. He was no *finocchio*.

The crowd parted with laughter as the spindly-legged fool stumbled forward. Those villagers closest by goosed Bobo's buttocks, slapped his thighs and tugged his ears, overjoyed to see the fool they thought they knew so well and the padre they barely knew at all go mano a mano. Though few villagers would admit such a thing, they held much affection for their fool and often spent days pondering his irreverent point of view.

The only problem when it came to Bobo was that nearly everything about him annoyed someone in some way. Those who thought a man should be broad, strong and hairy were put off by Bobo's spindly limbs, soft flesh and hairless face. Those who thought a man should be serious were put off by Bobo's complete disregard for seriousness. Those who thought a man should be straightforward in his speech were put off by Bobo's circuitous reasoning and roundabout rhyming. Those who thought a man should be industrious were put off by Bobo's sloth. Those who thought a man should be sober were put off by Bobo's affection for insobriety. Those who held themselves in high regard were put off at how quickly Bobo laid them low. And those who thought a man should stand and fight were put off by how quickly Bobo would go limp and run. The list of Bobo's annoying traits varied from person to person, but as long as one wasn't at the sharp edge of Bobo's razor wit, almost everyone agreed there was much pleasure to be had by his presence.

After a final slap upon his watery buttocks, Bobo hobbled forward and the crowd parted to reveal the extraordinary Good Padre to him for the very first time. Bobo never was much for churchgoing.

The Good Padre, who had heard much about Bobo but had yet to meet him, decided to get right in on the joke. "Come now, Bobo," said the Good Padre, "won't you eat one for a beer?"

A mere arm's length from the Good Padre, Bobo's knees turned to pudding and his brain flushed with the abstract thought that all the wine he'd drunk over his lifetime had somehow stained his eyeballs. He put his hands upon the enormous shoulders of the Good Padre to steady himself and confirm the reality of such a being.

The Good Padre's lips peeled back into a broad smile. "Come now, Bobo," the Good Padre repeated, "won't you eat one for a goblet of wine or pitcher of beer?"

"Oh, no," said Bobo with a slowness most unlike the rapid repartee that normally marked his speech. "Not today and not here."

"Why not keep your namesake, Bobo, and make a fool once more of this crowd's fancy?" said the Good Padre as he lifted a tomato from the stand. "Here, I shall eat one first, then you shall follow."

It was not a particularly large tomato the Good Padre held, but the fact it fit so easily into his mouth and was masticated and swallowed so effortlessly mesmerized Bobo.

"Now, Bobo," said the Good Padre, "you try, and I'll be first to fill your mug."

Though he saw the movement of the Good Padre's lips, Bobo's mind was elsewhere, entwined in an internal struggle between vision and thought, thought and vision, and he didn't register a word said. Goodness knows how long Bobo might have stood there staring had the sloppy barnyard voice of Benito not cracked his stupor. "Listen to the Good Padre, fool, and eat your breakfast."

It was just enough of a barb to return Bobo's wits to focus on what he'd been paid to do. "Oh, no," said Bobo, eyes riveted upon the Good Padre, "Bobo doesn't care for breakfast."

"Ha," mocked Mucca, "both a coward and a fool."

"Indeed," said Bobo, turning his eyes to Mucca, "for cowardice art my golden rule. Good and honest cowardice is what sets the fool apart, to wear upon his sleeve what most carry in their heart. For cowardice and suspicion is a good and natural thing, dear cousin. 'Tis why Bobo shan't eat one, till the priest eat a dozen."

The crowd released a rather uproarious noise, well pleased with the words and challenge their fool had poised.

"A dozen tomatoes?" mused the Good Padre with a laugh.

"Indeed," answered Bobo. "Let me make it simple, pointed and plain: there's more to suspicion than meets the common brain. For all animals, be they cows, bulls, sheep, fowl or pigs, know to avoid certain berries and rotted figs. But what in a beast we accept and abide—suspicion—in a human, we condemn and deride. Even animals do not eat from any hand in which food is thrust. No, 'tis time and constancy that gains their trust."

"Bobo is right!" shouted Vincenzo. "We all know, our fool is not so foolish."

"Ay," said Mucca, " 'tis spindly limbs on you, Bobo, but a fat brain."

"Indeed," said the Good Padre amusedly, "fat on fancy and fallacy. For this wit and this logic, and all that it begs, scrambles virtue and reason like eggs. To think, the ill advice you lend this hamlet."

"Well, one must crack some eggs to make an omelet."

My God, thought Davido—the speech, the rhyme, this village, that girl, those ankles—how wonderful, how unlike Florence.

"So Bobo sayeth again, dear cousins: I'll not eat one till the padre eat a baker's dozen."

"Now a baker's dozen?" said the Good Padre.

"Indeed. The number does know and will tell. For twelve is a number straight from the Book, plus, eat one extra, so not to be mistook. Twelve, a number of common yoke to both the *foreign* and local folk. As by the number twelve he shall imbibe the number of the Hebrew tribes. Plus, a little known fact of some surprise: twelve was the number of Moses's spies."

Davido looked quickly at Nonno for affirmation of the fool's last statement and with an upward crinkle to his thick eyebrows and downward bend to his lips, Nonno gave it. Some fool, thought Davido.

Bobo continued. "As twelve are the months that rule the year, as twelve are the Apostles we hold dear. Hmm, well, minus one. And let us remember not in the least, *dodici piu uno* are the days till our coming feast." Bobo pointed toward the statue of the Drunken Saint. "So, let the priest eat twelve, plus one. Then we'll wait a twelve-plus-one-day week and at the feast we'll have the truth we seek. So on the day of our patron saint, let us judge then if he be healthy or faint."

The crowd erupted with approval. It was a rousing performance by their fool and if it mocked them they weren't so aware of it.

"I will agree," the Good Padre said loudly so to be heard over the crowd, "for the people have spoken, but to this I'm to add a token. If in thirteen days both fruit and health are to be judged, then in thirteen days we bury this grudge, and all agree to honor my request, that at our feast the *Ebrei* be our guest. And if on that day my health be of perfect accord, you hereby vow before the Holy Lord, that at the Feast of our Drunken Saint, with the *pomodoro* each and every one shall acquaint."

Bobo imagined that this was just the kind of result Giuseppe was hoping for. It couldn't have gone any better, the priest was even foolish enough to say thirteen *aloud,* and Bobo shouted out to galvanize the crowd's sentiments: " 'Tis a fair shake through and through, if at the feast your health be without woe, then we all eat this fruit of the *Ebreo.*"

The Good Padre turned his gaze to Nonno and Davido. "And for you, our neighbors," he said, "do you agree to be guests at our feast?"

A thousand excuses flushed through Nonno's mind, not the least of which was his grandson's wedding, but before a single one could leave his mouth, he heard the voice of Davido.

"T'would be an honor." Davido spoke up so quickly he didn't even know it was his mouth that had uttered these words. But it *was* his mouth, driven by his heart to say or do anything that would keep him out of Florence on *that* day and keep him near the girl who had such perfect ankles.

"Then take heed, my sweet cousins," said the Good Padre as he lifted a tomato to the crowd's attention, "for the priest is to devour a baker's dozen. And as for you, gentle neighbors," he said whilst turning to Davido, "think up a recipe most sublime, for we all eat *pomodori* in twelve-plus-one-days' time."

With all eyes upon him, the physically enormous and mentally bewildering Good Padre bit into the first of his thirteen tomatoes and thought about the absolute deliciousness of the fruit and sublimity of God's creation. Giuseppe thought about his own brilliance, how perfectly the morning had unfolded and the various possibilities for his next maneuver. Benito thought about the little voice barking away inside his head, incessantly repeating that he was a villain and a coward, and that after what he'd done—the horrible, murderous thing he'd done all those years past—Mari would never love him. Nonno thought about his grandson Davido, all the damage he'd just done to family and reputation, and about the trip he'd have to take to Florence to postpone the wedding. Cosimo thought about the absurdity of his life, about the reflection of his beloved courtesan that he caught in the tomato boy's eyes and about the memories of a childhood playmate thought dead thirty years ago, now suddenly before him. Bobo the Fool thought about money and wine and how many coins his performance today might loosen from the tight fist of Giuseppe and how long those coins could keep him drunk. Luigi Campoverde thought about the Love Apples in his sack and wondered if his boss, who particularly enjoyed things that offended his wife and the Church, would like the fruit's flavor.

With eyes set solidly upon the sweet-looking tomato boy, Mari thought about how much she'd like to be the one eating his Love Apples and about how she would manage to survive for thirteen days without his face to gaze at. And Davido, well, Davido turned to look at the splendid olive girl, her sturdy wrists and strong ankles, and thought not of the relief of a ruined wedding or the fear of an irate grandfather, but of love— love and tomato sauce.

Parte Due

OLIVES

In Which We Learn the Unusual History of the Good Padre's Pigmentation

The story of how the Good Padre came to be such a shade of eggplant purple begins with Fuka-Kenta, a witch doctor from a small tribe of natives located in the western jungle highlands of the Dark Continent. Because witch doctors were commanded to live alone in the highest regions to be closer to their ancestors, Fuka-Kenta lived on the mountainous slopes a half day's walk from his people's village. Upon each full moon, Fuka-Kenta would venture into the village for three days to cure the sick, depossess the possessed and relay messages from the recently deceased, especially those who'd died with a stone still on their heart.

At about the time Fuka-Kenta reached the height of his powers, when he had seen the monsoon rains come and go more times than he could remember, he descended from the mountaintop to discover that a group of men with skin as pale and pink as the underbelly of a hippopotamus had settled in the village. Fuka-Kenta had only been away for one cycle of the moon, but he was concerned by how much sickness had descended upon the village in such a short time. It seemed that the fire demon Wimba, in a form Fuka-Kenta had never before seen, had afflicted many of the children and some of the elders. The demon made their bodies hot to the touch and caused their flesh to break with small boils and their stomachs to retch yellowish bile.

Fuka-Kenta had never seen men such as these, and he'd never seen Wimba come when the moon was full; for as long as he had lived, the fire demon had only appeared when the moon was hiding. The pale men did not seem war-like, but Fuka-Kenta could not see the light of the Asase Yaa in their eyes and this troubled him greatly. He had never known a man, be he enemy or friend, who did not glow with the Great Mother's light.

There was much about the pale ones that Fuka-Kenta found suspicious, from their heavy brown robes and the totems of two crossed sticks that they wore around their necks to their size, smell and behavior. They were enormous creatures, two heads taller than Fuka-Kenta's people, yet their flesh appeared soft and tender, and their feet, though large and hairy, could not carry them about unless covered in animal skin and wood. They lumbered when they walked and grimaced when they sat. They moved awkwardly about the jungle, banging their heads into vines and branches. They jumped when the monkeys howled and scurried whenever leaves rustled. In general, they seemed ill conceived and ill designed. But how could that be? For as monkeys have tails from which to hang and birds feathers so they may fly, the Great Mother created all creatures with perfection. Perhaps, thought Fuka-Kenta, Anansi, the trickster god, had dropped the pale ones from the sky or belched them up from the swampy lands to the east.

Fuka-Kenta hid from the pale ones until nightfall allowed for closer inspection. He was amazed by what he heard, smelled and saw. The pale ones made noise in their sleep, like a gaggle of warthogs—a sound so great it drowned out the chirping of night birds, the croaking of frogs, the creaking of insects and the howling of monkeys. Their bodies gave off an odor like that of female apes in the ripe of their springtime rut—a rank and sour musk. Their smell drew the insects to them, and even by the faint moonlight Fuka-Kenta could see that any exposed flesh was red and raw, swollen with bites and broken open from scratching. These pale ones had prodigious amounts of hair sprouting from their faces that looked and felt to Fuka-Kenta like the long and stringy moss that hung from Bubinga trees.

At dawn the pale ones would rise and chant strange incantations while moving beads with their fingers and touching the wooden sticks around their necks. Their ritual seemed to be some kind of worship, Fuka-Kenta assessed, but who could be foolish enough to stir the gods so early when it was well known they do not like to be awoken before the sun? And what gods would tolerate such joyless prayer? No beating of the drum, no slapping of the thighs, no dancing, no dressing in paint and feathers, no laughing of children, no telling of the stories that the gods love to hear.

With so much sickness among the villagers and with the strange men about, Fuka-Kenta returned to the mountaintop to ask his ancestors for a vision. He drank a tea made from the bark of young *hatta* vines, which opened his ear to his ancestors. But when their voices arrived, they carried no laughter or delight. Instead, the ancestors told Fuka-Kenta that the pale ones were from a land that did not dance to the drum or listen to the Great Mother's whisper. They were wayward sons, bound to bring much harm upon the Great Mother's land and children until the day they returned to suckle from her bosom.

Fuka-Kenta awoke from his trance knowing exactly what to do. He would share the sacred *hatta* tea with the pale ones to open their ears to the whisper and way of the Great Mother. This he believed would protect the village, please the ancestors and prevent the spilling of blood; but when he returned to his village and saw the condition of his people, a great rage filled him and he put the sacred powder aside. The fire demon Wimba had spread and nearly half of the villagers now burned and blistered with disease. But it was not sickness that enraged Fuka-Kenta and prompted his massacre. In fact, Fuka-Kenta did not know why he felt such rage, for the simple reason that his people and their language had no expression or term for shame. But it was with a sense of shame that the children of his village had come to look upon themselves. They had taken to wearing sheaths that covered their parts of joy and creation. The women, whose bosoms used to hang and sway openly, now wore garments to cover them. And the men, whose power and virility had made them both great hunters and loyal fathers, bowed their heads in defeat, too sick and weak to hunt and provide for their families.

Come nightfall, as the pale ones slept, Fuka-Kenta conjured the spirit of Kuli, the Great Lioness, and prepared himself for the ritual of *bringing death*. One by one, Fuka-Kenta approached the pale ones and plunged a sharpened and slightly curved buffalo horn into their hearts. Fuka-Kenta had searched throughout the village to make sure he had brought death upon every last stranger, when, in the stillness of predawn, he came upon our Good Padre tending to the sick in a hut on the outskirts of the village. Fuka-Kenta, who had been stalking and killing with the stealth of a jaguar, moved within inches of the Good Padre, when suddenly, he heard the goddess Kuli whisper in his ear. *Stop,* she said, *this life is not for the taking. Bring him to the mountain,* instructed Kuli, *and cast your magic upon him. Turn his skin like your skin, his mind like your mind, his heart like your heart. Then send him back to his people as a lion of the Great Mother's light.*

And so, with a handful of sleeping powder tossed into his face and the help of many men, the enormous pale one was carried to the mountaintop. There, Fuka-Kenta and his helpers fed the pale one potions and pastes of ground-up yams and *hatta* vines, which sustained his body, but also transported his mind to the timeless, painless realm of the ancestors and the spirits. Fuka-Kenta and his men broke the man's nose and stuffed a small gourd into each nostril, so that when his nose healed and re-formed it was like their noses. They rubbed a poisonous ointment made from tree frogs into his scalp, which would forever keep him bald. They tied a heavy stone to his penis to stretch it and make it long like theirs. They used the slenderest of bamboo needles to prick every inch of his pale skin with a million holes, then submerged him for months on end in a pit filled with the dark juice of the yamba[11].

For nine full trips around the sun that the Good Padre later would have only a vague, dream-like recollection of, Fuka-Kenta chanted prayers, whispered secrets and worked his transformational magic upon the Good Padre—magic that widened his nose, stretched his penis and colored his skin. Magic that opened the Good Padre's inner ear to the voice of the ancestors, the animals, the plants, the wind and lent him a power that he was entirely oblivious to. Magic that forever would confound the eyes and hearts of all the wayward pale ones and cause the Good Padre to appear an inexplicable shade of eggplant purple that reflected the light and laughter of the Great Mother upon every living thing.

---

[11] A large jungle beet distinct for its purple-black color, nutritional potency and brilliant dye.

In Which Temptation
Finds Two Takers

"What?" Mari stopped the motion of her arm as she wiped down an olive jar and turned to face Benito. Benito was sitting on the wagon-bed doing nothing while Mari broke down the stand, and though she was looking and speaking right at him, Benito's eyes and ears didn't register a thing. All his cognitive senses were currently overwhelmed by an awful jealousy churning in his stomach and a little voice barking inside his head. He had seen it all, every appalling instant. The way Mari came to the *Ebreo's* defense, the hesitant, amorous glances they shared, the way they both nearly smiled when the Good Padre invited the *Ebrei* to the feast.

"Good God, Benito," Mari said sharply. "Had I a mirror, even you would be appalled." Mari dropped her shoulders, let her posture slouch and her mouth fall open in mimicry of Benito.

"Huh?"

"You're staring," said Mari, "horribly staring."

In response, Benito straightened his posture and turned his face away from Mari. Lifting the jug of wine at his side, he took a slug.

"Now, please," Mari said, returning her attention to the stand, "move your ass off that wagon and get thee gone."

"Well," snorted Benito as he slid onto his feet, "after a long day's work a mug of ale does beckon."

Mari scoffed. "So the miscreant does reckon."

"The what?" said Benito, a touch of upset in his tone.

"Oh, shut up, Benito." Mari lifted an olive jar from the stand. "You heard well what I said and know well what I mean. A long day for you, maybe, but *work*, hardly." Mari frowned at Benito as she set the jar on the wagon-bed. " 'Tis a good thing the Good Padre was on hand and blood did not spill."

"Is that what you think," said Benito, "that I would commit such ill?"

"No, you, think? Hardly the wit and hardly the will. You are merely the mongrel who does his master's bidding. Now, fetch off to the tavern. I'm sure there is a bone in store."

"Benito does no man's bidding."

"Oh, good God, Benito, who are you kidding? Giuseppe doth keep you on a short, taut leash. And while you may be too deaf and blind a knave, 'tis a stupid fool who thinks he's free when he's a slave. Now, get thee gone. Your master awaits."

A stupid fool, laughed La Piccola Voce from inside Benito's head, *she sure enough has you pegged.*

"*Vaffanculo,*" Benito snapped back at the little voice.

"What did you say?" Mari turned around, her nostrils flaring.

Benito stood there with his mouth agape. He had not meant to speak aloud.

"You ingrate," snarled Mari, "you pathetic ingrate. 'Tis cruel to a dog to compare you to such and a waste of my breath to argue as much. So get thee gone. Scurry off to the tavern. Lap up the words that rot your brain. Swallow as praise what should be shame. But drink down *this* with your roguish stout: what my father did kindly take in, I'll one day put out. For what was mine by birth shall be mine in life. Now, get thee gone." Mari waved the back of her hand at Benito in a dismissive gesture.

Oh, groaned La Piccola Voce, *that was quite an onslaught and you deserved every word of it. Yes, indeed, you are a coward. A jealous coward who would need to drink four buckets of beer to subdue the truth this girl has spoken. To think, all that this girl's father did for you, and all the cruelty you have done unto her. You, you are less of a man than a twelve-year-old boy in a dress!*

Benito had no reply for Mari or the little voice inside his head. He watched her turn away from him the way one might turn away at a funeral from the corpse of a person he secretly despised. Benito grabbed his satchel and his jug of wine and shuffled away.

Mari listened to Benito's footsteps fall off into oblivion as she worked her cloth over the neck of an oil jug about the size and shape of a wine bottle. Her eyes closed as she gripped the jug's neck, hard, the way one might when a bottle suddenly becomes a weapon for bludgeoning. Her imagination erupted to life. An elixir of vengeance flushed through her veins. How good it would feel to chase down Benito and smash the jug across his head. But who was she kidding? Benito was merely an arm of the beast. And in an instant her mind's eye set upon Giuseppe, until both the bottle and Giuseppe's head were broke to bits, bizarrely shimmering with olive oil the very way her father had when he was killed.

Mari's jaw clenched as she opened her eyes, rolled her neck and looked to the sky. Her hand was still gripped upon the jug's neck, her mind ablaze in anger. Mari sighed. It was too much for her to process in silence and she found herself, as she often would, speaking her thoughts aloud. It was something her father had done and a behavioral trait common amongst the villagers. " 'Tis good to speak the thoughts aloud in private," her father said from time to time when she would catch him talking to himself, "for God can hear them more clearly."

"Does not God in heaven," Mari said in quiet fury, "see who's blameless and who's at fault as bloodless wounds of mine are rubbed with salt? Oh, father, if only fate had born me as a son, then by no man my inheritance undone. Must I stomach this womanly plight and lose what's mine without a fight? As curs'd law condemns me in servitude to pigs, yet if born a man, I'd snap their legs like twigs, and run the blood of he who'd dare to spoil all in life for which father did toil. Woman, though, must suffer and concede whilst law and land condones greed. But not I! By heaven, I'll have revenge upon the wretched knave who doth usurp with impunity and feast upon my father's grave."

⊛　　　⊛　　　⊛

Oh, how lewd! La Piccola Voce protested as Benito brought his hand to his mouth and wrung a thick globule of wine-scented saliva from his tongue. *How wretched,* the little voice continued, *how absolutely wretched.* The ranting, though, was of no use. Hiding there, in the shadow of a building's doorway, just off the piazza, Benito felt the desire in his belly swell as the saliva in his hand commingled with the sweat and grime of his body to form a most unsavory lather. He focused his vision upon Mari, beautiful Mari, alone in the piazza. It was as if there was a demon inside him that begged for release each time he left her company—a demon that ravaged his body and scorched his mind with wanton thoughts, and blazed too hotly for the little voice to hold any effective council. "Oh, shut up," Benito whispered sharply as he smacked his head against the wall beside him, knocking the little voice off its feet.

⊛　　　⊛　　　⊛

Across the piazza, Mari set an earthen jar of olives onto the wagon-bed, when something caught her eye. The lowering sun had moved directly into the alley space between buildings, and, in the periphery of her vision, she saw her shadow stretching across the piazza's cobblestones. Her shadow was huge and the image brought with it an overwhelming sensation that as a little girl, perched upon her father's shoulders, she had once before thrown a shadow across the piazza much like this one.

"Oh, my father," Mari repeated sadly, "what trick of gloaming does this light and shadow play upon the eye that memory serves so clearly all that's by and by? Is this the manner departed spirit takes sight, here to comfort me in time of plight? Does earthly desire once in heaven grow so mild that your spirit would not venture back to comfort child? Tell me, father, art there eyes in heaven? Does death not bring some reprieve, or do you look down on all that's lost and grieve? And what rest, what salvation could soothe the soul, when all thou built in life in death is stole? The land, the fruit, the daughter, the woman once your wife, all the fouled legacy of your life. No, t'would be better heaven blind than behold all that plagues my mind, for surely such rage corrupts your heavenly bliss with all on earth that is amiss. And there is much amiss here, father. There is much amiss."

With her eye still cast upon her shadow, Mari began to gather up the burlap cloth that draped the entirety of the olive stand and hung down to the cobblestones. Feeling something roll against her foot, she looked down, drew a quick breath and felt her heart flutter. There, resting against her sandal was a ripe Love Apple. She moved her head from side to side to make sure she was alone. Seeing no one, she dropped the bunched-up burlap upon the stand, knelt down and scooped the Love Apple into her hands. It felt good beneath her fingertips and palms; its skin was smooth and it had a meatiness to it that tempted her palette and brought to her mind's eye the delicious image of the tomato boy as clearly as the fruit before her. His skin, the color of honey; his eyes, as lovely and green as the Cerignola olives that Mari loved so dearly; his hair, a tussle of brown curls as enticing and unruly as a bowl of *papardelle* noodles tossed with butter and porcini mushrooms. And his lips—his beautiful lips—which seemed to struggle so valiantly against a desire to smile when they'd looked upon each other at market. Mari could already tell that he was sweet and wise and witty in a way no other boy of the village was.

Filled with thoughts of the tomato boy, Mari brought the Love Apple to her own lips. She thought nothing about the cleanliness of the cobblestones on which the Love Apple had rolled. She thought only of the tomato boy as her lips parted and slid across the fruit's taut skin. Only of him as her nostrils caught a whiff of the Love Apple's aroma—fennel tops, fresh basil, wet earth the morning after a rainstorm. Only of him as her jaw muscles engaged and the fruit's skin burst beneath her teeth. Only of him as a river of flavor fell upon her tongue and her eyelids floated shut. Oh, goodness! Juices ran down her lips and chin; she never imagined a thing could be so sweet.

🍅   🍅   🍅

Nor had Benito ever imagined a sight could be so bitter, but bitter it was, a bitterness that wilted the demon desire burning inside him and brought the ranting little voice inside his head back to life. It's one pain to know that the object of your affection does not love you, but it's a far worse pain to know that the one you love loves another. And what could it be but love, feared Benito, that could bring Mari to do such a thing? To bring a Love Apple to her lips and indulge it with all the wantonness of Eve giving in to the serpent. What could it be but love? thought Benito, as a tear of anguish streaked his grimy cheek.

17

In Which We Learn
the Old Bite Test

"Psst," came a whistle, and with a clown-like flair Bobo halted his stride. He was standing in the middle of one of the town's streets, just in sight of the tavern. "Psst," the sharp whistle rang out again, bouncing between brick and cobblestone.

With exaggerated effort Bobo began to search out the source of the sound. He looked left, he looked right, but the whistle was not to be found. He looked up, he looked down and let his head lead his body in a circle. He looked past corners and under his boots and in his shirt pockets. Search as he might, the source was elusive to Bobo's ear, until from a second-floor balcony came the call, "Mutton-head, up here.

"Yes, up here, fool," Giuseppe repeated from his stepdaughter's balcony some ten-plus feet above the street. Giuseppe tossed a small cloth bag down to Bobo.

The satchel jingled with coins as Bobo caught it. He held it up to his ear and gave the bag a shake. Bobo frowned. Not surprisingly, the satchel felt a bit light to him.

"Just open it," said Giuseppe.

Bobo undid the leather string that held the satchel fast and spilled its contents into his hand. Four coins in all, one bronze, two silver and one gold.

"Oooh," Bobo sighed as he raised the gold piece before his eye for greater scrutiny. He brought the coin to his mouth, placed it between his rear molars and gave it *the old bite test.*

"Of course it's real, you idiot," snapped Giuseppe from the balcony. "Now, piss off to the tavern. If I have any bidding for you, I will let you know."

Bobo bowed slightly, clicked his heels, slid the coins into his pants pocket and stepped toward the tavern. He walked a few paces, just out of sight of Giuseppe's balcony, and then, with complete nonchalance, pulled a ripe Love Apple from his pants pocket. He scrutinized it briefly then polished it against his not especially clean shirt. Bobo brought the tomato to his nose, gave it a slight sniff, then opened his mouth and took a large bite. "Mmmm," Bobo hummed, eyebrows raised in approval.

In Which Davido Contemplates
His Fate & Curses
a Roman God

"Cupid, curs'd, meddling Cupid!" bemoaned Davido, "'tis no wonder the name so rhymes with stupid. Pudgy, errant, pedant, fat with impish rhyme and reason, to set my eyes upon the fairest treason and shoot me full of this seditious nectar turning me to Paris when tradition demand me Hector. Oh, curs'd Cupid, such poor aim as to miss by a mile and set an *Ebreo* heart upon a gentile."

Davido had never actually cursed Cupid before. As a monotheistic *Ebreo,* he'd never given the mischievous Roman love god much thought; but considering the suddenness and irony of emotions that assailed Davido, Cupid seemed a natural foil. The trip home from the village had been brutal—brutally silent. Nonno hadn't uttered a word, but between the frequent heavy sighs of "Oy" and the constant pulling at his beard, Davido could practically hear what was on his grandfather's mind.

From the moment they packed up their stand and left the piazza, Davido understood the bind in which he had put Nonno. Indeed, for Nonno it was a winless choice between postponing the wedding or alienating and, even worse, possibly antagonizing the local populace. Not to mention the potential loss of the bride's price already paid, and the logistics and embarrassment of delaying a wedding a mere thirteen days away. But nonetheless, Davido's immediate feelings as the wagon rolled out of the village and toward home were ones of immense relief. In no way could he see himself marrying that skinny-ankled little girl; the day's events had, it seemed, delayed that. However, as their journey back to their farm continued, Nonno's anguish began to wear on Davido. So much so that by the time they turned onto the entranceway of their farm, the ramifications of Davido's desire and the day's drama were more than enough to return his feet to the ground and plant them firmly in a pile of *merda* of his own making.

"Tell me, Cupid," said Davido as he now walked alone between the rows of tomato plants, "when you dipped your arrow in amorous potion and set it fly in romantic motion, did you have not the slightest inkling about into whom your love arrow'd be sinking? To aim and shoot in such wretched haste, to undo a wedding and set a bride's price to waste. To conflict me so of heart and head, that I know not which more I dread—this sorrowful choice, both ways a sin: deceive my heart or deceive my kin? Why in heaven's name could you not bless my life and enchant me to love the one who's to be my wife? What have I done to deserve such a horrible, wonderful hex that you deal this *Ebreo* from a Roman text? For what choice have I but to risk all there is to spoil, as my veins, my heart, do run with olive oil?

"Oh, dear God!" said Davido suddenly aware of his own speech patterns, "my head's amok with foolish glory, my tongue rhyming like a *rimatori*. But to speak such thoughts aloud, to act upon this joy, would surely turn this patch of Tuscany to Troy. Yet why I do curse—should I not rejoice? Is not all this talk of Cupid but my secret desire's voice? Just this morning did I not arise convinced that Florence would be my demise? That better to set Nonno and all my kin to stew and rankle, than wed that girl of puny wrist and skinny ankle. Yet never did I imagine such power to manifest and call this Cupid to my behest, aiming my vision, perfect, 'tween the figs and melon, piercing me with this sight of Helen. So that in an instant, timeless and fleeting, my heart did know new reason for its beating. Transforming songbirds' call and all my eyes do see into the voice, the lips, the scar upon the knee. So that all I think, all I hear, all I see, speaks to me of one thing: Mari, Mari, Mari."

In Which We Learn
the History & Artistry of the
Sicilian *Dieci Dita* Marionette

S itting there on one of the tavern's bar stools, finishing off his mutton shank and fourth goblet of wine, Luigi Campoverde, chef for Cosimo di Pucci de' Meducci the Third, Grand Duke of Tuscany, suddenly realized that he hadn't been this drunk since his teenage years at the monastery when his Sicilian mentor *traded* a three-hundred-year-old il-luminated Bible for a double-magnum of sparkling wine from Piedmont. Luigi had not thought he was especially inebriated tonight, but as he turned in his seat and looked over the lively tavern, for an instant, through the crowd, he could have sworn he saw his boss.

Drunk or not, Luigi turned back to face the bar, know-ing that some curiosities in life are better left unsatisfied.

Perhaps, thought Luigi, I have the sitting drunkenness, or, more accurately, the standing drunkenness, where one does not realize the extent of his intoxication until he stands up and finds his knees weak, his head cloudy and the tavern casting about like a ship in rough seas. What else could explain the sight of Cosimo di Pucci de' Meducci the Third, Grand Duke of Tuscany, sipping ale at a crowded village tavern and sitting shoulder to shoulder with the barnyard rhymer who accompanied yesterday's pompous truffle broker?

Luigi had not planned on getting so pie-eyed when he first sat down at the tavern some two hours ago. He'd meant only to have a piece of cheese, a few olives and a glass of wine before the rump-numbing mule ride back to the villa. Truth was, Luigi was anxious to return to the villa. He was too suspicious and paranoid a fellow to much enjoy being away from his kitchen. The Meduccis had many enemies and Luigi would be damned if a poison was going to pass before his nose and into his kitchen. It was well known that a chef of a poisoned lord was certain to follow his master to the grave—culpable or not. The problem was, the wine, cheese and olives were so delicious that Luigi needed a second order to confirm his palate's first impression.

Two rounds of wine, cheese and olives would have been enough for Luigi, but when the spindly fool from the market sat down on the stool beside him and had a fragrant and succulent-looking mutton shank placed before him, well, Luigi wasn't going anywhere. Although now, with the shank eaten and his spine prickling with fear that his boss—should it really be him—may come to wonder why the lady duke's brocade was around the neck of the tavern keep, Luigi knew it would be wise to take his leave. The idea of leaving, though, was a sad thought and Luigi gestured to the tavern keep for one more refill of his wine goblet. The wine was good and free, and Luigi did, after all, hate the idea of missing the puppet show.

❂ ❂ ❂

Despite nearly twenty years of marriage and successfully fathering three daughters, Signore Coglione, the tavern keep, was suspected by most villagers to be something of a *finocchio*. His ancestors, who'd arrived in the village some three centuries ago and opened the tavern-brothel, were from Greece, and everyone knew that Greeks were ancestrally predisposed to man-love. This cultural stigma was furthered by an unfortunate childhood run-in with an ill-tempered goose and the resulting permanent nickname of Signore Solo Coglione. Not to mention, Signore Coglione's penchant for fancy tunics and flowery vests did not make him appear especially manly in anyone's eyes. Certainly, the colorful brocade he now wore around his neck would do little to masculinize his image. Nevertheless, eating, drinking and whoring were such cherished pastimes of the men of the village that none dared offend Signore Coglione. Thus, the suspicion that he was a *finocchio* was rarely mentioned.

Good-natured as he was and queer as he seemed, Signore Coglione was no pushover. He had a Greek's shrewdness and a way with money, and did not make a habit of giving things away for free; but it was such a lovely brocade and the stranger at the bar swore that it was from the Orient and had once been worn by the lady duke herself. Regardless, it was, without a doubt, the finest and most splendid piece of fabric Signore Coglione had ever felt, and to think he received such a gift for a few pennies' worth of mutton, wine and cheese!

As if the silk around his neck was not good news enough, the tavern was crowded and full of life and the prospects for a performance by Bobolito were excellent. Everyone was up in arms over the day's events at market and, as it had been done for centuries, the men of the village gathered at the tavern for a de facto forum. Even Augusto Po, the puckered-ass miser, was present. In short, everything was how it should be, how Coglione's ancestors would want it to be. Even Signore Coglione's nephew, Bertolli, was in the kitchen doing the dishes, busy learning the trade that he would one day take over. Coglione scanned the barroom smugly. Vincenzo, the self-important *cacasotto,* was still wearing his Love Apple-stained tunic from market with all the sanctimony of a false martyr. Coglione could see that Vincenzo was drinking fast and hard to muster his courage, as Vincenzo would soon be rising to address the tavern as he often did. It was just the kind of false bravado that often inspired Bobo to bring out Bobolito. And this, above all, had Signore Coglione bubbling with delight; for Coglione, as well as nearly every resident of the village, loved that puppet.

⚘   ⚘   ⚘

"Friend," said Cosimo di Pucci de' Meducci the Third, Grand Duke of Tuscany, turning to the gentleman seated next to him. "What is it that you're eat—"

"Friend?" Benito interrupted with a hint of gruffness meant to intimidate. Benito did not look up from the plate of lamb shank he was noisily devouring. "What reason have you to call Benito friend, or Benito to call *you* friend?" Benito tapped his knife against his near-empty mug.

"Ah," said Cosimo, a touch of fear flushing his veins. He had not spoken to a *rimatore* since, well, never. "I see. Dear lady," Cosimo gestured to the barmaid passing before their table with a large pitcher from which she was pouring, "another round for me." Cosimo paused and gestured to his right. "And for my friend."

"Friend?" said the barmaid incredulously. "One should choose their friends more wisely."

"And you should shut your mouth and fill my mug," Benito said whilst shoveling a hunk of shank into his mouth, "then go and ready your hairy honey pot for my fat *cazzone.*"

"*Madonna mia!*" groaned the barmaid. " 'Tis I who'll need be drunk."

My God, thought Cosimo, eyes transfixed upon the bosomy heap before him as she filled their mugs. Is she a whore?

"Are you going to propose?" said the barmaid sweetly.

Cosimo stiffened noticeably. "Excuse me?"

"Are you going to propose?" the barmaid repeated. "Because if you're not, then you best stop your staring and pay me."

Benito laughed hard and gave his new friend a solid clap on the back.

"Oh," said a flustered Cosimo. He'd never before in his life paid for anything and he now nervously patted his hands across the four pockets of his jacket. Oddly, Cosimo noticed, each pocket jiggled with coins. So too did the two front pockets of his trousers. Lots of coins, far more than he imagined his stableman would be allotted. Goodness, thought Cosimo as he plucked a coin from his breast pocket and set it on the table. Is everyone stealing from me?

The barmaid's eyebrows lifted at the sight of such a large and shiny silver coin. "Do you plan on getting drunk tonight?"

"Why not?" Cosimo shrugged his shoulders. "Him too." Cosimo gestured to the man hunched at his side.

The barmaid scowled as she assessed the coin. "If you're drinking ale, it's five mugs each; wine, seven goblets and not a drop more."

"Now," said Benito, as he lifted his mug and turned to face Cosimo, "you may call Benito friend."

The smell of his new mate's breath was horrible. The sight of his face up close—pounded nose; ruddy, pocked and abused complexion; thick lips glistening with lamb fat; slightly errant right eye—was unnerving, but his smile was broad and real and his gratitude as authentic as a child's. Happily, Cosimo lifted his mug and toasted.

🍅   🍅   🍅

Rapide y Edili, Rapids and Eddies, wrote the renowned 15th-century Italian dramatist Pozzo Menzogna in his eloquent treatise on drama *Il Trattato Definitivo sul Dramma,* which from time to time informs upon our story. In a play's second act, Menzogna's treatise emphasized, the plot should move like a river in the midst of the springtime melt, complete with rapids and waterfalls. Yet, between the moments of fast motion, the river needs also to pool into gentle eddies of insight and introspection. A place, wrote Menzogna, where readers may come to know with greater depth and clarity the world in which they visit.

Thus, Menzogna would assuredly want the reader to understand that almost all the villagers we have come to know were at the tavern, *Ebrei,* priests and women excluded. Though not all women: the barmaids were there, of course. Benito, especially, was mighty thankful for that. Downstairs, the barmaids saw to the slaking of thirst and appetite, but when they escorted a man through *La Porta delle Puttane*— The Whores' Door—and led him upstairs, they set about quenching an altogether different thirst. And it's only fair to mention that no one in the village spent a larger proportion of his or her income quenching that desire than Benito.

True, Benito was mostly crude and vulgar whilst in the tavern, but once upstairs, his behavior dramatically changed. He made love sloppily, with considerable moaning and some drooling, yet there was a gentleness to his efforts that endeared him to many of the *puttane.* Unlike a good many of the village men, Benito was never rough or abusive with *ladies,* nor did he encourage them, as Vincenzo and many others did, to be rough and abusive to him. What Benito craved, but never dared admit, was tenderness. And though the *puttane* laughed and complained to one another of Benito's barnyard odor and thickness of penis, they all found themselves stirred by the soft sobs and tears that accompanied his release and his transparent need to be held and petted tenderly afterward.

And though it is of little importance to our tale, Menzogna would indulge the reader with the story behind the tavern keeper's name, which was not by birth Signore Solo Coglione. Who in their right mind would give a child such a name? He was born Adriano DelGreco, and while most in the village knew that, no one but his wife called him such. The event that precipitated Adriano DelGreco's decades-old moniker happened in the company of Benito and Vincenzo, when, as a trio of eight-year-old boys, Vincenzo thought it would be a hilarious idea to collectively loose their bladders upon the DelGreco family's haughty and ill-tempered goose. Well, the prideful bird had no tolerance for such antics, and with an indignant and lightning-quick extension of its neck, the goose's sharp beak tore through the young DelGreco's soft scrotum, snapping off and swallowing one of his prepubescent testicles before the boys even had a chance to halt their streams. From that day forth, the sweetly natured boy of Greek ancestry whose father ran the tavern and who preferred playing with his sisters, was known as Signore Solo Coglione—*Mister One Testicle.*

But even more than the story behind the tavern keeper's name, Menzogna would most want his readers to understand and appreciate the exquisite beauty, craftsmanship and nostalgic significance of Bobo's marionette, Bobolito. For had it not been for this puppet, Bobo's life might very well have turned out quite differently. The tradition of string-manipulated, lifelike puppets called *marionettes* may have begun in medieval France, but history undoubtedly asserts that it was in Sicily where marionette puppetry was elevated to an exquisite art form. And nothing exemplified this mastery more than Bobolito.

Bobolito was carved from the *Moro Nigro,* the black mulberry tree of Sicily, whose wood was loved by artisans for its density, strength, distinct grain and durability. The marionette was about twenty-four inches high with large brown eyes, pronounced cheekbones and eyebrows that turned up in a slightly devilish fashion. However, what made the Sicilian marionettes so extraordinary was not merely the artistry with which they were rendered, but the manner of their manipulation. Unlike the French marionette, controlled by a rudimentary pair of sticks, Bobolito was made in the Sicilian *Dieci-Dita* (ten-fingers) style. In this tradition, ten individual finger casts with a five-inch prod off the tip are placed over each finger. Each prod is in turn connected to a string controlling a specific function on the marionette. The setup, though a bit bizarre-looking, allows the *manipolatore* (puppeteer) a near-life-like range of movements in which the puppet's eyelids can wink, the jaw can open and close, the back, elbows and knees can bend, the arms and hands can move. So remarkable were the Sicilian *Dieci-Diti* marionettes that a whole new art form called *Opera dei Pupi* was developed in which epic tales and stories were told on elaborate puppet sets.

Bobolito had been a gift from Bobo's father, brought back from Sicily where the *Cardinale* de' Meducci had been traveling. It was the only gift the cardinal ever gave Bobo and one of the very few times he actually acknowledged that the child was indeed his. In any event, Bobo took to the puppet like Michelangelo took to marble. He brought Bobolito to life, or more accurately, Bobolito brought Bobo to life, evoking in the young child wellsprings of passion and creativity. The marionette also aroused in young Cosimo di Pucci de' Meducci the Third, Prince of Tuscany and cousin to and constant companion of Bobo, great envy. And so it was that in a few weeks' time that Cosimo too received a Sicilian *Dieci-Diti* marionette. Only the problem was, the Meducci guard sent to Sicily to fetch a puppet for the spoiled prince died of dysentery in Palermo. Orders got confused, and when the marionette finally did arrive at the Meducci palace, it was a female. This, however, was of little concern to Cosimo and Bobo, who found that most *Opera dei Pupi* involved both a man and a woman. They named her *Bobalita*.

Within a few months, the pair of cousins had created their own *Opera dei Pupi,* with elaborate sets and numerous costumes, and were heralded for the excellent entertainment they provided dinner guests of the duke. Well-traveled dignitaries, royals and church officials visiting the Meducci palace claimed they had never seen a marionette come to life like Bobolito did in young Bobo's hands. For a time, all was well in the Meducci palace. The quasi-bastard and mischief-prone child of *Cardinale* de' Meducci, who would only respond to the ridiculous and inappropriate name Bobo, seemed to have finally found a constructive arena in which to channel superior wit and creativity. Even *Cardinale* de' Meducci, who never dared show any connection or affection for his child, found himself to be begrudgingly proud of Bobo's extraordinary skill and the enthusiastic reaction it received.

Alas, the affection was short-lived and ended in spectacular fashion on the night that young Bobo unveiled his masterpiece before a royal audience that included not only

Cardinale de' Meducci, but the King and Queen of France and the Holy Pope himself. The opera told the story of a young and ambitious cardinal of royal blood, and his mistress. Filled with song and dance, unwanted pregnancy, aristocratic foibles and follies and exquisite manipulation of the marionettes, the young cousins' play seemed to especially thrill the King and Queen of France, who giggled hysterically through much of the performance. It also included a new puppet manipulation, invented by Bobo, that not even the most deviant Sicilian marionette-maker had ever thought of. Perchance the royal enthusiasm might have been enough to counter the rage that boiled inside *Cardinale* de' Meducci as he watched his life sanctimoniously mocked and satirized before the eyes of the Pope; but at the opera's climax, as Bobo lifted a middle finger and the erection rose, tenting up the cardinal-red gown that costumed Bobolito, it proved to be both the peak moment of the cousins' childhood and its culmination. As Cosimo recalled, *Cardinale* de' Meducci may have smiled and laughed along with the other guests that evening, but in the morning he was gone and so too was Cosimo's favorite cousin—never seen or heard from again. That was, at least, until today.

🍅   🍅   🍅

"Neighbors," said Vincenzo rising up from his chair with a tipsiness that splattered droplets of ale upon Augusto Po's already stained yellow tunic. "Neighbors!"

The tavern-goers turned their attention to Vincenzo.

"Now," said Vincenzo, taking hold of Augusto Po's arm to help him to his feet, " 'tis not the company he often seeks, which means noble Po must wish to speak. There is much to discuss, indeed. So calm your tongues and let insults relent, for one wrong word and he'll raise your stinking rent."

It was a good rhyme and a nice rib to start things off, but the tavern did not react with its usual boisterousness, as there was more caution than humor in Vincenzo's words. Augusto Po was not a stranger to the tavern. In the late afternoon while making his rent-collecting rounds he would often stop in for a glass of wine and a small supper. However, Po was not comfortable fraternizing with his renters and tenants, and he would leave as the tavern filled.

But this evening was different; if there was one thing that could bring Augusto Po to mix with the locals, it was the fear of having his business impacted. Po had been to Venice; he had witnessed the *Ebrei* prowess in banking and money-lending, and with his uncle, the old padre, dead and gone, he was without protection from the Church. It was challenging enough to have Giuseppe gaining such property and wealth, and he had no desire to see a clan of money-grubbing *Ebrei* welcomed into the village.

"Neighbors," said Po, "unlike many here, I have traveled and know firsthand of the world. I have dealt and bartered with the unscrupulous Greek and know the forked tongue with which they speak. I have dealt with the Gypsy trader and the silk-selling Moor, and can attest to greater scruples in a three-penny whore. Idolaters, sodomites, be dubious of what's in store, for these are people who prefer the back door."

"They're not the only ones!" the bosomy barmaid who'd just served Cosimo and Benito yelled out.

Much to Po's surprise, the tavern broke out in laughter. He had meant *back door* from an ethical standpoint.

"Oh, for God's sake!" shouted Vincenzo, throwing his arms in the air. "Barmaid, mind your place."

The barmaid raised a hairy eyebrow to Vincenzo. "You sure have mined *my place.* You'd think my ass were made of truffles with all the burrowing you've done."

And with that, a pigpen of laughter and snorts exploded through the tavern as crusts of bread and suds of ale and droplets of wine splattered and bounced all about Vincenzo. He had broken the tavern's golden rule and he knew it: never, ever, should a whoremonger attempt to best his whore in public.

"*Basta, basta,*" said Vincenzo dropping his hands in defeat. "Can we just get on with it?"

The tavern quieted.

"Thank you." Vincenzo gestured to Po and took his seat.

Augusto Po looked around in disgust. "As I was say-ing," he continued, his garments speckled with ale and wine, "the Greeks have done the world little favor, but at least they have sense to share our savior. But the Gypsy, the Moor, the money-lending *Ebreo,* what quality of theirs do we know? Do not be so foolish as to place an ounce of hope upon he who denies both *Cristo* and Pope. I tell you, long and hot shall be hell's penance, to the *Cristiano* who turns our Eden into Venice. For be it a pound of flesh or ten percent, the *Ebreo* bleeds the *Cristiano* from money lent."

"Ha," laughed the Cheese Maker, undercutting Po's grumble of support. The Cheese Maker was not an educated man, but he knew the difference between what smelt like cheese and what stunk like shit. "T'would be a pleasure for which I would thank," he said in his full tenor voice as he rose to his feet, "to do my business in an *Ebreo* bank. For while I know not, it must be so, Po's far cheaper than any Greek, Gypsy or *Ebreo.*"

It was not often that one got to witness a well-deserved humiliation of Augusto Po, and the tavern-goers took full ad-vantage of the opportunity, rejoicing in a chorus of anony-mous laughter. Augusto Po tilted his chin upward and feigned a smile, but it was obvious he did not take kindly to ribbing, which only sweetened the laughter, and he took his seat.

"You confuse the message with the messenger," said Vincenzo in Po's defense. "I take his words to heart."

"Come now," the Cheese Maker continued good-naturedly, "you make too much of this. We are country folk and have not the spleen to hate so many sight unseen. I would think in the name of commerce we'd all be supporters, yet you make shar-ing our market tantamount to sharing our daughters."

Giuseppe's ears perked up. Now, there's an idea!

"Ay," shouted out Mucca from the corner, unable to help herself, "you'd think Vincenzo'd be happy to sell such bruised and ugly fruit."

The tavern crowd loosed a noise akin to that of a wrestler at the Easter Feast when he takes a low blow to the *coglioni.* Mucca was referring to Vincenzo's pair of daughters, who, though approaching marrying age, by looks and demeanor would seem to have few prospects. It was exactly the kind of comment that made Mucca the only female to be tolerated at the tavern.

"By God!" Vincenzo said, throwing up his hands in exasperation. "You flea-bitten harpy, have not you had enough of me today? You'd think a man need be married to a woman to be so pecked!"

Amazing, wonderful, delightful, thought Cosimo di Pucci de' Meducci as the tavern's habitués roared with laughter.

"And surely," said the Cheese Maker over the noise, "by God's wrath, would Venice have not long ago sank if these foreign *Ebrei* were truly so depraved and rank? Instead the city prospers. And why? Because Venice is keen enough to know the lesson that this decree does wish to sow: that whether a person be *Ebreo,* Greek or Gypsy, it's by food they're nourished and wine made tipsy. And it's by tools they'll farm from morn to night, and it's candles they'll need for evening's light. So why take as contention what I take to please: all the better to have more customers to buy my cheese."

" 'Tis not only your cheese that grows mold," said Vincenzo with a certainty that belied how little he really knew about the subject, "for all you think you'd sell would not be sold. The *Ebreo* belly is not so easy for us to please, for as surely as they don't eat pork, they'll neither eat your cheese."

"Is that true?" asked the Cheese Maker, suddenly befuddled. "Surely, there is no cheese from a pig."

Peering into the tavern from behind the kitchen door, Bertolli made a mental note to ask the Good Padre if it *was* true that *Ebrei* don't eat pork. And if so, thought the boy, did Jesus not eat pork? And if he didn't eat pork, then why do we eat pork?

Triumphantly, Vincenzo drained his wine goblet. "But the selling of cheese and pork, to me, is hardly the issue," he said, "as I'm more riled by the limpness of our local tissue; that this new priest, without council or vote, has the gall to force decree and *fruit* down our throat. And that our *wise* fool"—Vincenzo waved the back of his hand disdainfully in the direction of Bobo—"and our foolish priest, would give this offense such yeast and invite the *Ebrei* to our sacred feast. And that we, without protest or complaint, would spinelessly oblige the corruption of our Saint. Now, I know the word did pass by way of Holy Rome, but Rome is not the place that I make home. And as I am the king of my own castle, I'll not gladly play the Holy Roman vassal and eat willingly with knife and fork the fruit of those who killed our *Cristo* and defamed the pork."

Heads nodded; voices murmured in support. It was a good rhyme and well spoken, and a majority of the tavern-goers were now drunk enough to be stirred by such bluster.

"Bravo, Vincenzo!" shouted Signore Coglione from behind the bar as he set a wooden box upon the bar in front of Bobo. "Bobo, wise fool and poet, make us a toast. A toast of Vincenzo's pride."

The tavern erupted in gaiety as Bobo opened the wooden case before him. Cosimo felt his hairs stand on end and his life flash before his eyes. "Good God," he said softly, any doubt in his mind vacating. It *was* his cousin Bobo; for people can change and age to become nearly unrecognizable, but puppets always stay the same.

"Coglione," growled Vincenzo under his breath, "you had to fetch the puppet."

With a flurry of taps and a fluttering of arms, Bobolito came to life upon the bar. His big wooden eyes with their dark pupils stared intently at Vincenzo; his eyelids fluttered adoringly. "A toast," Bobolito's jaw opened and closed in near-perfect mimicry of speech. The marionette spoke with a slight falsetto—not quite man, not quite woman.

Cosimo looked about the tavern. To a person they were enraptured by Bobolito's peculiar, near-life-like movements, just as the Meducci court had been thirty years ago. Bobolito wore the costume of a medieval court jester, complete with yellow stockings, purple knickers, striped tunic and a three-pronged jester's hat with tiny bells affixed to it. As far as Cosimo recalled, it looked like the very costume that clothed the marionette when it first arrived from Sicily.

"Ah," said the puppet, "here's a ripe one. Ale to a hero." Pompously, Bobolito bowed to the crowd and then, in a very formal fashion, stepped one foot slightly forward, brought his posture erect and raised his right arm as if holding a mug. "Speak more than thou knowest, yet have less than thou showest. Do not what thou sayest, yet admit not thou a nayest. Do less and drink more. Think thou a king, when thou a whore!"

The tavern broke out in laughter. Crusts of bread, sprinkles of wine and droplets of ale bombarded Vincenzo.

"Bitter puppet," said Vincenzo, wiping drops of wine from his chin, "you speak through your liquor."

Bobolito looked offended. "Which makes my wit all the much quicker. For honest is he who knows he's a giglet, than to think he's a lion, when he's a piglet."

"You mock me, Puppet!"

Cosimo smirked. It was deeply satisfying to see how some things never change. Just as in Florence when they were youngsters, Bobo had trained the tavern audience to know well that when Bobolito comes to life, only Bobolito may be addressed.

"No, no." Bobolito's eyelids fluttered and his tone softened. "I pray thee, I merely confused a lion with a sheep, for the roar you make at tavern, at market, sounded more like a peep."

More laughter, bread, ale and wine pelted Vincenzo, and the vanquished man took his seat. "*Vaffanculo* puppet!" he said as he lifted his goblet and gulped down its contents.

The tavern-goers gasped! Suddenly, Bobolito looked very sad. His jaw dropped, his eyelids drooped and his posture went slack. "Aw," the crowd sighed. They had come to know that Bobolito was very sensitive.

"Apologize!" a voice in the tavern called out.

Bobolito did not move and hung sadly.

"No," mumbled Vincenzo.

"Say you're sorry."

"No."

"You pig-loving bastard," goaded Mucca, "if you don't say you're sorry the show won't go on."

"I'm not apologizing to a puppet!"

The tavern filled with boos and curses.

"It's a fucking puppet!" Vincenzo yelled desperately.

The crowd did not relent. Another round of boos, crusts of bread and splatters of wine and ale pelted Vincenzo.

"Enough!" Vincenzo sprung from his chair, "enough! *Faccia di merda!* I'll say I'm sorry."

The tavern quieted.

"Bobolito, I am sorry."

Bobolito did not look up. Weakly, his puppet arm lifted, bent at the elbow and tapped against his cheek.

Vincenzo looked to the crowd for sympathy. "Oh, for God's sake!"

"Go on!" the tavern-goers shouted back in near-unison.

"Ay." Vincenzo threw up his arms in defeat and walked over to Bobolito, slouched sadly upon the bar. Vincenzo bent over to face Bobolito. "Little puppet," Vincenzo said with sincere contriteness, "I am sorry," and then he leaned forward and kissed Bobolito on the cheek.

The tavern waited anxiously. One could never be certain with Bobolito; he was a temperamental puppet. Then, slowly, Bobolito's trousers began to tent up. "Ay!" the tavern erupted with jubilation.

Bobolito sprang to his feet and danced his herky-jerky *bastone* dance. "So, now's the time to rant and rave," Bobolito's squeaky voice sang out, "and bless the drink that makes us brave."

The tavern-goers raised their glasses, mugs and goblets, and joined Bobolito in song. "So raise your mug and hail," they all sang, "and bless the precious ale. Lift up your cup of wine and bless the sacred vine. Forget that you're a slave, forget that you're a knave. A pauper to a prince, a whore to a queen, drink the drink and dream. For tomorrow we may suffer, but tonight by drink we'll gloat, so raise your goblet high and pour it down your throat!"

And with that the entirety of the tavern emptied their mugs, glasses and goblets. *"Bravo!"* resounded the tavern as empty drinking vessels thudded upon table and bar.

Giuseppe caught Benito's attention through the crowd.

"Now," said Giuseppe, raising his voice over the tavern's ruckus, "there is still much to discuss. As a matter of purity, Augusto Po says no. As a matter of commerce, the Cheese Maker says yes. As a matter of pride, Vincenzo says no. Now, faced with this drastic choice, who else to raise their voice? I, for one, am undecided."

Cosimo di Pucci de' Meducci felt a hand press down on his shoulder for a little boost as his new friend rose to his feet.

"Ah," said Vincenzo loudly in Benito's direction, "you break for the whores' door."

"No," answered Benito indignantly over the smattering of laughter. "Benito wishes to speak."

"Yoooou?" mocked Vincenzo.

"Quiet, neighbors!" Bobolito angrily stomped its puppet leg upon the bar. "Simmer down!" Heads turned to Bobolito. The tavern quieted. "This forum is open to wise man and fool, and as some use tongue for speech, others for drool. So listen up, neighbors, show respect, make not a peep, for far better Benito in here than out *pleasuring* your sheep."

"Ay," said Benito over a chorus of *baa*s as he sat down defeatedly, " 'tis safer to be mocked by a man than defended by a puppet."

"Basta!" said Giuseppe with sufficient force to bring the flock to order. "Puppet, that is enough out of you."

Bobolito's head drooped and his body went lifeless.

"Come now, Benito," Giuseppe turned to his underling, "take not to heart what's made in jest; speak your speech like all the rest."

Benito strained to recall the gist of what Giuseppe wanted him to say, and therefore spoke with a hesitancy and ponderousness that was unlike his usual speech. But mostly, Benito was still thinking about Mari, and this did indeed lend a tenderness to his speech that caught the tavern by surprise. "Of these *Ebrei*," Benito began, "I too am riddled with suspicion, but must confess, my doubt does wilt through a common ill-nutrition. Oh, my head does too move against my heart, but I know the bitter taste of a life apart. For Benito, no joyous children, no faithful spouse. It's work at the mill, drink at the tavern, then home to empty house. And what for me is sour to swallow and goes down rank, does it not too leave an *Ebreo*'s heart blank? For hard enough it is for Benito to sleep in empty home, but at least this village, this tavern, I can call my own. Is it then right for Benito to do in kind, and make worse for them the loneliness that plagues my heart and mind? Is this what our *Cristo* would deem us to do, act unto another as you'd not like unto you?"

Well, that was not the kind of sentiment one had come to expect from Benito, and the tavern fell absolutely silent, Bobolito and all.

In Which We Contemplate
the Difference Between Dirt & Earth

"Bless me, Father, for I have sinned."

"Hmm," the Good Padre chuckled, "really?"

"Padre! Please, I have."

"Oh, Mari," he sighed amicably from behind the small rectangle of latticed iron that divided the confessional, "I don't believe it."

"Good Padre," Mari did her best to keep from laughing, "I'm supposed to be anonymous."

"Then what is the point of trust and friendship?"

The question stumped Mari and was an instant reminder why she adored the Good Padre. "Nevertheless," said Mari, "it's true, this time I *have* sinned."

"Well, I assure you, God will no doubt forgive a daughter who serves her mother so selflessly, and a farmer who deals grapes and olives so deliciously."

"But Good Padre . . ." Mari paused, desperate to tell him, to tell someone. "My . . . my . . . thoughts. My mind—"

"Oh, Mari," the Good Padre gently interrupted Mari's faltering speech. "The mind is a monkey. It leaps from branch to branch, tree to tree. The more you try to house it, the quicker it slips free. Concern yourself with actions, with kind words and busy hands. Rest assured, God more than enough rejoices in how you treat your mother and how you love your land."

Mari's heart swelled. Until the arrival of the Good Padre, Mari had been dead set against the Sacrament of Reconciliation. The idea of the old padre acting *in persona Cristi* sickened her. She went to confession the two times a year that she had to and no more, and she told only false trifles then. She would have sooner spilt her blood than given a true penance to that wretched old louse. But within a month of the Good Padre's tenure she began to take a weekly confession. She knew half the village could hardly form a coherent sentence in his presence, but for Mari just the opposite was the case. Yes, something about him was indeed quite baffling, but he emanated a love that loosed both Mari's heart and tongue. Heaven knows, her near-constant stream of vengeful, hateful thoughts toward her stepfather had begun to poison her mind, and one day, without plan or forethought, she found herself inside the church's confessional baring her soul to the Good Padre.

Today, however, was different. Truly, she was too enraptured to much condemn herself for what she was feeling, but she feared God and village might. And she sought confession to both share her excitement with someone and gauge the potential *unholiness* of her desire through the Good Padre's reaction. After all, if she really thought about it, which she didn't often do—she kept herself too busy with olives—the Good Padre was her only true confidant.

"Thank you, Good Padre, you are most kind. But my mind has been . . ." Mari searched for the courage to admit her feelings. "My thoughts have been . . . they have been replete with lust and desire."

"*Well,*" said the Good Padre cheerily, " 'tis certainly a nicer thing to think than thoughts of blood and vengeance, no?"

"But Good Padre," Mari paused, again delighted and inspired by his reasoning, "are they not *Peccati Mortali?*"

"Lust, desire, Mortal Sins?" the Good Padre asked rhetorically. "Well, I guess that all depends on what you desire."

"Please, Good Padre." Mari leaned in toward the lattice and brought her voice to a whisper. "Am I not being clear when I say *desire?*"

"Hmm, let's see. Do you desire a married man?"

Mari's eyebrows sprang with shock. "Goodness no!" she blurted. But then, her countenance dropped—*mio Dio!*—might he be married?

"Well then," the Good Padre continued, "do you desire a donkey?"

"What?"

"A donkey?"

"No," Mari answered quizzically.

"A goat?"

"No."

"A sheep?"

"No."

"A horse?"

"Good God!" exclaimed Mari. "What are you getting at?"

"Just what then do you desire that is so mortally wrong?"

"A boy!" Mari realized she had just about shouted. "A wonderfully handsome and beautiful boy about my age."

"Well," said the Good Padre, "do you think he is a good and honorable young man?"

"Oh, yes, Padre."

"Is he good to his family and the land?"

"Oh, yes."

"Is there love in his eyes when he looks at you?"

"Yes . . . I . . . I hope so."

"And when you look at him?"

"Oh, by heaven, yes." Mari beamed.

"And your heart, Mari, does it tell you that this love is true?"

"Oh, Good Padre, never has it spoken more clearly to me."

"Then what," said the Good Padre, "could be sinful about that?"

"But . . . but . . ." Mari struggled to give words to her thoughts. To confess to the Good Padre that the *boy,* the wonderful, beautiful, handsome boy who she could not stop thinking about, was—

"Listen, my dear," the Good Padre mercifully interrupted her stammering, "the *evil* that you think you've come to confess is the true direction of your heart's compass. There is nothing inherently wrong with lust or desire. They are the natural energies of life, God's divine fire. Yet in yourself you doubt what in nature you'd rightly trust. For does not the bee desire nectar, or the root for water lust? Without desire how would two sheep combine to make a flock, or eggs and chickens fill the coop without the lusty cock? Do you see, Mari? The energies of the body are replete with God's grace. Hence, our job as humans is not to judge, but to set them in the *right* place."

"Right place?" Mari murmured, overwhelmed.

"Hmm," the Good Padre continued after a moment's pause, "let me put it this way: the soil, the earth, in which you set cuttings and the farmer seed, bear the fruit by which man and village feed. In its place, it's perfect, it's life-giving earth, but when dragged by foot or hem of skirt, once in the house, we call it dirt. You see, the energy for which we wrongly pitch our mind to hell's fire is not the problem of the thing, but *where* we apply the desire. And I am certain, Mari, with your good and noble soul, that desire rightly moves your eyes to where your heart be whole. And, as odd as it may sound, as hard it is to trust, when rightly placed, there's God in your desire, Holy Spirit in your lust."

But... Mari heard herself say though her mouth could not bear to actually express the word. It was too delicious, too wonderful a notion to contemplate. To think, even for a second, that her olives and his tomatoes could rightly commingle—divined by God, blessed by Holy Spirit.

In Which We Learn
Mari's Father's Technique
for Curing Green Olives

When it came to the curing of olives, just about every village in Tuscany claimed it possessed the most flavorful and delicious olives in the land, and that its technique for curing was totally original and superior to all others. But the truth was, virtually all olives were cured using a saltwater brine bath, with the addition of some herbs and spices being the only local variable.

Mari's father, though, had created a technique for curing green olives that was truly unique to all of Tuscany. Instead of curing the green olives in an open container and changing the brine bath daily for ten days, as was commonly done, he sealed the container and let the olives ferment for ten days in a manner similar to fermenting crushed grapes to make wine.

The fermentation process softened the olive's skin more than the typical brine. It made the flesh juicier and its bite more pungent, even a bit cheese-like, which was both off-putting and enthralling in a way that only cheese can be, and certainly no other olive was.

In recent years, Mari had perfected the process further. She discovered that fresh-picked green olives were best left unwashed so that their naturally occurring yeasts could promote and enhance the fermentation. Here was how the process worked: the fresh-picked green olives were set into an enormous, chest-high earthen vessel and then mixed with sea salt, water and a few handfuls of leaves from a bay laurel tree. The vessel was then sealed with a heavy clay top with a small hole so the gases could escape and prevent the curing vessels from exploding (a phenomenon that had occurred on more than one occasion when Mari's father was first experimenting with the process). The vessel was then left to ferment for upward of ten days.

And so it was that on this Sunday afternoon of early September (six days since we left Mari at the piazza and Benito at the tavern, and one week to the day of the Feast of the Drunken Saint), Mari was busy at work inside the olive mill, bent over the large salt bin filling buckets in preparation for the fermentation of the season's first green olives. Outside the mill, Benito too was supposed to be busy working. Certainly, his body was where it was expected to be, standing before one of the enormous green olive-curing vessels with an equally enormous wood spoon in his hands as he mixed its briny contents of olives, water, salt and bay leaves. But as Benito looked up through the small window into the mill and saw Mari, other things began to stir in him.

With all the awareness of a six-year-old child, Benito pressed his pelvis into the olive vessel's curve to more fully experience the swelling inside his trousers. These were the delicious first moments of spying, the innocent, boy-like moments when Benito would disappear inside the world of his desire and before the swelling got so great that it would bring on the arrival of La Piccola Voce and its abusive mocking. Mari was, after all, so beautiful.

"Mark her well."

"Huh!" Benito's heart jumped.

Standing behind Benito, Giuseppe leaned his chest against Benito's back and brought his mouth close to Benito's ear. The added weight further pressed Benito's *mezzo bastone* against the vessel and made him very uncomfortable.

"Mark her well," Giuseppe repeated, paying no heed to Benito's shock. He'd been conjuring this idea for the better part of a week. "Mark her nose, her eyes and her pretty little face, for therein, Benito, lies our ace."

Benito was annoyed. "What is it you wish Benito to know?"

"The theme with which we'll play the *Ebreo*."

Benito grunted. It was all he could think to do.

"Ten years past when my life took hold," Giuseppe continued in a near-whisper, "I made the moves that were quite bold, and through those moves this mill and that *daughter* I did inherit, she who thinks no more of me than a ferret. But by the village Mari's adored, and it's for them my plan's in store. Now, are you positive of what you saw that market day?"

"*Ay,* the young *Ebreo* and Mari shared romantic play."

"And after market, forbidden fruit she did find and so quickly lose her mind that she bit into it, letting its juice ooze down her chin?"

"By my life, Giuseppe, 'twas the very sin."

"Oh, then we have the finest Italian theme with which to lay our cunning scheme. 'Tis epic, age-old, even biblical in style, an illicit love 'tween *Ebreo* and gentile. For what better way to make our case than to lay the shame upon my daughter's face? As we play the fear that in this town runs thick, that a *Cristiana* daughter has met with an *Ebreo* pri—"

"Ha!" Benito blurted. He could not stand to hear Giuseppe say the word. " 'Tis a fine plan," he lied.

"And thanks to our good and noble *stupid* priest, the thing's to commence at our coming feast. Now, at the feast we'll deepen our ploy by making a hero of this *Ebreo* boy.

Then, soon after, once we've come to trust, all will be undone by a most unholy lust. And the gravest of fears shall be proved so, that we've been deceived by the serpent *Ebreo*. And the love we did lend both true and free, the *Ebreo* will defile by eating the *Cristiana* Mari."

"But how," said Benito faintly, "how do you know she'll love him?"

"Oh, Benito," Giuseppe chortled, "you know much of whores, but nothing of girls. Like Venus locked in a cage, I know the turnings of a youthful rage. How anguish of heart is grieved through the loins, you watch the way in which they join. For as surely as the farmer does reap what he sow, there's more than one way to raise Cupid's bow. Pain. I will pain her heart and plague her mind and of the *Ebreo* speak unkind. I'll abuse and insult, torment and demean, commingling youthful love with youthful spleen. She is a local cow who doth love to chew the homegrown cud, so imagine her fear as I speak of sending her off to marry blue blood. Oh, I'll have it so nothing seems more splendid to her eyes than loving the very thing that I despise. And just as Eve was drawn to fruit of the forbidden tree, she'll flock to the *Ebreo* for hate of me."

Benito felt his mind fracture and through the crack, like molten lava scorching everything in its path, came the mocking little voice. *You coward,* it burned inside his brain, *you pathetic coward. First you kill the father and now you destroy the daughter. Take this spoon and kill him now. Bash his very brains out.*

Giuseppe heard the sound of a wagon and glanced over his shoulder. Bobo the Fool approached, conducting a two-horse-drawn cart that carried a good two dozen cases of wine. It was time for him to go; he had business in Lucca to attend to.

Giuseppe leaned in to Benito to quickly finish his instructions. "Now listen closely, for here's what you're to know, to make a hero of our young *Ebreo*. When the bravest men line up to start the Drunken Saint's Race, among them Benito will have a space."

The news squelched the little voice inside Benito's head and he turned to face Giuseppe.

"Yes," Giuseppe said, returning Benito's boyish smile with a smirk. "You will race the race."

And in an instant, as was so often the case, Benito loved Giuseppe. He had always dreamt of racing in the feast.

"But second shall be your place," said Giuseppe matter-of-factly.

And in an instant, as was so often the case, Benito felt all the love in his heart transform to hate.

"You will lose," Giuseppe continued, "lose so we may win. For in order to hate the sinner and avenge the sin, the *Ebreo* must first be a hero and the hero must win." Giuseppe put his hands on Benito's shoulders and looked into his eyes. "Now I'm off to Lucca. More details upon my return. But in the meantime, tell no one. Be shrewd. Deal with a sly hand, as now we start in earnest our play for *Ebreo* land."

🍅   🍅   🍅

"*Vaffanculo*," Benito whispered to himself as he watched Giuseppe and Bobo roll away from the mill in the wagon. Benito returned to the simultaneous actions of stirring the olive vessel and staring inside the barn at Mari as she prepped the salt and bay leaves for the next vessel. *Tist, tist tist*, La Piccola Voce clucked his demon tongue. *You know much of whores, but nothing of girls.*

"Oh, shut up," Benito murmured. "You'll see."

You, scoffed La Piccola Voce, *Giuseppe's willing whore? I would sooner entrust your vendetta to a boy in a dress. You'll do nothing of honor but much of shame. You will be as you've always been.*

"Oh, you'll see, and so too will Giuseppe." Benito took to stirring the olives with a bit more vigor. Again, he pressed himself into the vessel. "Crude Benito, here for all to mock. Lewd Benito, who's deflowered the flock. Benito, bawdy, lowly and rank, the butt of all childish pranks. So mock me, bring it all in heaps, say I copulated with sheep. Run me over with your large words, hear from me what you only want heard. For I remember, you coward bully, 'twas I who undid that pulley. And the act that gave you wife and land put nary a penny in my hand. But this time Benito shall not toil in vain to have Giuseppe make the gain. No, while he plays the *Ebreo* and plays Mari, I'll play along and play all three. So mock me, 'tis better I be mistook, for Benito's not as dumb as he might look. And whilst you laugh, I operate in stealth, for soon I'll be the man with wife and wealth."

22

In Which We Learn
of Little-Known Saint Rachel

"Surely, Priest," said the Meducci guard, "there must be a patron saint of lost causes and impossible odds?"

Davido felt his mouth go dry and his chest run with sweat under his heavy robe. Could this be a test, he thought, fearful that he knew not of such a saint? "With *Cristo* no cause is lost." It was all he could think to say.

"Ah," said the older and friendlier-looking of the pair of *Guardia Nobile di Meducci* who had stayed their magnificent horses before Davido's donkey-drawn wagon. "The priest is young, but wise."

Davido gave a slight bow of the head. "But I am not a priest."

"No?" said the older guard. "Well, what are you, then?"

"A novice monk, a friar of *Il Ordo Fratrum Minorum*," answered Davido in proper Latin, just as Nonno would have.

"Oh," said the older guard, genuinely pleased. "A Franciscan."

Davido nodded.

"Long ago, in Assisi," said the older guard, "I took a wound, and were it not for the Order of the Little Brothers, dare I say, I would not be here today."

Good God, thought Davido with a jolt of fear, he'll know more about the monks than I do.

"And what of him?" said the gruffer, younger-looking of the pair, who had yet to speak. He pointed to Davido's uncle, Culone, who was passed out asleep in the wagon-bed. He too was dressed as a monk.

Davido smiled. "The brother does like his wine."

"Ah," said the younger guard with a tart chortle, "a little brother of the drunken order."

The older guard ignored his partner's comment. "Well, your kin did aid me once, perhaps you can again? God knows we could use a blessing for this fool's errand."

Even through his panic, Davido could hear Nonno's voice inside his head. *Keep your mouth shut. Nod. Play the part. The less you talk, the wiser you'll seem.*

The older guard leaned forward and lowered his voice. "Will you swear to secrecy, young monk?"

"I swear only to God," said Davido, trying his best to be monk-like. "But if something troubles you, speak your piece. It shall not leave my lips."

"Well," said the older guard, seemingly impressed with the young monk's manner, "monks are not known to be big talkers, are they?"

"Only big drinkers," said the younger guard caustically.

The older guard nodded at Davido apologetically for his partner. "The Duke of Tuscany has disappeared from his country villa. Not seen for a week now."

"Who can blame him," said the younger guard, "with a *sticchio* for a wife and *frocio* for a son?"

The older guard's countenance turned suddenly fierce. He shot his associate a disapproving glance. "Enough!" he said and then returned his attention to Davido. "Have you seen him, perhaps," he asked, gesturing to the surrounding countryside, "along the road or in any of these rhymer villages?"

"Well, I know not his look, but I've been upon this road since morning," Davido lied convincingly, "when I set out from Siena, and I have seen only shepherds with their flocks and farmers in the fields."

"Ah," sighed the older guard, "then you see how hard our charge?"

Davido nodded.

"Then give unto us a blessing before we part, good friar."

"Well," answered Davido, mimicking exactly the line he'd heard Nonno use once before in a similar situation, "it is God and priests who bless and monks who meditate and pray."

"Then lead us in prayer." The guard did not wait for a reply and swung a leg over his horse and dismounted.

"Ay," grunted the younger guard, clearly displeased.

Davido saw the older guard's eyes widen with anger as he turned to his associate. *"Figlio di Puttana!* You will dismount your horse right now and bend your knee in prayer," commanded the older guard with a severity that nearly caused Davido to leap from his wagon seat, "or I will stuff your goddamn balls up your horse's ass."

Immediately, the hierarchy became supremely clear as the younger guard grimaced, but dismounted nonetheless.

"Sorry, Friar," said the older guard, and then, in a rather knightly fashion, he staked his sword into the earth with both hands, held tight its hilt and took a knee in front of Davido's wagon. "Come," he beckoned Davido and then bowed his head in supplication.

Davido felt his pulse quicken and the muscles of his body tighten. Usually these exchanges never went further than extending the sign of the cross to a passing stranger. On the few occasions when they had, Nonno had been there to handle the situation; but even in those instances, it had never gone this far. The travel ruse that Nonno had thought up long ago did not extend much beyond dressing like a monk in a heavy frock, wearing a large cross around the neck and knowing a few key facts about the order of Franciscan friars. Alas, Davido did not know a single *Cristiano* prayer.

The younger guard knelt alongside his partner and assumed the same knightly position. Gripped with fear, Davido could not take his eyes off the pair of guards. Though little more than their faces and forearms were uncovered, their potential for ferocity was well apparent. These were real men of war. Their hands and forearms were the stuff of Michelangelo's sculpture, heavy with muscle and vein, marked by the real-life scars and burns of battle. Their necks were thick from years of wearing weighty helmets that may have kept their brains from being bashed out, but did not spare their faces from the traumas of their vocation. The pair of them made the heartiest of farmers look like altar boys.

The older guard again beckoned Davido: "Come, young friar, we await your prayer."

Davido let go his donkeys' reins and rose from the wagon seat. *Good God,* he prayed first for himself, *sweet sister in heaven, help me.* It was the right spirit to beseech, and as Davido took a knee before the pair and closed his eyes, suddenly words came to his lips.

"Brothers in God," said Davido, recalling his favorite line from the *Talmudi*[12] and one of the few he had committed to memory, "it is said that the mind is the essence of man, and when we think holy thoughts we enter a holy place. So let us bring our minds to holiness. By thought let us turn this patch of road into the holiest of temples. By invoking her name, let us invite the presence of little-known Saint Rachel," said Davido, spontaneously elevating his sister to sainthood, "patron of impossible odds, seemingly lost causes, self-sacrifice and protector of donkeys. So that our prayers may be bet-

---

[12] An ancient record of rabbinic discussions pertaining to *Ebreo* law, ethics, customs and history.

ter heard and better heeded, we will pray in the tongue that Rachel spoke. The language of *Gesù il Cristo* and his Apostles." Davido lowered his head and so too did the Meducci guards.

Kneeling there, in the middle of the ancient road built by the Romans, and speaking in an even more ancient Hebrew, Davido softly sang Psalm 23, the Shepherd's Prayer. It was his sister's favorite prayer and, since her death, his favorite prayer too. A prayer he had sung a thousand times in the *Sinagoga* of Florence. In truth, it was the only prayer he believed in. For as surely as he had walked through the valley of the shadow of death, which as a boy he always took to be the plague that stole the life of his mother and father, something, some divine power had protected him. And as he prayed he realized all the ways that this prayer he loved so much had manifested in his life. That not a rod and staff, but a shovel and a hoe did comfort him. That he *did* lie down in green pastures, fields that grew ripe with *pomodori.* That the country air and rains had been like still waters restoring his soul. Surely, prayed Davido, goodness and mercy shall follow me all the days of my life and I will dwell in the house of the Lord forever.

Despite the fact that there was no Saint Rachel in the *Cattolico* lineage, nor any lineage, to the pair of battle-hardened Meducci guards the ancient Hebrew prayer sounded sacred and mystical. To the older guard, especially, the prayer was like a healing balm offering him the transcendent moment that his soul and psyche so craved. A moment in which all the battles he had fought and lives he had taken were pardoned and the delicious elixir of forgiveness washed over him.

The prayer finished and Davido allowed silence to fill the space for a moment. "May Saint Rachel guide us in the service of our lives and fulfillment of our duty," said Davido, returning his tongue to Italian. "Amen."

"Amen," repeated the Meducci guards.

Slowly, Davido opened his eyes. He noticed tears streaming from the eyes of the older guard.

"Thank you, thank you, Brother," said the older guard. He clasped Davido's hand and kissed it. The guard reached inside his tunic and took out a purse filled with coins and placed it in Davido's hands. "Here," he said, "I have done much ill in my years. I have waged war and taken the lives of many men. I have contradicted my conscience and fought for unworthy causes and been on the side of the unrighteous. You, though, and your brothers do the work of God on earth."

The older guard held Davido's hands tight to the purse, letting him know that a rejection of his generosity was not an option. He turned then to his junior guard and with a glance communicated what a thousand words could not.

A grimace crossed the younger guard's face as he reconciled himself to the inevitable. He reached into his frock and removed his coin bag. "Here," he said, handing the purse over to Davido, "for the worthy deeds you and your kind do."

Doing his best to appear more humble than amazed, Davido took the purses, bowed his head, then rose to his feet.

"Godspeed to you, young friar," said the older guard, and then he touched his heart. "You have given me my patron saint: Saint Rachel."

"And Godspeed to you both." Davido made the sign of the cross as the pair of Meducci guards spurred their horses and rode off.

🍅   🍅   🍅

Davido took a deep breath and as he exhaled he found himself chuckling: a chuckle of disbelief. He thought to himself proudly, I'm finally getting some interesting stories of my own! And like that, the stress of the last week lifted from his shoulders. It had, indeed, been a difficult week. The usual banter and laughter that characterized his relationship with Nonno was absent; in fact, the pair had spoken very little beyond discussing the practicalities of the farm. There was much on both their minds, and for most of the week Davido had been anxiously rehearsing the great battle of ideas he was expecting to have with his grandfather—Nonno advocating the importance of keeping the wedding date; Davido, the necessity of going to the *Festa* and honoring their neighbors. But to Davido's surprise, the battle never transpired. On Friday evening, after a few days of less than happy contemplation, Nonno simply informed Davido that on Sunday he would be leaving for Florence to postpone the wedding. "What's done is done," Nonno said to his grandson. "You've made certain of that. It would be foolish to give *the natives* an excuse to hate us. There is more to lose in offending them, than our own."

Davido knew instantly what Nonno meant. He had heard the stories on a number of occasions: how Colombo's ignorance and arrogance so often left behind a pile of bodies. Nonno then told Davido to prepare two wagons, four donkeys and four sets of monks' outfits for a Sunday sunrise departure. Upon one wagon, Davido and Uncle Culone were to travel south to Pitigliano to deliver to the community a wagonful of *pomodori* and other fruits and vegetables, and to inform Rabbi Lumaca, a longtime friend to Nonno and to whom Nonno was greatly indebted, that the wedding was postponed until "a later date." Nonno also handed Davido a sealed letter that he was to deliver to Rabbi Lumaca. Upon the other wagon, Nonno and Uncle Uccello would be setting off for a few days in Florence to do what needed be done there.

"A later date?" Davido had questioned with a combination of relief and apprehension.

"Yes," said Nonno with a touch of exasperation.

"When?"

"The autumn and winter are far too wet and miserable for an old man to be traveling back and forth to Florence," said Nonno. "We will see what comes with the spring when we go to Florence for Purim."

"The spring?" repeated Davido. "But what of the *pomodori*? Seeds need to be germinated, soil tilled and amended, seedlings planted."

"Believe it or not," said Nonno, "there is more to life than your tomatoes."

Maybe so, Davido conceded as he now conducted his donkey-drawn wagon along the road, but what am I to tell my heart? What am I to tell my head, which, since the sight of those glorious feet, those beautiful ankles, that wonderful scar upon her left knee, has thought of little else but Mari? Would

Nonno ever understand such a thing? Safety, preservation and love of family and people—this was what mattered most to Nonno. How could I ever explain to him, thought Davido, that I cannot fathom marrying without love and I cannot fathom marrying anyone but—

In the distance, the homeward sight of the Apuan Alps came into focus and interrupted what was left of Davido's thought. Truthfully, it was such a dangerous thought that he was scared to even think it and grateful to use the mountains as a distraction. Davido loved the sight of those mountains—how the whitish marble of their peaks always made them appear snowcapped—and he estimated that he was little more than one hour from home.

Davido found himself at a fork in the road. To the left was the safer, longer way that skirted the village and eventually led back home—the way they always went. To the right, the more direct route passed along an olive orchard and mill before leading into the village. He'd only taken the direct route one time—accidentally—nearly a year ago, and he hoped his memory served him correctly. Davido turned his head to take in the angle of the sun; he figured that he had at least three hours until darkness. Looking over the other shoulder to check on his uncle, drunk and sleeping sloppily in the wagon-bed, he figured he had at least three hours before he would be awake. Davido felt the purses filled with coins jiggle inside his robe. He felt the heavenly graces of *Saint Rachel* still upon him. He thought of wrists and ankles and feet and a little scar upon a knee. He had time enough to make a detour.

In Which We Learn
Mari's Technique for
Curing Black Olives

It was late Sunday afternoon and Mari was alone. She ducked into a corner of the mill, under the stairs and below the second-floor office that Giuseppe had built into the barn some years after he took over. He liked for his office to look down upon his workers, something Mari found repugnant and something her father never would have done. The area underneath the office was a shadowed nook used for storing empty olive-curing vessels and the perfect place to hide something.

Mari moved between some of the larger pots, crouched under the steep angle of the stairs and removed a bucket-sized earthen vessel that she had hidden. Finally, she hoped, they would be ready.

On Sundays Mari would put in at least a half-day's work at the vineyard-orchard; then, by early afternoon, she'd turn her attentions to getting things together for Monday's market. Giuseppe cared little for the village market as there was far more money to be made exporting oil and wine to the wealthy monasteries and lords throughout Tuscany. Hence, operating the stand was entirely Mari's responsibility. To that end, she liked to get everything in order on Sunday afternoon. That way, come early Monday morning when she arrived at the barn, she would have little to do but attach the mule to the already loaded wagon.

Mari understood Giuseppe's mind well enough to express disdain over being forced to work on Sundays, but in truth, she relished being alone in the mill. Prepping and loading the wagon with olives, olive oil and wine in preparation for the village market had been something her father had seen to and taken great pride in. Not surprisingly, Mari took pleasure in replicating many of those same tasks. One such task was to use the quiet of Sunday afternoons in the empty mill to experiment with grapes and olives. Mari remembered well the Sunday afternoon when she and her father first tasted the small batch of green olives he had cured through fermentation. What a flavor that was—buttery, salty, a bit of cheese-like musk—and as she now lifted the lid from the bucket-sized vessel of olives in which she was working her own experiment, the nostalgia of paternal approval washed over her. The olives were beautiful: plump, purple, late-season Frantoi, picked last December at their very ripest.

Here was how Mari had cured them: first, she handpicked several dozen fat and exceptionally ripe olives, which she then salt-cured for twenty-one days, drawing out their bitter water and causing them to prune from dehydration. Next, Mari had set the olives into a bath of red wine, salt, rosemary and dried bay leaves. Her hope was that the olives would rehydrate and swell with the brine's flavor. And as she now lifted the lid, this was exactly what had happened. Thank God for that, thought Mari, because it sure took longer than she had originally calculated. Even after six months, the last time she checked, the olives weren't quite ready. But now it was month eight, and as Mari dunked her fingers into the vessel and plucked out a plump purple olive, it felt just right. She brought the olive to her mouth; its flesh was meaty and firm enough under tooth, easily separating from the pit. The flavor was excellent—a balanced integration of the olive's butter and the brine's salty red-wine pungency. As Mari swallowed, she could not help but wonder if *he* was a lover of olives too?

Suddenly, this seemed like the most important question in the world. It had been that way for much of the last six days. In fact, ever since seeing him at market, nearly everything Mari did was accompanied by a corollary thought of the tomato boy and the curiosity—*the hope*—that her likes and dislikes would concur with his. I wonder if he likes wine, Mari would think as she drank wine, or cheese when she ate cheese, or anchovies; and she certainly hoped that he was no fan of raw onion or sanguinaccio[13], which Mari found disgusting.

"Whoa!"

A voice and the noise of a horse-drawn wagon coming to a halt outside the barn's eastern door startled Mari. Immediately, the pleasant sensations in Mari's mouth and mind soured from fear. Fear that she was doing something wrong and fear that her olives would be discovered. Mari stilled her breath as she made herself small under the staircase. She heard someone dismount the wagon and footsteps approach. She peered between the open spaces in the steps as a silhouette entered the barn. It was Giuseppe and he was carrying an elaborate contraption comprising tubes, a copper teakettle and a glass wine bottle. She had no idea what it was.

Mari held her breath as the brown leather of Giuseppe's overly fine Florentine boots flashed before her eyes and his wood heels clacked upon the wood steps leading up to his office. She heard him open the door and step inside.

Mari exhaled with relief; her olives were safe. Above, she

---

[13] A Tuscan specialty: pork blood pudding flavored with anise, cinnamon, cloves, raisins and pine nuts.

heard the clang of metal as Giuseppe set the contraption down, and then the door of the office's small furnace open, the tossing in of kindling, the strike of a match. Hmm, she thought, 'tis a warm afternoon for the lighting of a fire.

Quietly, Mari placed the lid upon her jar of olives. She wanted to go home. Not to the place she shared with Giuseppe and her stroke-crippled mother, but to her home of ten years ago. A time before the death of her father. A time before Giuseppe's usurpation of the orchard and her mother. A time before her mother's apoplectic undoing rendered her lame and mute and left only her sad, watery eyes to speak of relentless heartbreak.

Mari slid the olives back under the stairs to hide her creation from the man who would no doubt usurp this too. That was his pattern: to first arrogantly dismiss any idea she may have, thus demeaning the fruits of her endeavors, only to later commandeer the very idea and claim it as his own. Dismiss, demean, usurp—that was how it was with Giuseppe.

A clang from the office above her snapped Mari back to the present moment. Why not on this day a little vengeance? Giuseppe had no idea she was anywhere near the mill and it was as clean a shot as she would ever get. She felt her pulse quicken with excitement. Softly, Mari stepped over to the wagon loaded for tomorrow's market and removed a jug filled with olive oil. She slunk back underneath the stairs, pulled the cork from the jug and drizzled a cup's worth of oil all over the third stair from the bottom. Not so high as to maim, merely to bruise. With her fingertips, Mari massaged the oil evenly about the stair. She smirked: the old wood felt slick as ice. But then she heard the mill door creak and the smirk slipped from her face.

Mari looked up; she thought she saw a little tuft of Benito's dirty hair dart out of view behind the mill door. *"Testa di Cazzo!"* Mari said under her breath. Even her minor act of vengeance had been foiled by that ogre. Dear God, she thought, if Giuseppe learns of this there'll be hell to pay. Terror turned quickly to fury, a gurgling, roiling volcano aimed at Benito.

That vulgar beast, thought Mari, as she lowered herself onto her hands and knees and, hidden from sight, crawled out the mill's western door, the one opposite Benito. Outside and hidden from view, she picked up a wooden bucket by its iron handle and walked down the slight knoll to where Benito kept his truffle sows penned up. She stepped into the pen and filled the bucket with an altogether vile combination of pig manure, rotting food slop and the putrid, muddy muck in which the pigs liked to roll around to cool their bodies.

Mari set her jaw in a determined clench as she walked past the large olive-curing vessels sitting alongside the south side of the mill. She did not care that her footsteps were not especially quiet or that the bucket full of slop was splashing about and soiling her hand. She was going to carry out this deed like a proud and charging knight who looks not for cover as he storms into battle. She quickened her pace as she neared the barn's edge. The sun was setting and the light was poor on the eastern side of the barn. She turned the corner, and, just as she suspected, he was ten paces off, his back to her, hiding in the shadows and peering into the barn.

"*Vaffanculo!*" Mari yelled as she let fly with the bucket's contents. "*Faccia di merda!*"

⁂   ⁂   ⁂

Run! his instincts urged. Surely, she had heard the barn door squeak. Run, you fool! It would not look good to be found spying. But he could not bring himself to leave before getting one more chance to gaze upon her. His eyes beheld her beauty for only an instant before she slipped into shadow. But, my God, even sweaty and soiled from a hard day's labor, she was more beautiful than any girl he'd ever seen. Run, his instincts commanded again, yet his body disobeyed. He could not bear to leave such beauty in the shadows.

And then it was too late. First came the footsteps from behind him. Then the onslaught of curses. So he turned, as anyone would, in absolute panic to face his attacker. He did not know what came toward him, but he did see *her*, ever so briefly, before his survival instincts closed his eyes, sealed his mouth and raised his arm to shield his face. He'd seen Mari, and it was wonderful.

⊛   ⊛   ⊛

Mio Dio! Mari gasped as the bucket of pig slop exploded across her target's throat and chest. It was not Benito, definitely not Benito.

Davido felt something cool and foul crash over his chest and drip down his neck. Thank God the monk's frock came nearly up to his chin and that he still had the hood up and that his instincts were fast enough to raise his forearm defensively. Quickly, he wiped his sleeve across his face to clear it of the splatter. Then he opened his eyes. There, standing along the east side of the barn, next to its open, squeaky door, Mari and Davido beheld each other for the second time in six days. For an instant, they knew intimately of their shame. Davido for being dressed as a monk and furtively spying upon Mari, and Mari for acting rashly, for cursing him and then dousing him with a bucket of slop.

For a moment, a brief moment, these were the prevalent emotions and they crippled both speech and movement. But then, a new emotion took over, one far more powerful than shame. For the very thing in life that both Mari and Davido desired more than anything else was suddenly before them. And it was enormous and overwhelming. A feeling so great as to obliterate all other feelings, so that no thing needed explaining, no apology or excuse needed to be given. Not even their skin and noses could perceive offense in the smell and feel of muck. It was as if Davido and Mari were not themselves, or maybe for the first time ever they were entirely themselves—raw and honest and fearless.

There was a shared breath—a quick inhalation. A critical launching-off point, and then, without a word spoken, Mari and Davido rushed into each other's arms—desperate to eradicate any distance between their lips. Though they had never kissed before, not each other nor anyone else, a sublime instinct took over. Something that had them turn their heads to just the perfect angle, both tilting slightly to the right, something that had them press their bodies against each other and slide their hands past cheeks and around necks to tenderly secure the seal of their mouths so their lips and tongues could dance and devour one another in perfection; something that unbound them from the earth and sent them spiraling heavenward, so that they did not know nor care what was up or what was down.

⊛   ⊛   ⊛

It is impossible to say how long the kissing lasted, as kisses such as these are not easily assessed by the parameters of time, but suffice it to say that as the wooden heel of Giuseppe's left boot slipped upon the freshly oiled third stair from the bottom, pitched his legs out from under him and sent his buttocks spectacularly crashing into and through that very third stair, well, the racket did also bring Mari and Davido crashing back to earth.

And as suddenly as their lips had met, they also parted, breathless and gasping and stinking of muck and *merda*. The couple looked toward the mill, where the racket had come from, and then back at each other. A delirious moan came from inside the barn, prompting Mari to bite her lip and raise her eyebrows. Then, her lip slid from under her tooth and her mouth stretched into a wondrous, bewildered and embarrassed smile that in an instant had Davido smiling too. Neither Mari nor Davido knew what to do or say and somehow they both had the awareness and good grace to do the exact same thing at the exact same moment. The only thing one really could do after such a first kiss. They ran; Mari into the orchard of her father, and Davido down the road to where his wagon and sleeping uncle waited.

24

In Which We Learn the Fine Art of Steam Distillation

Giuseppe moaned. It all happened so fast. The onslaught of curses from outside the mill that caused him to drop his apparatus and rush down the stairs; the sudden burst of panic as his feet slipped out from under him; the awful jolt of pain; and then, darkness. He was not sure how long the darkness lasted, but within the darkness, there it was, gleaming like a gem. He was at the Feast of the Drunken Saint, watching the men race their donkeys round and round the piazza, stopping only to drain their goblets of wine. Wine that he'd provided for this year's race, wine that was laced with *Fungi di Santo*.

Earlier in the day, he and Bobo the Fool had traveled to Lucca to visit with the owner of a local perfumery and see about acquiring a steam distillation apparatus. It was not an entirely unexpected visit, as Giuseppe had a business relationship with the perfumery. Each December, for the last six years, Giuseppe had sold the perfumery of Lucca the vineyard's pressed grape skins that were left over from the wine-making process. The perfumery would separate the tiny grape seeds from the skins and then press a delicate oil from the seeds. The oil was then used in the making of fine soaps, cosmetics, body lotions and shaving creams.

For Giuseppe, selling the grape skins was an excellent way to squeeze every ounce of profitability from the land. While pressed grape skins were not hard to come by, the owner of the Lucca perfumery deemed the oil from Giuseppe's seeds exceptional and was therefore more than happy to barter an old and rarely used steam distiller for the coming season's grape skins.

As a teenager, Giuseppe had frequently distilled mushrooms, barks, roots and other poisonous compounds. Hence, as he arranged the steam distiller in his office, the whole poison-making process returned to him in a flash of memory. 1) Crush the dried fungi into a fine powder with a mortar and pestle. 2) Set the fungi dust into the copper distillation kettle along with a bottle of red wine and a spoonful of honey. 3) Set a fire underneath the kettle and bring the honey, red wine and mushroom dust to a slow boil. 4) Wait for the liquid to turn into steam. 5) Trap the steam and run it down the steam-distillation tubing so that it may cool just enough to form droplets of liquid. 6) Collect the liquid into a glass bottle at the device's other end. 7) Test a drop on the tongue to make sure all bitterness and mushroom flavor has been removed so that *not even the most skilled food-taster*—Giuseppe recalled his uncle's words with a clarity that startled him—*could tell the wine was tainted.*

Yes, Giuseppe knew exactly what he was doing when it came to distilling the *Fungi di Santo* mushrooms he had chanced upon last Sunday whilst foraging for truffles with Benito. He just wasn't certain *why* he was doing it. Of course, he reasoned, a non-lethal yet debilitating toxin might come in handy at some time or another, possibly even in his current scheme to usurp the *Ebrei* land. However, he had no specific plan in mind until he crashed through the stairs and the perfect idea came like a light shining through the trauma: taint the racers' wine with *Fungi di Santo* at the Feast of the Drunken Saint; guarantee the *Ebreo*'s victory by drugging all the competitors but the tomato boy and Benito.

And then the pain arrived, a pain that overwhelmed any and all visions of narcotized donkey riders and a victorious *Ebreo*. At first the pain seemed to emanate from every part of his body and he feared that his back might be broken. He had crashed in such a way that his buttocks broke through the stair, collapsing his knees and chest into one another, and brutally wedging his body and right arm between the second and fourth stairs. *Everything* hurt. His hamstrings felt pulled and his back bruised and raw. His stomach pressed uncomfortably against his thighs and he realized that had it not been for his potbelly and general inflexibility, he would have folded and fallen straight through the stairs like a limp noodle.

Giuseppe took a short and painful breath and did his best to assess his situation. He was stuck, stuck like an animal, as if a man-sized bear trap had folded him in half, leaving only his ass to dangle. He had seen a man break his back once—tossed out a third-story window by his uncle—and it occurred to Giuseppe he should attempt wiggling his fingers and toes. Thank God, he thought, as he felt his digits press against the soles of his boots, I am not crippled. Slowly, the shock began to wear off and the pain began to localize. It hurt most in one place.

It was an unbearable position and he squirmed and fought to free himself from between the stairs. He could not stand being so vulnerable and he worked desperately to extricate his limbs. In his efforts, Giuseppe keeled abruptly to his right and smashed his right cheek against the sideboard that framed the stairs. *"Faccia di merda!"* Giuseppe hollered as he lay there stuck and panting. Curiously, his right hand made contact with an object underneath the stairs. It felt like a small olive-storing vessel, the kind people kept in their kitchen. He pushed on the vessel. It was solid and provided some extra leverage to help free his hips and buttocks. Now he leaned to the right, wiggled his hips and back, pressed harder against the olive vessel and, with a great show of effort, managed to roll all the way over his right shoulder. With a grunt and a thud, he fell to the ground on his left hip and shoulder.

🍅   🍅   🍅

Partially underneath the stairs, Giuseppe laid in a semi-fetal position, his face upon the cool earthen floor, catching his breath. Finally, he could see the broken and splintered wood in front of him; the third stair had split right in half. His right buttock pulled one way, his left buttock pulled the other, causing his poor little asshole to stretch and tear. He noticed a droplet of oil dangling from a splinter of wood. He reached out and touched it, rubbing the oil between his fingertips. Fresh oil? *Testa di Cazzo.* What idiot would spill oil on the stairs and not clean it up? Next to the broken stair Giuseppe spotted the small olive vessel that his hand had discovered. This was not the proper place where jars this small were stored. He reached out and slid it closer to him. It was full of something. Liquid? Olives? With a groan, he sat up and lifted the lid from the jar. Indeed, there were olives inside: plump, purple and floating in brine. They didn't look like any olives his mill produced. He popped one into his mouth and immediately everything became clear. *Figlia di puttana,* he thought. That little bitch!

In Which We Learn
the Recipe for Tuscan Toast
with Fig Jam & Cream

"No," said Luigi Campoverde, "I will not call you Princess Margarita, and you know that very well. You have a perfectly good and regal name—Gian Gastone di Pucci de' Meducci, Prince of Tuscany and sole heir to the dukeship."

The boy frowned and said sadly, "It seems I may be duke sooner than I would like."

Luigi felt a rush of anxiety tighten his muscles at just the instant he was to crack an egg against the lip of a bowl. "Tsst," Luigi snapped his tongue against the roof of his mouth as a fleck of eggshell fell into the bowl and some glop of egg white slimed over the bowl's rim and onto the table. "Do not say such things."

"Where do you think Papa could be?"

"How should I know?" Luigi answered without looking at the boy.

"Well, do you think Papa is dead?"

"Dead," repeated the chef as he used a larger piece of egg-shell to scoop the smaller fleck from the bowl. "How should I know if the duke is dead? I am a chef, not a teller of fortunes."

From the corner of his eye, Luigi noticed the boy's face deflate. Good God! Luigi felt his own heart wilt. He knew what it was to lose a father and the idea that the young prince was imagining such a scenario unnerved him greatly. He had, after all, just seen the duke five days ago: this past Monday, at market, when he ventured back to the village to stock up on provisions—actually, to *barter* for them. And there, he spotted the duke looking like a peasant in his dulled and soiled stableman's outfit that he'd worn for a week straight. Behaving like a peasant too, doling out olives as he gladly assisted the pretty young girl who ran the olive stand. Already, the duke's body looked leaner and his face darker than Luigi had ever seen it—and with an untidy week's worth of facial hair. Even from a fair distance, the duke appeared to Luigi to be happier than he could ever recall in the two years he'd known him.

"No." Luigi now turned to face the peculiar little prince. "I do not think the duke is dead."

Young Gian, still wearing his sleeping gown, gave a half-hearted smile. "How do you know?" he asked.

Luigi Campoverde felt something odd stir inside him, a feeling he resented yet could not ignore. Annoying and queer as the boy may be, he was about the only person that Luigi could ever recall looking up to him and depending on him for something other than his next meal. "Here." Luigi patted the stool beside the kitchen counter, indicating that the prince should take a seat.

Gian sat down, resting his elbows on the counter, facing the chef.

"Pay attention," Luigi said to the boy, gesturing to the bowl with the raw egg in it. Luigi poured a touch of cream into the bowl and then proceeded to narrate his actions. "A pinch of salt, a small grating of nutmeg, then cinnamon, then clove. Be especially sparing with clove." Luigi looked at the boy as he grated a fine dust of clove into the bowl. "Too much clove will ruin any dish. Then beat the egg and spices together."

Luigi reached for a yellowish loaf of semolina egg bread. Then he set his knife at a slight angle to the loaf before cutting. "Slice the bread on a bias, it's prettier that way. Not too thick, nor too thin, about as wide as my thumb. Set the slice of bread onto a plate and pour the egg mixture over it. Flip it over a few times so that the bread can sop up as much of the egg as possible."

Luigi wiped his hands on a cloth then added a dollop of butter to a hot pan on the stove. "Tilt and rotate the pan so the melted butter spreads about and do not let the butter burn. Now," he said to the boy as he reached his fingers into a mortar filled with a crushed something or other, "this is my little trick. Finely, very finely, crush some toasted hazelnuts and chestnuts then sprinkle them atop the bread. Dust it, like this. Don't coat it entirely."

Luigi set the slice of bread into the pan. "Do you hear that sizzle? That's what you want. The pan should be hot, but not too hot or you'll burn the nuts and ruin the flavor. Then shake the pan very quickly, like this, to make sure the bread isn't sticking to the pan. Count to thirty and then it should be ready to be flipped."

Luigi took a thin-lipped wooden spatula from a vase set on the counter. He held the handle of the pan with one hand and the spatula with the other. "When it comes to flipping," Luigi continued, "don't be timid. Make a strong and confident move. Position the lip of the spatula under the bread and then lift it up a bit to see that the color is proper. Then flip the bread away from you, using the lip of the pan to prevent splattering. Always, always flip away from yourself—that way if grease is to splatter, it will splatter away from you. Do you understand?"

Gian nodded.

"Good." Luigi peeked under the bread to see that it was

cooked properly then flipped the bread onto its other side; butter sizzled and bubbled at the edges of the bread. "There, do you see that color?" Luigi glanced over his shoulder to make sure Gian was paying attention. "That's what you want."

Luigi left the bread to cook. He took a clean plate off the shelf and set it on the counter, then pulled a knife and fork from a drawer and set it before the boy. Reaching for a pitcher, he then poured a glass of milk from it. "Fresh," he said whilst sniffing the air, "you can still smell the grass."

Gian did not smile. Luigi pursed his lips in a moment of internal deliberation. He had come to know the young prince well enough to understand that if not even fresh milk and a lesson on Tuscan toast could undo the boy's concern about his father, then he must truly be suffering.

"Let me tell you a secret that all good chefs know," Luigi said to the boy. "A secret I learned many years ago when I was about your age, about how food and flavor can tell the future."

Luigi turned to face the stove and with another quick move of the spatula lifted the cooked bread from the pan and set it on the plate. From the cupboard he took a jar of jam and flipped its metal cinch-top open. Discerningly, he brought the jar to his nose and sniffed twice. "Ah, fig jam," he said, and then spooned some atop the bread. Next, he sunk the spoon into a bowl of fresh whipped cream and shook a dollop of it upon the plate as well. Quickly dipping a knife into a pot of honey, he then drizzled a thin stream of the sweet nectar over the toast in a back-and-forth pattern. Finally, he slid the plate before the prince.

"Here," he said, looking into the boy's eyes. "This is how we'll know if your father is still alive. This is the secret that all true chefs know. You see, when someone you love dies, even if your eyes have not seen it, nor your ears heard of it, your belly will know of it."

The young boy raised his eyebrows.

"It's true," Luigi answered the expression, "your stomach has a mind of its own. And if someone you love has died, even the sweetest and most delicious foods will taste like *merda*."

Luigi gestured to the plate, letting the boy know it was time to sample the dish.

Tentatively, Prince Gian Gastone picked up his knife and fork and sliced into the toast. He was a refined eater for a boy his age and made sure to get equal amounts of fig jam, cream and honey upon the fork. Slowly, the boy brought the fork to his mouth.

Faccia di Merda, thought Luigi Campoverde, as he watched the boy's face light up, this could assuredly cost me my job. But Luigi knew that he had no choice but to fetch the duke from hiding. A boy deserves his father, after all.

In Which We Learn
the Divine Reason
Behind an Unruly Child

Wonderful, thought Cosimo di Pucci de' Meducci the Third, Grand Duke of Tuscany in peasant disguise, *absolutely wonderful.* He was working in tandem with the colossal and perplexing Good Padre. It was only yesterday that Cosimo had such an extraordinary experience in the Good Padre's company, and he felt something akin to a childlike excitement just being in the man's presence again. Cosimo was particularly giddy about all the commotion going on around him. It was the day before the feast and nearly the entire village was present in the piazza, arranging tables, festooning donkeys and setting up all manner of decorations and preparations for the great day. Cosimo and the Good Padre themselves were busy lifting hay bales off a wagon and helping in

the construction of a hay-bale-lined oval track that circled
the statue of the Drunken Saint.

Cosimo had been living with the villagers for nearly two
weeks now and, ironically, had found that he was almost as
useless a peasant as he was a duke. This realization, though
a touch disheartening, hardly undid his newfound joy in being among the common folk and working the land. How easy
it was for Cosimo to shed the falsity of his life as Duke of
Tuscany and so heartily adopt the falsity of his life as a village peasant. Even the ribbing he received as an inept farm-
hand was oddly droll when compared to the humiliations he
suffered as the duke. Not a single bone-tiring day of work
over the last two weeks left his soul anywhere as exhausted
as the simplest day spent as the Duke of Tuscany. Even the
mockery dished out by the locals carried but a fraction of
the venom that poisoned even the pleasantries doled out in
the corridors of power. No, among the villagers, Cosimo found
that insults and ridicule—lavishly lobbed about—were not so
much meant to demean their recipient, but rather to provide
a collective moment of amusement.

The work, however, was grueling and shattered the romantic fantasies Cosimo had so ripely held for much of the
last two years. If only I were a farmer, he would so often
repeat to himself to counter the toxic melancholy that ate
away at his soul, if only I were a farmer. Well, now Cosimo
was a farmer and what he'd imagined as joyous hours spent
working the land with the sun bronzing his face, a peasant
song ringing in his ear and his stomach never far from a
hunk of cheese and a bottle of wine, proved a touch overide-
alized. Indeed, there was often wine, cheese and song, but
so too were there chilly mornings, sweltering afternoons and
back-breaking labors.

In fact, every part of Cosimo's body ached, every muscle
and joint—even places where he had not known there was a
muscle or a joint. But the ache of Cosimo's muscles proved to
be a pittance in comparison to the soreness of his self-image.
Cosimo was not so deluded as to perceive his soft flesh and

paunchiness as Atlas-like, as many aristocrats did, but he had no idea that he was such a spongy, unfit and ill-coordinated twit. Hefty sacks of salt that Benito would easily toss over each shoulder and then effortlessly carry through the mill, Cosimo would have to drag one at a time. A row of six olive trees that Mari would have picked clean in three hours would take him nearly all day. Even the de-pitting of green olives (a task reserved for the retarded and infirm) proved daunting. So much so that Benito's drooling cousin, who had been kicked in the head by a mule many years past, could remove four olives of their pits before Cosimo could de-pit a single one. And when it came to hoisting the pulley to load the wagons with barrels of wine and olive oil (something of a virility challenge among the men of the vineyard), Cosimo was so pathetically weak that the workers would gather round to marvel and mock his futility (except Mari—she never laughed when it came to the pulley).

Yes, Cosimo was weaker than a woman, as inexperienced as a child and less dexterous than a drooling retard. But he was happy, happier than he had been in years. True to his imagining, hard work proved a panacea to his soul. And the locals, for their part, seemed not to mind his presence at all— except for Bobo the Fool, who found himself befuddled and oddly tongue-tied in Cosimo's company. Indeed, even those like Mari who were suspicious of anyone whom Benito took a liking to found themselves won over by Cosimo's enthusiasm, his odd manner of speech (the poor man had not a stitch of rhyme to offer), his gentlemanly disposition and his gleeful subservience to all. He seemed, without a doubt, the easiest person in the entire village to get along with. Even Giuseppe, who until four days ago found Cosimo contemptibly useless, did a quick turnabout. It happened like this:

"Benito," said Giuseppe pointedly upon seeing Cosimo struggle under the not-so-significant weight of a sack of salt. "Should you desire to employ this useless foot-licker, then you shall pay his wages."

"Very well, sir," said Benito.

"What do you mean, *very well?*"

"I mean what I mean," said Benito, "and it is very well what I mean."

"Well, it's not to me!" Giuseppe seemed in no mood for foolery; his torn anus had turned his disposition especially foul. "Between the insatiability of your gullet and groin, from where do you spare a coin?"

"Well, sir," said Benito, with a touch of fumble and delay as if he had a card up his sleeve, "the thing is . . . *eh,* the point being . . ."

"*Faccia di culo!* Get to the point."

"Well," said Benito, "the man asks for no wage."

"Ah," Giuseppe smiled, patting his underling upon the shoulder, "excellent hire."

And with that, not even Giuseppe objected to Cosimo's presence. The sole person who seemed to object to Cosimo's new-found life, only most recently and only a little, was Cosimo himself. When he first ran off, Cosimo believed that his life as the Duke of Tuscany was over and that he would simply disappear from that world entirely. All the anguish and pain and sadness that had beset him since the murder of his beloved courtesan had been a ceaseless murmur in his mind, pleading with him to escape, to run away from it all.

Only a simple life as a farmer could cleanse his mind and heart of all the sorrow that plagued him. At least, that was what Cosimo had hoped. And amazingly, it was proving true. As he lay in bed, dirty and bone-tired, after a full and exuberant day preparing the piazza for tomorrow's feast, Cosimo found that the myriad regrets and miseries that for years had churned his sleep into a nightmarish mess had almost entirely receded. There was only one longing that interrupted his fatigue as he drifted toward sleep: Cosimo longed for his child, Gian. Of all the revelations and realizations of the past two weeks none had been as profound or shocking to Cosimo as the fact that he had come to miss his boy. This was odd, because while Cosimo was decent and kind to his son, he loved him only with half his heart, the way one loves an ugly, embarrassing little dog.

Oh, Cosimo had tried to love his child in the manner he imagined a proper father should, but to him the child was a living affirmation of his own inadequacy. Every time he looked upon his son he saw the boy not for who Gian was, but for what he, Cosimo, was. And that was a fraud and a weakling and a coward. The kind of man who bore a child with a woman for whom he had not an inkling of love (nor she for him). The kind of man who could not even father a proper and manly child at that, and through whom the distinctly Meducci disease of spawning queers and sodomites had come to such spectacular fruition.

But that was yesterday, the past. For even Cosimo's understanding of his own child and the very nature of love was now reborn. It had happened the other day, on the afternoon of *L'Iniziazione dei Bambini*[14], as he worked an olive tree free of its green fruits alongside the Good Padre, Bertolli the altar boy and Bertolli's grandmother. Cosimo could not help but notice that Bertolli was not a good boy—not a good boy at all—but that he was a perfect boy, full of life and vigor, mischief and curiosity. Cosimo could also not help but notice that Bertolli seemed to have initiated a covert war of olive-throwing amongst the children and that every so often a ripe green olive bounced off the back of his head. While the Good Padre, in all his infinite grace, seemed to pay no mind to the mischief going on about him, the same could not be said for Bertolli's grandmother. The old woman appeared to be growing so angered by the boy's antics that Cosimo felt she might spontaneously cure the olives with the acid of her frustration. Finally, the plump and feisty *nonna* could take no more and, with a cat-like agility that belied her age, she took hold of Bertolli's ear and bent it to debilitating effect.

"Mio Dio!" the old woman exclaimed as the boy howled. "Why in heaven would the Lord make a child so useless and unruly?"

---

[14] The Initiation of the Children: so sacred were olives and grapes to Tuscan village life that it was tradition for a village priest to gather all the children and lead them in a day of work upon the village's primary orchards and vineyards at the beginning of the harvest season and to perform a series of blessings over the vines and trees.

With hardly a hitch in the workings of his hands as he too picked olives, the Good Padre said, "So we may learn to love without condition."

"Gian," sighed Cosimo. Every hair of his body stood on end. He turned his head and caught the eyes of the Good Padre. They seemed to be waiting for him—massive, brown, preternaturally radiant. Cosimo felt a ray of light explode inside his chest. He thought he was dying. A death without pain. It felt like an orgasm, not of the loins, but of the heart. As if his heart were exploding! His body went weak. His knees buckled. He crumpled to the ground. No, he crumpled *into* the ground, like he and the earth and the olive tree and the sky and the old woman and the boy and the priest were all one. He began to sob. Sobs that seemed to undo all the anger and sadness that bound his heart. He felt an overwhelming sensation of being loved and of loving, and that everything in life was somehow perfect and existed to be loved without condition. "It's beautiful," Cosimo mumbled as he sobbed, "so beautiful."

As he now lay in bed, listening to the nearby humping and panting of whores and men—very likely his friend Benito—Cosimo reconciled himself to the fact that it would all be over soon, his foray into peasant life. No good thing goes on forever. Indeed, it would no longer be good if it did. He would give himself a bit more time, maybe a week. No question, he was learning a great deal about himself, the land and the common folk. His soft flesh was at last beginning to firm from all the hard work and it was nice to be around his long-lost cousin Bobo, even though they had yet to share anything but an occasional quizzical glance. But Cosimo missed his son, odd as the boy might be; he was excited for the second chance he knew he'd been given—a chance to love his son properly.

In Which We Learn the Best Way to Rob a Donkey of His Vigor

It was early, several hours before the village would arise and begin to gather in the piazza for the *Festa*, yet nearly everything was set—Giuseppe's plans included. It had always been the custom to put the piazza in order on Saturday, hold the feast on Sunday and leave the cleaning of the piazza until Monday. This was done to allow the men of the village a rare morning of leisure and the women more time to cook up their dishes for the evening feast—an extravagant communal affair.

It was commonly thought that the one-armed Drunken Saint arrived in the village in the late afternoon. Accordingly, the donkey race, which commenced the *Festa*, would not begin until the sundial's shadow touched five. After the race, tables would be arranged, the women of the village would bring forth their dishes and a great meal would be shared among the entire village, with special attention lavished upon the winner of the donkey race. As night arrived, torches would be lit, minstrels would take up their instruments and the dancing would commence. The wine, however, followed no timetable. It would flow from morning well into the night, as it was both tradition and expectation that each vineyard and winemaker would provide a fair share of their best juice and that every villager would get spectacularly drunk.

The absurdity of twelve riders racing twelve donkeys and gulping twelve wine goblets for twelve laps around a make-shift track with their right arms tied behind their backs whilst pummeling one another with their left hand was not lost on the villagers. But it was also a serious matter in which not only pride and bragging rights were at stake, but a good deal of coin. In actuality, it was common for each *Capitano dei Quadranti* to wager a great deal on the success of their rider.

Capitano dei Quadranti? Ah, yes, this tradition was believed to have been started by children playing in the piazza. The piazza was the geographic center of the village and at the center of the piazza stood the statue of the Drunken Saint. Among the many marvels of the statue was the goblet held in his left hand; it had been sculpted and positioned in such a way that it served as a perfect sundial. It was believed that a century or two past, a group of boys playing bocce in the piazza had divided themselves into teams according to the specific hour of where they lived as indicated by the sundial's shadow. By the time these boys had grown into men, a tradition had started and the entire village had divvied itself into hourly quadrants (*quadranti*), each represented by its unofficial leader (*capitano*), usually the most powerful and wealthy man of their little slice of village, or at least the best bocce player. It wasn't long until rivalries, more friendly than vicious and usually involving bocce, emerged between the various *quadranti;* for instance, the *One-Hours* felt themselves superior to both their neighbors at twelve and two, and so on.

However trivial the rivalries between quadrants may have

been throughout the year, in the days leading up to the Feast of the Drunken Saint they would gain in energy and by feast day come gloriously to life. A week before the feast each *Capitano* would nominate *Un Cavaliere di Quadranti* (a Knight of the Quadrant) to jockey a donkey and race for the glory of his hour-quadrant. Over time, each *Quadranti* also adopted a color, and on feast day the donkeys and *Cavalieri* would arrive in the piazza dramatically costumed in the colors of their quadrants and with their hours prominently displayed on their chests. The race, in fact, had come to be known as *La Battaglia degli Orari* (the Battle of the Hours).

The *Cavaliere* who won the annual race had a wreath of olive leaves and grapevines placed upon his head and was named *Santo Del Giorno*. As Saint for the Day, the victorious *Cavaliere* was treated like royalty, awarded eleven months' worth of wine and oil by the eleven losing *Quadranti* and given a trio of kingly duties that he must perform: *Brindisi, Richiesta e Degustazione*. To toast, request and taste. First, the triumphant knight would raise his victory goblet and lead the village in a toast honoring the Drunken Saint, beseeching him to bless the year's crop of grapes and olives. Second, he would assume the role of village sire and make a kingly request that could not be denied. It was tradition that the request be humble so to minimize the likelihood of acrimony on feast day and it usually involved something harmless, like making public one's affection and asking a favorite girl for a kiss upon the cheek. Though, on occasion, if the winning *Cavaliere* felt especially bold (as was the case with Mari's father some twenty years prior), he might ask for a woman's hand in marriage. ·

And finally, before the great meal was served, the victorious knight was blindfolded and the village's leading winemakers, six in all, would set a cup of their best juice before him. The knight would sip from each cup and then declare one wine superior. For the winemakers, almost always captains of their quadrants, this was a high-stakes contest. The winning winery was awarded the yearly papal contract to supply wine to both the village church and the Vatican in

Rome—fifty cases with nine bottles per case. Not only was this a great honor, but a well-paid contract and the opportunity to visit the Vatican as a guest of the Holy See for an evening.

The tasting contest was also an entirely crooked event and the underlying reason why the various *Capitani* so desired to see their *Cavaliere* win the Battle of the Hours. In the weeks leading up to the race, each *Capitano*—including those without a prominent winemaker, but aligned with one— would spend hours training their *Cavaliere* to distinguish the wine of their quadrant from all the others. Hence, on race day, even the drunkest *Cavaliere* could pretty well discern the wine of his quadrant.

The feast that followed the race was the collective work of the women of the village, all bringing a dish or two. Wine for the enormous communal meal was supplied by the various winemakers of the village, but wine for the Drunken Saint's race was the singular responsibility of a *Capitano*. Each year a different captain had the duty of bringing forth his finest wine, thirteen *Jeroboame*[15] bottles, twelve for the riders and one precautionary extra should the Saint come back to life. This year that duty fell to Giuseppe, captain of the Twelfth Hour. And so it was that Giuseppe, *Capitano della Dodicesima Ora,* on the morning of the Feast of the Drunken Saint, rolled his horse-drawn cart into the empty piazza, carrying thirteen *Jeroboame* bottles of his finest red wine (well, not exactly his finest; those he'd sold to a count in Pisa), eleven of which were infused with a potent extract of *Fungi di Santo.* He would drug the *Cavalieri*—all but Benito and the *Ebreo.*

🍅   🍅   🍅

Giuseppe crinkled his brow, surprised to find anyone in the piazza at this early hour, let alone Benito. God knows, given the chance, the man slept like a pig in cool mud on a hot day.

---

[15] Jeroboam was the first king of the ten tribes that comprised the Kingdom of Israel. The name Jeroboam means *increase of the people,* and for reasons uncertain was the name given to triple-sized wine bottles that held three liters, or the equivalent of twelve goblets of wine.

But even from across the piazza Giuseppe could tell it was his underling slinking about and intuited immediately that Benito must be up to something. *Figlio di Puttana,* thought Giuseppe, detecting an odd bob and gesticulation to Benito's movement. Curiously, Benito was in the pen where the donkeys were kept the night before the race, held there so they would be equally rested and well fed before the competition.

What is he doing? thought Giuseppe as he neared the pen. He was in no mood to be dealing with Benito at this early hour. He was nervous as is and his bruised buttocks and torn anus ached immeasurably. It made walking unpleasant, sitting difficult and the taking of a shit a supremely brutal act. And to think that his own stepdaughter had done this to him—*that wretched bitch!*—only made the pain worse. And now, reflected Giuseppe as his wagon drew closer to Benito, I've got my other asshole acting up.

"Oh, yes," Benito whispered salaciously into the donkey's ear. "That's it, good donkey. Think happy thoughts, happy-naughty thoughts of green grass and mares in rut. That's it, sweet donkey, think the thought that cracks your nu—"

"Good God, Benito!" gasped Giuseppe, truly astonished. Not even he could have imagined this.

A burst of nerves shot through Benito as he turned to find Giuseppe just outside the pen; he hadn't even heard the wagon approach. *"Vaffanculo,"* Benito sighed. The motion of his arm paused. His grip loosened. His heart pounded.

"What are you doing?" asked Giuseppe.

Benito shushed Giuseppe angrily. " 'Tis all part of playing the *Ebreo."*

"This?" Giuseppe's eyebrows lifted incredulously.

"Little do you know," answered Benito. "No donkey does well a day's rigor when in the morn it spills its vigor."

"Ah, I see."

Benito returned his full attention to the donkey at (and in) hand. His arm was already aching and he didn't have the time to waste explaining himself to Giuseppe. It was far harder work than he'd envisioned and he was only on his third donkey, with three more to go. (The five she-donkeys

were currently separated, in an adjacent pen.) The problem for
Benito was that he-donkeys were temperamental creatures,
not easily brought to erection, let alone climax. One could
not simply masturbate a donkey. No, a he-donkey needed a
bit of romance. Before the beasts could grow anything close
to a proper *bastone* they had to be seduced with a blindfold
over their eyes and a cloth scented with the pungent musk
of a rutting female draped over their nose. And then there
was the motion, a long, arm-exhausting stroke that required
a firm grip, a thorough slathering of olive oil and the tiniest
pinch of clove. All of which led to an explosion that dangerously bucked and tossed Benito from side to side. It was hard,
messy and dangerous work, but a necessary part of his mas-
terful plan, and the last thing Benito wanted was that arrogant bastard screwing it up.

"You'll see," said Benito derisively. "Come the race, six of
these he-studs, robbed of nectar, will move like duds. But my
donkey," Benito made a quick gesture to his donkey in the
corner, "heavy of sack and full of vigor, will lead the attack."

"Well," said Giuseppe, sniffing warily, "be quick about it.
And cover up too this musky stench. Let no nose catch whiff
of skunk that Benito is anything but his usual bawdy drunk.
But be not drunk. Sip much but do not imbibe, save your
kidneys for the ride. Before the race, the less you're deemed of
merit the more you stand to inherit. For he who's overlooked
is he who overtakes. Now, in terms of the crowd, between me
and the fool we'll loosen both tradition and rule, and raise
the doubt and speak the speech that puts the *Ebreo* within
your reach. Then, Benito, it's up to your wiles and might, to
protect the *Ebreo* and squash every other knight. Ride, drink
and battle like a roguish lout, make the *Ebreo* in contrast appear honorable and stout. The more you take the role of brut-
ish Goliath, the more the crowd to the David aligneth. Yes,
give him some lumps, but let him land some too, for the battle
must appear contested and true. I know, of course, you're the
man of greater wit and power, but for us to profit the *Ebreo*
must win the hour. So as you round the final bend, keep in

mind the bigger end, and give not temptation the upper hand. Let him have the victory then we his land."

Giuseppe sat up in his wagon seat. "Remember, Benito, often is the man with more, he who's shrewd enough to lose a battle so to win a war." Giuseppe gave a snap to the reins. His wagon lurched forward. "Adieu, till the feast."

Benito nodded, and grunted his good-bye, eyeing Giuseppe as he rolled his wagon across the piazza.

Giuseppe then dismounted next to the wine table set up aside the track. It was a long table with the numbers one through twelve etched into it, and the place where the riders would stop during each lap and gulp down their goblet of wine. Giuseppe now unloaded the wagon, placing each enormous wine bottle upon its proper hour. Earlier he had marked the two untainted bottles with a small drop of wax and was sure to place one of them now atop Benito's number: twelve. He had not let Benito know about tainting the wine bottles with *Fungi di Santo*. The man had too much foolish pride and would certainly take drugging the competition as a slight to his own abilities. In any event, Giuseppe reasoned, the less he knows the better.

Giuseppe bent down and set the other untainted bottle, the one for the *Ebreo* boy, underneath the table. The movement, however, caused his anus to spike with pain. He gritted his teeth and thought of Mari and of the *Ebreo* boy. You two, I'll undo with the drug of lust.

❊   ❊   ❊

"Figlio di puttana," Benito spat as he watched Giuseppe mount the wagon and leave the piazza. "You'll see." Benito slathered his hand with olive oil, added a pinch of clove and set his grip upon a new donkey. "You'll see. Twelve laps and twelve wines that make the match is where my double-cross I'll unhatch. Six he-donkeys will be slow upon the course and those who ride the shes I'll finish off by force. Now for the *Ebreo,* curs'd swine, I'll put hot pepper in his wine. I'll twist his gut and bend his ear, I'll rot his belly with pepper and fear. And, yes,

Giuseppe, as part of my trap, I'll take the *Ebreo* to the final lap. But the brute Goliath of which you hope to persuade will seem the noble *Cristiano* on Crusade. And in Benito the crowd will align and forgive as I take two lumps for every one I give. Then we'll see, Giuseppe, which way goes the crowd, as Benito battles true and proud. Even Mari will see the boy she did formerly seek compared to Benito is feeble and weak. And through this Battle of the Hours, you'll see, Giuseppe: I'll capture her heart and assume your powers. For all you've planned, today I'll rebuke, as Benito leaves the *Ebreo* in his own puke. And with my victory wish, I'll break our creed and unveil the depths of your heinous greed. Before Mari and all the village I'll reveal your murderous idea to loose that pulley wheel. So think low of me, Giuseppe, hold me as least, for by day's end 'twill be Benito who wins Mari and wears the wreath."

In Which We Learn
of Donkeys & Purim

Davido felt like an overripe tomato decomposing on the vine. All the notions and desires he had felt so clearly were suddenly turning to mush. Surely, Davido's mind reasoned as the wagon's wheels bounced incessantly, today's donkey ride to the village must be worse than the unwanted walk down the wedding aisle he was originally set to do? Really, would it be so bad marrying that skinny-ankled girl and living in Florence for a year? he pondered. He knew Florence, he knew what to expect there. But as he and Nonno rolled along the road toward the village—toward the feast— baking in the late-afternoon sun, everything he was heading toward was a mystery, and a terrifying one at that.

"Tell me the story," pleaded Davido, "of you and Colombo and your years in *Il Nuovo Mundo*."

Nonno clucked his tongue dismissively. "What, you need a story?"

"Oh, come on, Nonno." Davido needed something, a story, a tale, *anything*, to stay the decomposition and keep the tomato of his mind from falling entirely off the vine. "The anxiety is killing me."

"Ha," Nonno sniggered, "we'd be lucky today if anxiety is the only thing that seeks to kill us."

Davido brought his hands to his head in anguish. He was sure *she'd* be there. It was her village's feast, after all. And while this thrilled him, he was petrified that her father, or brother, or suitor, or *suitors* would be at the feast too. Of course, he wanted to see her, but *dear sister in heaven,* he thought, I kissed a *Cristiana* village girl, and if one of hers doesn't kill me, if Nonno finds out, he will.

"Oh, for God's sake!" Davido blurted. "Then practice on me again, so I may one day tell my children and grandchildren."

Nonno let go one hand from the reins and pulled at his beard. "That's very manipulative."

"Well," Davido asked, "did it work?"

"Fine," said Nonno begrudgingly. "But I'm not speaking in that moronic country rhyme. God knows, we're sure to hear enough of that blabber today."

"So be it. Proper Italian, then."

"And I'm not going to speak of Colombo, either. God knows, we've got enough lined up against us today without invoking the memory of that madman."

"Good God," said Davido, "just talk of something to distract us from the mess we're about to enter."

"I'll speak about the donkey."

"Very well," replied Davido.

" 'Cause you're an ass too," said Nonno with a smirk.

Davido laughed, thankful for the distraction.

Nonno drew a deep inhalation. In truth, he was happy to have something to talk about as well. A proper man, he always felt, should be a good storyteller and relayer of insights and information and contain in his lexicon a breadth of subjects upon which to hold court. Without so much as saying, Nonno was pleased that his grandson seemed to think so too, and he secretly liked the idea of his stories living on after his death. Not to mention, Nonno loved donkeys and considered a good donkey, like the one that pulled his wagon now, to be something of a talisman. A donkey was all Colombo left him with those many years ago when he was abandoned by that scoundrel on the hot and forested island of Guanahani. Had it not been for the exquisite she-donkey, Nonno never would have survived.

And so Nonno began, as he had a hundred times before, usually to the entertainment of children, secretly hoping that one day his Davido would recount the wonders of the donkey to his grandchildren in much the same way. "In the order of all things equine," Nonno said as he sat up a little straighter on the wagon seat, "donkeys are naturally smarter than horses. They have larger brains, live longer lives, have better eyesight and hearing and a vastly superior digestive system to that of horses. In fact, a donkey's belly can extract nutrition out of virtually any plant. Barbed shrubs that would lacerate a horse's gut and kill it, a donkey will merrily eat and prosper upon. Even the milk a she-donkey produces is more easily digestible and nutritious than that of any cow. And donkey cheese—oh, to taste a thing so fine!—sweeter and creamier than the best mascarpone in all of Lombardy!"

Davido cocked his head to the side with Nonno's last statement. That's a new twist, better than mascarpone?

"When it comes to brain power," Nonno continued, "few creatures rival the donkey. They have an intelligence and temperament far more sophisticated and resilient than that of the horse. Unlike their larger cousins, a donkey cannot be spooked. When startled, the donkey will not bolt and abandon either human or pack; it will simply remain still, assess the situation and then act accordingly. Additionally, the largely held belief that donkeys are stubborn is a misconception. What may appear as obstinacy is actually evidence of the creature's intelligence. Unlike a horse, a donkey will not walk where the footing is loose, will not drink from unclean water, such as a filthy horse trough, and will not willingly engage in any activity that it deems contrary to its well-being."

Davido smiled to himself. It had been some time since he'd last heard Nonno wax rhapsodically over the donkey, but it was still clear, the old man's opinion of the horse had certainly not changed.

"Indeed, if one takes a closer look, is it not revealing that even the Bible hints at the donkey's near-supernatural intelligence and loyalty? Of all the creatures mentioned in the Torah, it is only the donkey through which God takes voice, chiding the prophet Balaam to be more patient and respectful." Nonno turned to Davido. They could hear the sound of music and revelry and see the village entrance. "Pay special attention to this next part, it's important that children understand."

Davido nodded, though both he and Nonno knew he was not really listening.

"To the Children of Israel," Nonno continued anyhow as they passed through the village's large open gate, "the donkey has always been revered. From the moment the Romans expunged us from our homeland, the donkey has been the only pack animal available for us. Even as the centuries passed and our people settled in the villages and cities of Europe, we've maintained our connection to the donkey. During the holiday of Purim—that joyous celebration that recalls the biblical story of Esther—*Ebreo* communities the world over hold donkey races and donkey pageants so that every *Ebreo* child is raised to value and adore the donkey. For if ever there was a beast akin to our people, with its sagacity and knack for survival, it's the don—"

And then the sounds of revelry and the pounding of their hearts grew too loud, so that Nonno could hardly hear himself think, nor Davido hear his grandfather speak. But it was all true, everything Nonno had said about the donkey, especially the part about Purim. So much so that when Nonno and Davido rolled their wagon into the piazza, pulled by their

own beloved donkey, and saw the assemblage of festooned
donkeys and costumed riders parading about the piazza,
there was a wonderfully familiar quality to the scene.

"Like Purim," Nonno leaned over, close to his grandson's
ear, and then added dryly, "if Haman[16] had won."

"Ay," said Davido, as he too saw the connection. *Like Purim,*
he meant to answer, but just then he made the other connection—the one his eyes and heart sought. His vision found her,
there amid the crowd, filling a goblet from a wine barrel. And
it *was* like Purim; only, Queen Esther could not have been
half as beautiful.

Mari too looked up, and found Davido's eyes; and from
her eyes to her heart to her lips, she could not help but smile.
She had not seen him since their kiss of last week. He was so
lovely, she had been longing to see him, even scheming to see
him. And if, as she'd prayed every night, he *did* come to the
feast, she had a plan at the ready. Beginning with the wine:
Mari had not watered it down as Giuseppe had commanded.
Instead, she poured it full-strength and had brought two more
barrels than Giuseppe had ordered. She'd tapped the barrels
earlier than in years past, then filled goblets and bottles by
the dozen so that, even now, she could see the elated effects of
strong wine upon the spirits of the crowd. She would get them
drunk, every man and woman of the village. So drunk that
their eyes would go bleary and their memories faulty. Thus,
if by chance any reveler may happen to see Mari and the
Ebreo boy sneak down an alley to share a kiss, surely they'd
dismiss such a sight as the play of too much wine upon the
mind.

"Like Purim," Nonno repeated.

"Oh, yes," Davido agreed, as he pried his eyes from the
girl, "like Purim." To Davido, the whole scene really *was* like
the *Carnevale di Purim* back in the ghetto Florence, the way
he remembered it from his childhood—the food, wine and
minstrels; the men dressed in their ridiculous costumes and

---

[16] Villain of the biblical Book of Esther who attempted to destroy the *Ebrei* of Ancient
Persia.

mounted upon adorned donkeys. Even the antics of the spindly fool, babbling about something or other and riling the
crowd, reminded him of the way the villainous Haman was
portrayed and mocked at the Purim festival in Florence. But
then the fool's eye caught sight of the "guests" rolling into the
piazza and he moved his tongue in their direction. And suddenly, for Davido, it didn't seem like Purim at all.

In Which We Come
to Better Understand the
Symbology of the Drunken Saint Statue

Heads and eyes turned. The strumming and drumming of the minstrels petered out. The crowd went quiet with disbelief. *They had come.* There, before the villagers, escorted by the Good Padre and Bertolli, as many had feared but prayed would not be so, were the *Ebrei* and their wagon full of forbidden fruit.

"Welcome! Welcome, at last," Bobo repeated as he gestured to the *Ebrei* and then to the Good Padre. "My, how *twelve-plus-one* days did pass quite fast."

"Indeed they did," said the Good Padre. He had made sure this time he was a better host. He and Bertolli had waited for the *Ebrei* at the village gate and then personally escorted the young man, his grandfather and their wagon full of *pomodori* into the piazza.

"And your health?" said Bobo with a quick pat of the Good Padre's belly. "The question of our anticipation."

"Never better," answered the Good Padre. "Not a stitch of constipation."

Bobo raised his eyebrows inquisitively. "Hmm, not the runs, the shits, cramps or gas?"

"No."

"Or desperate sprints to the outhouse with fire in the ass?"

"No."

"Not boils, or seizures, or fits of cold sweat?"

"No."

"Or waking at night with your gown soaking wet?"

"No."

"No locking of jaw, aching of joint or loss of sight?"

"No."

"No reeling, no writhing, no fits of devilish fright?"

"No."

"You mean," said Bobo, "after twelve-plus-one days and twelve-plus-one accursed berries, not a moment of ill health, not a pain, not a worry?"

"Exactly," said the Good Padre. "I'm healthy as can be." The Good Padre reached his hand into the back of the wagon and took out a tomato. "Here, after all your talk, you should be first."

Bobo lifted his hand and exuberantly wagged his finger. "Oh, no, no."

"Is Bobo not a man of his word?"

"Depends which words," answered the fool, with raised eyebrows.

Nervous as he was, Davido almost burst out laughing.

"Come now," said the Good Padre, patting his belly affirmatively. "Do you not trust what you see before your eyes?"

"With you," Bobo pointed from the priest to the *Ebrei*, "or them? The eyes tell their lies."

"My goodness," said the Good Padre. "What, then, does Bobo need?"

"I will tell you." Bobo looked suspiciously from the Good Padre to Davido. "Foreign fruit, foreign face, I'd trust it more if he raced the race."

Who is this damn fool, thought Nonno, as he moved his eyes about the crowd. There were hundreds packed into the piazza, certainly every villager and nearby farmer, far more than he saw at market last. Nonno's vision searched until he found the familiar faces awaiting his gaze. They nodded back to him. Thank God, Rabbi Lumaca had gotten the letter he'd sent with Davido last Sunday and honored his request. They were the toughest *Ebrei* of Pitigliano (not that the *Ebrei* of Pitigliano were especially tough): butchers and blacksmiths and masons, dressed today like any other gentile peasant. Truthfully, Nonno did not think his life or his grandson's was in jeopardy. He found Italians tended to mix wine and revelry well, growing more amorous than vicious with their drunkenness. Nevertheless, Spain had left its scars, and Nonno was too old and wise to venture naked into a lion's den.

"Oh, by heaven!" The Good Padre threw up his hands in mock exasperation. "Join the donkey race? Only if he rides upon your back. For who could be a bigger ass?"

"Listen to your fool," Bobo said, addressing the crowd's laughter. "Foreign fruit, foreign face, it'd serve us all if he'd race the race."

The crowd began to boo and jeer. Davido felt his skin bristle as the fool, again, gestured in his direction.

"Do you see, Good Padre?" Bobo gestured to the crowd. "Do you not hear? Go ahead, serve the fruit, but we'll taste only fear. And then what good the bet, what good the bite, if we honor word but taste only fright?" Bobo turned to the crowd. "I ask you all: is this how this day among days was meant to start, by opening the mouth yet closing the heart? Is this how we would taint this day of our greatest pride? No, I say, better to open first the heart, then the mouth after the *Ebreo* does ride."

"Pride?" scoffed Benito from atop his donkey. "When our fool claims pride, 'tis time to run and hide."

The crowd broke into laughter and Benito sat upright on

his donkey, sucked in his belly and puffed up his chest. He felt almost regal in his purple *Cavalieri* outfit with its fine silk, fancy colors and large Roman numeral twelve upon his chest. Giuseppe, however, was not so pleased. *You deluded, blubbering idiot,* he thought, *what are you doing?* Contrary to his orders, Benito was not acting nearly drunk enough and now, as he had explicitly told him not to do, Benito was running his stupid mouth.

"No, no, do not say that, friend," said Bobo with a surprising earnestness as he stepped forward and took hold of Benito's left wrist. "I am not so horrid and ill-natured a fool to undo the day in which goodwill should rule. T'would be to the spirit of Saint and village a great disgrace, if a thirteenth rider didn't join the race."

Giuseppe inhaled the wine-scented air. *Thirteenth rider* was his cue to enter the fray, but as he opened his mouth, another voice emerged.

"But an *Ebreo*?" spat Vincenzo from atop his donkey. "This puny *Ebreo*?" He gestured dismissively toward Davido. "T'would be a double dishonor to Saint and vine."

My goodness, thought Davido, recalling the last time he saw the pork merchant, what have I done to this man?

"True," said Benito mockingly toward Vincenzo, "best to shorten the field for the old, fat swine."

The crowd laughed. It was true, and Vincenzo's fat face—stuffed and bulging under his red hat—turned crimson with anger. He was already married and too old to be racing in a young man's event, and his yearly participation in the race had become something of a village joke. But as *Capitano del Quadrante Otto,* Vincenzo could appoint as *Cavaliere* whomever he liked, and for the ninth year in a row, he liked himself.

"*Vaff,*" Vincenzo scoffed at Benito. "You too have your share of years and fat."

"But not such a share as that," replied Benito as he reached out with his left hand and gave a soft squeeze to Vincenzo's fleshy bosom. "I say, let the puny boy run, for all I care."

"You will pay for that upon the track," said Vincenzo.

"Really?" said Benito as he raised one finger before

Vincenzo's face. "Not even one lap 'fore you're off your donkey and on your back."

"Is that so?" said Vincenzo as the crowd howled with delight.

"*Ay.*" Benito smiled, knowing firsthand the prodigious sum Vincenzo's donkey had ejaculated just this morning. "Not even one lap."

"Care to wager?" asked Vincenzo.

Che stronzo! thought Giuseppe, through the hooting and howling and snorting of the crowd. *These idiots shall make a mockery of my intentions.* He could risk no more of this. "Oh, you flap-mouthed fools!" snapped Giuseppe with a poorly veiled air of lightheartedness. He stepped between the parade of donkeys. "I would wager that all this good wine go sour before either of you paunchy slobs takes the Battle of the Hours. Now," Giuseppe pointed to Bobo, "king of all fools, can you not find a better forum to take your pleasure?"

"But Bobo speaks to the common treasure," answered Bobo.

"Treasure? My God." Giuseppe looked to the clear sky above. "I fear a sudden thunder; our fool seeks to protect and not to plunder." Though many were privately weary of Giuseppe, he was not without his charms, and his unique ability to take the piss out of Bobo brought many to laughter. "As they have their feasts, we have ours, and it's not for an *Ebreo* to battle among the Hours. We agreed not to brotherhood, only to taste, so hold your fool's tongue and its treasonous haste."

Bobo frowned. "Do not mistake the truth for treason. Bobo does love his village, Saint and season."

"Love?" said Giuseppe with a chuckle. "Oh, I see. It is by love and not foolish tricks that you toss the *puny Ebreo* into the mix."

Again with the puny, thought Davido rather self-consciously. He did not like being degraded before the girl and subtly squeezed his own thigh to confirm his manliness. Though, it was hardly the beefy haunch of the purple-clad ogre before him, it was not the bookish chicken leg it used to be, either.

"Yes," said Bobo. "It is by love."

"And what today," asked Giuseppe, suddenly concerned that he was doing too well in an argument he need lose, "of all days, does inform our fool to speak of love and not of scorn?"

"Our very Saint," said Bobo as he gestured to the sculpture of the one-armed Drunken Saint at the center of the race oval.

"Oh, this should be good," said Giuseppe. "Tell us, then, fool, what secret and symbol in our Drunken Saint do we not see?"

"Notice," all heads turned as Bobo pointed to the statue, "but one *heart's arm*[17] to do less harm; belly full, fat with the good of life; countenance sweet, devoid of strife; satchel brimming with fruits of tree and vine; goblet overflowing with sacred wine. And as if to prove this merry lack of greed, he rides—as we race today—upon the humble steed. By donkey, grape and goblet our patron does slyly teach the earthly length of heaven's reach. Yet how by Saint are we to revel free of heart and mind, when here we see and soon we eat what is not of our kind? Hence, to keep sweet grape and Saint from turning sour, the boy must do battle as the thirteenth Hour. Our Saint would want it so."

Even Benito knew a perfect opportunity when he saw one, and in the midst of the collective silence he dismounted his donkey, stepped to the table adjacent to the race track, lifted from it his enormous wine bottle—the one to which he'd added a great deal of finely ground hot pepper—walked over to where the *Ebreo* boy sat atop his donkey-drawn wagon and extended the bottle to the boy.

Davido thought of the last Purim festival he'd attended some two years ago in Florence, in which he competed in the donkey race and was promptly and ignominiously knocked off by a boy not even his own size. That was before he became

---

[17] According to Etruscan tradition, the *heart's arm* was the left arm and was considered the peaceful side of the body that evoked the heart's energy, while the right arm was called the sword's arm and was used for wielding weapons and tools. Throughout Italy it was considered unmanly for a boy to be left-handed, and children who showed such inclination had it quickly trained out of them.

a farmer. He hoped he was stronger now—he certainly was more familiar with donkeys. His sister was still alive then, which naturally led Davido's thoughts to her. She'd had a bit of a wild streak and would have relished the situation her brother was currently in. This led Davido to think of the girl he was meant to marry on this day; she seemed to possess no adventurous side. And this thought moved Davido's eyes to find Mari's—eyes that seemed to be waiting for his. And then the run of Davido's thoughts halted and fixated upon one. "I will race," Davido heard himself say as he reached out and took the *Jeroboame* wine bottle from the man who held it. Davido saw the lips of the girl he adored curl ever so slightly upward, as if she was proud of him, and this, but for an instant, made Davido feel invincible. "I will race!"

"And so it is!" shouted the Good Padre, and the crowd erupted, *"Bravo!"*

Perfect, thought Giuseppe, absolutely perfect. Vincenzo, however, did not like the idea of being outdone by Benito. He also did not like the idea of having staked his pride against Benito—the man was strong as an ox—and he saw for himself the perfect opportunity to opt out of the race with honor. He dismounted his donkey, took hold of the wine bottle on the table set before the Roman numeral eight, his number, and with an air of formality offered it to Benito. "If one does not ride today," said Vincenzo, "it should be I." And for once, all in the village—all but Giuseppe—applauded Vincenzo.

With the bottle barely passed from Vincenzo to Benito and the air still loud with applause, the Good Padre felt a tug upon his frock. Bertolli pointed under the stand to the extra *Jeroboame* wine bottle. Of course his altar boy knew—he knew so many things—that it was tradition for the prescribed *Capitano* to bring an extra wine bottle to the race. He even knew, as few did, the real and ancient impetus for bringing an extra wine bottle: in case the Drunken Saint, observing the revelry happening in his honor, should decide to reappear.

The Good Padre bent down and lifted up the massive bottle. "By spirit of bless'd Saint," he said as he handed the extra bottle to Vincenzo and in so doing robbed the aging pork merchant of the very thing he so desired, "be it then twelve plus one, as Vincenzo stays in, and the *Ebreo* joins the run!"

For the villagers, all but Vincenzo, Giuseppe and a little piece of Mari, a fever of excitement stirred them. Yes, Mari too felt her share of exhilaration, but her enthusiasm was laced with concern. Of course, she was excited that the boy she adored appeared to have some guts, and certainly, his entry into the race would afford her an unadulterated opportunity to marvel upon his beauty. Nonetheless, she was equally concerned about his well-being. He did not seem to be a brutal boy—not with those soft and kind eyes—and the race was a rough affair, bound to be even rougher with this year's inclusion of Benito. Historically, the race was marked by knocking and punching and jostling and a ridiculous, near-belly-bursting abundance of drinking, none of which—and yet all of which—she desired to see her tomato boy put through. Then there was Giuseppe, who felt not a shred of amity and was instead roiling with the horrible acid of a plan gone awry. All Giuseppe could hope for was that somehow the mind-twisting distillation of *Fungi di Santo* in the bottle of wine that Benito would *now* be drinking might not affect a mind so already twisted.

"Then get the boy off his wagon and upon his donkey," shouted Vincenzo in what would prove to be his last moment of glory for the day, "and let us race!"

In Which We Learn
the Unusual Manner in Which the
Battle of the Hours Crowns a Champion

The crowd loosed another *"Bravo!"* as they pressed in and around Davido, undoing the ropes that bound his donkey to the wagon. Others took hold of Davido's arms and legs, until he found himself hoisted from his wagon seat and set onto the bare back of his donkey, with the wine bottle still on his lap. From the corner of his eye Davido saw his grandfather's bewildered expresson as he too was lifted from his wagon seat and set gently upon the ground. Then Davido felt his body react against a tug on the wine bottle and suddenly realized the excessive firmness of his clench. Embarrassed, he looked to the Good Padre, who smiled back at him. Davido loosed his grip and watched the enormous bottle pass through the crowd until it wound up in the hands of Nonno. It was heavy and he hoped Nonno would not drop it. Then Davido felt something cool and wet upon his skin—a sensation he thought for an instant to be the precursor of great pain, but quickly realized it to be the coolness and wetness of paint as the Roman numeral thirteen was painted onto the front and back of his tunic in bright red. No sooner had that sensation receded than Davido's body again twanged with panic; he felt a loop of rope tighten around his right wrist. But the act was done without brutality and Davido's sudden rush of anxiety receded as he looked up and saw that all the other racers had their right hands tied behind their backs in a similar fashion. Thank God, thought Davido with a clarity that startled him, I'm a lefty.

⊛   ⊛   ⊛

"Merda!" gasped Mari as she suddenly remembered her mother sitting there. Though it nearly killed Mari to give up such a fine vantage from which to watch the action, she knew it was too dangerous a spot for her mother. With her attention so fixated on the boy and her hands so busy filling wine goblets, the area around her wine barrel was now precariously overcrowded. One good jostle of the crowd and the half barrel upon which her mother sat would no doubt topple over. Quickly, Mari closed the spigot on the barrel and saddled up to her mother. *"Maggio!"* (short for *formaggio*), Mari shouted, purposefully catching the Cheese Maker's attention.

"Oh, goodness!" said the Cheese Maker, bushy eyebrows vaulted with concern as he shuffled over to Mari and her mother. *"Uno, due, tre,"* he nodded to Mari as he took hold of the crippled woman's right arm and together they helped lift her to her feet and usher her out of the crowd.

As always, there were a few benches set up on the roof of the bakery so the old and infirm could have a safe place from which to watch the action. It would take an able-bodied person hardly two minutes to make it there, which meant it took her mother, even with help, at least twice as long. *Mio Dio!* Mari felt a cleaver of guilt and desire split her in half. It was just too long to be away. "Please?" Mari looked desperately to the Cheese Maker and then gestured to the bakery's roof. "I've got to get back to my wine barrel," Mari lied. "If Giuseppe sees it unattended, I'll be in an awful heap."

"By all means, love," answered the Cheese Maker, both sweetly and urgently. "Go, go! I'll see to your mother."

🍅   🍅   🍅

Now Davido heard the strum and beat of the minstrels' lute and drum, and the crowd pushed in more forcefully. A man whom Davido might one day come to know as Signore Solo Coglione, the tavern keep, smiled at him warmly as he took hold of Davido's donkey's rein and paraded the boy, with all the other outlandishly adorned *Cavalieri,* around the piazza. Everything was happening so fast. It seemed to Davido like pure chaos, but he could tell in the ecstatic faces of the villagers and the coordination of their actions that there were centuries of purpose and tradition informing every move.

The parade continued about the piazza, while the villagers began to divide and cluster together by color around their quadrant's *Cavaliere* and donkey. The townspeople frolicked and gulped from wine-filled goblets, jugs and bottles. They sprinkled knight and donkey alike with wine, not unlike priests sprinkling parishioners with holy water, until it seemed as if it were raining red wine. They kissed the donkeys' noses and scratched lovingly between their ears, and many, to Davido's surprise, even rubbed their donkey's testicles in a way similar to how Davido had seen Catholics rub the bald head of Saint Francis statues for good luck. The villagers now pumped their fists in the air as each *Quadrante* took turns shouting out their number at the top of their lungs: *"Numero Uno, Numero Due, Numero Tre . . ."* and so on. Davido's ears perked with expectation as the piazza rung with *dieci, undici, dodici,* but alas, not even one voice called out in support of number thirteen. And before Davido knew what was happening he found himself coaxed into position, side by side with all the other *Cavalieri* into something of a starting line.

Davido did not turn to look—he was too nervous to do so—but on his right he glimpsed the beefy ogre of a man who had given him his wine bottle, and on his left, the pork merchant who seemed to dislike *Ebrei* immensely. This did not strike Davido as an especially promising starting position. Then a rope was pulled before the racers to keep the donkeys from moving forward. The crowd was pushed back to the hay- and dirt-lined edges of the track until they formed a perimeter of humanity ten persons deep, creating a perfect race oval, with the statue of the Drunken Saint at its center.

The noise echoing throughout the piazza was overwhelmingly loud as the crowd continued shouting out the cycle of numbers time and again: *"Numero Sei, Numero Sette, Numero Otto . . ."* Davido scanned the crowd to find the stabilizing face of Mari. He could not locate her, but his vision found his grandfather just as the Good Padre positioned Nonno beside the wine table and placed a wine screw in his hand. Davido held his grandfather's eyes, hoping to glean from them any strength and insight he might have to offer. Slowly, Nonno's lips broke with the slightest of smirks and in an instant Davido got what he was searching for.

'Tis strange, thought Davido through the noise and chaos, that a smirk can reveal so much. On the surface, Nonno's smirk did exactly what a good smirk does: it mocked Davido's current predicament and reproved him for ignoring the wisdom and cautions of his grandfather. But beyond the mockery, there was a crinkle of the lip and a glint in the old man's eyes that revealed how it was that his grandfather had survived Colombo's voyage, the desperate years living among the *Indiani* of the New World, the decade spent hiding throughout Italy, the plagues, the heartbreaks and everything else. Put simply, his Nonno was mad. Not mad as in angry or crazy, but mad in that he possessed a cultivated and indomitable life force that was somehow greater than the circumstances life threw at him, no matter how dire. In that moment Davido saw that there was something about Nonno that could not be broken. He hoped to God that he too possessed such a madness.

The Good Padre walked past the line of *Cavalieri* and up to the statue of the Drunken Saint. Then he turned toward the *Nobiluomi* table and raised his hulking arms. Instantly the reveling of five hundred villagers stilled, just as Bertolli said it would (this was, after all, the Good Padre's first time presiding over the *Festa* and he had relied on his altar boy a great deal). The silence was startling to Davido—the proverbial quiet before the storm—and a good part of his being wanted nothing more than to run from this crazed village all the way back to the safety of his farm. But then, just as one might expect in a tale such as this, the drunken, sea-like swaying of the crowd parted and Davido found his eyes locked upon those of Mari. The sight stiffened Davido's resolve and he remembered precisely his motivation for why he'd come to the feast. For such eyes, such a look, were worthy of risking life and limb for.

In the midst of the silence, Bertolli, dressed in his finest altar boy cassock, made the ceremonial walk past the line of *Cavalieri* and up to the Good Padre. He carried a pillow upon which sat a wreath made of olive and grape vines and leaves and an ornate aspergillum filled with holy water. The Good Padre lifted the wreath from the pillow, held it high for the entire crowd to see and then, with a great ovation from the crowd, turned and set the wreath upon the Drunken Saint's bald head. Next, the Good Padre lifted the aspergillum from the pillow, spoke a few words in Latin, and then sprinkled the first *Cavaliere* and his donkey with holy water.

Davido had never been sprinkled with holy water and looked anxiously to Nonno as the Good Padre made his way down the line of *Cavalieri*. Nonno returned his grandson's gaze with a slight shrug and lift to his eyebrows that seemed to say: *when in Rome . . .* Davido felt the cool water sprinkle upon his face. A drop ran down his cheek, perched on his lip and sent a ripple of conflict through his psyche. The confusion, though, was short-lived, as quickly Davido sucked the holy water into his mouth, figuring he could use all the luck he could get today.

The Good Padre raised his arms again and the crowd fell silent. Standing before the wine table, he commanded: "*Nobiluomi del Vino,* reveal the sacred juice." Swiftly, the men who manned the wine table set their corkscrews to bottles and Davido saw that even Nonno fell in line as corks were pulled. With the wine bottles open, the Good Padre again addressed the table and said, "Squires of the Wine, pour forth the first goblet." In near-unison the *Nobiluomi* tilted the great bottles and filled the goblets before them. Davido noticed that Nonno did not spill as much as some of the other men.

Now the Good Padre turned his attention to the riders on the track. Slowly he stepped to the side, out of the direct line of the racers' path. The men holding either side of the starting rope across the track pulled it especially taut. Davido felt the muscles of his donkey twitch with urgency. With his free left hand, he gave a gentle, reassuring pat upon the coarse hair of his donkey's neck. The beast bristled defiantly, as if he knew that it was not he who needed the reassurance. This was just one of the ways that Davido found the donkey to be a lot like Nonno: still full of piss and vinegar and with no tolerance for placation.

The donkey Davido sat upon was the obstinate old male first introduced in the opening page of this story—the one most favored by Nonno: Signore Meducci. Named thusly because he appeared to have been left by the Meducci winemakers years earlier, the creature roamed about the farm with an air of entitlement that was nothing short of regal. The old donkey listened to and seemed to respect no one but Nonno. He pretended to be deaf when called, but always seemed to hear well the hoof-steps of his favorite female.

Despite his somewhat haughty and cantankerous demeanor, Signore Meducci was old and slow and thought to be blind in one eye. Worse still, the old beast had begun to lose control of the muscles that keep a donkey's penis drawn up tight to the belly, so that when he walked, his prodigious *cazzone* would often waddle and knock between his bony thighs. However, on occasion, he could still muster some spirit. Nonetheless, it had not been Davido's idea to harness him to the wagon this morning, but Nonno deemed Signore Meducci something of a talisman. The conversation about Nonno's choice of donkey had gone like this:

"Buono," said Nonno as he and his grandson regarded the swayback, penis-dangling, sorry sight of old Signore Meducci begrudgingly harnessed to a wagon full of tomatoes.

"Good?" repeated Davido incredulously.

"Indeed," answered Nonno, " 'tis always best to appear humble before gentiles."

Merda di toro, Davido thought. He knew his grandfather too well to take a half truth for whole—better to have a senile old donkey dangle his fat *cazzone* before a village of rhymers was more like it. Indeed, by all outward appearances Signore Meducci could not have seemed more unfit for the challenge ahead; but like Nonno, the old donkey was tough and shrewd and seemed to share a penchant for survival.

"Cavalieri," the Good Padre's voice now boomed as he raised his arms. The crowd looked on anxiously. This was all part of the ritual and they knew well the words to come. "By bless'd Saint and sacred season, gather all for holy reason." Many voices from the crowd began to join the Good Padre as he led the ancient invocation. "Gather for grape and wine, gather for olive and oil, gather to honor Saint and soil. Gather young men of honor and power; gather to battle for the hour."

The crowd roared with applause. The Good Padre continued as more voices joined in. *"Quadranti* and *Capitani* send forth your knights and hear the rules to race it right." Five hundred voices now rang like thunder through the piazza. "Twelve laps, twelve goblets drunk, he who's dropped is he who's sunk." Davido felt his hair stand on end. He took a quick, panicked gulp of air. It was happening. "First to finish in twelve laps' time; first to finish his bottle of wine; first to place a hand upon the shrine; is he who wears the olive and vine. So raise your goblet and *Cavalieri* set your mark, for the Race of the Drunken Saint does hereby start!"

⊛　　　⊛　　　⊛

Attraverso Gli Occhi di un Estraneo, wrote Pozzo Menzogna in his eloquent treatise on drama, *Il Trattato Definitivo sul Dramma.* The idea being, according to Menzogna, that when faced with a large and compelling scene (an epic battle, or perhaps a donkey race) filled with familiar faces, it is, on occasion, insightful to establish the scene and relay the action *through the eyes of a stranger.* This need not mean an absolute newcomer to the story, which Menzogna argued would be quite distracting, but a character or player familiar to the tale in general, and yet unfamiliar—or *strange,* as Menzogna put it—to a particular environment. The introduction of *strange* eyes to a familiar environment affords the reader a heightened sense of objectivity and increases that all-important quality of verisimilitude. Additionally, witnessing an event through *strange eyes* eradicates the need to move between numerous perspectives. This intensifies the wonder and immediacy of the action at hand and allows for a more natural compression of linear time, for instance, as may happen here, moving straight from the first lap of the donkey race to the penultimate. Finally, viewing events through the eyes of a stranger makes for a telling juxtaposition when in the climactic moments the perspective shifts back to the familiar and subjective eyes of the story's hero: *Attraverso Gli Occhi dell' Eroe.*

Hence, with Davido and Benito directly involved in the action and Mari, Nonno, the Good Padre, Giuseppe, Bobo the Fool and Cosimo di Pucci de' Meducci the Third all pressed in among the exuberant throng and overtly or secretly hopeful for one outcome or another, and with Mucca, Signore Coglione, Bertolli, Vincenzo, Augusto Po and the Cheese Maker all present but not significant enough to our story to entrust the retelling of such important events, Menzogna would assuredly recommend that we look through the eyes of Chef Luigi Campoverde to recount the opening lap of the Drunken Saint's Race, for Luigi, familiar as he may be to the reader, had no idea what in the world he'd just happened upon.

Luigi had arrived in the village just an hour ago, yet he was already disappointed in himself for getting drunk so quickly. Of course, rolling into the village on what happened to be its most raucous and celebratory feast day proved compelling even to a tightly bound elitist adamantly averse to keeping company with lowly rhymers. And yes, the sight of the profoundly pleasant priest, or Good Padre, as he seemed to be called, prompted Luigi to drain his first two goblets with great urgency. Plus, the wine was free and delicious, and the girl who served it a delight to look upon. But what should happen to him if the duke were to find him in such a debauched state? Certainly, he'd be out of a job.

God knows, Luigi's original intent for visiting the village was harrowing enough. He had not come to the far-off hamlet to shop or *barter,* as one might expect of a chef so inclined to bargains and petty thievery, but to inform the duke-in-hiding that his son, Prince Gian, missed his father dearly and feared that he was dead. But then the race started and Luigi Campoverde, snobbish, guarded, paranoid and peculiar as he may be, became totally engrossed in the action just like the Duke of Tuscany and all the lowly *rimatori* in the piazza.

What's this? thought Luigi Campoverde, as his head and shoulders felt suddenly wet. There was wine everywhere. No sooner had the starting rope dropped and before a single donkey had taken a step, the entire sky turned crimson with red wine as each and every villager threw the contents of their goblets in the direction of the *Cavalieri*—no matter how far they were from the action. One could get drunk by drinking the sky, thought Luigi, as red wine continued to rain down. The donkeys and riders, dripping of wine, set off down the track and Luigi found himself startled again, this time by the sloppiness of the race's start. Hardly ten strides into the race, the *Cavalieri* began to beat and pummel one another with their left hands. The action was more comical than brutal as uncoordinated blows missed their marks, slipping off noses and cheeks, heads and shoulders.

Wine bottles passed through the crowd so that no one need be empty of goblet for drinking or for tossing, and Luigi quickly refilled his travel goblet. Drunk and most unlike himself, he burrowed deeper into the crowd, managing to squirm his way closer to the action.

Unintentionally, Luigi found himself just a few feet behind the young *Ebreo*'s grandfather, who, along with the other

Nobiluomi del Vino, manned the *Jeroboame* wine bottle set upon the long table aside the track. He was surprised to see that while ten of the *Cavalieri* were nearly halfway through their first lap, the other three riders had barely stepped from the starting line. Why, he thought, would anyone choose such lazy donkeys for so important a contest? The crowd, especially those from opposing quadrants, found the three donkeys' indifference rather hilarious and mercilessly heckled and drenched the desperate riders in wine and insults. Upon the track the other ten riders were rounding the bend on their first lap and it wasn't looking so good for the *Ebreo* boy—Luigi didn't expect it would go well for him.

Seated upon his trotting donkey, Vincenzo the pork merchant reached across his own body and secured a firm grip on the *Ebreo* boy's collar and was now attempting to drag him off his donkey. The poor boy had a look upon his face of utter bewilderment; still, his legs and left arm clenched firmly around his donkey. "Look at that!" Luigi pointed and shouted to no one in particular as the *Ebreo*'s donkey suddenly dropped his *cazzone.*

"Ay!" The crowd gasped in amazement at the simultaneously pathetic and awesome sight of the old donkey's colossal *cazzone* dangling and bouncing between his gnarled knees. (Marveling at the size of a donkey's *cazzone* was something of a village pastime.)

You idiot, thought Luigi, as he watched Vincenzo vainly look to the crowd, *they're not cheering for you!* It was just enough of a pause to allow the *Ebreo* boy to reach out and cuff his left hand around the heel of Vincenzo's boot. "Ay!" the crowd erupted in near-unison as the *Ebreo* boy quickly sat up, swinging his left arm and Vincenzo's right foot in a wide and skyward motion. From the look upon his face, Vincenzo's mind seemed unable to fully grasp what was happening to his body as his own foot suddenly swung above his head. And, just as predicted, in a spectacular backflip that tossed his feet over his head, rolled him backward off the ass of his donkey and pitched him face-first upon the hay- and dirt-strewn track, Vincenzo fell off his donkey, a mere seven strides short of one lap.

"Bravo!" the crowd exploded in a spontaneous show of emotion based not on any affinity for the *Ebreo,* but on the sheer uniqueness of the move. None of the villagers had ever seen a donkey-heel-flip before. Luigi noticed a look of delight upon the old *Ebreo's* face and was utterly surprised to discover he was clasping the old man's hand in an act of shared drunken joy.

The hand-holding didn't last long, as a jostling in the crowd knocked Luigi to his right. Instinctively, Luigi looked to his left and witnessed a mad scramble by the crowd to grab what had just been Vincenzo's wine bottle. It appeared that once a *Cavaliere* was off his mount the prized wine inside his *Jeroboame* bottle was up for grabs. And before Luigi knew what was happening, a pair of youths were pouring wine directly from the enormous bottle into every nearby mouth, open or not.

"Uh-oh," sighed nearly the entire crowd. Quickly, the youths lowered the bottle from Luigi's mouth and all three returned their full attention to the track. The crowd could see what was about to happen. Nine *Cavalieri* rounded the final bend and trotted speedily (donkeys do not gallop) toward the wine table and straight toward the three *Cavalieri* whose donkeys had yet to move from the starting line area. The three were sitting ducks! But it was the actions of the stout troll that caught Luigi's eye. What was his name? Luigi scanned his memory—the one who'd accompanied the truffle merchant that day. Ah, yes, Benito. He was the one who led the charge, with the most cunning and vicious efficiency. Rather than attack *uomo a uomo,* Benito encouraged one of the other riders, *Cavaliere Sette,* to attack first and then he attacked *Cavaliere Sette* just as *Cavaliere Sette* was about to dislodge sitting-duck *Cavaliere Tre.* That's a lot of numbers, yes, but suffice it to say that with a most untender face grip, Benito made certain that both riders Seven and Three were rudely tossed from their donkeys. Maybe he's not as dumb as

I first thought, mused Luigi. And like that, the pack of thirteen was down to seven.

With four *Cavalieri* now dumped from their donkeys, another wild scramble ensued and Luigi found himself pushed
and bumped until he was virtually on top of the old *Ebreo*.
He had never been so close to an *Ebreo* before. Odd, thought
Luigi, he doesn't have horns or smell like a goat. "Like
Purim," Luigi overheard the old *Ebreo* say wryly amid the
sea of noise as Nonno handed a full wine goblet to his grandson. Luigi didn't know what the word meant, but it obviously
had some meaning between them as it took the edge off the
boy's panic-ridden face. "Like Purim," the boy answered as he
grabbed the goblet and quickly drank down its contents.

"Blah!" went the *Ebreo* boy.

Luigi reared back, fearing an explosion of vomit when
the boy pulled the drained goblet from his lips and threw
his mouth wide open as if he'd just drunk a cup of fire. The
old *Ebreo* grabbed the goblet from his grandson and brought
it to his nose to smell; he winced and Luigi clearly saw the
fine remnants of hot pepper flakes. *Figlio di puttana!* Luigi
thought, someone spiked the boy's wine bottle. The old *Ebreo*
gritted his teeth and leaned in toward his grandson. "Not a
peep," Luigi heard the old *Ebreo* say with a look that carried
far more meaning than any three words might. A look that
even inspired Luigi to stand up a little straighter and stiffen
his resolve. To applause and shouts the *Cavalieri* finished off
their goblets and headed back onto the track. Even the old
Ebreo smacked the donkey on the ass and gave it a push.
"Ride hard, Meducci," Luigi swore he heard the old man say,
though he doubted it immediately.

Again, Luigi felt a jostling on his left side as four *Jeroboame*
wine bottles were lifted from the *Nobiluomi*'s table and held
up to the crowd. Pairs of men held the bottles shoulder-high
and began to sift their way through the sea of bodies, pausing
to pour the prized wine directly into the mouths of a hundred
villagers. Delicious, thought Luigi, as he set a hand upon
the neck of the bottle, steadied his lips to the smooth glass
and did for a third time what an hour ago would have struck

him as utterly appalling: share his lips upon the same bottle as a hundred foul-breathed rhymers. Such is the way of feasts, when it is so often the tightest wrapped who come the most undone. And as the laps mounted and the *Cavalieri* fell one by one, Luigi pressed his lips to every bottle lifted from the *Nobiluomi* table, no matter whose lips preceded his and, gratefully, greedily drank down the succulent juice.

This was different wine, he thought—the best he'd ever tasted. It warmed his joints and made his body feel so wonderfully fluid that the swaying of the crowd gave him the sensation of being an infant, secured with a soft shawl between his mother's large and bouncing bosoms. This was different wine, he thought—sweet as honey, rich as butter—and it defrosted his mind and melted the ice that encased his heart. And as the laps mounted and the *Cavalieri* fell, while the *Ebreo* boy bravely survived, Luigi found he was falling in love with him and his sweet grandfather, and wanted more than anything in the world for this boy to win the race. Oh, Luigi mused, savoring his final thought before we leave his eyes, if only somebody had loved me the way this grandfather loves his grandson.

⊛   ⊛   ⊛

Attraverso Gli Occhi dell' Eroe: "Ay!" Davido heard the entire crowd groan in unison. Why, he thought, why are they making that noise? But then came a feeling from the depths of Davido's stomach, and he understood why. I am afraid, thought Davido, a portion of his mind oddly detached from time and the immediacy of his experience, that I shall not enjoy spicy food again for quite some time.

Much happened in the shared blink between our *stranger's* and our *hero's* eyes. As to be expected in a tale such as this, by the final lap the race was down to Davido and Benito. Benito had been a scourge upon the track, leveling nearly the entire field and doing what needed be done to protect the *Ebreo*. And Davido, despite the fiery bucketful of hot-peppered red wine sloshing about his belly, had managed to outlast much of the field. Two things had worked immensely in

Davido's favor to keep him in the race. The first, obviously unbeknownst to Benito, was that capsaicin, the chemical that makes some peppers hot, has a slightly mitigating effect upon alcohol. So much so that Davido, not an especially prodigious drinker, would have surely come undone by his ninth goblet had Benito not added crushed hot pepper to his wine. The second was that *Ebrei* did not subscribe to the same superstitions regarding left-handedness as *Cristiani* and allowed their children to favor whichever hand to which they were naturally inclined—a fact that made Davido defter at deflecting blows than many stronger riders were at delivering them. This was not to say that Davido didn't absorb a good many whacks—he did—and survived a few near-calamities, some with the last-second assistance of Benito. But Davido had done well for himself and even managed to undo another rider in the ninth lap using the same heel-flip technique he'd utilized earlier with Vincenzo.

At the point our tale returns to the track, Davido and Benito had drunk their last goblet, dismounted their donkeys and wrestled their way to the foot of the Drunken Saint statue, a mere arm's-length from victory. They were on their knees, engaged in a desperate, drunken, one-armed battle. Davido pushed with all his might to squirm and free himself from Benito's clasp upon his collar. Benito's smell was horrible, his clasp like iron and the manner in which he mumbled to himself—bizarre and horrible things—was rather terrifying. But they were drunk (capsaicin or not), drenched and slippery with wine and sweat, and it was not easy wrestling with one arm tied behind one's back.

Suddenly, now, Davido felt Benito's clasp upon his collar release. Instinctively, Davido's body reacted. He stretched forth his left arm, his whole body lengthening to touch the statue and claim victory. Then Davido heard a noise—a deep, empathetic groan. He felt his torso go limp, as if all the breath in his body had been suddenly plunged out. Some part of him, a part that seemed to be a few feet removed and a witness to the event, told the other part of him that he'd been punched in the stomach. This same part told the other part that, with his left arm outstretched, his rib cage lifted and his belly bloated with wine, Benito's blow was solid and devastating and that something awful was now about to happen.

🍅   🍅   🍅

Oh, you foul, vile, cowardly, murderous idiot, shouted La Piccola Voce from inside Benito's head, *what a stupid place to punch this boy!* For nearly all the other *Cavalieri* and many in the crowd too, the effects of ingesting good red wine tainted with *Fungi di Santo* was rather delightful. As the laps and goblets mounted, colors grew brighter, sounds more crisp and clear, touch more titillating, experience more immediate, observation more nuanced and emotions more inclined to laughter and goodwill. And as Benito bested nearly the entire field—one by hair and one by ear, one by nostril and one by neck—even for the vanquished there was sublimity. Muscles worked as never before, so that even the most portly felt like Hercules battling valiantly through one or another of his Twelve Labors. Hands and fingertips, though engaged in harsh battle, felt as alive when brushing against the coarseness of a man's beard as they ever felt upon the softness of a woman's *fighetta.* Human thighs conjoined with the animals they rode created a sense of bestial unification so overwhelming that, by the sixth lap, four of the *Cavalieri* felt as if they were a new breed of centaur: half man, half donkey. Even the pain was glorious.

But poor Benito felt none of this delight. The *Fungi di Santo* had transformed the little voice inside his head into a raving demon. It turned the faces of the other *Cavalieri* into his face, only worse—with horns and fangs and thick eyebrows that squirmed like maggots upon raw meat—so that in beating the other racers he was beating himself. Moreover, in the ninth lap, when Benito's eyes caught sight of the dangling *cazzone* of the *Ebreo*'s donkey, the phallus grew and came to life like a serpent. The huge serpent *cazzone* slapped upon Benito's cheeks, writhed over his ears and pissed on his face. The serpent *cazzone* cursed and mocked him for defiling the other knights' donkeys and for sabotaging the *Ebreo*'s red wine. *Not man enough to win by merit,* taunted the giant pink donkey dick as it tried to slither its way up Benito's nose.

And then, when he and the *Ebreo* dismounted and battled to within inches of victory, La Piccola Voce tormented him from inside the *Ebreo's* stomach, moving Benito to punch the boy in the unwisest of places and then mocking him for doing so: *Eat his vomit, you horrid, murderous coward.* The little voice rang so loudly through Benito's head that he did not hear the voluminous, disgusted groan of five hundred villagers. *Open your mouth and swallow his vomit,* the voice screamed, and Benito dropped his jaw in acquiescence. *Eat!* it shouted as a crimson torrent of predigested red wine and hot pepper exploded from the *Ebreo's* mouth directly into the face and open mouth of Benito. *Eat, it is the meal you most deserve!*

31

Sobbing & Laughing, Part I

"**A**nche *Il Santo ci beffa,*" Davido heard or dreamt through the blackness, *the Saint mocks us too.* He could not quite place the voice, but there was something familiar about it, something that made him think or dream of a cow. He wondered, or dreamt, if perhaps *he* was dead. He wondered why an angel would say such a thing?

It was the voice of Mucca, and she, along with Augusto Po, Signore Coglione, the Cheese Maker, Bertolli, six *Ebrei* from Pitigliano, Vincenzo, Bobo the Fool, Luigi Campoverde, Cosimo di Pucci de' Meducci the Third, the Good Padre, Giuseppe, Nonno, Mari and roughly four hundred and eighty-two villagers and peasants were standing in a tightly packed circle around the statue of the Drunken Saint and the two prone, vomit-splattered and semi-unconscious *Cavalieri.* "The Saint mocks us too," Mucca repeated.

It was frighteningly quiet in the piazza. All the drunken revelry of a moment ago silenced by the conundrum of what they'd just witnessed. The *Ebreo* had clearly won. No doubt, with his arm outstretched, he'd touched the statue of the Drunken Saint, then fallen over and passed out. *IL FESTA DEL SANTO UBRIACO* HAD BEEN WON BY AN *EBREO!*

Standing there, looking down upon the mess (though far enough away so as to not tarnish his shoes), Augusto Po wondered if it was a legal victory. There were no formal rules regarding such things, yet technically speaking, the *Ebreo* did vomit up his goblets before he'd touched the statue, which could be grounds for disqualification. But then again, he'd been punched in the stomach, and considering the current state of Benito, Po thought it best to hold his tongue. Still, his was a sentiment shared by most, and the very confounding root of the matter. Was it better to have a seemingly virtuous and little-known *Ebreo* who had just vomited win the beloved race, or a well-known, entirely unvirtuous boor, who had just eaten vomit?

Of course, the six *Ebrei* from Pitigliano wanted Davido to win. So too did Luigi Campoverde, as well as Giuseppe and Mari, though for very different reasons. Bobo, on the other hand, could have cared less who officially won. To him, the mere fact that the race had come down to Benito and the *Ebreo* was in itself a gloriously sacrilegious victory. And as if that weren't enough, to have the *Ebreo* vomit directly into the open mouth of Benito lent the affair an exquisite poetry that not even Bobolito could have dreamt up. Cosimo di Pucci de' Meducci, all too used to humiliation, felt tremendous empathy for his friend Benito, but the *Ebreo* boy looked so much like Cosimo's beloved courtesan that he could not help but hope the boy would be declared the victor. For Nonno, there really was no question: the *Cristiano* should win. Certainly, grandfatherly pride was a factor, but for Nonno a controversial defeat was better than a Pyrrhic victory. Of course, during the race he'd wanted his boy to win, but now that the race was over Nonno was calculating the long-term implications, and by those criteria he saw more harm than good coming from an *Ebreo* victory.

"Acqua," shouted Giuseppe as he pushed his way through the crowd, "water!" Giuseppe never was one for group consensus.

The crowd made space for Giuseppe. They were relieved that the current quandary might be settled by someone. Not that it was Giuseppe's decision to make, but he was the only one speaking up, and as the village's largest employer, Captain of the Twelfth Hour—for whom Benito rode—and the supplier of wine for this year's race, his opinion carried a certain magnitude.

Acqua, Davido heard through the blackness, *acqua.* And he dreamt of water. Cool and clean water. What a bizarre dream, that water should feel so real. The water flooded his face, filled his nostrils and transformed his dream to one of drowning. Then, with a startle and a cough, the dream ended. The water was real.

"You two," said Giuseppe, pointing at a pair of men who happened to be standing closest to Benito's feet and then pointing to the prone and vomit-covered Benito, "off with him." The men dragged Benito away by his boots.

Giuseppe now emptied a second bucket of water upon Davido.

Davido coughed as he came to awareness.

"Don't just stand there," said Giuseppe to one of the workers from his mill, "help the boy up." Giuseppe turned his head to the right, "And you too," he said to what looked like the fittest man close by.

The men stepped forward and grabbed the *Ebreo* from under his arms, helping him to his feet. The boy was unsteady and the two men looked to each other for a kind of assurance. It was at that very moment that Luigi Campoverde, chef to the Duke of Tuscany, realized that supporting the *Ebreo* boy's other arm was his boss, the duke. Luigi felt his knees weaken as every intoxicated nerve of his body rang with alarm. *Surely I'll be out of a job now!* Cosimo too was similarly startled, but the feeling was quickly overwhelmed by a sensation far more powerful. Beneath the odor of vomit and wine, Cosimo's olfactory sense deciphered a scent that instantly transported him from the task at hand and placed his memory acutely where his nose had once been: the soft armpit of his beloved courtesan after a warm evening spent drinking wine and making love. My God, thought Cosimo, as he felt himself entirely dislocate between what is and what had once been, the boy smells just like his sister!

🍅   🍅   🍅

"You drunken idiots," barked Giuseppe to the pair of men who had suddenly and simultaneously crumpled to the ground and brought the *Ebreo* boy down with them. "This is no way to treat a champion!"

Dutifully, the Good Padre and many from the crowd moved in and helped all three men to their feet.

"*Bene, bene,*" said Davido softly as he steadied his legs under him. It seemed safer to stand on his own.

Giuseppe lifted the olive and grape vine wreath from the Drunken Saint statue and raised it to the crowd's attention. "Behold," he said with a great air of formality, "*Il Vincitore!*"

Davido looked about in disbelief as the entire crowd encircling him dropped to one knee as if the Duke of Tuscany himself had just arrived.

"Let me be the first," said Giuseppe as he held the wreath over Davido's head, "to state here admittedly the wrong I've done this brave boy of Italy. For never was a braver race ever run and never by a braver knight was it ever won. So let all here recognize and accept without complaint: the hero, the victor, champion of our beloved sain—"

"Look!" shouted a shocked Bertolli, as he pointed to the donkey that just moments ago had carried its rider to victory. The poor beast was in the throes of death, foaming at the mouth, twitching his lips and flailing his tongue in an entirely unnatural manner. Heads turned. The noise was horrible and sublime at the same time. There was a pounding of hoof, a wheezing inhale of a *hee* and then a short and desperate burst of *haw*. But the *haw* was not complete—the sound suddenly drained of life—as the donkey collapsed to the ground.

"Ay!" Davido cried out as he leapt out from under the wreath and toward the noise. "Signore Meducci! Signore Meducci *e morto!*"

The animalistic wail, the pained look upon the boy's face, the sound of dead weight dropping to the ground sent a ripple of confusion through the tightly packed crowd. "The duke?" said a skeptical voice in the crowd. "The duke is dead?"

"Who is dead?" said Mucca as a chorus of "Ehs?" and "huhs?" and "whats?" and "whos?" fluttered through the crowd. Instantly, there was a great reorienting of the mass to see what had happened.

Vaffanculo, thought Giuseppe as the crowd's attention entirely shifted focus.

Luigi Campoverde heard the cry of *Signore Meducci* echo through his drunk and drugged mind. He felt his heart sink, *My boss is dead?* Could it be? I was just looking at him! Poor Gian, he thought, I have failed my prince. What am I to tell the boy? Surely I'll be out of a job now.

Cosimo di Pucci de' Meducci the Third, also drunk and drugged, felt his heart sink: *I am dead!* Instinctively, he moved his hands over his back and kidneys to feel for the knife wound—the assassin's knife always comes from behind! It was not the first time Cosimo had heard the phrase *Signore Meducci is dead.* He heard it when his father died, and when uncles and cousins had been murdered or passed away. He always imagined it would be the last thing he would ever hear. Who would have thought that death would be so painless?

Only Nonno immediately understood the true meaning of what was said, and his heart sank too.

"Oh, no," sighed Davido as he dropped to his knees beside his fallen donkey, "oh, no." The boy's grandfather shuffled over and dropped to his knees beside his grandson. They placed their hands upon the head and neck of the donkey, stroked his hair and together began to sob.

The crowd fell silent. These were superstitious folk, and death, especially the death of the victorious donkey, seemed a bad omen. It was a sad sight too. The beast, old and gnarled and dangling of *cazzone,* had raced hard and well and carried the boy to victory. And while the crowd may have had reservations about the rider, they were not at all conflicted in their admiration of the old donkey. They were also drunk, drugged and Italian and therefore predisposed to effusive displays of emotion.

Giuseppe looked about the crowd. It was eerily silent but for the muffled sobs of the two *Ebrei.* He noticed eyes welling with tears, and not just his stepdaughter's, but nearly the entire crowd. My God, he thought, this drug I've rendered is true.

It was difficult to know for sure, perhaps it was Cosimo di Pucci de' Meducci, or maybe his chef, or possibly Mari who first joined Davido in sobbing, but once the crowd heard the Good Padre's cries, a wave of emotion spread until the entire piazza became a great sea of tears. They sobbed, at first, for reasons separate from them, but the sobbing began to open that wellspring of sadness that all humans hide within their heart. For who has not suffered?

Mari found herself sobbing because her heart was bursting with so much love and sadness for the tomato boy that she had no choice but to weep. Cosimo sobbed for his dead courtesan, Luigi for his parents killed by the plague, and Bobo for the secret that lay buried in his heart. The Good Padre sobbed because the spirit that moved him was moved to sob. Mucca sobbed for her own dead child, who, if he'd lived past infancy, would have been about the *Ebreo* boy's age. The Cheese Maker sobbed for his favorite cow, dead and gone, whose teats produced the sweetest cream he'd ever tasted. Vincenzo sobbed for all the pigs he'd slaughtered and how sad and terrified they always looked as he slid the knife across their throats, and for how much he hated his task. Signore Coglione sobbed for his long-lost testicle and the fact that he loved men more than women and that his whole life felt like a lie. Even Augusto Po sobbed, suddenly mourning his recently deceased uncle, the old padre, who despite being nasty and cold-hearted was the only family he'd had. Only Giuseppe didn't cry, his heart alone among the villagers too calcified to crack.

The assembled crowd sobbed for mothers and fathers and sons and daughters and brothers and sisters and spouses and friends and lovers and courtesans and horses and mules and goats and sheep and donkeys and cows and cats and dogs and dreams and desires that had died in flesh or spirit. They sobbed for things said and unsaid and for love and efforts unrequited. They sobbed because life is nothing if not a constant reconciliation with death and sadness and loss that leaves one no choice but to sob—sob or lose one's mind. They sobbed because in sobbing even the vile and villainous, the most closed-hearted and closed-minded may come, even for an instant, to find their humanity. They sobbed for the holy and cathartic sake of sobbing itself. Even the children sobbed, and not just because their parents were doing so, but because even children can sense that life can be cruel and unfair and an ordeal entirely worth sobbing over.

And then, after who knows how long, the sobbing began to miraculously transform into laughter. It began subtly, with a chuckle, perhaps from Davido or Nonno—a chuckle tucked between sighs and moans, but a chuckle nonetheless. And the chuckle spread like a contagion that brought with it the realization that while life was indeed cruel and sad and burdened with anguish, it was also absurd and joyous and a thing worth laughing over—a thing that *must* be laughed over!

At first people chuckled because the Good Padre chuckled and because they remembered what began all the sobbing. A donkey had died, yes, and that was sad, but it was also absurd. With a *hee* and *haw* and a huge *cazzone* dangling 'tween its thighs, a donkey had died, which proved to one and all that God was not without humor. A donkey named after the Duke of Tuscany had died, which allowed the lowly to mock the mighty (this was what made Cosimo laugh most), and showed to all that *Ebrei* too are not without humor.

And the chuckle grew to a laugh. The gathering of festival-goers laughed at first for reasons outside themselves, but rather quickly the laughing opened in each and every one that wellspring of laughter that all humans share; for who has not a pain that craves the balm of laughter? And the laughter spread into something that could not be controlled: a plague of laughter. They laughed for mothers and fathers and sons and daughters and brothers and sisters and husbands and wives and friends and lovers and courtesans and animals and dreams and desires that had died in flesh or in spirit. They laughed for things said and for things unsaid, and for loves and efforts unrequited. They laughed because life is nothing if not a constant reconciliation with death and sadness and loss that leaves one no choice but to laugh or to lose one's mind. Even the children began to laugh and not solely on account of their parents' laughter, but because even children know that life is cruel and unfair and an ordeal worth laughing over. Adult and child alike laughed because in laughter even the vile and villainous, the most closed-hearted and closed-minded may come, even for an instant, to find their humanity. They laughed for the holy and cathartic sake of laughter itself. They laughed because life is something that cannot be endured without laughter.

The villagers laughed as Giuseppe finally managed to lay the victor's wreath upon Davido's head, because what could be funnier and more ironic than an *Ebreo* winning the Race of the Drunken Saint and being declared *Il Santo del Giorno*? They laughed as Davido made his blessing over the crowd and asked the Drunken Saint to bless the year's harvest. They laughed as Davido made his *request* of the people that they should all eat a tomato. And then they laughed as they bit and chewed, as tomato juices dripped from their lips. They laughed as they swallowed and laughed at their fears, that a thing construed so evil would prove to be so delicious.

They laughed as they drank and as they toasted. They laughed as they ate and danced. They laughed as the stars grew bright and they laughed as the sky went blue with dawn's first light. They laughed as they grew more and more drunk until their bellies could hold not another drop of wine or laughter. Some laughed as they stumbled home and fell into bed; others laughed as they crumpled to the piazza floor and passed out. They laughed as they fell asleep and then went right on laughing in their dreams.

Mari laughed because she did not fall asleep and Davido laughed because Nonno and every *Ebreo* from Pitigliano had. Together, Mari and Davido laughed, because as the entire village fell with sleep and intoxication, they remained standing. And they went right on laughing as they snuck off down an alley. Laughing that a plan unspoken could come so perfectly together. Laughing as their arms and hands and lips and tongues slithered and constricted around one another, proving that love too is a thing worth laughing over.

In Which We Ponder
Four Types of Death

Nonno was in the lead. He was too old to sleep in a wagon-bed with a group of drunken men half his age and younger. Illuminated by the dawn light, he was conducting a pair of donkeys along the road that led from the village to his farm. Behind him, in the wagon-bed, lay his beloved donkey. Behind him farther still, two other wagons, each pulled by donkeys and conducted by half-asleep men from Pitigliano. It was a good thing that the *Ebrei* from Pitigliano had been there at the feast. Had they not, Nonno and Davido would never have been able to transport all the crates of wine and oil back to the farm, let alone deal with the task of moving Signore Meducci so he could be buried in the very ground he considered his rightful property.

Davido had been given much: eleven cases of the finest wine, eleven cases of the best olive oil, with nine bottles per case. The wine wasn't kosher, but to Nonno, that fact made it all the sweeter. True, he had reservations about Davido being declared the victor, but he was, nonetheless, the proudest he had ever been of his grandson. The boy had some fight in him, a touch of madness too! He had bested a village full of gentiles and a miracle such as that was more than enough to make kosher any *Cristiano* wine.

Nonno peered over his shoulder and noticed that the rigor mortis that had set in within hours of Signore Meducci's death had yet to relent. Like a comically macabre statue, the poor dead beast was frozen in the position of his last moment of life, including his enormous *cazzone,* petrified in its final semi-erect state. Yes, it wrenched his heart, but Nonno nearly chuckled at the look of annoyance calcified upon the donkey's face; that death should visit him at such a public and inopportune moment.

Of all the beings that Nonno had loved and who had died, this was the best death. He had seen many deaths, some honorable, some pathetic and some horrible. He once saw a starved and syphilis-mad sailor aboard Colombo's ship chase a rat right off the stern, plunge into the ocean and be consumed by sharks—a pathetic death. In *Il Nuovo Mundo,* he watched, bound and helpless, as the *Indiana* woman he loved sacrificed herself so he might live—an honorable death. And then, many years later, he witnessed his second wife, son and daughter-in-law die slowly and miserably of plague in the ghetto of Florence—a horrible death.

Yet with all the death Nonno had witnessed, he'd never before been privy to such a good and perfect death, a death in which a being takes leave of this world in a manner both glorious and entirely consistent with how it lived. Such was Signore Meducci's: a perfect donkey death—proud, defiant and ridiculous in a way that only an old donkey or old man can be. Nonno only hoped that one day he would have such a death. Perhaps, thought Nonno, I too should have died at the *Festa* along with my favorite donkey. I could have died laughing.

Parte Tre

SAUCE

33

In Which We Learn
of Tossing Crumbs
& Furthering Plans

O nly Benito never laughed. He could not stop sobbing. He'd been dragged off into the dark of an alley, where he lay unconscious, his body blanketed in vomit, his dreams wracked by a demented orgy of demons. And when he awoke hours later and spotted the entwined bodies of Mari and Davido kissing in the alley, his sobs turned to cries. Deep and horrid cries that lasted through the dawn and into the next day. Cries that did not abate with the sunrise as most cries do. Cries that ran his body dry of tears, until all that remained was a pathetic, fluidless whimper.

"For *Cristo*'s sake," said Giuseppe with a quick smack to Benito's left cheek, *"basta!"* Enough.

Remarkably, Benito stopped his whimpering; his hatred

of Giuseppe instantly halting his sobs. The two men were now sitting across from each other at a table in the tavern, a mug of ale before each. It was Monday, dusk, the day after the feast, a day of rest and cleaning. It was considered offensive, even sacrilegious, not to participate in the cleanup; hence, by early afternoon, even Giuseppe could be found sweeping, lifting and cleaning every last vestige of dirt, hay, vomit and donkey poop from the previous night's revelry. It was both village tradition and an integral part of tomorrow's religious procession to take a handful of dirt and crumbs from the piazza's cobblestones on the day after the feast and secret it in one's pocket until the next day's ceremony. Of all who lived in the village, only Benito did not come to the piazza to clean. In truth, no one expected him to.

By early evening the piazza was clean and most of the villagers, especially the more devout, stumbled on home to prepare themselves for Tuesday's ritual of *Per Gettare le Briciole*[18]. A few headed to the tavern.

"Giuseppe," said Benito with some difficulty, his hand shaking as it gripped the handle of his mug. "I . . . I . . ."

"Oh, shut up, man. You're perfectly fine, just a tad hungover."

But Giuseppe knew Benito was not merely recovering from drink. He looked horrendous. Giuseppe had seen this look before, how too strong a dose of *Fungi di Santo* unhinged the mind. For the two hundred or so persons at the feast positioned behind the *Nobiluomi*'s table who shared a few gulps from the bottles of fallen riders being passed about, the effects of the narcotic seemed slight and rather delightful; but Benito had drunk down an entire *Jeroboame* bottle himself, and even Giuseppe feared what that might do to Benito's mind. He still needed him, after all. "Nothing a good ale or two and

---

[18] To Toss Crumbs: an ancient Etruscan ritual that followed a village's grape and olive feast, whereby the devout filled their pockets with crumbs and dirt, then traveled to a river and tossed the crumbs into the water as a symbolic act of purification. Once the crumbs had floated off, the devout would then plunge into the river. This was done so one could approach the sacred acts of grape- and olive-harvesting clean of conscience and spirit. With the spread and adoption of Christianity the ritual also came to include a baptismal procession led by the local priest.

a romp with your favorite *lady* won't cure," said Giuseppe as he dropped a pair of silver coins before Benito.

Benito watched the coins as they hit the table. He had little desire for ale or whores.

"Now," said Giuseppe, "are you certain what you saw?"

"*Eh,*" said Benito as he lifted his mug, " 'twas a lusty lip-lock."

"Good, for soon she'll have those lips upon his co—"

There was a loud clang as Benito's pewter mug slipped from his grip, crashed upon the table and splattered the last few drops of ale upon himself and Giuseppe.

"Good God, you idiot!" Giuseppe leaned back and removed a handkerchief from his pocket. "Get a grip on yourself." Giuseppe wiped a droplet of ale from his chin and patted down a few others dotting his vest. "Barmaid." Giuseppe snapped his fingers and pointed at Benito's empty mug.

Benito readied himself for some quip as the barmaid refilled his mug—some awful jab about yesterday's humiliation, but none came.

"Piss off," said Giuseppe to the barmaid the instant Benito's mug was full. "Now," Giuseppe returned his attention to Benito, "with our plan that lies twofold, 'tis the other route we take hold." Giuseppe tapped his ring upon the table deep in thought. "Hmm, what to do, what to do? Bobo!" he shouted across the tavern. "Come hither with paper and a quill"—Giuseppe turned back to Benito—"so I may play this through."

Giuseppe snapped his fingers before Benito's face. "*Eh,* pay attention now. Take from Coglione a case of good wine—ours. Then upon my horse-drawn wagon to the *Ebrei* in double-time. Have Bobo do the bidding, whilst you do the waiting. Bobo will say that the wine is from me, a victory bequest, whilst Bobo slyly does his mistress's request and drops the young *Ebreo* a secret note, which for his purposes my step-daughter wrote. Now, tonight, I'm off to test her will and guarantee that tomorrow she'll be at the mill. Then, while all are off tossing crumbs and cleansing soul, tomorrow, in hiding, you'll play the mole." Giuseppe reached inside his vest and removed his recently acquired three-segmented telescope. He placed it before Benito.

Benito looked wide-eyed at Giuseppe.

Nodding at his underling, Giuseppe signaled that he was indeed trusting him with his prized possession. "In the distance, upon Mari spy, lie in wait. We've set the trap, Benito, now let the *Ebreo* take the bait."

Bobo the Fool sauntered over carrying paper, ink and quill.

"Sit," commanded Giuseppe. Benito slid over. Bobo set the paper down and dipped his quill. "Now write," Giuseppe went on. "Tomorrow. Morning. At the olive mill." Giuseppe paused, searching for the right words. "With bated breath." Giuseppe was especially curt when it came to letter-writing.

Bobo looked up with eyes that seemed to say, *That's it?*

Giuseppe's expression grew stern. He did not like revealing so much to the fool. "Sign it," said Giuseppe, "Mari."

Bobo raised his eyebrows inquisitively, but he kept his mouth shut. He knew well that Giuseppe masked his near-illiteracy not only with bullying but overpaying.

"Give it here." Giuseppe took the paper and pretended to peruse it.

Bobo and Benito shared a quick glance at the ridiculousness of this gesture.

"You write like a woman," Giuseppe said snidely. Giuseppe folded the paper into the shape of a proper letter. He reached for a candle and dripped some wax onto it, forming a seal. After blowing on the wax to quicken its drying, he slid the letter back to Benito, stood up and reached into his pocket. "Half each," said Giuseppe, dropping a money purse before his underlings. "Now," Giuseppe looked to Benito, "is there anything for which you lack?"

Benito slid the telescope into his pocket, placed his hand upon the letter and shook his head.

"Then fill in the fool and move this play to final act."

In Which We Learn
of Broken Stairs & Spilled Olives

"**B**irds chirp and vineyards bloom and I float like the plume." It was a warm and delicious evening as Mari strolled amidst the olive orchard, heading for the mill. By all practical accounts, Mari should have been exhausted. She'd hardly slept last night and then done nearly a full day's labor cleaning the piazza, but it mattered not. She was beside herself with happiness and bubbling with energy. Her lips still tasted of tomatoes and Davido; her fingertips were still imprinted with the outline of his flesh. It had been quite a kiss and the possibility of going home and ruining such a rhapsody of feeling by crossing paths with Giuseppe was so totally unappealing that she'd set out for a walk in the orchard, found an eagle feather lying upon the ground and then, like her father before her and so many in this story, she began to speak of her joy aloud:

"The plume carried upon the winds of love, the plume that falls from tail of dove. The plume adrift on these warm currents, the plume that sets my soul a-errant. To plume and wander lost amidst the timeless moments of our tryst. To ride and float, plume and careen, to plume myself on pleasures unseen. Oh, Father in heaven, I have met the noble soul who fits my half into a whole. And now I plume, plume and blush, on what so moves my heart to flush and sets my mind to plan and scheme that I may once again kiss the dream. But more than kiss, oh sweet plume dipped in ink, write the tale into which I sink. A story whereby true love transcends all who might condemn, and he and I and our sweet fruits commingle to meet a happy, happy end."

Mari held the plume to her heart as she rounded the corner and entered the olive mill, her spirits soaring. But her flight of fancy was short-lived. There, sitting on the steps leading up to the office, was Giuseppe. Mari's heart sank, her plume fell to the ground and the sweet taste in her mouth soured. He sat on the fourth stair from the bottom, just one step above the still-broken third stair. Next to him rested a bucket-sized clay jar of olives. He was looking into the jar, poking around with his fingers.

"Amazing," he said, a twinge of menace to his tone, "the things one can find beneath a broken step." Giuseppe plucked an olive and popped it into his mouth.

Mari felt her body flush with rage. Giuseppe was defiling the very olives she had spent the better part of a year curing, the ones she wished to share with Davido. Mari did her best to ignore Giuseppe and strolled through the mill in silence as if she had a specific reason for being there.

"You have no greeting for me, daughter?" Giuseppe spit the olive pit out of his mouth and onto the floor.

Mari was silent. She busied herself with the straightening of some equipment in the corner; a broom, a long, stiff-bristled brush for cleaning the olive press. It was all she could think to do.

Giuseppe clicked his tongue against the roof of his mouth; his fingers picked another olive from the brine. "What is it with mine women, I do beseech, that hath so withered their organ of speech? Your mute mother has excuse at least, as it's only language that distinguishes women from beast." Giuseppe popped the olive into his mouth. "Ah, but perhaps a good beast could put my womanly woes to end," he said whilst obnoxiously chewing on the olive, "for 'tis true what they say, that dog be man's best friend. And gladly I to suffer some shit and piss upon the floor than endure such silent barking a second more."

"A dog?" shot back Mari. She could not help herself. "T'would think Benito was more than 'nuff the mutt."

Giuseppe spit out the olive pit. "And he doth have such puppy dog eyes for you."

The comment irked Mari. "What do you want, *Step*father?"

"Funny you should say that."

"Say what?"

"*Step*," said Giuseppe as he looked between his legs at the broken third stair. Giuseppe leaned to his right, lowered his hand and knocked over a board, mallet and a dozen nails that rested against the side of the stairs.

Mari felt her throat tighten.

"Do not," Giuseppe looked directly at Mari for the first time, "embarrass me. I am all that stands between your mother's penury and you in a nunnery."

Mari scowled. "Are you threatening me?"

"Goodness no, daughter, I am merely stating the reality of the situation."

"The reality," repeated Mari, "is that you're a fiend who does little more than repossess that of others, including their land and their mothers."

Giuseppe clucked his tongue remonstratively. "To think such ill thanks you bequeath and reduce my gesture to common thief?"

"Oh, no, far more evil than petty thief is he who preys upon a widow's grief."

"Watch your tongue, you ingrate girl," said Giuseppe,

obviously trying to control his temper. "Lest you forget: you and your mother'd be destitute had I not married that crippled mute. A widow and her impish daughter with not a coin in hand. Po and the church would have scoffed up this land."

"Your kindness is lost on me, sir."

"Be that as it may, my fury is not. Do not embarrass me."

"One cannot embarrass the shameless," Mari sneered.

"You will not," repeated Giuseppe severely, "embarrass me."

"Good God, *Step*father, of what do you speak?"

"I have housed and fed you for ten years—"

"Upon land fattened by another," Mari interrupted.

"Shut up, girl!" Giuseppe yelled. " 'Tis bad enough I have to waste a dowry on you."

"What?" Mari flushed with panic. *Does he know of Davido?*

"I will have my recompense."

"For what?" shot back Mari.

"For the bread my labors have fed you. For the roof and shelter I've afforded you. For the dowry I am forced to give."

"Bread I have always baked, a roof my father tarred and shingled. And as far as a dowry, I would not assume so much of you."

"Shut up, you insolent girl!" Giuseppe violently stomped his foot upon the bottom stair. "You are of marrying age. I have been in contact with suitors, older men of wealth and means; fine, fat, rich and boring. Men whose blood runs blue."

Mari glared at Giuseppe. She felt her life was being drained from her. "I would sooner take a knife to my heart."

"Then best you whet your blade." Giuseppe stood up. "You will marry whom I command, when I command, and you will go to your wedding bed a virgin. Blood will mark your nuptial sheets or I will pitch you to a nunnery to rot, and toss that crippled mother of yours to a dank asylum." Giuseppe glared at Mari so to better burrow his words into his stepdaughter's head. "Rest assured, what I lose in coin, I will gain in title." Then he stepped off the stairs, letting his right hand trail behind him, catching the lip of the olive jar with his index finger and insouciantly tipping it over.

Mari watched the olives and liquid spill and splatter onto the floor.

"A little salty," said Giuseppe as he made for the barn door.

Mari heard the door swing shut.

"Fix the step," she heard Giuseppe say as the iron bolt slid into place. She was locked in.

In Which We Learn
of Rivers, Oceans & Sauce

Better to a nunnery, thought Mari as the first rays of sun shone through the windows and she heard the dead bolt slowly slide open and the mill door creak. It had been a long and angry night on a dusty floor. Yes, she fixed the third stair (she was not a stupid girl), fixed it perfectly, so perfectly that Giuseppe would hardly think to check the fifth stair, which Mari made certain would surely come apart in the near future. She would be damned if she would marry a monster of Giuseppe's choosing. Better to a nunnery, better to Davido—much better to Davido. I too will have my recompense, thought Mari, as she readied her bucket and waited for the door to open. Ten years of abuse has been enough.

Davido had hardly slept. It was a word and a wagonful of excitement that kept him awake. *Tomorrow,* that was easy enough to understand. *At the olive mill,* yes, he knew where that was. *With bated breath.* Oh, *mio Dio,* to think that Mari was waiting for him with such eagerness was itself over-whelming. But *morning,* that was the part of the note that confused him. What did she mean by *morning*? Morning is made of many hours, especially for a farmer. Was Tuesday not a work day, he thought? Will I not be seen by a dozen millworkers? Can I really take such a risk? How can I not? For her, how can I not?

Thank heavens, at least, thought Davido, Nonno had gone off to Pitigliano on Monday for an overnight stay and had not been present when the fool dropped off the wine and note. To visit with a *Cristiano* village girl, Nonno would have none of it. Just the idea that a village girl had the temerity to write such a note and have her servant deliver it could have very well meant a year in Florence for Davido and certain marriage to that skinny-ankled girl. But *morning,* what did she mean by *morning*?

All night the question plagued Davido, right up until this very moment as he approached the olive mill. He had chosen early morning. Actually, it had chosen him. He could not sleep; he could not stand the wait, so he put on his monk's robe, laid the heavy cross around his neck, mounted a don-key and trotted off with the first hint of sunlight. The morn-ing air was cool and crisp, but underneath the heavy robe Davido's stomach was aflutter with butterflies and he could feel the drops of nervous sweat gathering in his armpits. The anxious perspiration carried with it a stink too, a body odor that added to Davido's nerves. He fanned fresh air into the robe every few minutes and even pulled some cypress needles from a tree as he strode by and rubbed the rough green and fine-smelling fur under his armpits—anything to smell better for her.

The mill was empty—*grazie Dio!*—but the door was bolted shut. Why, thought Davido, is she not here? Is there another entrance? Let me just have a look inside. Madness, yes, I know. Nonno would not approve. But how can I not? For Mari. Dear sister in heaven, bless me, he told himself as he slid the bolt and pulled the door ajar, just enough to peer his head inside. And then, out of the shadows, it came! Panic-stricken, Davido inhaled and sucked the burning oil right into his mouth. It blinded his eyes and burned down his neck. I am dead, he thought, I am dead!

Mio Dio, Mari gasped, I have done it a second time. She dropped the empty bucket of oil and ran to him with a purpose even greater than that which she'd heaved the oil. Ran and jumped into his oil-drenched arms. Pressed her lips onto his oil-covered lips, ran her tongue into his oil-covered mouth and kissed him.

I am not dead? Davido's mind questioned itself as it sorted through that moment of confusion when one cannot distinguish the very cold from the burning hot. Davido's oil-coated eyes opened and he saw the blurry figure of his attacker moving toward him. He felt a body lean against his chest as twice-familiar arms wrapped around his torso and twice-familiar lips pressed onto his. *I am alive,* every sense of his body affirmed, as his mouth opened in return and olive oil and lips and tongues commingled and danced for a third delicious time.

❊   ❊   ❊

Ed il fiume deve fluire verso l'oceano, wrote Pozzo Menzogna in his eloquent and definitive treatise on drama. *And the river must flow to the ocean.* Menzogna was writing, of course, about the importance in a third act to narrow the action around the story's main characters and their dilemma. To increase the narrative's current and build a sense of urgency as the story flows toward its "ocean of resolution," as Menzogna put it. Accordingly, Menzogna postulated, by *Parte Tre,* the audience should have a keen understanding of the inner workings and desires of a tale's characters and therefore the time is past for elaborate asides, introspection and excessive detail.

And so, while it may be an interesting current to follow,

Menzogna would in no way recommend we divert the balance of our tale's current and dwell unnecessarily upon the procession of villagers en route to the river on this Tuesday morning of *Tossing Crumbs.* The reader will know in an instant that while Giuseppe's pockets may have been filled with crumbs (as he trailed along with Mari's crippled mother at the rear of the procession), it was only appearances he was keeping up and that he had no room in his heart or space in his mind to actually believe in such a foolish rite.

In a state of mind very different from that of Giuseppe, Cosimo di Pucci de' Meducci the Third, Grand Duke of Tuscany in hiding, also walked the processional, cast his crumbs into the river and then surrendered himself to the Good Padre's baptismal plunge. There, as the cool waters washed over him, Cosimo felt the final burdens of sadness that had plagued much of his life simply wash away.

His chef, Luigi Campoverde, still not of right mind from all the tainted wine he drank at the feast, was also amongst those walking the processional. He was walking out of sight of his boss, of course, but walking nonetheless. He had been unable to bring himself to leave the odd little town that he imagined to be so like the village of his birth, and he thought that a blessing from the priest might help restore his mind and ensure his job security.

Benito, feeling soiled and foul and likewise unstable of mind, did not obey Giuseppe's orders to spy upon Mari. La Piccola Voce would not let him. Instead, he walked at the head of the processional—well away from Giuseppe's sight—desperate to be rid of his guilt and the little voice that was ruining his mind.

Bobo, who was like a cat when it came to water, could not bring himself to be a part of the processional, and while he did not loathe the Good Padre as he had the last priest, he had too many secrets to hide and no place in his heart to forgive the Church.

Bertolli, the Cheese Maker, Mucca, Vincenzo, Signore Coglione (always hopeful that a miracle might bring back his lost testicle), Augusto Po and all the other villagers made their way to the river where their indescribable Good Padre waited for them in waist-deep water like a giant yet gentle hippopotamus, washing away sins and absolving guilt; all the while fulfilling the divine curse cast upon him centuries ago—to shine a sliver of the Great Mother's light upon each and every pale one.

No, Pozzo Menzogna and his eloquent treatise on drama would not recommend we spend much time at the river. On the contrary, now is the moment to jump into the current of our young lovers' day. To glean all that drove them into each other's arms. To learn of how they kissed and slathered themselves with olive oil until Mari had the good sense to break the kiss. "It is not safe here," she said, "we must go to another place." To which Davido had the good sense to place his monk's robe over Mari and hurriedly escort her back to his farm like a hired servant leading an old monk between monasteries. Of how the hours went by in each other's company. Of how Mari spoke of the death of her father and the living death of her mother, the annoyance of Benito and torments of Giuseppe. Of how Davido spoke of the plague in Florence, his parents' demise and the death of his sister (though he did not say how she died). And of how finding someone who could relate fully to the sadness that always sits in the heart of a child who's lost a parent brought them both a feeling of emotional kinship that equally matched their more lusty desires for each other. Of how Davido kept stealing downward glances to gaze upon Mari's wondrous little toes, shaped like baby eggplants, her ankles, not too thick, nor too thin, but perfect and strong. Of how Mari breathed in a little deeper each time she passed near Davido and how his musk of body odor mixed with the slightest scent of cypress formed a smell so delicious to her that if it were a pudding she would have eaten a bucketful. And of how their simple lunch of tomatoes and olives and cheese and wine and figs and bread and olive oil was the tastiest meal either of them had ever experienced.

And how it all began so innocently as Davido shared with Mari his difficulty in making a proper sauce from the tomato, given that cooked tomatoes became too acidic. And of Mari's simple suggestion to do what she did for the olive and add red wine. Of how they emptied basket after basket of ripe tomatoes into the enormous cauldron at the center of the barn. Of how it was Mari's idea to crush the tomatoes the way women crush the grapes, rolling up pants and skirt and climbing into the cauldron. And of how titillating it felt to hold each other up and balance on each other as the thigh-high heaping of tender tomatoes burst under heel and squished between toes. How it was Mari who first squished a tomato onto the side of Davido's head. Of how their tomato fight grew into tomato wrestling, their bodies slipping and wriggling against each other. Of the energy that grew inside them and between them, until that energy took on a life of its own and they were no longer Davido and Mari, but something else, something ancient that seemed to know the other in a way that transcended knowingness, and of how this energy was like a madness. Of how Mari used her fingers to paint tomato pulp across the lips of Davido. And of how their lips then came together mixing tongues and tomatoes as they kissed. Of how they kissed and licked each other with mouths so open that it was as if they wanted to eat through the other's flesh. How kissing in itself was not enough. How clothes— anything that kept their bodies apart—became an enemy to them until they finally felt their naked flesh press against each other for the very first time. How the shaft of Davido's *pisello* pressed against the soft muff of Mari's *farfalla*. And of how, as their bodies slid downward into the mash and pulp of tomatoes, something else rose upward, spinning and reeling and twisting and turning until neither Davido nor Mari knew what was up or down, only what was together. How they pulled onto and into each other's bodies, smashing tomatoes between their bellies. How the moan that came from Mari's mouth was the greatest sound Davido had ever heard. And of how the act did not last long—a thrust, a sigh, an ecstatic clench—yet seemed to last forever. How time melted away as if there was no such thing. How their bodies twitched and spasmed as an eruption rose up through them, between

them. And of how, for a sublime moment, they entirely disappeared into each other, losing all sense of where their bodies
began and ended.

This is what Menzogna would want us to know. How it
was that Davido and Mari made love for the very first time in
a cauldron filled with crushed tomatoes.

⁂   ⁂   ⁂

They had been cooking for hours. It had been Mari's idea.
It was just too many good tomatoes to waste. They'd stoked
the fire and swung the cauldron atop the iron fire ring—an
invention that Mari found quite incredible. They'd peeled and
roughly chopped half a bucket's worth of garlic. They added
olive oil and salt and oregano and bay leaves and chili flakes,
the same spices Mari used to cure her olives. And once the
mass of crushed tomatoes had begun to simmer they'd emptied four bottles of red wine into the cauldron, just as Mari
had suggested. And then they waited—waited and stirred and
made love, twice more and less frantically—allowing time for
the crushed tomatoes, garlic, salt, herbs and red wine to simmer, reduce and thicken into a sauce. They also washed their
clothes, scrubbing and beating and pounding until nearly all
the olive oil and tomato juice was rinsed out. And after four
hours, by early afternoon, a few hours before Davido expected
Nonno's return and their clothes were dry, Davido took the
cauldron off the fire and swung it onto the iron cooling rack.

⁂   ⁂   ⁂

And it was done. The sauce was burgundy-red and flecked
with herbs, glistening in olive oil, yet thick enough to nicely
coat the piece of bread Mari dipped into it and then fed to
Davido.

Davido smiled with delight. They had done it! Mari was
right: the red wine and long, slow cook time had stewed the
acid out of the tomatoes, leaving the sauce robust and the
slightest bit sweet. It tasted of the sun and earth, and was
exactly the flavor his palate had been searching for. Hungry
after so much cooking and lovemaking, the two ate a whole

loaf of bread, torn into pieces and slathered with sauce, careful this time not to soil their clothing.

✻   ✻   ✻

Davido sat on an overturned bucket, digesting the bread, the sauce, the immensity of his feelings for Mari. Mari was up, moving about the barn, and caught Davido staring just as she grabbed an earthen clip-top jar off a shelf, the kind of jar she'd filled with olives on a thousand occasions. "Just one," she said playfully to Davido as her empty hand reached for a ladle.

Davido's eyes widened. "With sauce?"

Mari let her smile reply.

"It seems not a decent thing to do."

"Well," answered Mari, sinking the ladle into the sauce, "he is not a decent man."

Davido's expression crinkled.

"What's the matter," asked Mari mischievously, raising her left eyebrow—a gesture Davido had already come to adore—"have you not the nerve to feed the wicked the dish they most deserve?"

Davido couldn't help but smile. "And what will you tell him as to how you acquired it?"

"I will play to his vanity," Mari replied formally as she struck a pantomime of servitude. "Look, sir, what the *Ebreo* boy delivered to the mill in return for your kindness at the feast." She held the jar forward and bowed her head. "A sauce made from the tomato."

Davido looked at Mari gravely. "He treats you that poorly?"

Instantly, Mari's countenance went heavy with sadness and her eyes welled with tears. She did not answer. She did not have to.

"Then let him eat," said Davido. "Serve the knave a bucketful!"

Mari's expression lifted with a smile.

"Now," said Davido, intentionally lightening his tone, "what of the rest? I fear this sauce will go to waste. Are there not a hundred more scoundrels to serve?"

Again, Mari's lips turned upward with mischief.

"I was only joking," Davido answered her look.

"Why not?" Mari shrugged her shoulders as she glanced from the cauldron to the shelf that held a few dozen randomly sized jars. "Jar it up and bring it to tomorrow's market. You are the hero of the feast; they will eat anything you serve."

"Serve the sauce?"

Mari bit her lip. "Our little secret."

"Really?"

"Oh." Mari waved her hand nonchalantly as if to wipe the concern from Davido's brow as she stepped in his direction. "If grapes are squished beneath feet, then why not tomatoes between bellies? Besides, all things are purified by fire and boiling." Then she kissed him upon the lips. "What harm in our little secret? Is it not a greater shame to waste something so delicious? Truly, no one will ever know. Plus, we should do it for us. Your feast day heroics opened the villagers' hearts and minds, now let your sauce sway their stomachs in kind. Believe me, should we be courageous—or foolish—enough to make this anything more than a heartbreaking tryst, we'll need to throw our prayers, our passions and our *sauce* into the mix."

Nervous, Davido glanced upward and caught the angle of the sun gleaming through a slat in the wood. " 'Tis time," he said.

"Hmm," hummed Mari as she leaned in and kissed him on the lips. "Sadly so. Quick, let us don the monk robes and escort me to the outskirts of my orchard. Then return and ready yourself for tomorrow's market." Mari smiled. "And bring our tomato sauce."

Davido returned her smile tenfold. For her, how could he not?

36

In Which We Learn
to Discern Between
the Guilty & the Innocent

"*Avete scopato mia figlia in quella salsa di pomodori?*"
Everything stopped—all the talk, all the chattering, the bantering, the bartering, everything. Davido felt his heart stop too, and his entire body erupt with heat, as if his blood had just turned to lava. His mouth fell open in disbelief. He thought to speak, but the lava, the hot and molten fear, dried his mouth to a silent crisp. What a horrible twist of fate, was all he could think. Everything had been going so well. Villagers were actually approaching his stand and buying tomatoes, congratulating him on his feast day victory. And the tomato sauce, well, already Nonno had twice replenished the small pieces of bread that surrounded the crock of tomato sauce set upon their stand for sampling.

Though the sauce was a bit spicy for Nonno's taste, the villagers' reaction thrilled Davido and, begrudgingly, also pleased his grandfather. Piece after piece of bread was being dunked into the rich red sauce and scoffed down. Yes, there was some hesitancy at first, but the Good Padre was not afraid to try it and his reaction cleared the way for all to follow. And follow they did, with wonder and delight and moans of deliciousness and question upon question as to how the sauce was made and what best to use it for. No one had ever tasted anything like it, and by the time the Good Padre paid for his basketful of tomatoes and headed off to continue his shopping, a sizable group had gathered around the stand. Throughout all this activity Davido kept stealing glances down the market row, finding Mari's eyes for an instant, flashing a smile, raising an eyebrow, doing all he could with his face to say *I adore you, you're beautiful, and, yes, you were right, it was good to have brought the sauce.*

But then, Giuseppe slammed the small clip-top jar that yesterday Mari had filled with sauce onto the stand and repeated, "Did you fuck my daughter in that tomato sauce?" and everything went suddenly bad.

The silence was immediate and horrible. There was still chatter all about the market, but the area around the tomato stand was like a soundless island. Davido could hear his voice creaking and cracking, straining to say something. "I . . . I . . ."

Finally Mucca, *blessed Mucca,* short and fat, bosomy and bawdy, interrupted the boy's stutter. "Have you lost your mind, Giuseppe?"

Giuseppe ignored Mucca. He glared at Davido, *l'occhio diabolico,* the dead-eye stare he'd learned from his uncle years ago. He'd been mentally rehearsing this look since last night and knew exactly how to play it; once the Good Padre cleared off he was ready to make his move. He felt he had no other choice but to take matters into his own hands. Yesterday, Benito had failed him entirely. He disappeared for the day, did not spy on Mari as ordered and even lost Giuseppe's telescope. Goodness knows, if Giuseppe had not arrived home yesterday evening to find the half-empty clip-top jar and a bowl of pasta tossed in the red tomato sauce waiting for him, all his scheming thus far may have proved for naught. But the jar—the sauce—put all the pieces into place for Giuseppe to make his boldest play. Finally, Giuseppe spoke, repeating for a third time, *"Avete scopato mia figlia in quella salsa di pomodori?"*

"Good God," said Mucca, "what are you talking about?"

"This," said Giuseppe as he reached into his vest's small breast pocket.

The crowd leaned in.

"What," said Mucca, "your palm?"

"No," said Giuseppe, using his left thumb and index finger to lift the short and curly hair from his right palm and hold it up.

The crowd leaned in closer.

Giuseppe made certain to look haggard and aggrieved. He was known for dressing smartly and always keeping the lines of his beard well shaped and shaved, but on this morning his tunic was wrinkled and untucked, his vest unbuttoned, his hair was disheveled, his beard unkempt and his eyes especially dark and bloodshot—a drop of grappa in each one, an old Roman trick. *Italians,* Giuseppe recalled the words of his wickedly cunning uncle from many years ago, *are always more apt to believe a grand lie, well told and well sold.*

Dear God, thought Nonno, as his own blood turned to lava.

"What is it?" said Mucca.

"Un pelo pubico," said Giuseppe, "and it's from his *cazzone.* And it was in that sauce. And it was in *my* mouth!"

The crowd gasped. Augusto Po and several others looked in horror at the crusts of bread slathered in tomato sauce that they held in their hands. Several others stopped in mid-chew and spat the now semi-masticated blobs of sauce and bread from their mouths. Sweat began to bead upon Davido's brow. He strained his vision to catch a glimpse of Mari, but the crowd around the stand was now packed tightly and he could not see a thing.

"But you haven't had any of this sauce here," said Mucca. "I've been here the whole time."

"I had some last night."

Mucca's eyebrows rose. "How?"

Giuseppe pointed to the clip-top earthen jar that he'd just slammed upon the stand. He flipped the metal cinch, lifted the jar and poured the remaining half cup of tomato sauce onto the stand itself. "Mari had a jar. Claimed the boy dropped it by the mill."

"Is that so?" Mucca asked Davido.

Davido gave a slight nod of agreement.

"Why?" Mucca asked Davido.

"To say . . . to say thanks."

"For what?" asked Mucca.

"For being kindly at the feast," answered Davido.

Giuseppe glared at Davido. "How did you get to my mill?"

"What?" answered Davido. "I don't under—"

"How did you get to my mill!" Giuseppe interrupted. "By horse, by wagon, by mule?"

"By . . . by donkey," stuttered Davido.

"That's what Mari said too."

Davido nodded.

"But it's not true!" Giuseppe snarled. "Last evening, I ate the sauce. I pulled this hair from my mouth. I thought for a moment. By donkey, my daughter said. I took a lantern. I went to my mill. I searched the tracks and dust leading to its entrance. I saw the tread of a wagon. The imprint of feet. The wide outline of a horse's cleat. And though you and she claim it as excuse and proof, I looked everywhere, but found nothing approximating the slender shape of a donkey's hoof."

Davido felt the eyes of the surrounding crowd narrow guiltily upon him. A bead of sweat ran down his temple. Though his mouth was bone dry, he swallowed hard. He opened his mouth to speak, but no words came.

"So I ask you," Giuseppe actually lowered his voice, "how did my daughter get this jar of sauce?"

"What's going on here?" said a voice pushing through the crowd.

All heads turned.

Giuseppe's head turned too. "Why don't you tell me?"

The crowd widened to make room for the stepdaughter to confront her stepfather.

"Tell you what?"

"Avete scopato questo ragazzo in questa salsa di pomodori?"

Mari's countenance lit up with fury. "How dare you say such a thing?"

Oh, no, thought Nonno as he turned his eyes from Mari to Davido, his worst fear now proved true. *How could you be so stupid?* Nonno understood how to immediately discern the guilty from the innocent. It was a skill he had picked up years ago and one he sorely hoped Giuseppe had not acquired. As time and observation had taught him, the vast percentage of the time the guilty will immediately question the audacity of the accusation (*How dare you say such a thing?*) while the innocent will answer the accusation (*I did no such thing!*).

"Then how did this get in my mouth?" Giuseppe held the telltale curly hair before Mari.

Mari recoiled. "God only knows what goes in that mouth of yours."

Mucca and several in the crowd could not keep from chuckling.

"It was in the sauce," said Giuseppe. "The sauce you served me."

"And from that you make such an accusation?"

"No," answered Giuseppe, "from this." Giuseppe reached into his vest's opposite breast pocket and removed another hair.

The crowd leaned in.

"Oh, *mio Dio,* you've lost your mind," said Mari.

"Giuseppe, please," said Mucca, "two hairs in one sauce should not cause such alarm. Surely they could be from a head or arm."

"They're not the same hairs!" Giuseppe turned to face Davido. He sensed that it would be easier to break Mari if he went after the boy. He held up both hairs before Davido. "They're *not* the same hairs. This one's brown and curly, the other black and wavy. They match neither your head nor arms, yet they wound up in the gravy."

Nonno could not help but notice how nearly all the heads in the crowd turned to take note of Davido's brown and curly hair and Mari's black and wavy tresses.

"Tell me, boy, how did such different hairs end up in my mouth?" Giuseppe inquired menacingly. "From size and shape 'tis obvious from where they came, so if not your *cazzone* and her *farfalla,* then what else to blame?"

Davido felt the glare of a hundred eyes. The lava coursed hotter through his veins. His hairs stood on end, his complexion crimsoned. He tried to speak. "I . . . I . . ."

"Stop it!" shouted Mari. "Stop it!"

"Ah, see how she protects you?" Giuseppe taunted Davido. "How a girl protects you?"

"Giuseppe, please," said Mucca.

"Well, boy," Giuseppe ignored Mucca, "you have hardly said a word. Prove your innocence, boy. Pluck me a hair from your *cazzone.*"

The crowd gasped.

"Stop it," Mari repeated. "You're embarrassing all of us."

"Why do you not speak, boy? Does the truth have your tongue?"

"Stop it!" Tears began to well up in Mari's eyes and she pushed Giuseppe's shoulder.

"Can you not defend yourself, boy?"

"Leave him alone!" said Mari.

"Or must a girl defend you?"

"Shut up!" Mari yelled.

"Do it, boy, reach down your trousers and give one a pluck. Prove to me that you and my daughter didn't fu—"

Mari smacked Giuseppe across the face, knocking the word from his mouth.

Women shrieked. Men gasped. Bertolli ran to find the Good Padre.

"I am not your daughter!"

Slowly, Giuseppe turned to face Mari. *"Lo . . . avete . . . scopato?"* Did . . . you . . . fuck . . . him?

With her left hand Mari smacked Giuseppe. Hard as she could.

Giuseppe's head snapped to the side. Slowly, he turned back to face Mari. His eyes glaring so intensely they could burn holes in wood. *"Lo avete scopato?"* he repeated.

With her right hand Mari smacked Giuseppe.

Davido wanted to do something—lunge across the stand and choke the life out of the bastard—but he couldn't bring himself to move. The fear made his limbs too heavy.

Giuseppe's face began to redden, blood trickling down his nose. *"Lo avete scopato?"*

Again, Mari smacked Giuseppe.

"Lo avete scopato?"

Tears streamed down Mari's cheeks, her body quivering with fury. She went to smack Giuseppe again, but this time he caught her wrist.

"Lo avete scopato?" he said, twisting her wrist.

"Yes!" Mari screamed, "I fucked him! I fucked him in that sauce and you ate it!"

And then Giuseppe smacked back.

37

In Which We Learn the Significance of the Church's *Dictum Coitus di Chastatia*

It did not last long, but it was brutal and it was awful and it had many in the crowded tavern feeling soiled and conflicted—none more so than Cosimo. Here he was the Duke of Tuscany and he didn't even have the courage to stop a lowly rogue like Giuseppe from beating a wonderful girl like Mari or the brother of his beloved courtesan. All he could do was watch. Even his chef had the courage to act—recklessly, ridiculously—throwing his face in front of Giuseppe's fist.

And now Cosimo could not get what he'd seen and heard out of his mind. The way Mari's entire body had crumpled from the force of Giuseppe's open-palmed smacks across the side of her face. The ferocity with which Giuseppe lunged across the tomato stand, grabbed the bewildered *Ebreo* boy by the hair, twisted his neck and pummeled a half-dozen hard punches into his face. The pathetic manner in which the old *Ebreo* slipped and fell to the ground as he tried to pull his grandson away. The horrible sound of Giuseppe's hands as they pounded against innocent flesh. The combination of jeers and gasps that tellingly divided the crowd between those who craved vengeance and those who sought mercy. And then, the worst sound of all, the sound that Cosimo could not purge from his head: the sound of young lovers being torn apart while calling out each other's names.

Thank God the Good Padre was quick to the scene, pulling Giuseppe off Davido with such facility that a raving adult seemed suddenly like a squealing child, or who knows what may have happened. Even so, it was not a good ending, with Giuseppe cursing the Good Padre and "the wicked *Ebreo*" as he dragged Mari off by the hair, and the Good Padre escorting the old *Ebreo* and his beaten grandson onto their donkey-drawn wagon and hurrying them off.

And now, with the onset of evening and only an old mule as his transport, Cosimo was afraid there wasn't time enough to return to his villa and muster up a legion of guards to keep the next travesty from occurring. For Cosimo had little doubt another travesty *would* occur. He knew Giuseppe's type too well; whether they wore the clothes of a petty landholder, politician or pope, such men were dispassionate, shrewd and adept at exploiting tragedy for great personal gain.

It was depressing to Cosimo that so many in this village that he had come to adore seemed just as vile and cowardly as the aristocrats he had left behind; indeed, as cowardly as himself. Not a single man in the crowd, save for Luigi, raised a finger toward Mari's defense. Only the Good Padre and Mucca, blessed Mucca, dared to confront Giuseppe. And, to Cosimo, a startling number of villagers actually seemed to share Giuseppe's outrage, raising their fists and voices in approval, as if Mari's feelings for the boy were a threat to their very existence, her virginity a communal possession.

Of course, Cosimo knew that fathers often place a foolish pride upon their daughters' chastity, but Giuseppe was

hardly a father to Mari. Neither was this a case of rape or sa-
lacious seduction. No, from the manner in which Mari called
after Davido as she was dragged away, and he after her, the
truth of their feelings was undeniable: young and innocent
and beautiful love. Indeed, it made Cosimo sick with despair
and self-loathing to think that he had let such a thing be
killed before his very eyes.

⊛   ⊛   ⊛

"Order! Order!" Vincenzo took off his shoe and pounded it
against the table. "Po shall be heard!"

The tavern quieted. All heads turned to Augusto Po.
"Vincenzo is right," said Po smugly, pointing to a specific page
in the large book he held. "The Church's *Dictum Coitus di
Chastatia*[19] does clearly state that if a virgin Catholic daughter be deflowered before wed and out of faith, then in payment for the aggrieved family's disgrace, the perpetrator is to
pay by forfeiture of his estate."

"There!" shouted Vincenzo over the grumbling of the
crowded tavern. "There you have it. Giuseppe does have his
rights, and we here have no right to act against a deceived
father or our Mother Church."

"Oh, hypocrites! The lot of you," said the Cheese Maker as
he rose from his seat. The room drew quiet. "Sanctimonious
blowhards seething over a ruined virgin bed, all blind to the
lives and lies you've led. Feigning holiness as if we have not
shared a life; I know many here who rolled in hay with another
'fore you bedded your wife. And now you spew this venom
toward a deed you seemingly abhor, when who amongst you
has not turned another man's daughter to whore—or at least
longed to?" The Cheese Maker looked about the room and
then softened his tone. "Please, good neighbors, this is Mari
we speak of, daughter of our deceased friend, yet we brand
his child a harlot and contemplate such end. She is but a
young woman, who in the folly and hotness of youth perhaps
did err, but banishment and forfeiture?"

---

[19] A papal edict written in 1299, and adopted by much of Europe, that governed sexual
behavior, improprieties and punishments.

"Have you no shame?" said Vincenzo disgustedly. "No pride? Nor even eyes to see the sin? A serpent hath slithered into Eden and deflowered our kin!"

"I saw only love," said the Cheese Maker.

"But what of the sauce?" shouted Vincenzo.

"Is it even true?" questioned the Cheese Maker.

"Now you call Giuseppe a liar?" Vincenzo's face crinkled. "Are you blind? Were you not there? Could there be a greater sign of culpability than her temerity and his timidity?"

The tavern went quiet. Even the Cheese Maker said nothing.

"Ah," scoffed Vincenzo, "even our milk-hearted friend is at a loss to defend the malicious act of the *Ebreo* coward, who would serve us to eat as food the *Cristiana* he deflowered."

"Please," said the Cheese Maker as he looked about in disbelief, "this is madness. It was an act of the young, the foolish and imprudent, but to answer with forfeiture and banishment? My God, this is Mari we're speaking of, flower of our village."

"Hmm," it was Augusto Po who broke the mortifying silence, "a flower now plucked."

"Shut up," Mucca snapped at Po. "You nasty, heartless miser."

There was a grumble in the tavern. Some on the side of Mucca, others seeming to side with Po. The Cheese Maker looked about, desperate to make eye contact with anyone, anyone but Vincenzo and Giuseppe, but throughout the room heads were lowered in shame and confusion. "Bobo," the Cheese Maker shouted across the tavern, "please, wise fool, say something. Surely you must see the truth here?"

All heads turned to Bobo. Slumped upon a stool at the bar, he barely lifted his head to face the room. "Bobo says nothing."

"Ha," blurted Vincenzo, "what a pleasant surprise! Besides, the laws that govern premarital carnality care not of the coupling's mutuality. The law is the law and the law is with Giuseppe. And as we, his kinsmen, shall abide his word, let Giuseppe be heard."

Still in his tomato-stained shirt and seeming much the maligned father, Giuseppe slowly stood up. "Tomorrow," he said without passion or menace, "a militia's to be raised to exact the penance: she's to a nunnery and the *Ebreo* from Tuscany to Venice." And then Giuseppe snatched up Vincenzo's shoe and hurled it directly and squarely into the face of the Cheese Maker.

The sound startled Cosimo and put the fear of God into his belly. He had never heard the awful cracking sound of a nose breaking.

38

In Which We Learn How Michelangelo Dealt with Sadness, or How Pizza Came to Be, Part I

Nonno sliced the cheese, ladled some tomato sauce from a pot on the stove into a small bowl and cut a piece from the focaccia he'd brought back from Pitigliano. It was the only food they had in the house. Though it was of little solace, Nonno knew for certain that Davido had gone and made an additional pot of sauce. He'd been there in the evening as Davido made it. At least Nonno had that to comfort him, that his grandson had the decency not to serve the villagers the tomato sauce in which he and the girl had made love. Nonno set the food upon a tray. Davido had not eaten since morning. He'd not even wiped the blood from his face. He'd done nothing but sulk before the fire for hours. Though Nonno wanted to berate the boy for his utter stupidity, he figured food would do his grandson more good. They would be leaving at tomorrow's dawn—the whole clan, all thirteen of them, leaving for Pitigliano.

This was the kind of thing that *Ebrei* were killed over and Nonno couldn't risk that. Had it been Spain, Davido never would have made it out of the market alive. They would spend the autumn, maybe even the winter, in Pitigliano. Nonno didn't believe that any of these villagers would come looking for Davido there, but he couldn't imagine the farm a safe place, at least for the time being. After the new year, Nonno would send a messenger to the Good Padre to gauge the sentiment of the villagers. If the Good Padre reported back that it was safe and the farm had not been razed, then, and only then, would Nonno and his kin return. Davido, however, would not. He would be sent to Florence, to marry and live out the next few years in the ghetto.

How could he have been so stupid? thought Nonno. There wasn't an *Ebreo* in all of Europe who didn't know better. This was why Nonno didn't chastise his grandson, because he knew that Davido did not act from lust or stupidity, or any base desire, but from love. It was plain to see. The girl was beautiful and brave, and Nonno was not so out of touch with the idea of youth to discount the notion that, as a young man, if he'd met such a girl, she would have surely stolen his heart too. Indeed, in *Il Nuovo Mundo,* Nonno *had* met such a girl when he was but a few years older than Davido, and that, like this, did not end well. It was all painfully evocative of the love he'd lost a half century ago. And the way his grandson and the girl called after each other, it was enough to break his heart. But it was a love that never could be and certainly was not worth dying over and Nonno knew that from his own experience.

Nonno did not believe in dying for a cause, but rather in *living* for one, and he always looked at the numbers. That's the horrible lesson he'd learned in Spain, the thing Torquemada[20]

[20] Tomás de Torquemada: First Inquisitor General of Spain and the man universally credited with fomenting and leading the Spanish Inquisition.

had taught him: *Ebrei,* no matter where they lived or how assimilated, were but a minority, and, whether by rancor or whim, if sentiment turned against them their only salvation was to flee. This was the thing, Nonno believed, that an *Ebreo* must accept—that his Davido must accept: there were certain forces an *Ebreo* couldn't resist, certain battles an *Ebreo* couldn't fight, certain loves he couldn't have, no matter how much he desired, as it would be his very death and the death of all he loves. An *Ebreo* has no choice but to reconcile himself to survival and all the awful demands, choices and emotional scars that come along with it. The *forever sadnesses,* as Nonno called them, which forevermore stain the heart and mind.

Though Nonno never spoke of it, he had come to believe that there were two types of sadness: temporary sadness and the forever kind. Temporary sadness may burn very hot at first—for years even—but, over time, it was a sadness that the mind could reconcile and a pain the heart could forgive. Forever sadness, on the other hand, was that sadness that created in the heart permanent embers: cinders of anguish that smoldered away in perpetuity and could at anytime burst into flame, igniting a pain nearly as fresh as the day it first arrived.

The awful truth that life had taught Nonno was that forever sadness was born of guilt: that the pain that forever blistered his heart was not caused by randomness or the force of God, but by cowardice—that if only one had acted with greater courage or cunning the outcome could have been different. This was why the death of his granddaughter, of all the sadnesses that Nonno endured, and there were many, lay heaviest upon his heart. For he could have chosen differently; he did not have to let his granddaughter become a courtesan, especially one to the Duke of Tuscany.

As Nonno now lifted the tray of food and headed toward his grandson, he saw there, glowing before the fire, a young man in the throes of sadness, a sadness, Nonno feared, that would last forever.

"Eat, Davido," said Nonno, as he set the tray of food on

the footstool near where his grandson sat. "You must eat something."

Davido did not respond. He sat before the fire, comatose, still in his blood-and-tomato-stained shirt. The fire crackled before him, throwing glimmers of light across his beaten face. His cheeks were red and raw, his right eye and lips puffy and swollen.

Nonno stood there for a moment waiting; assessing the room, the fire, his grandson, the situation, his own memories. "Do you think," said Nonno, breaking the extended moment of silence, "that I was not young once? That I do not know this pain you are in? I do, Davido, I do. More than you will ever know. But you must remember, child of my child, life is long and the winning is in the living. Now eat." Nonno pushed the tray a bit closer to his grandson. "You will need your strength. We leave for Pitigliano in the morning."

Nonno began to leave, but then stopped. He didn't want to say it, to so state the obvious, but perhaps his grandson needed to hear it from him. "You are an *Ebreo*, Davido, and she is a *Cristiana*." And then he turned and shuffled from the room, knowing that after that, nothing more need be said. Nonno was only twenty or so feet away, opening the door to his bedroom, when he heard the tray come crashing to the floor. Nonno paused for a moment, contemplating what he should do. Then he stepped inside his room and shut the door. Some things, he knew from experience, can only be dealt with alone.

※   ※   ※

Michelangelo was in his mid-sixties when he met and fell in love with a beautiful and charming fifteen-year-old boy named Cecchino dei Bracci. When Bracci suddenly died a year later, it was said that Michelangelo fell into such a fit of despair that he wrote more than fifty love poems dedicated to the boy and sculpted the boy's elaborate tomb—from marble—in less than a month, an unheard of feat. Certainly, the spasm of creativity that now impelled Davido was hardly on par with that of Michelangelo, but it was driven by the same despair.

That horrendous feeling that something holy and sacred, something that one values more than his own life, has been ripped from him, and the mind, in a confused and desperate effort to maintain sanity and provide an outlet for the grief, erupts in a torrent of creativity.

And so it was that Davido lay upon the warm stones before the fire in absolute anguish. In his fit, he had knocked the tray of food over, slid from his chair and collapsed to the floor. What a coward he considered himself. He had just stood there while that monster beat Mari. Now he was sobbing, heartrending sobs. The salt from his tears burned his raw cheeks; vomitus acid scorched the back of his throat. He sobbed with such ferocity that he felt as if his guts might explode from his mouth. Surely, if there'd been any food in his stomach, he would have ejected it upon the bricks before the fire. Instead, he vomited up bile and sadness. All the sadness that sat in the pit of his stomach, sadness over the death of his parents, over the death of his sister, and now this new sadness, the seeming death of everything he loved—Mari and tomatoes. But mostly Davido sobbed for himself and for that calamitous moment when he most needed to be courageous, how he proved to be an utter coward.

Davido lay there for a long time, until a loud pop from the fire drew his attention like that block of marble must have drawn Michelangelo's. There, two feet before him, lying upon the hot bricks, Davido beheld the sight of the tray's spilled contents. A bit of tomato sauce had splattered upon the focaccia; a slice of cheese hung partially over the bread and had begun to melt. Davido's tears paused. He sat bolt upright and slid his body closer to the focaccia. Reaching for the bowl of sauce, with his hand he scraped what remained on top of the focaccia and spread it about with his fingers. He took the slice of cheese that lay partially upon the focaccia and centered it on the sauce-covered bread. He slid the sauce-and-cheese-topped square of bread closer to the fire and watched as the cheese began to melt, brown and bubble. He rotated the focaccia several times to cook it evenly on all sides. From a bundle of herbs he had set above the fire some weeks ago to dry, he sprinkled some oregano on his creation.

Gingerly, Davido lifted the toasted focaccia from the hot stones. The crust burned slightly against the tips of his fingers, and through his swollen lips, he blew to cool it. Davido brought the slice to his mouth and bit down. His lower teeth cracked through the toasted crust. His upper teeth broke through the layer of warm, soft cheese and bread. He began to chew. His swollen lips shimmered in the firelight. His eyelids closed as every ounce of sensate awareness transferred to his palate. At first it was the primordial satisfaction of teeth crunching into warm food that enthralled him but, as he chewed, the sauce and cheese and crust melded and blossomed into a flavor so extraordinary that only one thought, the highest praise Davido could possibly offer, overwhelmed him: "Mari," he gasped, "Mari."

In Which We Learn
the Meaning of *La Punizione*

You shameless coward, shouted La Piccola Voce from inside Benito's head. *He defiles you and you do nothing. He does not even bind your hands and feet, yet you take it like a sheep. How can you let him do this? Do you have no honor? No dignity? How can you not fight?*

Because, as Pozzo Menzogna stated in his eloquent treatise on drama, *comedy without tragedy is irrelevant.* And how else to explain the tragedy of Benito's mind, his self-hating subservience to Giuseppe, unless we glimpse the wicked means employed by Giuseppe that ruined Benito's mind. Giuseppe called it *la punizione,* just as his uncle had. It had been a long time since he had last doled out *the punishment* upon Benito, some ten years. But there are certain things one never forgets. The first time Giuseppe dealt Benito *la punizione* was when Benito was just thirteen, after he had sided against Giuseppe in a disagreement with the man who would one day be Mari's father. After that, Giuseppe used *la punizione* throughout Benito's teenage years, to break him and mold him into the kind of loyal underling he desired. Giuseppe had not used the sadistic form of discipline in years, not since shortly after the *accident* that killed Mari's father. But then, like now, Giuseppe had risked too much and stood to gain too much to abide any disobedience from Benito.

Benito, bent over a barrel of olive oil, crumpled to the ground like a sack of grapes. Sobbing and sniveling, Benito lay there upon the cool floor of the olive mill, his hairy buttocks hanging out, drool and tears issuing from his mouth and eyes.

"Oh, shut up," said Giuseppe as he wiped his brow with his handkerchief and tucked in his shirt. "Stop that pathetic whimpering and take your punishment like a man." That's what Giuseppe's uncle used to say to him. "And pull up your trousers."

Benito did not move.

"I said, pull up your goddamn trousers, murderer."

"No," whimpered Benito through the mucus that clogged his mouth. "You made me. You tricked me."

"I did no such thing," answered Giuseppe. "You always loved Mari and hated her father. It was you who rigged the pulley system. You who killed him."

"No," cried Benito.

"Oh, yes, Benito. You killed him and I am the keeper of your secret. You owe me your very life. You would be drawn and quartered should the village ever discover the truth. Your flesh would be torn from your bones and left for vultures. Your name would never be spoken here again. It would be as if you never lived. And Mari, the one you love so much, she would spit and curse whenever a thought of you arose."

Benito writhed upon the floor as if the words Giuseppe spoke proved a second defilement.

"And it is I, and I alone, who protects you," Giuseppe continued with a chilling calmness. "You shall not fail me, Benito. You shall not fail me ever again."

Giuseppe stepped back from where Benito lay. He walked over to the base of the stairs that led up to his office and picked up a wine bottle sitting there, a bottle infused with a massive dose of *Fungi di Santo.* He returned to Benito and knelt down. "Listen to me," Giuseppe said with an odd tone of tenderness. "Pull up your pants and sit up."

Benito did as he was told.

Giuseppe now set the bottle of wine before Benito. "This is a very special bottle of wine, my finest. Tonight, you are to bring it to the Good Padre. Tell him it is a gift from me, an apology. Tell him I am sorry, that I beg his forgiveness. Tell him I have forgiven Mari, that she has forgiven me, and that all is well in my house. Tell him I will pay a visit to the church in the morning and make my confession. Then you are to open the bottle of wine and insist on sharing a toast with him on my behalf. Tell him you cannot leave until you and he have toasted to peace. Fill his goblet full and watch him drink it down. Then share with him another toast, for the wine is good." Giuseppe stared into Benito's eyes. "Do you understand what I ask?"

Benito nodded yes.

"And you shall not fail me?"

Benito nodded.

"Serve me well and you will be much rewarded." Giuseppe extended the back of his right hand before Benito's face. "Now kiss my hand and tell me that you love me."

Bite it, screamed La Piccola Voce, *bite the filthy hand that ruins you, that has stolen your life from you. Scar him as he has scarred you!*

But the little voice that ranted away inside Benito's head could not undo the bizarre loyalty that bound him to Giuseppe. And with both his hands Benito took hold of Giuseppe's hand and pressed it to his lips. *"Ti amo,"* he said. "I love you."

40

In Which We Learn How Bobo & Benito Came to Hug for the Very First Time

"**D**ove?"

The focaccia and cheese and tomato sauce made him do it. How could he not tell Mari what he'd made with their sauce? He was in such a state that he hardly recalled the donkey ride into the village. Thank God the moon was nearly full and the road to town free of bandits. He tied off his donkey in the brush outside the gates then snuck stealthily into the village. There, he saw the glow and heard the noise coming from the tavern. He figured here, in the shadow of an alley, with one eye on the tavern, was as good a place as any to lie in wait.

"Where?" Davido repeated an instant after reaching out from the alley's shadow, collaring the fool, snatching him into the darkness and pinning him against the wall. Davido had been hiding for over an hour and the fool was the first person to exit the tavern whom he recognized.

It took Bobo's eyes an instant to adjust to the darkness of the alley and the shock of being grabbed in such a manner. But as he made out the face before his, he knew immediately the meaning behind his abduction. Bobo saw the desperation upon the boy's face and something inside him cracked. "There," Bobo offered without hesitation; he pointed to a balcony some twenty paces off. "That's her room," he said in a whisper. "I believe she is there, and I know Giuseppe is not."

Davido looked hard into the fool's eyes, searching his face for the truth. After a moment, he loosened his grip upon the fool's collar. "Are you truly a villain or do you just play at such?" Then Davido craned his neck to see if the coast was clear and headed off to Mari's balcony.

Bobo leaned back against the alley wall and slowly slunk down as if he'd been deflated. The boy's words echoed in his head: *Are you truly a villain or do you just play at such?* The question combined with the boy's desperation pierced him like an arrow through his heart. Now he watched as the boy struggled to get a grip upon the building's stones. It was not an easy face to climb. The bottom three feet were smooth marble and the boy's foot kept sliding, making too much noise for such a risky operation.

He couldn't stand it anymore. Bobo sprang up and ran to where the boy stood. The boy turned in panic. Bobo offered him a slight, conspiratorial smile then dropped onto his hands and knees, creating a stool of sorts. The boy now stepped onto Bobo's lower back. Bobo felt his slight frame buckle—he never was much for physical labors—but his spine held true. At last, the boy found a handhold and the weight upon Bobo's back lightened. Bobo stood up and pushed against the boy's feet, helping him crest the balcony. Leaning over the balcony the boy nodded gratefully down at Bobo, then turned and gently rapped upon Mari's door.

With haste, Bobo shuffled back to the alley and stepped into its shadow. Peering from around the corner, Bobo could not help but watch as the shutter doors opened and Mari stepped onto the balcony. He heard a noise: a sound like a metal chain rattling against stone—had Giuseppe shackled her by the ankle?

It was an archetypal sight for Bobo, something read about in countless stories, seen in plays and reenacted with Bobolito in puppet shows from the time of childhood: the star-crossed lovers in a desperate, moonlit embrace upon a balcony. The image cut to Bobo's very core, and though he knew it was indecent to spy upon two people during such an intimate moment, he could not look away. "Bitter, bitter fool," Bobo whispered to himself as tears welled in his eyes, "look what you have done. Lent a willing hand in killing the only thing worth living for. Cruel, heartless fool, look how they love. What deed more wicked and worse, than to have played in the destruction of love so to hide myself and fill my purse? Is this the fool, is this the creature I've become, to stuff my face whilst love's undone?"

"Huh!"

Bobo's heart sank as he heard the breathy gasp come from the street just beside the alleyway. He knew that grunt anywhere. Bobo pressed himself against the wall to remain hidden and turned his head to find Benito, standing with a bottle of wine in his hand and his mouth agape, also dumbstruck by the sight of the lovers embracing on the balcony. Surely, thought Bobo with an immediacy and horror that was not at all in step with his temperament, if Benito were not dealt with quickly this would be the end of Mari and Davido. Something in Bobo snapped. All his wit, all his cunning and all his cowardice suddenly fled his being, and for the first time in his life, Bobo clenched his fist in violence and struck Benito squarely across the chin.

The blow was excruciating and Bobo felt for an instant that he might faint from the pain coursing through his hand. Benito, on the other hand, appeared to hardly register the punch whatsoever. Slowly, he turned in the direction from which it came. He seemed hesitant to take his eyes off Mari and Davido embracing upon the balcony, as if that was more important than suddenly being knocked across the face. But when he turned to his side and saw Bobo standing there, Benito's emotions flooded not with pain, shock or anger, but desperation. And then Benito did the oddest thing: he stepped into the shadow of the alley, lifted his arms and pulled Bobo close into a tender hug and began to cry. And Bobo, for reasons he could not rightly explain, hugged Benito back and began to cry too.

In Which We Learn
the Difference Between
Knowing Long & Knowing Well

"I will kill him," said Davido in the faintest of murmurs. "I will take a knife from the cupboard, sneak into his quarters and stab him through the heart."

It was late. Mari's exhausted body lay upon him. Davido could feel the cuff and chain binding Mari's ankle scrape against his shin. They had been holding each other and making love off and on for hours. Quiet lovemaking, with their bodies squeezed so tightly together that their passions were nearly soundless, their voices muffled by lips pressed to cheeks. They did their best to keep the chain from rattling against the bed frame to which it was locked. They had no choice but to suppress both their ardor and angst, as they could faintly hear Giuseppe's snores wafting from down the hall.

"No, my love," answered Mari with a poignant smile that Davido felt against his raw and swollen cheek. Though she had not known her lover long, she knew him well enough to be certain he was no killer. "Killing him would mean only certain death for you and all your kin."

"Then what?" asked Davido. "Do we take our own lives? Do we set a knife to our wrists?"

Mari inhaled deeply and then sighed. "I do not think you or I are made of such stuff." She pressed her lips against his ear. "And I am not yet without hope."

Davido smiled, sadly, ironically. "How can it be," he said, "that I know you so little, yet feel as if I've known you forever?"

Mari felt the space where their cheeks touched moisten, their tears commingling. He was crying, which made her love him all the more. "I know not, my love."

"Do you feel this too?"

"I do, my love, as if I have waited lifetimes to be with you again. Like some part of me that I did not know to be incomplete suddenly felt whole the moment I set eyes upon you."

It was both the greatest and the saddest sentiment Davido had ever heard. "Then how," he asked as he kissed her softly upon the cheek, "how can God permit a thing so heaven-sent to be denied on earth?"

"God," Mari whispered, "permits what man allows."

"And are we allowing this?"

"Well, we do not fight it."

Davido turned his head slightly. He felt suddenly ashamed. Mari felt the shift in her lover. "What, my love, is wrong?"

"Oh, Mari," Davido sighed, "so much is wrong. I am an *Ebreo*. You are a *Cattolico*. What do I know of fighting? *Ebrei*, we do not fight. We run, we hide, we broker, we bribe, we do what must be done to survive. How can I fight? There would be so many. How can I do something I know nothing of?"

"How can we not?" answered Mari.

"I," Davido began several times as if his desire to speak preceded the formation of his thoughts. "I . . . I will track you to the nunnery where you are sent. I . . . I can acquire the money—we have much of it hidden. I will buy your freedom. I have seen Nonno bribe many. I know how such things are done. I will buy your freedom. We will run, Mari. To Venice, to Genoa, to . . . to anywhere. We'll take passage on a ship, to an island of Greece, to Cyprus, to Macedonia. Anywhere we can start anew."

Mari leaned up on Davido's chest and looked directly into his eyes. Her lips bent with a slight, sweet smile. She let her fingers linger as she brushed a bit of hair off his forehead and then said, "No."

"No?"

"No, Davido. I will not flee like some fugitive."

"But Mari—"

"I shall not play the part of criminal. I shall not give *him* the satisfaction. This is my rightful home. Olives and grapes my ancestors planted, wine my grandfather made, oil my father pressed. We are not felons that must run from a crime."

"But Mari, I am an *Ebreo,* and you, you a *Cattolico.*"

"So what of it?" Mari held her hands upon the sides of Davido's face, their lips so close they shared the same breath. "What worth is my life if not lived with you? What matters of God or religion true, if I go to nunnery yet pray only for you? Every day, every moment of life, a torture, if I took a false husband and you a false wife. Is this what God wants, is this religion's point and forum, to deceive the heart and live by paltry decorum? Is this what it means to be an *Ebreo,* to be a *Cattolico?*"

Davido felt as if he were suffocating. A horrendous fit of images, real and imagined, spun before his mind's eye. He saw his farm and the fruits he loved; his Nonno as a young man stealing away from Colombo's ship with a sackful of tomato seeds; a memory of his sister as she left home for her *Courtesane* training; the skinny ankles of the girl he was arranged to marry; the children asleep between the rows of tomato plants; his father and mother lying in bed and dying of plague. He felt three thousand years of ancestors standing on his heart, and two awesome forces ripping him apart. Again he said, "But Mari, I am an *Ebreo* and you a *Cattolico.*"

"And so what of it?" Mari too said again. "Though it may seem so, in our hands does not rest our religions' fate, one less will not make their numbers any less great. Neither does threat of hell seem such a curse. I'll risk it in the afterlife rather than guarantee it here on earth. For what could be a more gruesome hellfire, than by cowardice to squander our true love, to waste this right desire. We have, Davido, only to live for ourselves. And folk and village will in time care not whether I went to your side or you to mine, but will see the truth my heart tells me looms above, that if we choose each other, God will protect us, for God is real and God is love."

"We should run, Mari. This is not a battle any man was born to win."

"I cannot, my love. Running before fighting would prove a double sin. Giuseppe would appear the aggrieved and keep my lands, and as vengeance, take yours from your kin."

Davido felt a great weight upon his chest, ten thousand pounds greater than the weight of Mari's body. He felt such the coward. He had never raised a fist, never fought for any-thing. The only fight he'd ever won, he won by vomit. "But so many will rise against us."

"Not so, Davido. There is less here than you think to dread, the monster has but one head."

"But what weapon would I wield?"

"Your heart! Your love, and if need be, your fists too."

Davido looked desperately to Mari. His mouth fell open as if to speak, but no sound came out.

"Fear not, my love," Mari said tenderly as she stroked his face. "I believe in you. You have more than enough heart to stand against this villain. I know this village. They may be cowards, but they are not killers. *He* is the coward, the petty tyrant who bullies and abuses, but he engenders the hidden scorn of all he misuses. If you stand against him and I stand with you, the villagers will choose and choose what's true."

"Do you think, Mari? Do you really believe so?"

Mari smiled at her lover, a smile so strong that it poured courage into Davido's heart. "Oh, yes, my love, I do. It must be so. If not, what the point of life? How another moment proceed if not held by the secret belief that somehow, some way, good will succeed? Our love will win, Davido. It's already done, my heart knows it as fact. For why would God make our love so perfect if God did not want us to act?"

Mari sunk her lips into his, and the lovers began to kiss fully, deeply, hopefully—tasting both the salt from their tears and the sweetness from their soon-to-come victory. Davido slid his hands down Mari's back and once again was overcome by that sublime feeling that his fingertips were each a living and breathing entity. Her skin, how could he describe such a feeling? He let his fingers luxuriate in the detail and nuance of her flesh; the rise of her muscles that ran along her spine; the upward roll from her lower back to the mounds of her backside—mounds of heaven! The two most wonderful, ripe and luscious things he had ever touched. He would compare them to tomatoes, but no tomato could withstand the wondrous kneading and pulling like Mari's ripe fruit.

Davido began to swell to life. A swell that pressed and parted the second lips of Mari's love. She was still warm and wet. Mari moved her hips from side to side and then slowly slid down upon him, swallowing him fully inside of her and exhaling the slightest of moans into his ear. This thrilled Davido, the fact that she slid onto him: that a woman so beautiful and wonderful desired him.

Dear God, Davido took a deep breath and squeezed her tightly against his chest—his will suddenly set like iron, his heart like a lion! For the chance to love a woman so wonderful, he thought, there is not a thing in the world that I wouldn't risk, no battle I would not fight! *For her,* thought Davido, as he felt the weight upon his chest lighten and the elixir of victory proliferate his heart with courage. For her, how can I not?

How Pizza Came to Be, Part II

At the river, during the crumb-tossing procession, when the enormous priest put his hand upon his head and dunked him under the water, Luigi Campoverde, chef for the Duke of Tuscany, felt a sublime light shatter his body, blinding him from the inside out. He felt, for the briefest instant, that he was not separate from anything, that the river water, the hand of the Good Padre, the stones beneath his feet, everything and anything that existed was intricately a part of him and he a part of it. The feeling was so extreme that Luigi lay for hours upon the bank of the river, crying and laughing and mumbling to himself: "*E cosi bello,* it's so beautiful, so beautiful."

It was true that Luigi had not known much love in his

life, given his parents' deaths when he was so young and the harshness of the orphanage where he was subsequently raised. Nonetheless, what he felt as he lay there upon the riverbank transcended even the vague remembrances of love that he'd received from his own mother. A spontaneous revelation, an all-encompassing feeling, that not only was he loved, but he was made *of* love. That God was love and all life sprung from this love.

When Luigi awoke on Wednesday morning he was so grateful to the Good Padre and the altar boys who'd fed and sheltered him for the night that he spontaneously gave all his bodily possessions to the Church. These included the mule and cart he had arrived upon, a bag full of coins and the dozen or so items carried off from the Meducci villa that he had planned to barter at market. All Luigi asked in return was for the Good Padre to make a breakfast of the same meal he'd consumed for supper the previous night: a thin wheel of dough laid with sliced tomatoes, a few olives and some shavings of pecorino that were quickly baked in a hot oven, "until," as the Good Padre said out loud, "the dough begins to *pizea*[21]."

Once removed from the oven, the *pane pizea* (Bertolli's name for it) was drizzled with olive oil, sprinkled with salt, laid with some freshly torn pieces of basil and then immediately eaten. True, by Tuesday evening Luigi had gone a full day without a morsel of food and his senses were both tender and heightened. Nevertheless, the *pane pizea* was the single most delicious thing that Luigi had ever eaten and he would have gladly given all the gold in the world for the chance to eat such a thing again.

To say that Luigi awoke on Wednesday morning a changed man was something of an understatement. He was so transformed, so in doubt of his previous life that he may never have returned to the Meducci villa had it not been for the viciousness of the beating he witnessed a bit later that morning. He had seen people beaten before—indeed, many of the

[21] Ancient Etruscan word describing the blackening of bread in an oven.

monks in his childhood orphanage had seemed to take great delight in beating the young Luigi—but he had never seen anyone beaten for the crime of love. And as the blows landed upon the poor boy's head and the smacks across the girl's face, they impacted Luigi far more than any wallop he'd personally received. How, pondered Luigi's fragile mind, could mankind be so cruel? The couple seemed to be deeply in love and the tomato sauce they'd made possessed a flavor so exquisite that Luigi felt a just and caring God would send an army of angels to guarantee their protection.

But the miracle never transpired. The sight and sounds of slaps and punches and screams horrified Luigi, and as he saw the crock of tomato sauce upon the stand begin to sway and tumble from the tumult, Luigi took action. He stretched forth his hands and lunged with his body, his deluded mind convinced that the souls of the two lovers and everything that was good and beautiful about life was somehow held inside that crock and that it must be saved. But Luigi's coordination was not as keen as his intent, and as his hands reached for the crock, his face passed right before Giuseppe's flying fist. There was pain and an instant of blackness as the blow struck his cheek and pitched him to the ground, but not so much that he did not hear the crack of the crock upon the cobblestones. He felt the warm splatter of tomato sauce upon his neck and then he, in turn, felt himself crack too.

Luigi did not move; he couldn't. The sound of the lovers' wailing paralyzed him. He could do nothing but lie there, partially under the tomato stand, being kicked and stepped upon as the crowd swayed violently above him. He felt his right eye begin to swell, his chest constrict, his breath shorten and a great, ungodly ache emerge from his heart. He was certain this was the death of him. *"E cosi orribile,"* Luigi mumbled as he began to sob with the exact converse of the energy that he'd experienced at the riverbank. "It's so horrible."

Luigi lay there sobbing as the screams of the girl grew distant and the wails of the boy ended with a clatter of hooves and the roll of a wagon wheel. As the piazza went quiet with shame, Luigi did not get up. He laid there awaiting his death, until he felt something bump against his face. There, in front of his nose, was a tomato. Suddenly, a thought entered Luigi's mind—a thought worth living for. He sat up, untucked his tunic and gathered up as many fallen tomatoes as he could manage to hold between his longish shirt and belly. Then he stood up and began to walk. He walked from the piazza and he walked from the village. He walked past farm and forest, walking through the night, arriving back at the villa just before dawn, thinking the entire time the one thought that had saved his life: that young Prince Gian Gastone would very much enjoy a *pane pizea* for breakfast.

⊛   ⊛   ⊛

But there would be no breakfast. "*E cosi orribile!*" Luigi cried out as he let go his shirt-end and the tomatoes fell to the floor. He ran to the prince and cradled the convulsing and near-ruined boy in his arms. There was vomit, blood and diarrhea covering the child's sheets. The left side of the boy's face had fallen, wilting with paralysis. Blood ran from his nose and his eyes. It stained his thin linen pants as it leaked a trail down his legs. It was as if his very organs were being cooked to soup inside his body; but it was the retching and the reeling fits of pain that made Luigi feel as if his heart would shatter into a thousand pieces.

Poor Prince Gian had been alone in his quarters, abandoned by his mother and staff for fear that it was the plague, but Luigi knew the effects of poison when he saw it. He had been trained at the monastery to keep an eye out for such things. "Dear God," lamented Luigi as he eyed suspiciously an empty jar of fig jam sitting on the boy's nightstand. Poison was a slow and awful death and Luigi knew the prince's worst hours still lay ahead.

The prince looked up at Luigi; his eyes were opaque and running with tears and blood, yet they seemed to register the face of his beloved chef.

"Oh, my little Margarita" was all Luigi could think to say, "how you would have loved the *pizea*."

43

In Which We Learn the Meaning of La Dolce e Piccola Morte

Among the courtesans of the Sisters of Esther they called it *la dolce e piccola morte*—the sweet and little death—and while Davido's sister may have known of it, neither Davido nor Mari had ever heard of or experienced such a thing and they knew not to be on the lookout. And so they slept, the sweet and delicious sleep that occasionally follows perfect lovemaking. It had been sublime, the wave-like buildup, the way their bodies and hearts and minds—even their souls—seemed to meld and explode into one another. And then sleep came over them, like a perfect and painless death, and the lovers drifted from orgasm to unconsciousness with their bodies still entwined and without the least bit of awareness.

Usually, as Davido's sister may have attested, the sleep would last for but a few exquisite moments and was more often than not a male-oriented phenomenon—the end result of a heaving, humping, grunting, sweating mass of flesh suddenly erupting and then just as quickly cooling off and passing out. As one might imagine, this was often a rather unpleasant experience for the woman. One moment, she was doing her best to endure a torrent of thrusting, jostling and panting, and the very next, near-suffocating under an intractable blanket of blubber. But in instances of inspired lovemaking, when true love is involved, and especially when the woman's body was atop the man's, the few moments of sleep that followed the couple's climax often proved to be a transcendent siesta for both. Such was the case with Davido and Mari. However, after the physical and emotional trauma of the day, the late hour, the repeated lovemaking and their total exhaustion, what normally would have been a short siesta went on a good bit longer. Had it been a moment or a lifetime? Davido knew not as he was stirred to semi-consciousness. It was that good and deep a sleep, but he wondered—or perhaps he dreamt—why would Mari wake him in such a manner, with her fingernail digging sharply into his neck?

⊛   ⊛   ⊛

Giuseppe knew the smell. He had been about to enter her room when the scent stopped him in his tracks. *Could they be so stupid?* He was imagining that the day and events to come would be much more arduous: gathering up Mari and making a bit of a scene as he led her out of town and banished her to the nunnery at far-off Assisi, then rallying some villagers, mostly men under his employ, to storm the *Ebrei* land. But this, thought Giuseppe, as he took one more sniff of the musk emanating from his stepdaughter's room, this would make everything easier. Quietly, he walked past Mari's room to his own bedroom. Delicately, he opened the door one-third of the way. He reached in and removed the key, then closed the door and locked it. It wasn't much of a lock, but Giuseppe imagined it would be more than enough to keep his wife in her place. After all, the last thing he needed was a hysterical invalid disrupting his plans. Giuseppe slid the key into his pocket and strode to his study. He lifted his crossbow off its wall mount, cranked back the bow and slid an ivory-tipped bolt into the chamber.

☩   ☩   ☩

"Get up, boy."

Davido heard a voice, an awful voice, and then he heard the panting and screaming of Mari as her weight suddenly, violently lifted off his body. He opened his eyes only to find himself blinded. Sunlight filled the room. What was going on? Had he slept so long? He was naked, he knew that. Mari was screaming and it was not, he realized—as the pointed pain against his neck increased and the crossbow came into focus—Mari's fingernail pressed to his throat.

Giuseppe turned and glared at Mari. "Shut up," he said, forcefully pressing the arrow end of the crossbow against Davido's throat. Davido squirmed. The arrow broke the skin; a trickle of blood ran down Davido's neck and stained Mari's bedsheet. Mari quieted; she understood Giuseppe's point: you scream, he bleeds.

Davido strained his eyes to catch Mari in the periphery of his vision. The panic etched upon her face told him that the situation was not good, that his life was in grave danger. Davido trained his eyes back on Giuseppe. He opened his mouth to speak, but the pressure of the arrow tip against his throat stole his voice. Davido knew not what to make of the pair of brown eyes behind the crossbow. They seemed to express emotions other than hate. Davido prayed that his eyes could do all the things his voice couldn't—declare his love for Mari, claim that she was blameless. *Please God,* he thought, *do not let me die naked and helpless, slaughtered through the neck like a sheep.*

And the prayer was answered, or so Davido believed. Slowly, the fierce pressure of the arrow against Davido's throat relented. Odd, thought Davido, noticing the tense pursing of Giuseppe's lips give way to something like a smirk. He looked pleased, genuinely pleased. And then, in a blur, the arrow end of the crossbow spun away from Davido's throat and the blunt, solid-wood handle came crashing into the side of his head. Davido thought he heard Mari cry, thought he felt something like pain, and then everything went black.

⊛   ⊛   ⊛

"Oy," groaned Nonno, pushing open the door to Davido's room to find the bed empty and unslept in. Please God, thought Nonno, may I find him sleeping among the tomato plants. Nonno made a quick pass through their small home. Clearly, Davido was not in the house. Nonno slipped on his boots and jacket. It was early morning, the air was chilly and the ground was still wet with dew. He stepped outside toward the bushy green rows and their red fruits. As he feared, there was no sign of Davido sleeping, walking or working among his beloved tomato plants. *Could he be so foolish?* Nonno sighed his morning's second "Oy" and then quickly walked the twenty paces to the barn, only to find that it too was empty.

Since the death of the donkey Signore Meducci, they had but three donkeys left, only one of which was still tethered to the far side of the barn. *Could he be so foolish?* Yesterday's donkey was still attached to the wagon and the wagon-bed was still full of tomatoes. He and Davido hadn't even thought of detaching the donkey or unloading the wagon when they limped home from yesterday's debacle.

Nonno placed his foot upon the side step and readied himself to mount the wagon when he suddenly thought better of it. He hurried back into the barn, pushed aside a pile of hay in the corner and used an iron crowbar to remove a pair of floorboards. Reaching down into the hollow, he lifted out a burlap sack. From the sack he removed a white and seemingly weighty quilted vest specially designed for holding sums of money in an inconspicuous fashion. Nonno jiggled the vest and quickly judged by its weight that it held enough coin. He removed his jacket and tunic, brushed a little dirt from the vest, laced his bare arms through the money vest and secured its buckles against his chest and upper belly. Who knows, he thought, what kind of trouble I may need to bribe Davido out of today?

44

Sobbing & Laughing, Part II

It was Thursday, not one of the main market days of Monday, Wednesday and Friday, but still a dozen merchants and food vendors filled the piazza. There was some produce to be found, but the emphasis was clearly on breakfast, and nearly all of the hundred or so villagers milling about the piazza were there to fill their mugs with hot tea or scoff down hard-boiled eggs with olive oil and salt for dipping, or, perhaps, the most popular and traditional breakfast in the village, yesterday's bread sliced thick, spread with honey and laid with cheese.

The mood about the piazza was unnaturally pensive. On just about any other day, there was an unspoken agreement to engage in as much conversation and folly as possible before heading off for the drudgery of work in the fields, mills, trade shops and stores; but with nearly half the piazza momentarily heading off to work at Giuseppe's vineyard and mill, the idea of conversation carried an ironic burden that could not be lifted. Hence, most in the piazza looked to their feet or overly fretted about the hotness of the tea or staleness of the bread, anything to avoid talking about the very thing that weighed most upon their hearts and minds. How could Mari have done such a thing? Why in the world would the *Ebreo* boy serve that sauce? And what was to be done about Giuseppe's desire for banishment and forfeiture?

Alas, Bertolli, walking through the piazza on his way to the church, was not so fortunate to avoid the thing that weighed equally as heavy upon his heart. He had always liked Mari, and after his experience eating tomatoes with the Good Padre and the shock of the *Ebreo* winning the Feast of the Drunken Saint by vomiting into Benito's face, Bertolli couldn't help but admire the *Ebreo*. So it was that Bertolli was the villager who noticed them first, and the sight stopped him on the spot. He squinted to better focus his vision over the distance between where he stood and where they were entering the piazza. Could it be? Was such a thing possible?

THE *EBREO* WAS NAKED. His hands were bound with rope before him, blood dripped from his neck and the side of his head. Right behind the *Ebreo,* Giuseppe followed with his raised and loaded crossbow, occasionally jabbing the *Ebreo* in the back and prodding him forward. Close behind Giuseppe trailed Mari, apparently tied and bound upon a long-eared donkey.

The short, sharp moans of pain grew louder and began to capture the attention of others besides Bertolli. Heads turned, conversations ceased and mouths fell agape. It was a shocking sight and quickly brought to the surface the array of conflicting emotions the villagers harbored. Just about all mistrusted Giuseppe, at least a little bit, and conversely adored Mari, but that did not make her love affair a right or accepted thing. Neither did they want to lose Mari to a nunnery.

However, what approached was more than just a startling

sight. It was an archetypal image, and though no villager was conscious of it, something about the scene profoundly struck their psyches. With his lean body, bruised and bloodied face, bound hands and utterly helpless nakedness, the *Ebreo* boy was a near-phantasmagorical likeness of *Cristo* incarnate reliving the *Via Dolorosa,* and this brought the entire piazza to a silent, almost reverent halt.

Bertolli looked to Mari. Her hair was a mess, she wore a white sleeping gown and her hands were bound with rope and tied to the donkey's bridle. Her ankles were also bound by rope, secured to each other under the donkey's belly, trapping her upon its back. Mari lifted her head and caught Bertolli's eye. Immediately, Bertolli understood what the terror in her eyes was beseeching him to do and he ran from the piazza to fetch the Good Padre.

Giuseppe marched his prisoners forward. The sound of the donkey's hooves clattering and the slapping of Davido's bare feet against the piazza's cobblestones played eerily against the flabbergasted silence. No one moved, no one spoke, no one even dared swallow the food in their mouth. To Augusto Po, Vincenzo and a few others, the sight was unsettling, but they convinced themselves that the *Ebreo* deserved such abuse. To Mucca, the Cheese Maker (with his broken, swollen and purple nose), Signore Coglione and many others, the sight was alarming and awful, but to Cosimo di Pucci de' Meducci the Third, the sight of the naked and beaten Davido and his bound lover was entirely devastating.

"Look here!" Giuseppe proclaimed as he prodded Davido. "Behold his naked guilt. I have caught the rat red-handed."

"Lies!" screamed Mari. "All lies."

"Do you see," Giuseppe retorted, "do you see how he's bedeviled her?" Giuseppe positioned Davido in the center of the piazza. The statue of the Drunken Saint lay ten paces to his left, Mari upon the donkey was just behind him and the gathering of food stands and villagers were before him. Giuseppe scanned the crowd. Vincenzo and Augusto Po were there, along with twenty or so men who made their living working at the mill—that was good. Benito and the Good Padre were not there, and that was even better, leading Giuseppe to think that Benito and the *Fungi di Santo*–tainted wine had done the trick.

"You lie!" shouted Mari, her hands and feet struggling madly to free herself. "You are a filthy liar!"

"It is you who is filthy," shot back Giuseppe. "Did I just not find him in your bedchamber, your naked body strewn upon his?"

Mari looked to the crowd desperately. "He lies. I swear it. He has beaten and kidnapped the boy. Ripped him from his farm."

"Ha," scoffed Giuseppe, secretly pleased. "A likely story. I stole the boy and his donkey too." He had purposefully left Mari's mouth ungagged, assuming that her vociferous protests would only further incriminate her. "It is you who is bewitched and full of lies. The only place I ripped him was from 'tween your thighs."

Mari opened her mouth to respond, but the sound of a donkey's hooves and a wagon's wheels clattering against cobblestones stole her words. Heads turned and jaws dropped for a second time as the old *Ebreo* pulled up on the reins and brought the donkey to a stay, just ten feet from his naked grandson. Nonno had seen much in his long life, but nothing he'd seen prepared him for the prospect of his grandson standing bound and bloodied, in the midst of a crowded piazza, surrounded by gentiles, with a loaded crossbow pointed at his back and naked as the day he was born.

Like mice smelling cheese, heads began to peer out from windows and balconies and alleys and stores as more villagers were keen to see what the ruckus was about. Davido, however, could not stand to look up. He knew from the crowd's collective gasp that it could be none other than Nonno.

"Please," said Nonno as he rose to step from his wagon, "he is a stupid boy, I know, but he—"

"Stay where you are, old man!" Giuseppe cut him off.

"He made a different sauce." Nonno looked desperately at several faces in the crowd. "He may be guilty of love, but he made a different pot of sauce. He didn't serve you the sauce that—"

"No!" Giuseppe raised his voice to thwart that of Nonno's. "Just to me, he did."

Nonno turned to face Giuseppe. "You, sir," Nonno said wryly, "seemed to deserve it."

"Shut up, old man, or I will put a bolt through his brain. This grandson of yours, the villain, the ruin of my daughter."

Mari looked to Nonno and then to the crowd. "What the man says is true! Davido served you all from a fresh sauce. It was I and only I who served Giuseppe."

"Shut up!" Giuseppe barked over his shoulder while keeping his eye and the crossbow focused on Davido's back. He glanced upon a few faces in the crowd and could see their mental wheels spinning in a direction he did not like. "Do you see how my daughter disgraces me, disrespects me?"

"I am not your daughter!"

"You certainly are not!" Giuseppe yelled back at her. "For no flesh of mine would grow to be such a *puttana*!"

"Do not call her that!"

"What?" said Giuseppe, raising his crossbow and refocusing his attention upon Davido. "You dare speak? He who's turned my daughter to a harlot?"

Davido shifted to face Giuseppe, mortally embarrassed that his naked buttocks now faced Nonno and much of the crowd. At least his hands were bound before him, providing a slight bit of coverage to his genitals. He had no doubt he would be dead soon, and he hoped that that certainty would take his attention off his own pain and pathetic nakedness. Alas, such was not the case, and as he spoke up to defend Mari, resolved to what he must do, he was acutely aware of it all: the splitting ache in his head, the throbbing arrow-pierced holes in his neck and back, the shame that he had brought upon Mari, the devastation to Nonno. "Do not call her that," Davido repeated firmly.

"You, villain," roared Giuseppe as he stormed forward, "are in no place to make demands." Giuseppe spun the butt-end of his crossbow around and jammed it into Davido's gut.

Mari screamed; Nonno yelled; Signore Coglione moaned;

Cosimo, Mucca and a hundred others gasped. Davido dropped to his knees, the wind knocked from his body.

Now Giuseppe raised the crossbow and held it directly between Davido's eyes. "Admit your guilt, villain, and I may spare your life."

"My life," said Davido, gasping for breath, "what do I care for my life? But leave her be. She is innocent."

"Innocent?" mocked Giuseppe. "Would an innocent serve a sauce so crude? Would the innocent be found laying in the nude?"

"It is all my doing," said Davido. "She is blameless."

"Not true," said Mari pleadingly. "My love, why do you say such things?"

"You know not what you say, girl!" Davido shouted. He was desperate and panting; saliva and blood dripped down his face. "Do not blame her. Her heart and mind are not complete, for I have swayed them with devilry and deceit. I have used *Ebreo* potions. I have bewitched her with Love Apples and ancient spells. I have used the blackest magic, the darkest *Ebreo* art to lower her virtue and steal her heart. Punish me. It is I who you must kill, for she did not act from her free will."

Giuseppe had not expected the *Ebreo* to say such a thing. He'd imagined the puny boy would plead for his life, and he had no immediate response.

"Not true," said Mari, breaking the brief silence. "He did nothing of the sort. He lies to protect me. He lies because he is brave and good."

Davido glanced pleadingly at Mari. Why, his eyes seemed to ask, will you not let me run this ruse and spare you this misery?

"Oh, shut up!" Giuseppe snapped. "Look how the illicit lovers protect each other. But it matters not. The crime, the guilt, is all the same."

"Then punish me," Davido spoke up, "kill me, for it is I who's most to blame."

"If the law permitted me to kill you," said Giuseppe, "I

would for the indignity you've brought upon my name. But I will exercise no more revenge or might than that which is my legal and paternal right." Giuseppe retreated a few steps back from Davido. "Now get up, get off your knees. Go to your grandfather. Get thee from this village. Pack up all that belongs to you and be off your land by sunset tomorrow. For you and all your kin will pay the price for this great sin. As fatherly judgment and papal law permit, she's to a nunnery and your land to forfeit."

Every stomach and heart in the crowd twisted and fluttered with fear, none more so than Nonno's. Nonno felt so suddenly old—old and scared beyond reason—and he knew not what to do. He opened his mouth to speak, to say something on his grandson's behalf, but another sound came first—the sound of laughter.

"Is that what this is all about?" Davido said between laughs, albeit a gasping, swollen-lipped and slightly delirious laugh. "My land?"

"Shut up, boy," growled Giuseppe.

"A thief." Davido's laughter grew. "A lowly thief. This is not about immorality and abuse of chastity—"

"I said, shut up, boy!" Giuseppe now aimed the crossbow at Davido's throat.

"—or a vengeance-minded father driven by grief. This is about land, and you're a thief."

Giuseppe tightened his finger on the trigger. "I said, shut up, boy, or you'll be dead."

Naked, beaten, bloodied and upon his knees, Davido lifted his head to face Giuseppe. "Oh, the thief does murder too?"

"As you have ruined my daughter!" Giuseppe roared.

"Mari," Davido looked directly into Giuseppe's eyes, "is not your daughter."

Mari felt her heart swell.

"Get up." Giuseppe motioned with the crossbow for Davido to stand. "As fatherly judgment and papal law permit, she's to a nunnery and your land to forfeit."

But Davido did not rise. He remained on his knees, glaring into Giuseppe's eyes, unmoved by the crossbow's bolt trained upon his throat. "No. Better you slaughter me like the thief and butcher you are."

"By the devil, I'll do it!" Giuseppe said furiously. "As fatherly judgment and papal law permit, she's to a nunnery and your land to forfeit."

The crowd fell deathly quiet. Giuseppe braced the crossbow against his shoulder. His left eye closed to better focus his right. His finger tightened.

"It is not his land to give away." A voice, not Davido's, broke the silence.

Giuseppe and his crossbow turned. All heads followed suit.

"You," said Giuseppe incredulously.

"Yes, I, Cosimo di Pucci de' Meducci the Third, Grand Duke of Tuscany," said Cosimo in his most regal and powerful voice as he stepped forward from the crowd. "And as your sovereign, I do hereby prohibit this forfeiture from taking place. Besides, you vile, ignorant moron, all law, papal law, is subordinate to will and judgment of the Meducci. All land of Tuscany is my land. I dole it out only by the goodness of my heart. And I pardon any and all wrongdoing here and order that you cease this inquisition at once."

"You," Giuseppe chortled menacingly. "The Duke of Tuscany, the vagrant wretch who works my land for free? The itinerant fugitive who survives only by the good graces of Benito? Oh, this is too much."

The crowd, however, did not laugh. No question, the idea that the odd, sweetly natured character who had wandered into town a few weeks earlier was the Duke of Tuscany was indeed laughable, but the crazy fool had put himself in harm's way and no one saw fit to join Giuseppe in laughter.

Neither did Cosimo laugh. He narrowed his eyes, lifted his chin and gazed upon Giuseppe with an aristocratic sort of contempt. "You dare deride the Duke of Tuscany, you petty, pathetic, arrogant beast? I will have you stripped and flogged and pitched into the dankest, darkest dungeon of my choosing. I will destroy you and usurp all that you own and give it to whom it pleases me. I will make of this day a great feast.

Children will play games that scoff and scorn your memory. Adults will gather to drink and eat and celebrate the vanquishing of the loathsome, bullying little tyrant who once tried to get in the way of a love so true."

The crowd was stone-silent, their guts gripped with tension. No one had ever spoken to Giuseppe in such a fashion, and the style with which it was done had more than one villager believing that the bizarre interloper might just be the Duke of Tuscany.

"Now put down your weapon," continued Cosimo, "and leave forever this place. You are banished, exiled, hereby forbidden from ever setting foot in this village again. You will find no home or peace in my Tuscany. You will walk south. I catch the Roman in your tongue. You will return to that turgid place from which you came. This is my command and I pity the fate that will befall you should you dare be here tomorrow when I return with my guard."

Giuseppe felt himself bristle with rage and fear. He had never told anyone that he was from Rome, and the fact that his long-buried accent had been so easily recognized troubled him even more than what the deranged interloper had said. Could it be? he thought to himself. Impossible.

Shoulders back, chest forward, the way a king carries himself, Cosimo strode over to Davido and stood before him, his back to Giuseppe. Taking off his stableman's waistcoat, he set it over Davido's shoulders.

"You dare turn your back on me?" Giuseppe yelled.

Cosimo did not reply nor did he turn around. Instead, he put his hands on Davido's shoulders and helped lift him to his feet.

"You dare turn your back on me?" Giuseppe barked again.

Cosimo ignored Giuseppe as he looked Davido in the eye. "I knew your sister," he said softly for only Davido to hear, "and I shall not let the same fate befall you."

No sooner had these unimaginable words landed upon Davido's ears than he heard the snap of the crossbow and the horrendous sound of an arrow pierce and burst through skin and muscle. Right before Davido's eyes, the duke's expression exploded with pain as the hands upon Davido's shoulders gripped him in anguish.

There was a scream from the crowd. The duke fell forward onto Davido's naked chest, his hands gripping desperately against Davido's shoulders as he slowly crumpled to his knees. Looking down, Davido saw the arrow lodged into the duke's right buttock and blood pouring from the area, drenching his pants leg and turning it crimson.

Giuseppe dropped his crossbow, strode over to the kneeling duke and, with appalling insouciance, stomped him with the sole of his boot between the shoulder blades. The blow smashed the duke into Davido, knocking him backward and the duke face-first to the ground.

"Now," said Giuseppe as he quickly knelt down and removed his gleaming, ivory-handled dagger from inside his boot, "enough games." Giuseppe then grabbed Davido by the hair, bent his head back and placed the dagger to his throat. "You will be gone, or you will be dead, and your land is forfeit!"

Splat! Davido heard the screams and felt the blood burst and splatter upon his face, filling his open mouth and blinding his eyes. Though it seemed that everyone in the piazza cried out in unison, he clearly heard the two voices that mattered to him most—Nonno and Mari. *I am dead,* he thought as Giuseppe's firm grip upon his hair slackened. Shame of all shames, I am dead. So much I wanted to do . . .

But in an instant Davido recognized that the taste in his mouth was not blood, but *tomato.* Opening his eyes, Davido saw Giuseppe, a mere eighteen inches before him; the tyrant looked stunned with the remnants of a tomato pasted across the right side of his face. Giuseppe shook his head to regain his wits, apparently equally stunned by the blow and the notion that someone had the gall to attack him. Slowly, he turned his head in the direction from which the blow came. There, seeming more giant than ever, Giuseppe saw who dare oppose him. It was the Good Padre.

"Benito," Davido could have sworn he heard Giuseppe mumble, "you failed me."

Giuseppe now squared his shoulders in the Good Padre's direction and the crowd fell absolutely silent, petrified with fear. True, the Good Padre was enormous, but Giuseppe had a knife and seemed far more the killer between the two. He took a step forward when suddenly a heartrending moan filled the air and a feebly thrown tomato bounced off Giuseppe's shoulder. The blow, though harmless, stopped Giuseppe in his tracks.

"You?" Giuseppe said with a wicked crinkle to his lips as he beheld his wife, Mari's mother, standing on the side of the wagon opposite the Good Padre and already reaching to grab another tomato.

The delay proved just enough. *Splat!* As if fired by cannon, another tomato blasted into the side of Giuseppe's head. Davido heard the crowd gasp; a cripple and a priest were leading the charge. Again, the Good Padre reached into Nonno's wagon, lifted a tomato from it and hurled it. This time the tomato struck Giuseppe in his raised dagger hand and knocked the blade into his face, opening a small cut upon his cheek and sending the dagger clanging to the ground.

Mari, Mucca, the Cheese Maker, Signore Coglione, Bertolli and dozens of villagers let loose with a great roar. The crowd converged upon the wagon, hands extended so to grab a tomato and follow the Good Padre's lead. Tomato after tomato began to bombard Giuseppe, blows paltry and punishing alike. Davido caught the expression on his grandfather's face—the single most incredible look he had ever seen! To call it delight or bewilderment would have ignored its spiritual component: the epiphany on Nonno's countenance that he would live to see the day that a crowd of simple rhymers came to the defense of his grandson. Davido then looked to Mari; she too seemed equally enthralled that her mother, her beaten and broken mother, could rise to such heights of courage.

The entire crowd now hollered a great battle cry as they continued their assault upon Giuseppe. Bertolli, Mucca, Signore Coglione and a half-hundred others near the wagon threw tomatoes. Those about the market grabbed and launched what was closest at hand. The Cheese Maker lifted a firm smoked mozzarella from his stand and with devastating accuracy did to Giuseppe's face what yesterday had been done to his. Even amongst the din, Davido heard the crack of Giuseppe's nose and saw it collapse to the side. He watched in disbelief as dozens of tomatoes and hard-boiled eggs and onions and hunks of cheese and whatever else one had at hand pummeled Giuseppe. The revolt was contagious, and perhaps by virtue of village sentiment or some shred of personal decency, even Augusto Po and Vincenzo entered into the fray, bombarding Giuseppe with the hard-boiled eggs on the stand before them.

Strangely, Giuseppe did not try to cover or protect himself. He simply stood there hollering as things both hard and soft exploded into him; hollering, as if he could not fathom that a man as great as he could be undone in such a ridiculous fashion. Giuseppe was stout and took quite a pounding until a viciously thrown hunk of pecorino cheese came crashing into his left ribs. The blow knocked the wind out of him, perhaps even cracking a rib, and comically altered Giuseppe's defiant holler into a dismal moan.

At last, Giuseppe keeled over, staggering like a drunken fool whose body was torn between a desire to walk and an urge to vomit. His feet slipped and shuffled on the puddle of food-slop surrounding him. To no avail, his discombobulated hands attempted to swat the tomatoes and eggs and onions flying toward him as if they were gnats swarming around his head. It appeared to Davido, who was closest by, that Giuseppe was mouthing the words *basta, basta,* but that he had not even the breath to say, "enough, enough." Finally, Giuseppe could take no more and he dropped to his knees as if his legs were made of water. Another tomato or two bounced off Giuseppe's head and shoulder, but it was clear the villain was finished and the crowd's attack petered out. He was a bloody and beaten mess, his nose and ribs broken.

The crowd came to a halt—an exquisite moment of stillness before they burst with elation. Giuseppe had been brought to his knees by tomato and onion, egg and cheese. But not even this odd victory could prepare the villagers' eyes, for that which came next took all by surprise. There, parting the crowd, without clothing or single shroud, together upon a lone donkey and naked for all to see, came Benito and Bobo the Fool. But wait! In a delicious twist of fate, sure as sagging bosoms sway by donkey's gait, appeared the naked truth that only the duke knew: Bobo the Fool was a woman. And by *Fungi di Santo*'s magical glory, last night must have been some story, for all the rancor their relationship was formerly made of now appeared transformed into a sweet, sweet love.

The entire piazza stared. There was no denying it: Bobo's naked flesh was too close at hand, passing right before the eye. Perhaps by age, or more likely from decades of flattening, Bobo's bosoms hung like the teats of an old cow milked half to death; but they were bosoms nonetheless. And by virtue of Benito's blissful demeanor they seemed more than good enough for him.

Benito halted his donkey as close to Giuseppe as the mash of food surrounding him would allow. With what little awareness Giuseppe had left, he too gazed at Benito. The donkey lowered its head and began to selectively feed upon the weapons of Giuseppe's destruction. Benito blithely took little notice of anything other than Giuseppe and let the donkey eat freely. Bobo kept her arms wrapped around Benito's barrel-like belly, her cheek resting lovingly against his back. Even to Davido, who knew him little, but especially to those who knew him well, Benito appeared transformed, like a large, naked, hairy and adorable cherub.

"Poor love-lost Giuseppe," said Benito without a trace of rancor; the little voice inside his head vanquished as surely as Giuseppe had been. "By willing hands and supple head you've played me through a life of dread. And while the plans and profit have been all yours, sadly, it's been I who's done the chores. You, the shameless, beguiling bully, deceived me into undoing that pulley. The deed that killed Mari's father. And now you aim to twist love with wretched lies, and once again, look to profit by love's demise. But love, Giuseppe"—

Benito paused and looked pityingly upon his former boss—
"love must win."

Benito lifted his gaze from Giuseppe and regarded Mari.
"Sweet girl," he said contritely, "I am sorry, so very, very sorry."
And with that Benito gently prodded his donkey and the pair
of naked lovers began their slow exit from the piazza.

"Cousin," said Bobo playfully as she turned her head to
look upon Cosimo. "Wouldn't this all make for a lovely *Opera
dei Pupi?*" And that was all she said, keeping her eyes and
smile on Cosimo for one last moment.

Cosimo, who was lying on his side being tended to by
Mucca, could not help but smile back. "Yes," he said softly, "it
certainly would."

The crowd watched as the fool and the slob they thought
they knew so well waddled off together upon their donkey,
arms wrapped around each other. It was quite a bit to take in.
All that had transpired in the past few minutes was a lifetime's
worth of secrets, deceits, treacheries, revelations and reunions.
And, as the donkey carrying Bobo and Benito cleared the piazza, all eyes returned to Giuseppe: the villain, the usurper,
the murderer of Mari's father.

Mucca stood up from the side of Cosimo and gathered
Giuseppe's fallen dagger from the ground. She shook the slop
from it and walked over to Mari. Using the dagger, she cut
the rope that bound Mari's hands and feet to the donkey. The
Cheese Maker approached Davido, removed his own large
apron and tied it around the boy's waist, covering the parts
of his nakedness that Cosimo's coat had not. He then took a
small knife and cut the rope that tied Davido's hands.

The crowd stood in silence as Mari rolled off her donkey and rubbed her sore wrists. She could now do whatever
she wanted. The awful truth had been revealed: Giuseppe had
killed her father and he'd planned this current ruse to destory
both her and Davido. She could kill him if she chose to—even
use Giuseppe's own dagger and stab it through his heart—
and no one would act to stop her. Mari stood there, taking
in the evil that for the last decade had been her stepfather.

She'd spent years imagining Giuseppe's destruction, how she would love to see him humiliated and vanquished, and how she needed to be the one to do it. But now that he lay beaten and crumpled upon the ground, wheezing for breath, Mari saw Giuseppe for what he really was: a friendless, petty tyrant. A peasant, really, just like all the villagers, though a peasant with two coins to rub together. However, now that the illusion of wealth and power was broken, Giuseppe *had* nothing, he *was* nothing. And the one thing that makes life bearable, *love,* Giuseppe had not even that—not for anyone, nor anyone for him. And this, Mari understood—as she thought of Davido, of her father, her mother, the Good Padre, the village that had come to her defense—made Giuseppe a creature truly worthy of pity. And so Mari did nothing, for Giuseppe was *nothing.*

She lifted her gaze, looked to the crowd. She found the eyes of the Good Padre; they were waiting for her, bright, wide, loving and baffling as ever. She smiled at him, and he at her, a smile worth a lifetime of gratitude. Mari then looked to her mother. Her eyes were also waiting for her daughter's gaze, but her eyes were different now, brighter, wider and more resplendent with love than they had been in a decade. Mari then turned to Davido. *Of course* his eyes were waiting, waiting with ten thousand arrows of love that Mari instantly felt pierce her heart. She was not sure that the village's vanquishing of Giuseppe equaled a sanctifying of her love for the *Ebreo;* nevertheless, she could not stop her feet from following her heart.

The crowd stood there watching as Mari walked to the boy and then kissed him sweetly upon the cheek; stood there mesmerized as the boy blushed and despite his cuts and bruises looked suddenly like the happiest man in all of Tuscany; stood there thinking precisely what Nonno also thought, that there are times in life when it's possible to believe that a just and fair God rules the world. First Bertolli, then Mari's mother, then Mucca, the Cheese Maker, Vincenzo, Signore Coglione and the entire crowd turned to look at the

Good Padre, and saw that he too was looking and smiling in the direction of Mari and Davido, that their wonderful, baffling, mind-boggling priest seemed to approve of this love and sanctify it in the eyes of Church and God. And then, like a bottle of Lambrusco, that odd, sparkling wine that the people of Parma prefer to drink, the cork of triumph popped. Mari leapt into Davido's arms. The crowd exploded with merriment, and the couple kissed with the exact and perfect zeal that Cupid reserves for lovers who have just overcome great odds!

And the crowd too followed Cupid's bow. There was spontaneous hugging and joyous slaps upon the back, laughter and tears of joy. Mucca and Vincenzo hugged, as did the Cheese Maker and Mari's mother, Bertolli and his uncle Signore Coglione. Even Augusto Po, who had not hugged another human in forty-three years, found himself improbably—delightfully—wrapped inside the huge, warm arms of the Good Padre. But just then, as the entire town frothed and bubbled with jubilation, an incredible clatter of hooves dispirited the celebration and a dozen gleaming stallions came galloping into the piazza.

The cadre of Meducci guards drew their horses to a halt and the crowd recoiled nervously. Most in the village rarely, if ever, had seen a Meducci guardsman and the sight of a dozen battle-hardened, elaborately adorned soldiers atop their fierce horses turned the mood from gaiety to anxiety in a heartbeat. Cosimo, however, feared he knew why his chef would take such a risk.

"My lord!" cried Luigi Campoverde upon finding his boss lying on his side with a bolt stuck in his buttock and a cloth compressed against the wound. He quickly dismounted and hurried to the duke's side.

"Just a scratch," Cosimo answered his chef, waving off his concern. But the look of desperation upon Luigi's face could not be waved off and Cosimo felt his heart sink.

"My lord," Luigi repeated, hardly able to say the words, "your son."

The Meducci guards dismounted and scanned the crowd for dangerous elements. The lead guard stepped forward and a burst of nerves swam up Davido's spine. He recognized him. It was the older guard whom he'd led in prayer and who'd given him a pouch of gold coins just eleven days ago.

The lead guard rushed to Cosimo's side and gestured to the crossbow bolt sticking from the duke's buttock. Cosimo flicked his chin in the direction of the bloodied and beaten man sitting in a pile of food muck, mumbling deliriously. The lead guard nodded to the duke, then removed a cudgel from his belt, approached Giuseppe and whacked him across the back of the head.

Mari, Davido and the entire crowd groaned, not with empathy for Giuseppe, but more at the ruthless efficiency of the guardsman. The fierce soldier cracked Giuseppe across the head the way a skilled chef cracks an egg one-handed: deft enough to spill the yolk without getting a trace of shell in the bowl. And just like that, Giuseppe fell face-first into the slop—unconscious, but not dead.

The lead guard restashed his cudgel then returned to the duke's side. He took a leather bit from a satchel attached to his belt and handed it to the duke. With haste, Cosimo placed the bit between his teeth and braced his hands upon Luigi's arm.

The lead guard now set his hand on the bolt and eyed Cosimo. "I'll pull on three," he explained, suggesting to all present that this was not the first time he'd dealt with an arrow sticking from someone's flesh. *"Uno, due . . ."* The lead guard pulled on two.

"Ay!" Cosimo reeled and his jaw clamped down on the leather bit.

"Mi scusi," said the lead guard as he held the bloody arrow.

Cosimo nodded approvingly, knowing his man had done the procedure exactly right. The lead guard then took out a small vial of honey, scooped some onto his finger and pressed it into Cosimo's wound. Next, he undid the burgundy sash from around his own waist and tied a figure-eight knot, weaving it around Cosimo's hips, waist and thighs, effectively securing and compressing the wound. All told, the operation took hardly a minute and thoroughly impressed the village folk.

Luigi and the lead guard now helped the duke to his feet. "Cosimo di Pucci de' Meducci the Third," the lead guard announced, "Grand Duke of Tuscany!" And then he rapped his sword three times upon the cobblestones and all the members of the Guard dropped to one knee and bowed their heads.

Mari looked to Davido, Mucca looked to the Cheese Maker, Augusto Po looked to Vincenzo. It was true! The odd vagrant in their midst was who he claimed to be. Accordingly, every villager in the piazza followed the guards' lead, lowering themselves onto one knee and bowing their heads.

"Raise your heads," commanded Cosimo, acting decidedly more like a king than a farmer. "Guards," he gestured to where Giuseppe lay, "take this man. Bind him and toss him in the dankest, darkest and most dismal prison in all of Tuscany. There he shall stay, and there he shall have a special sentence. These fruits of red that lie about him, they are called tomatoes, and they are all he shall be fed. And when it is winter," the duke looked to Davido and paused for a moment, unsure of what to say next, "he will eat dried tomatoes—tomatoes dried by the sun."

Now, there's an idea, mused Davido and the Good Padre at the very same instant: *sun-dried tomatoes.*

"He will have only water and tomatoes for the remainder of his days. And so it is." The duke flicked his wrist in the direction of Giuseppe, indicating that he was through addressing that subject.

The lead guard pointed to a pair of junior guards, and then pointed to the criminal in question. The junior guards sprung to their feet, dragged Giuseppe from the food mess and began to bind him up.

"Now," continued Cosimo, loud enough for all to hear, "the olive mill, the vineyards, the orchards that were wrongfully his, I return rightfully to Mari. And as for you two," Cosimo proclaimed while limping over to Mari and Davido

and gesturing for them to rise, "I do not care much for religion, but I care a great deal about love. And your love will
be protected as long as I am duke. But we Meduccis are not
known for our longevity, so I would suggest that you choose
one religion. Which one, I do not care. But be of that, marry
in that and live in that. And know that a life lived for love is a
life lived in God." Cosimo leaned in and lowered his voice for
only Davido and Mari to hear: "I will keep an eye on you both
and may your sister in heaven keep an eye on us all."

Cosimo then smiled as he stepped away from the couple and, with the aid of his chef, hobbled toward the battalion. The pair of guards who had bound Giuseppe now
heaved him up onto a horse's back and secured him there
with rope. Subsequently, the lead guard and two others lifted
Cosimo onto the back of his exquisitely muscled horse. All
the Meducci guards followed suit and mounted up, some of
them, including Luigi, mounting up two per saddle. Davido
caught the eye of the lead guard as he settled into his saddle
behind the duke. A glimmer of recognition crinkled the old
warrior's brow, followed by the slightest of smirks.

From atop his horse, Cosimo gazed down upon the gathering of villagers who, for the last three weeks, had been his
peers—his salvation. "Good-bye, my friends," he said with a
raise of his hand, "you have been so very good and kind to
me; indeed, you are the noblest kin in all of Tuscany." Without
even realizing that he had rhymed his language like a peasant, Cosimo gave a nod and the lead guard stirred his horse
to action. Please God, thought Cosimo, as the entire battalion
galloped from the piazza, let me see my son one last time.

⌘   ⌘   ⌘

"Look," said Bertolli, breaking the extended silence. They
had all been mesmerized: Davido, Mari, the Good Padre, the
Cheese Maker, Mucca, Signore Coglione, Vincenzo, Augusto
Po and all the villagers gathered in the piazza—gazing in
the direction where Cosimo di Pucci de' Meducci the Third
and his *Guardia Nobile di Meducci* had just galloped from
the piazza. Of all the things unimaginable just one hour ago,

none was more fantastic than the realization that for the last three weeks the Duke of Tuscany had been living and working among them.

"Look!" Bertolli repeated more urgently. Heads turned and Davido felt his heart tumble. It was Nonno. Davido ran to the wagon; Mari followed and everyone closed in. Apparently, Nonno had fallen from his seat, fallen backward and landed in the wagon-bed upon the few tomatoes that had not been thrown. Moreover, he'd landed in such a way that his head had squashed a ripe tomato and splattered its red, watery innards into something like a nimbus of pulp and seeds.

Nonno was dead—he had to be. As Menzogna wrote: *How taste the sweet with the bitter?* He had died with his eyes wide open—as if he saw death coming—wet and misty with tears. He had died with a grin, profoundly pleased that life had given him just enough answers: that people could be good and righteous, that his granddaughter had not whored herself to a scoundrel and that the duke was an honorable man. The grin too expressed Nonno's equal pleasure that life had left him with just enough mystery: not to have to live to see whether his grandson became a *Cattolico* or his granddaughter-in-law an *Ebreo*.

Davido began to sob, because it's the tragedy of life that hits first and hardest. They were all dead now—his mother, his father, his sister and now Nonno. Old as his grandfather was, Davido never imagined that Nonno, who'd evaded death on so many occasions, would one day succumb to it. All that was good and glorious about the day instantly evaporated and Davido plummeted into a sea of sadness. Davido's emotional descent was powerful and its tide pulled Mari into it, and she began to sob too. She sobbed at first because Davido sobbed and he was her family now. She sobbed for the seemingly sweet grandfather she would never know. She sobbed because now she knew the truth: that her own father had been stolen from her and that the murderer had then usurped everything her father had built, and that was a tragedy that demanded sobbing.

All the villagers in the piazza began to sob as well. They

sobbed for the old man because he seemed sweet and brave and as loving and loyal as a grandfather should be. They sobbed for Davido, because he seemed to love his grandfather so very much. The sobbing grew, because Mari's plight was something that made every villager weepy and ashamed. Her father had been murdered and despite suspicions and ill feelings toward Giuseppe, either by reason of cowardice or coin, they'd all turned a blind eye to everything that was bad about him. They sobbed because the Good Padre sobbed, and because the morning had carried with it such an array of emotions that sobbing felt like a natural thing to do.

At first, those present in the piazza sobbed for what was before their eyes, but then the villagers began to sob for themselves, over things unseen. They sobbed for parents and grandparents who'd passed away, and for children and friends and anyone else who still needed to be sobbed over. They sobbed because life is nothing if not a constant reconciliation with death and sadness and loss that leaves one no choice but to sob—to sob or lose one's mind. They sobbed for the mere and holy and cathartic sake of sobbing. They sobbed because life can be cruel and ironic and because the perfect resolution had been stolen from them: just when evil was vanquished and goodness restored, a sweet old man had died and salted their comedy with tears.

The communal expression of sadness continued for some time, until the moment Davido felt Mari's hand touch his and her farm-strong and olive-oil-soft fingers interlace with his. The touch was enough—more than enough—to initiate Davido's transformation from sobbing to laughter. He was not alone, for as surely as something had died, something else had been born. And just as his sobbing had been a descent that pulled all around him downward, his laughter was an ascent of even greater power. Davido began to laugh, because it's the comedy of life that tends to hit second and softest, and, God willing, stay with us the longest. He laughed because he could now see all that was ironic and sublime about Nonno's death. The old man had died upon a bed of Love

Apples, after all, with a nimbus of crushed tomatoes around his head and a gathering of *Cattolici* to mourn him. He'd died with his hand upon his heart and a grin upon his face. Died knowing that his granddaughter's paramour was a just and decent man, and that his grandson had found a love that was good and true. Died in nearly the exact way and in the exact spot that his favorite donkey had died just a few days earlier, and what could be more hilarious than that?

Mari felt Davido's fingers tighten around hers and she too began to laugh, because, just as there was a tragedy to sob over, there was also a comedy in which to rejoice. Giuseppe had been vanquished, the olive mill returned to her and her love for Davido sanctified by the Duke of Tuscany himself. All in the piazza began to laugh. At first they laughed for Davido, because he was a comical sight, bloody and beaten, yet wise enough to recognize that his grandfather's passing was an exquisitely ridiculous death that had to be laughed over. And the laughing grew, because Mari laughed, and this was something every villager could celebrate. Her father's murder had been avenged and not with daggers and blood, but with cheese and eggs and onions and tomatoes—strange, new, glorious and delicious tomatoes.

They laughed because the Good Padre laughed, and because the morning had carried with it such an array of emotions that their minds and hearts and souls needed the release of laughter. They laughed in joy for Davido and Mari's triumph. They laughed because Bobo was a woman and now everything about him—*her*—made sense, and because Benito had been naked upon a donkey, yet chivalrous as a knight upon a stallion and seemingly adored by Bobo. And what could be more worthy of laughter than that? They laughed because it really *was* the Duke of Tuscany living in their midst and Giuseppe had shot him in the ass with an arrow! They laughed because life is nothing if not a constant reconciliation with death and sadness and loss that leaves one no choice but to laugh—to laugh or lose one's mind. They laughed for the mere and holy and cathartic sake of laughing itself. And they laughed because those things that all decent people adore—love, justice, olives, tomatoes and a happy ending—had won the day, and these were things worth laughing over.

🍅 *Fine* 🍅

Acknowledgments

If my gratitude is to begin anywhere, it should start with the Tuscan hills of Matraia, outside the city of Lucca, where in 1995 I was working the grape and olive harvest of a charmingly chaotic, little-known family vineyard. My de facto chaperone, a roguish, sex-crazed, failed Italian race-car driver, and I were headed to the farmhouse for lunch, when he plucked a ripe tomato from the vineyard's garden and introduced me to the heirloom variety of a fruit I thought, up until that point, I knew well. Alas, from a Tuscan tomato to a loving Noodle, many have helped me over the course of writing *Tomato Rhapsody;* none more so than my wife, whose ragu of unwavering belief and keen perception kept me well fortified over the years of effort. Heartfelt thanks as well to my dear friends and mentors, Leonard Chang, a constant source of support and insight, and David Carlson, whose vast knowledge, general impatience and easy annoyance only made the novel better. I offer a huge nod of appreciation to my literary fairy godmother, Laurie Fox, whose wit, wisdom and passion bless every page of this book, and to Linda Chester of the Linda Chester Literary Agency. I am also greatly indebted to the following people: Nita Taublib and Kate Miciak for their extraordinary belief and encouragement; Randall Klein, my exquisitely talented and irrepressibly enthusiastic editor; my mother-in-law and the ten thousand rosaries she said on the novel's behalf; my friends Saundra Benassini and Milo Clow for their editorial input; Marina Mann, my resource for

Italian curses; Tom Dieterle for a job well done; Char Sol and JK for making the introductions; the Friday ride crew, whose grueling rides and dulcet vulgarity do much to replenish my spirits; Guru Singh and Dr. Michael Beckwith, whose spiritual teachings laid the foundation upon which the character of the Good Padre was largely built; and finally to my mother, father and brother (Lynne, Michael & Angela too), who always loved a good story and passed that love on to me.

ABOUT THE AUTHOR

ADAM SCHELL holds a master's degree in creative writing from Antioch University. He played inside linebacker at Northwestern University, has made two award-winning short films, worked as a screenwriter, directed commercials, cooked professionally, picked grapes and olives in Tuscany, got fired as a food critic, then moved to the *left* coast with his wife, where he works as a yoga teacher and writes.